De facto
Pathfinder

De facto Pathfinder

a novel by

CW3 Cesare Giannetti U.S. Army (Ret.)

kindle| Direct Publishing ©
Amazon.com, Inc.

For Isabella,

my daughter and shining light

———————

I
HO HUM LIFE

"When I was 5 years old, my mother always told me that happiness was the key to life. When I went to school, they asked me what I wanted to be when I grew up. I wrote down 'happy'. They told me I didn't understand the assignment, and I told them they didn't understand life." –John Lennon

"Take care, Chris," a regular at the Oklahoma state-run VSA (Veteran Support Agency) said with a quick wave goodbye to him before heading out into the oppressively hot afternoon sun. Chris Longo politely peeked up at the aged veteran and replied uninspiringly, "Have a good one."

Chris wasn't feeling motivated. It was the first week in August of 2018. The dog days of summer for sure. *Perhaps I'm just not motivated because it's 97 degrees outside?* He then shrugged and continued shuffling some more paperwork which would then be sent off to somebody else for further shuffling. *It wasn't supposed to be like this.* He had served a five-year stint in the Army right there in the Sooner state at Fort Sill. He was proud of his service as a young Field Artilleryman. Very proud. But that was two decades ago. Today, he was just a regular middle-aged man working at a dull office job. Stuck and bored.

Yes, the job did have its occasionally gratifying moments, like when he got to work directly with the veterans. And the job did pay his bills, *most of them anyway.* He thought of the many years he worked in medical equipment sales after his army time was over and the ups and downs of working in sales. *Sucked.* Now he was here, just a few years, but still, something was missing with the job, and he finally accepted, with his life too. *Okay, fine,* his divorce four years ago and the estranged relationship he had with his only child from it—a fifteen-year-old girl named Sara—didn't help matters any. But those were different issues than his job, he unsuccessfully tried reasoning to himself. Either way, he thought, he needed a change. A fresh start.

Later that evening, Chris called his Aunt Sophie for her hopeful reinforcement of his plan, or *epiphany,* if you will. He was a little disturbed that at just two years shy of fifty, he had no one else to confide to. Not his ex, not his kid, not even his mom who was too old and too much of a mom to listen. His dad would have taken his call and handled it easily, but he was no longer around after losing his long fight with cancer three years earlier.

I guess it'll have to be good ole' Aunt Sophie to save the day. Again. Or at least listen to me bitch and moan.

As he phoned her, Chris felt both anxious and relieved.

"Hello Christopher. How are you feeling?" she asked him in a way that only an aunt could, which was warm and inviting but not *too* intrusive. The way a parent or sibling can often be.

"I'm feeling fine, Auntie," he told her but knew, or hoped, that she wouldn't buy it.

"Oh, come on, you know you can always talk to your Aunt Sophie about what's bothering you. What is it, hon?"

"I'm thinking of quitting my job at the VSA."

"Good heavens, why would you do a thing like that? I was under the impression you liked working there?"

"Well, I do, or *did.* It's just I've been feeling disconnected lately. I think a change—a big change—would do me some good. I feel I need to do it—something different, that is. Do you know what I mean? Everything in my life just seems so...I don't know...Ho-hum."

"Christopher, I believe there's a name for what you are going through or feeling in your middle age."

"I know, and I thought of that, but deep down, I don't feel that's the case here. So, what ya think? Do you support me going for this change? New Job? New Life?"

"I assume you haven't told your mother about this yet. I also assume that you have figured out your finances so that you'll be able to leave your job before having a new one lined up. I mean, you do have Sara to consider financially you know."

"I have a few dollars saved for a rainy day—nothing too impressive, mind you. But enough to, well enough, I guess."

"Before I give you my go-ahead, I want to warn you that a decision like this often comes with consequences like failure and regret before finally getting to your accomplishment, but you are, of course, old enough and hopefully wise enough to know this already. I just want to remind you of that. But there is a bright light at the end of the tunnel, that is, if you carry on through all the pitfalls along the way. You will achieve what I think we all want or *should*, happiness and peace. In any case, I commend you for listening to your inner voice and going for what you want. Come to think of it—as an old history teacher—this reminds me of what the Native Americans referred to as a 'vision quest.'"

"A *vision quest?* Really? And what exactly is that?"

"From what I remember, it's when a young man would seek advice from a higher power or guardian spirit (me in this case) before going out on a journey into the wilderness to seek his spiritual being or higher calling in life. Then, (if successful) a sign or signal from the Gods would reveal itself in the form of an animal or bird, thus providing the young man with a vision and identity of his true purpose in life. How exciting is that, Christopher! So, yes, as the guardian spirit of your 'vision quest,' I approve of you going for it! Just promise me you won't go off to Mexico and get a tattoo."

Chris felt better now that he had his Aunt Sophie's approval for his vision quest, or whatever she was calling it. He was now all in on going through with his plan for a change. But that was the easy part. He still had to tell his ex-wife about the plan, and his boss, that he was quitting.

Great, just when I was feeling good about my plan or vision thing, now I have got to deal with them about it....

On his first day back to work, Chris approached his boss, Mr. Arnold, and told him that he needed to speak to him in private when he had the chance. Bob Arnold was a tall, thin man in his mid-fifties who was completely bald and always seemed irritated about something. Chris figured the reason for his crankiness was due to his mandatory relocating from his hometown of Boston, Mass, to Oklahoma City so his wife could be closer to her family—*or maybe he was truly just an ass.* Whatever the reason, he wasn't a pleasant fellow in anyone's eyes. For this reason, Chris wanted to get this conversation with his boss over quickly.

"What is it, Longo? Can't you see we're swamped today?"

"Mr. Arnold, I need to talk to you in private," he repeated.

"Okay, fine, meet me in my office in half an hour and don't be late, it's a very busy day."

"Yes, sir."

Twenty-eight minutes later, Chris was standing in front of his boss's door. He knocked on it three times.

"Come in, Longo, take a seat."

"Thanks, sir."

Mr. Arnold remained silent as he continued pecking loudly at his keyboard from behind his oversized monitor, which blocked Chris's view of him, except for the top of his shiny oval head. Chris looked around the modestly sized office. It was neat. *Too* neat. He then noticed a small but colorful Boston Red Sox pennant hanging discreetly in the corner. Mr. Arnold then began speaking in his typical crappy demeanor. He stopped his finger pecking, looked around his monitor, and squawked, "What is it? Whatta-ya-need?"

"Mr. Arnold, I'd like to put in my two weeks' notice. I'm leaving the VSA." The news now grabbed all of Mr. Arnold's attention. He moved his chair around his desk and monitor so

10

that he could be in full view of his quitting subordinate.

"Umm, okay. But are you sure you *really* want to do this? I remember just four short years ago; you were hired here after what? Fifteen years in sales? Which I believe you didn't much care for. And now *this?* You're not getting any younger, you know. You have a stable position here with a reputable state-run agency that helps veterans like yourself. Why leave? The veterans like you, and you like them. I don't get it. So, before you put in your two weeks' notice, can you at least tell me why—I mean really why—you are doing this?"

Mr. Arnold's eyes were now locked onto Chris's. *Maybe he thought he could change my mind by running down my past.* But Chris's heart and mind were already made up.

"Well, it's like this, it's true, I do like working with my fellow veterans—though, my position doesn't afford me that much time with them since, as you know, it is more paperwork intensive than actual face-to-face time with them—regardless, I just don't think I'm making a real difference here, for them, or me. Besides, I'm not a VSA social worker, nor do I want to be. Anyway, it's not just about the job. I've been feeling increasingly disconnected with everyone in my life, and even with the veterans here."

"—As well as with your daughter?"

The comment took Chris by full surprise and partial offense.

That's none of his business, and where does he get off saying that to me? But Chris then realized that he was, of course, right.

"Yes, as well as with my daughter...," he muttered back.

"You know, Longo, most of us yearn to be doing something else, or *be* someplace else. What makes *you* so special to go for that? You don't think *I* would rather be somewhere else? *Do* something else?"

And just when I thought he may actually be a decent person, he turned back into his old jerk self.

"I'm not trying to do anything revolutionary here," replied Chris. "All I know is that I need to do this simply for my self-preservation. That's all."

"Then, as a VSA supervisor, I must remind you that as a veteran, you have support here, even mental health support available to you. All you need to do is ask."

Although obligatory, Chris appreciated his boss's response. *But in the end, he was still a jerk.*

"Well, if there isn't anything else..." Mr. Arnold went on, "I will let HR know about your two-week notice—after you fill out these forms," he said while handing Chris a set of stapled papers. "I do hope the grass is greener on the other side for you Longo, and don't forget to shut the door on your way out."

Tell the boss I'm quitting my job. Check. *Tell the ex-wife. Crap.* Chris knew Jessie, or *Jessica*, as she now insisted that he call her ever since the divorce, was going to be a pain about it. He just knew it. But some things in life are just unavoidable.

Back home at his apartment, Chris opened an old photo album of Jessie and him together. During their happy, more carefree times before their marriage when it seemed for a brief, blissful period that the only people who could make them wholeheartedly content were each other.

Some photos stood out more to him than others. He focused on those. Like one of them back in 1999 when they first met at a bowling alley in Norman during a league game on opposing teams. Chris had just finished with the service months before. They had the common denominators of age and outlook: both were hitting thirty soon and both were awful bowlers, and both didn't care that they were. Playing in the league was just a fun, social drinking event for them.

At the snack bar that night, they giggled at some of each other's teammates who they felt took the game and league far too seriously, like bringing their own brightly colored bowling balls or having their names sewn into their bowling shirts. And the kicker that had them red-faced with laughter was the hilarious accoutrements of the over-the-shirt back support girdle coupled with the bowling wristband. They quit the league two weeks later after they started dating.

He recalled her alluringly beautiful, amber-colored hair, mixed with gold that reminded him of the actress Diane Lane.

She had creamy skin, bedroom eyes, and a lean yet shapely body with legs like anacondas. Chris turned past the courting period photos when he was beginning his sales career and frequently traveled around the Great Plains states. She would mind the place with their cat, Moses. But Jessie was also a few years into her own career, working in finance after graduating from the University of Oklahoma with honors. He recalled her fanaticism with the OU football team during those early years, and who could blame her? With them winning the National Championship in 2000 and all, the two would spend many a Saturday afternoon watching her beloved Sooners.

On some occasions, they would also attend OU home games, as their apartment was in Norman, which the Sooners called home. But mostly, they just preferred to lay in bed together, all day, intertwined, with her sporting OU school pajamas, or sometimes nothing at all. Chris loved that Jessie had so much passion for OU football, but he also felt envious of it. His family came from lesser economic means, so he could only afford community college in Oklahoma City. Five years after high school and all he could show for it was an associate degree in business. Being in his mid-twenties, he figured since he hadn't accomplished that much academically or relationship-wise, why not join the service and be all he could be? And so, he did.

With the photo album now on a page of them kissing on their honeymoon in Puerto Rico, he called Jessie from his cell phone.

Maybe that old love would float from the picture, permeate through the phone, into her ear, and into her heart.

"Hey Jessie, how are you?"

"You mean Jessica?"

"Oh yeah, I forgot. How are you, *Jessica?*"

"I'm doing fine," she said. "Haven't heard from you in a while, nor has Sara, for that matter."

"And how's *Fred?*" Chris said sarcastically.

"It's Frank—for the zillionth time."

"Sorry, how's *Frank?*"

"Why did you even call me?" she asked him, clearly annoyed.

13

"If you want to talk to Sara, just call her. God knows you rarely do."

"No, I called for you," Chris replied. "Jess, I need to tell you something. Something important for me." Jessica knew that whenever Chris called her "Jess," he was genuinely sincere in what he was saying.

"All right, Chris, what is it? It's way too hot out for arguing."

"Well, I don't know how to say this, but I've been in sort of a funk lately. A pretty bad one, to be honest with you. Anyway, this all leads me to tell you that I'm leaving my job at the VSA. I feel I am in bad need of a change."

There was a long pause on the line as if Jessica was letting the information sink in. Chris couldn't take the prolonged silence, so he hastily began talking again.

"I know what you're thinking. Do I have a job lined up? And if not, why the hell am I doing this now with Sara in high school and needing more and more things, like, I don't know, new clothes, a car soon, and a college education."

"That's *exactly* right, Christopher," Jessica said sternly.

Conversely, whenever Jessica called Chris 'Christopher' it had the opposite effect of when he called her Jess—she felt distrustful of what he was saying. But after so many years together, he could, on occasion, persuade her to feel that he was just being Chris. So, he did what he always did during these contentious conversations with her; he soldiered on.

"Look, I have some money saved up—only *some* money, mind you before you get any wild ideas of asking for some. I am going to try a new start in life. A fresh one."

"So, you're going to search for your Density?"

"Ha-ha, yes, Jess. That's right, my Destiny."

"Okay fine, as long as you keep up with the child support, go ahead and find whatever it is you're searching for. Perhaps if you do, you'll return to being a better, more involved father to Sara, like you were when she was younger."

After hearing her say this, Chris felt a twinge of guilt in his stomach for not calling or seeing Sara more often over the past few years.

How did I let this happen? Why did I let this happen?

Chris felt at least grateful, if not surprised—considering his distance from Sara lately—that Jessie was at least somewhat amicable about his fresh start idea.

"Thanks for your support on this," he said, "—whatever *this* is."

She then robotically replied, "Keep me posted on your new job and life. Goodbye, Christopher."

The phone hung up before Chris could say goodbye.

I guess she's heard enough, granted it was a lot to take in.

And so, with his old job behind him and new freedom in front, Chris was now ready for his change. But to what? And how? He hoped that that would reveal itself sooner than later, for his budget and ex-wife, wouldn't allow him too much time to find it. And especially not his daughter.

II
A FRESH START

"Whatever you can do, or dream you can, begin it.
Boldness has genius, power, and magic in it."
–Johann Wolfgang von Goethe

It was mid-September, and although Chris had only been out of the VSA for a couple of weeks, he was already feeling better. Even the weather had finally cooled, outside of a string of four days—from the 17th through the 20th—where temperatures reached up into the nineties. But this didn't matter to him. His spirits were high, regardless of the weather. He relished his new time off and his new outlook on life. And he was extremely optimistic about landing a position in the private sector, maybe even one that would have him traveling a little. Worst case scenario, he figured he could always apply for a government position at Tinker Airbase, located just eleven miles east of downtown Oklahoma City. Tinker was a huge base that offered many good jobs, especially for those with a veteran preference hiring advantage. Nevertheless, Chris was careful not to apply for any jobs he felt would bore him and make him quit too quickly. He wanted to do this change thing right. He may not get a second chance at it, he thought. On the other hand, he didn't want to be too picky either; monthly bills remained, so he did what he could, like working with headhunters to help him land something he liked. *Whatever the hell that was.*

The following week Chris got a surprise call from Pat, an old friend from his salesman days. He asked Chris if he wanted to watch the upcoming Oklahoma-Army football game together.

"Hey, Longo, I know you don't care too much about OU football, but I thought since they were playing Army, you might like to go to the game. It's at 6 on Saturday night. Or we can go watch it at a sports bar?"

"Thanks, but I don't want to go to the game. With my luck, I'll run into my ex-wife and her boyfriend there. I'd watch it at a sports bar, though."

"Cool, how does Lumpy's sound?"

"Sounds good. See you there Saturday night, game time."

The football game, Chris thought, would be a good distraction to keep his mind off his job hunting and the anxiety of trying to find that new something in his life. If nothing else, Pat was always good for a few laughs, as he never took things too seriously. It was something Chris had always admired about him, and it was something he thought he should do more of himself.

Lumpy's Sports Grill was your ordinary modern-day sports bar. Nothing too exciting, but nothing too dull either. It was a lively and comfy place to spend a relaxing weekend evening. An array of flat-screen TVs hung from the largest room walls so nobody wouldn't (or couldn't) miss a play of the game. Most patrons donned OU gear, from jerseys and T-shirts to ball caps and visors. OU *loves* its college football team.

Pat arrived at the bar first and was seated at a nondescript small square table. Chris came soon after, just before kickoff.

"What's up? Sorry for this crappy table, but the bar was full," said Pat. "Hell, this *whole* place is full. Lucky we even got this."

"This is fine," said Chris.

"I ordered us some beers," added Pat. "I know you're not a big drinker, but I ubered here; my ass is getting *drunk.*"

"Same old Pat. Anyway, how's the family? Wife, the boys?"

17

"You know Chris, we're good. Really. I mean, it's nothing too exciting, but no complaints. The boys are almost finished with high school; college is next, *hopefully*. And Stacey has been a real trooper during all my traveling. Remember those days, Longo? I'm thankful I'm not traveling that much anymore since I've advanced a bit. And Stacey said she's looking forward to us spending more quality time together when the kids are out of the house. I'm looking forward to it too. Life is good."

The positive news about Pat's life made Chris feel glad for his friend, but it also reminded him of what he was missing in his own life and of what he no longer had—a close family, a satisfying job, and something to look forward to in his fifties and beyond. His goal of "searching" for that happiness, gratifying work, and elusive love, was again on his mind. He tried to focus on the game, which turned out to be a surprisingly competitive one. The score was knotted at 21, entering the fourth quarter. It stayed that way until Oklahoma scored on a 10-yard touchdown pass to put the game away in overtime. The bar went nuts.

"So, how about you?" asked Pat. "Work? Family?"

Chris wanted to open up to Pat or anybody near his age, but deep down, he knew that he, like almost everyone else, was too busy with his own life and issues to want to hear the details about his. Besides, they were never really close, more like good coworkers. And now, it was just the occasional get-together. Nevertheless, Chris felt obligated to tell Pat something about what he was going through.

"Well, I've decided to move on from my job at the VSA and look for something else."

"Really? I thought you liked it there?" Pat said.

Wow, does everyone I know think that?

Chris cringed inside and wished he didn't have to explain to somebody else why he was moving on from a job that wasn't that bad.

"Just time to move on, ya know?" he replied.

"Sure, I get it. Whatever floats your boat—I bet *she* can float *my* boat," said Pat, pointing his beer toward their waitress.

"Huh?"

18

"Come on, she's *hot.*"

"What? You're drunk," sneered Chris.

"Guilty as charged! But all kidding aside, if you ever want to come back to sales, just let me know. We have openings, and business is good. Hell, the *economy* is good, there are a lot of excellent jobs out there right now," Pat said encouragingly.

"So, I hear. Thanks, but no thanks. I have already submitted a handful of applications for various positions. I'm just not a hundred percent sure of what I want to do. All I know is that I want to do something else."

"And your daughter? How's she?"

"Sara's doing fine. I need to see her more, but... I just need to see her more. Anyway, how about that game, huh? Army almost pulled it off. Now *that* would have been one for the ages."

"OU was never *really* in trouble," Pat said unconvincingly.

"You're probably right," said Chris. "Hey, I'm taking off—you need a lift?"

"Thanks, but nah. I'm going to have another beer—*or three.* You take it easy. And good luck with that job hunt."

"Thanks, bud, and you better not stay out late, or Stacey will give me hell."

"I love that woman!" yelled Pat.

"Yep, she's the best," Chris said in full agreement.

"No, I mean our *waitress!*" Pat said as he smacked an open hand on the table.

"Same old Pat," Chris said, shaking his head, "good night."

"Night, Longo."

The following day, Chris took a long walk along Lake Hefner, located in the Northwest part of Oklahoma City. It was officially the first day of Autumn. Although it wasn't prime fall foliage season, some trees had already begun changing from their ordinary shades of green to cascades of bright and cheerful colors of lively oranges and reds to warm yellows and tans. It was also a pleasant and leisurely day for a walk with summer's scorching heat all but gone.

A walk would do me some good. Clear my head. Think of what I want to do. Maybe even see my vision quest out here.

But the walk ended up being only partially successful in achieving what Chris had hoped for as it failed in helping him think of what he wanted to do. It also failed to display any kind of sign or signal—*that Aunt Sophie sure had me going on that one.* Yet, the long walk was successful in clearing Chris's head. Afterward, he sat down on a bench to rest. He then looked down and rubbed his knees which had begun aching. When he looked back up, he saw a father holding his young daughter's hand. The sight reminded Chris of earlier years when he would often bring Sara to the lake on weekends. He thought of all those special times they had shared there and how much joy it gave him. *Them.* Like when she had first learned to ride a bicycle on her own, without training wheels. She was only four and looked so adorable in her white protective helmet. On that day, he remembered her being exceedingly triumphant of her achievement with her joyfully wide smile. It was the best time of Chris's life. He yearned to feel needed like that again. To be wanted like that again. To be loved like that again.

He decided to call Sara finally.

"Daddy?"

"Hello, Sara? How are you? How have you been?"

"Okay, I guess."

An awkward silence followed. Chris then thought that his daughter might be—and justly so—upset with him for not calling her and seeing her much lately. The thought that he didn't think of this that much before made him feel selfish. He then tried clumsily to address the issue first. "Um. I..., um, just wanted to tell you how sorry I am for not calling you and not coming out to see more of your games in the past."

A momentary silence re-emerged, then ceased.

"What's wrong with you, Daddy? Why are you acting like this? Was it something I did? Something Mommy did?"

"No, it's not like that at all! And I wish I could give you some reason as to why I am behaving this way. But I can't—at least not a good one. I can tell you that I haven't been feeling myself lately, but I'm trying to change that. Actually, I'm trying to change a lot."

20

Sara then abruptly changed the topic.

"Anyway, our volleyball team stinks this year; by the way, did you watch the OU-Army game last night? Mommy and I did."

"I did too," said Chris, "but don't rub it in; I know how much your mom *loves* her OU football, which I guess means you do too, huh."

"No way. I was rooting for Army all the way."

Chris's heart skipped a beat when he heard her say that.

"Mom was pissed that I wasn't cheering for OU and that they almost lost to Army. Hey Dad, I need to go."

"Wait a second. I want to ask you a quick question. Do you remember when you were little, and I used to take you to Lake Hefner?"

"What, Dad? I was so young then. Bye"

"I love—"click, and just like that the phone call was over.

She was going for Army. And she seemed hopeful in me. Us. Although she's still disappointed in me, it feels as if I still have a chance of fixing this—a real shot. But Chris then remembered that he couldn't do that until he fixed himself first.

Easier said than done.

III
NO, REALLY, A FRESH START...

"Try not to become a person of success, but rather try to become a person of value." –Albert Einstein

Fall came and went, with the Red Sox winning the World Series that year; this had Chris thinking *that surely had put a smile on Mr. Arnold's face*, though on second thought, he doubted it. As for the Oklahoma Sooners, they had a stellar year ending up one of the country's top four teams and reaching the illustrious College Football Playoff National Championship. They, however, got bounced out in the Orange Bowl by powerhouse Alabama. That result *did* put a smile on Chris's face, as well as the fact that the Army football team finished the year 11-2, ranked 22nd in the country, and closed out the year with a romp of Houston in the Armed Forces Bowl. Chris wondered if Sara had followed Army football throughout the season.

Unimportant. The fact that she rooted for them against OU was enough.

After all the Bowl games were played and Clemson University was crowned as the National Champs, it was the winter of his discontent for Chris as it seemed to drag on forever. It was now

January 2019, just four months removed from his departure from the VSA, but to him, it felt like years, for it was now decision time. Time to decide on what job he wanted—or what job he *had* to choose from—as there were many. But which one would make him happy? *Why couldn't everybody do what they loved? But then again, many people don't even know what they love. Anyway, bills needed to be paid, and my savings were almost up. Life goes on.* Chris thought of calling Aunt Sophie, or Jessie, or even for a moment, Pat. But those conversations, like passing ships at sea, had moved on. Some decisions just need to be made alone. Chris knew this but didn't like his choices *or jobs. Maybe this wasn't the best plan.* In reality, it wasn't even a plan—just an idea. *And what a great idea it was: quit my job and hope something I love to do will simply pop up in front of me, change my life, and make me happier, as well as improve all my relationships. How dumb of me to think that could happen so easily. What have I done? Nothing to do now but go forward.*

Always forward.

Over the following weekend, Chris cut down his list of jobs that most appealed to him to three, or at least to the ones that had called him back. The first was as a Training Deployment Coordinator. The second was in Inventory Management. And the third was in General Business and Industry. All were located at nearby Tinker Air Force Base.

Chris thought long and hard about which job he would finally settle on, but beggars can't be choosers. *Let's see... Training Deployment Coordinator? I don't know. I mean, I served in the military, but I never deployed before. Think. I'm no combat vet. What do I know about coordinating a deployment? —scratch job one. Next, Inventory Management? Isn't that just a fancy way of saying counter-keeper? Sounds dull —scratch job two. Okay, last one now, General Business and Industry? At least I have some formal education in the field. That's the one! Decision made.* After the weekend, Chris would call HR about obtaining that job. No need to delay. Still, something didn't sit quite right with him. He didn't sleep well for the remainder of the weekend.

The following week, Chris was awoken on one early, quiet snowy morning by an unrecognizable 405 local area phone call. Who could it be? Another job return call? Nope. His mother had recently purchased a new phone, and with it came a new telephone number. "How are you feeling, Chris?" she asked him. "You seemed down over Christmas, so I wanted to ensure you were okay."

"I'm fine, Mom," he responded, "it's just...I'll most likely be starting a new job soon, so I've been a little stressed lately. Things haven't turned out the way I thought they would but I'm okay. In fact, I'm going to call my prospective employer today. And sorry for not telling you about my leaving the VSA and all but I didn't want to bother you."

"Sometimes, son, it feels like I never understand you; just make sure you bring over Sara soon so I can see my little girl."

The conversation between Chris and his mother marked the last 'proverbial' hurdle before he could begin his new job and life. He didn't want to tell her, but he knew that it was necessary— *though she never understands me.* Besides, she would have found out eventually, which would have insulted her since she hadn't been told by him directly.

Whatever. She knows now. It's over.

Later that morning, Chris called Tinker Airbase about the General Business and Industry job. He wasn't surprised when the polite yet brief woman on the line informed him that he had all but secured that position after his second interview.

This is it. New beginnings. A Fresh start. So why don't I feel excited about it? Chris then again felt the need to call Aunt Sophie. He felt compelled to tell her he was starting a new job soon after waiting four months for a sign or something new in his life to occur, but neither of which did. *I wonder what she'll say about that —vision quest, my ass.*

"Hello, Christopher? And Happy New Year, before I forget!"

"Hello, Auntie."

"So, to what do I owe the pleasure of your phone call, hon?"

"I called to tell you that I've finally landed a job. It's over at

24

Tinker. It's in Business and Industry."

"That sounds wonderful! Are you not pleased?"

"Honestly, Aunt Sophie, I'm not. I know I should be grateful and appreciative that I have something, at least. But I don't know, I feel like I wanted to do something more…more…."

"Valuable?" she inquired.

"Yes, more *valuable* and more *meaningful,*" he replied. And what of this sign you said I would see? The vision thing. Do you remember?"

"I do remember. And I also recall telling you that when you decided to change your life, with it would come consequences, like failure and regret, before finally achieving what you set out to accomplish. It almost *always* does. Do you remember that?"

Chris did, vividly. But someone else had to be at fault for his failure and the negative feeling he had besides himself; at least it would make him feel a little better, he thought. Regardless, he knew that Aunt Sophie was only telling him the truth. Tough love.

"You're right. Sorry. I'm just feeling discouraged. I really don't want this business-type job. And I know it's a fine job and all, but as I said, I want to do something of value."

"I understand you, Christopher," she said, then paused in deep thought before continuing. "Did you, by chance, see the Solar Eclipse last weekend?" Chris heard something about it on the news but didn't physically see it.

"No, I missed it. Why?"

"Well, there is a lesson here that fits your present situation. Listen, as you know, a Solar Eclipse occurs when the moon passes between the Sun and the Earth, thus blocking the view of the Sun to us on Earth. At this point, the Moon, Sun, and Earth are all aligned, creating what's known as a cosmic coincidence."

"Are you saying that *that* was my vision quest?"

"No, that's not what I'm saying; that's something only *you* can determine and decipher. What I mean is that sometimes, on rare occasions, like a cosmic coincidence, for instance, things that you would normally see so big and clearly can get blocked out so you no longer can."

"Okay. But what can, or can't I, no longer see clearly?"

25

"Again, that's something only *you* can determine."

"Sounds complicated."

"Life's complicated."

"Wow, Aunt Sophie, you're taking this guardian spirit role seriously."

"Well, your life is a serious matter. Look, Christopher, I'm not going to tell you what to do, but I will tell you to follow your instincts and heart. It will ultimately lead you to the right path."

"I get you, Aunt Sophie—that doesn't mean I know what I'm going to do—but I think I get it. And thank you for being there for me. Also, before *I* forget, Happy New Year to you too."

After Chris hung up the phone, he sat down, closed his eyes, and thought...*what to do, what to do...*Then it hit him. He would *not* take the General Business and Industry job because it was *not* what he wanted to do. He decided he was somehow going to make what *he* wanted to happen. And he felt damn good about it. A sudden peacefulness came over him—which he thought was strange, considering the odds against him.

But nobody gave Army a shot against OU either, and they pushed them to overtime. Chris was going to push it to overtime too—fortunately for him, however, he wouldn't have to, for like the Moon moving past between the Sun and Earth after a Solar Eclipse, Chris would soon see big and clearly what he would do just hours after talking to his Aunt Sophie. It came in the form of a phone call from another unidentified 405 area code number which turned out to be his previous employer, the VSA. But what did they want?

"Hello, Longo. It's Mr. Arnold from the VSA—but I'm calling on behalf of the DoD (Department of Defense). They'd like to talk to you about a new program they are implementing. They, apparently, think you would be the right man for the job."

"Mr. Arnold, I don't know what to say...? Why would the DoD, a federal agency, work with the state-level VSA?"

"That's above my pay grade. And to be frank, I don't care why. I know Mr. Montrose wants to speak to you here at 0900 hours sharp next Monday. If you have any more questions, save them for him. I'm just the messenger here."

"Oh, I have questions...," said Chris. "Please tell him I will be there, and thanks for the call, Mr. Arnold."

"No thanks needed. I *had* to do it."

"Nevertheless, thank you."

And just like that, out of nowhere, Chris had his hope restored. But at this point, that's all it was, hope. That was until he got the specifics from Mr. Montrose on just precisely what the job was. Many people say that hope is not a strategy, but not Chris. To him, it certainly was one and more, like free will, a better way of life, or even happiness. In other words, *everything*.

The following Monday morning, on the drive into the VSA, Chris wasn't sure how he'd feel being back there. It would be his first time returning since he had quit his job back in August. Would he feel happy? Glad? Sad? Or maybe just indifferent? But did that matter now? he thought. He had left *that* job and *that* place. He had moved on. He was done with it. He was back now for a different reason, for a different job. But what? And where?

The VSA center was busier than usual when Chris walked through its doors at 0830 hours. Curiosity began to get the best of him as he stepped up to a clerk's desk, which was divided off for privacy like all the other neatly aligned desks which faced the incoming veterans. Chris came upon a female clerk who he didn't recognize and asked her if Mr. Arnold, or Mr. Montrose, were ready to see him. The young woman, who had wide jet-black hair that had a unique shape to it, told him, "I'll go find one of them, no problem." She then sprung up, conducted an about-face of sorts, and hurriedly walked off in excessively tall heels which made Chris wonder if they caused her any pain when she walked.

The young woman returned just as quickly as she had left.

"Mr. Montrose will see you in room 101, located in the back of the lobby," she said with her finger pointing behind her. She then waved eagerly to the veteran standing behind Chris, who she was finished with.

Room 101's door opened just as Chris was about to knock on it. He was greeted by a fit fortyish black man in khaki pants and a

27

white, long sleeve dress shirt that had a blue DoD emblem on the right side of his chest. It consisted of an American bald eagle clutching three horizontally crossed arrows by its talons. To Chris, the man seemed enthused to see him.

"Chris Longo. Hello, I'm Michael Montrose; nice to meet you. And please, call me Michael," he said as he held his hand out for a strong handshake.

"Hello, nice to meet you too," Chris said politely.

"Please, have a seat," said Michael.

"Thank you," Chris replied, sitting in an uncomfortable plastic chair in the small windowless room. There were no pictures on the sterile greyish-blue walls. A large notebook and a pitcher of water sat on a rectangular desk in the middle of the room. The two men sat facing each other.

"So, thank you for coming in. I assume Mr. Arnold told you why I wanted to speak with you."

"Oh yes, well, some," said Chris, "something about a new program and a job? He didn't go into it much further."

"That's right, Mr. Longo."

"Please, call me Chris."

"All right, Chris, let me explain. As you have been told, I'm with the Department of Defense. And yes, we are implementing a new job—or *pilot program*. We partnered with state-run veteran agencies, such as the VSA, to combat veteran wellness and personal recovery issues."

"Doesn't the VA handle that? —*those issues?* And why would the DoD, a war-fighting agency, work on Veteran Affairs issues? I mean, the VA is *huge*. Are they not getting the job done?" Chris asked, puzzled.

"Short answer, no, they are *not* getting the job done. Did you know that we lose roughly twenty veterans a day to suicides? Twenty! There are, of course, many other serious veterans' issues as well that need immediate attention. But I'm preaching to the choir here. I'm told you've been with the VSA for four years. You're surely well aware of these issues."

"I am," Chris said glumly.

"Then you understand that this is unacceptable, especially in our great country. That's why the President sent down a directive, or order, to the Secretary of Defense and the Secretary of Veterans Affairs to fix this *ASAP*. The VA has been far too much money with far too few results for our fine service members and veterans to continue having with all these issues. So, that's why I'm here. And it's why you're here too, *we hope*."

"But still, the DoD?" Chris asked persistently.

"It's really not *that* crazy of an idea," Michael replied. "The VA is a reactive agency. They primarily deal with veterans and soldiers *after* they have served. The DoD, as you said, is a war-fighting agency. They deal with soldiers *while* they are serving. Besides, the VA has too many leadership and bureaucratic red tape issues right now to help with this new program, so the Secretary of the VA, along with the President's directive, pushed it down to the state level—enter the VSA, which brings me to why you're here. Weeks ago, when I arrived, I was asked to bring on a VSA employee for this new program. Someone who had a 'connection' with veterans. Someone whom the veterans genuinely liked, listened to, and respected—*someone like you*."

"Me? Who said so?"

"Well, for starters, Mr. Arnold did."

"Really? That surprises me."

"As a matter of fact," said Michael, "he spoke very highly of you. If I recall correctly, he said you were of 'great value to the veterans here.' He also had many customer surveys that reflected you in a positive light. We feel you're the right man for the job."

"And exactly what job is that?"

"Yes, of course, let me elaborate. First off, it's a one-year term position that pays reasonably well. Also, there is a chance of full-time hire afterward. The first six months are all travel, but it does include an excellent per diem package, so you will not be spending much of your salary while on the road. There is no travel for the last six months of the term, during which you will work with the DoD at Tinker Air Base. The travel period would consist of meeting with six veterans (one per month) around the country who need help. Ones who have—for one reason or another—lost their way. With your ability to connect with veterans, we feel you

29

you could be the X factor that will hopefully bring them around to...," Michael said, then was suddenly at a loss for words.

"To...*what?*" asked Chris, who now grew even more curious.

"To...to finding themselves again, so to speak," said Michael. "We are trying to help them find their path back, back from what is presently ailing them. It could be anything, from feeling isolated and detached from people and society to alcoholism and being angry at the world. And there are, of course, PTSD and suicide prevention cases, just to name a few."

"So, basically everything," Chris said flatly. "But what am I supposed to do for them?" he asked, perplexed. "Talk with them? Be their Dr. Phil and give them a warm and fuzzy that'll fix all their problems. Sorry, but it doesn't work that way. It's not that easy."

Chris also thought about how hard it would be to be away from his daughter for six months, but then rationalized that perhaps this was not only an opportunity for him to grow but also for their relationship to somehow improve if he could somehow improve himself as well. And he would, of course, also be helping his fellow veterans. So, the travel time away wasn't a deal breaker but he had other concerns as well.

"And besides," Chris continued, "I'm not a social worker. I'm not qualified to handle those sensitive issues."

"True," said Michael, "you are not, but in some ways, you are *more* qualified than they are: *You* are a veteran. *You* have worked for several years at the VSA, and *you* have shown to make a positive connection with them. That is the essence of what we hope this new pilot program can accomplish here; that connection and that comradery with them. We know there is no easy solution to their difficult problems. But like I said, we have largely failed as a government (and as a nation) to help them. And to heal them. "

"But I'm still not qualified to...," Chris began saying before Michael then cut him off. "But that's not your concern," he said. "These veterans all have social workers who know the details of each of their cases. They will brief you accordingly. You, in turn, will brief us on your findings and observations after your time with them. There will also be follow-ups, of course, as needed."

"Do you really think I can help them?"

"You could try."

Chris thought about this for a moment. Michael was right. He could try. He then thought about the recent conversation he had with Aunt Sophie about wanting to do something of value. Plus, he had already passed on the General Business and Industry job.

If I don't take this one, what the heck was I waiting for?

"I'll do it! I'll accept the job of...by the way, what's the title of the position I just accepted?"

"We don't have one for it yet. I told you this was a brand-new position. But don't worry about the job title, OPM (Office of Personnel Management) will assign one eventually. For now, think of it as along the lines of a veterans' counselor or confidant."

"Well, you said that I was brought on to help some veterans find their way back? —No, you said to find their *path* back."

"I did. And?"

"Hmm," said Chris looking off in thought. He then turned back and asked, "How about Default Pathfinder? You know, since the position came to me in a way by default. What do you think?"

"I like Pathfinder. It's accurate and direct. But default? —ehh, not so much," replied Michael with some small shakes of his head. "It sounds like you won a consolation prize."

"I got it!" exclaimed Chris. "How about *De facto Pathfinder*?" Michael thought hard about it for a moment, "That's it! That's the one! You'll be their De facto Pathfinder!" And so, it was.

After completing the formalities that accompany most new jobs: training, filling out tax documents, insurance forms, and direct deposit information, Chris was now ready for his journey to begin. Informing Aunt Sophie and Pat was the easy part, as they were both excited for him. His mother wasn't as keen on the idea, but in the end, gave her lukewarm approval. It was predictably Jessie and Sara who were the least impressed with the job and its sacrifices. But when the time came for Chris to leave, Jessie seemed to come around and appreciate not only the monetary support that it would provide for their daughter but also the fact that Chris would be doing something that he had a real passion for, as well as helping others in need. And, she thought, that it would be healthy for Sara to see her father in a positive light; perhaps even as a role

31

model to emulate one day. Unfortunately, Sara did not see it that way. Not yet anyway. She still did not understand why her father had to be gone for an entire six months. He tried one last time to explain it to her and say goodbye as best he could.

"Please remember Sara, that although it may not seem like it today, your happiness is more important to me than anything else in this world," he said while holding back tears. Sara hugged him tightly with tears slowly rolling down her face. She then abruptly let him go and ran off to her room.

This time away was seen as a means to an end, as big sacrifices can reap big rewards—and that's precisely what Chris, his mother, Sara, Jessie, Michael, Pat, and Aunt Sophie, were all hoping for.

IV
THE JOURNEY BEGINS

"Start where you are. Use what you have. Do what you can."
–Arthur Ashe

The euphoria and excitement that Chris had felt since landing his new job with the DoD were now mostly gone. It seemed the reality of his situation had changed his point of view. Pessimistic questions and concerns took the forefront position in his mind as he prepared to leave for his six-month mission to help some veterans in need. Chris wanted concrete answers that he still didn't have, like, *what if I don't connect with the veterans? Or what if I cause them more harm than good? Or what if they don't like me? And where exactly am I going first? And why couldn't Michael tell me more than two days in advance? All he talked about was how the weather was where I was going—cold. Very, very cold. Well, that sounded a little disturbing, and awful. And where was that sign from the animal or bird that Aunt Sophie had told me about which was to confirm my purpose? —Nowhere.*

Absolutely nowhere.

Only two days remained before Chris was about to embark on his travels, so he was fully expecting Michael's call that day.

"Hello, Chris. Are you packed, ready to go?"

"I'm ready," he replied assertively.

Hell, I've been ready.

"But *how* again is this all exactly going to work?" he then asked, sounding more anxious than assertive. "And why are the locations to where I'm going so hush-hush?"

"Well, that's done for a reason," Michael responded, "exactly why I don't know, but that's not my call. Look, I apologize for the lack of specifics, but try not to worry about the where's, why's, and what's until you've reached each location. All the information you need will be provided to you by the veterans' social worker, respectively. And I'll be in communication with you throughout the mission, should you need any assistance. Remember Chris, this is a 'pilot program,' an experiment if you will. So please, don't put too much pressure on yourself or stress yourself unnecessarily before you have even started. Your job is to do the best that you can with the abilities that you have. The rest will all fall into place. Your journey starts now. Embrace it. I'm sure you will make us and your family very proud."

"Wow, thanks for those encouraging words. I really needed to hear them. And I do want to do right by you, as well as my family."

"That's the spirit!" said Michael, "And half the battle!"

"By the way, now that I am leaving, can you *finally* tell me where I'll be going first?" Chris eagerly asked.

"Sure, you're headed North to the future!"

"Where?"

V
ALBATROSS IN ALASKA

"To understand the man, you have to know what was happening in the world when he was twenty." –Napoléon Bonaparte

On the long flight to Anchorage, Chris was still in disbelief. *I can't believe I'm going to Alaska, and in the middle of winter!* Concerns within him persisted: *am I adequately packed for the weather? And what the hell am I doing there for an entire month?* To get his mind off his predicament Chris closed his eyes and tried to relax with a nap. He soon drifted off and found himself in a dream. He was standing outside a closed large black wrought iron gate. *Am I in heaven?* The gate then slowly began to open. He glanced around but everything was unclear, fuzzy. After the gate was fully open, he walked through it and into...? Chris still had no idea where he was going. At the moment when he was just about to worry, he saw a wooden sign off to his left with a word carved in it painted in white, ZOO.

    Okay, finally something. A point of reference. I'm at a zoo! This isn't so bad; though Chris, of course, didn't know he was in a dream, *still who doesn't like the zoo?* So, he continued, walking slowly past the entrance where he then saw a cashier booth off to his right. He stepped up to it and, lo and behold, sitting there in a chair behind the glass was his Aunt Sophie. Chris gasped and said to her, "Auntie, what the heck are you doing here?"

She responded with a wink and then slid to him, under the small opening in the glass, a zoo entry pass for one. She then put her right index finger over her lips and gestured "shhh" then, with the same finger, pointed in the direction of the zoo.

Oh, I see. Chris now remembered. *She was my guardian spirit. She was here to help me find my sign, (animal or bird) there at the zoo.* He took the pass from her, winked back, and then entered. Chris looked around and saw that in front of him were several big black cages lined along the zoo's main thoroughfare. *Perfect. I will surely see my sign there.* But as Chris came upon the cages, he saw that the first few were empty. He then looked and saw some further down. Again empty. *Perhaps the animals were inside, hidden, or sleeping?* But that wasn't the case. The cages were *all* empty. Chris continued looking around. He didn't know what to do so he quickly ran back to the front of the zoo to go talk to Aunt Sophie, but she was no longer there. He then went back to the cages to look again. He walked slowly. Very slowly. He then heard something. It sounded like the rustlings of leaves in a cage down on the left side. Was it a monkey? A tiger? An eagle? He didn't want to lose sight of it. He felt that this was his best shot at seeing his sign. He finally reached the front of the cage, where he then heard a branch break as if something had stepped on it. And some more rustling of leaves. Suddenly, he saw something. But it remained unclear as to what it was as it was hidden from vegetation inside the cage. Chris stood still and silent. He focused his eyes, so as not to miss anything. Then, to his shock, out stepped, *himself?*

Chris jumped back so fast that he almost fell. He then did a double take, sure enough, it was *he* who was looking back at him from inside the cage. Chris's jaw dropped in horror. He then felt a hand from behind him touch his shoulder, it began shaking him, harder and harder until he finally awoke.

"Are you okay?" asked an elderly man from the seat behind him on the plane. The man then peered between the seats and said, "You sounded like you were having a bad dream. You were breathing heavily and twisting your head from side to side. Are you sure you're all right?"

"I'm fine, sorry about that—like you said, bad dream," said Chris, who was sweating profusely. The dream shook him far more than the old man had. *What was the meaning of it? Did it even have a meaning?* Chris decided to stay awake for the rest of the flight. He wasn't in the mood to go back to the zoo today.

It was dark and late when Chris landed in Anchorage. He looked out the window expecting to see something, anything, but he was disappointed when all he saw was blackness. Chris then picked up his luggage and rental car and proceeded to his DoD lodging located next to the city of Anchorage called Joint Base Elmendorf-Richardson (JBER), which was previously an Army fort (Fort Richardson) until 2010, when it merged with Elmendorf Air Base.

There were several inches of snow on the ground on Chris's short drive to the base, but the roads were clear. After checking into his dull, yet sufficient room, Chris fell into a deep sleep until morning, where he then met up with his first veteran's social worker on base at 0930 hours.

"How was your travel here?" a wiry, white-haired woman, Chris guessed to be in her early sixties, asked him.

"Fine, fine, thank you," he said. "All good, just...well, it's just so cold here. How do you do it?"

"Alaska's *beautiful,*" replied the social worker. "And yes, it's really cold here in the winter, but it's truly a magnificent land. Look, at the risk of sounding rude, we're not here for small talk Mr. Longo. We're here for Tim. So, let me go over his case and details with you so you can begin doing what you came here for."

"Tim?" replied Chris. "Okay, but do I get his last name?"

"Tim's last name is in his file, which I will give you. But let me give you some advice. Don't worry too much about his last name. You don't have that much time to bond with him. You need to be on a first-name basis right off the bat. Time is not on your side for this task, nor is it on Tim's side for that matter. Understand, Tim's in a bad way. I'm not sure if Mr. Montrose had told you but he will probably be your most difficult case. Tim has been in and out of homeless shelters—a tough life for anyone but especially so for someone turning seventy. And Tim is a disabled veteran who lost his right leg (just below the knee) in Vietnam. He has a prosthetic leg and uses a cane. His other issues range from PTSD, alcoholism, and isolation to possible suicide.

"Jeez," Chris said lowly, "he is in a bad way." When hearing of Tim's situation, Chris worried even more about how or if he was going to be able to help this veteran in any way, as he seemed almost beyond help. But he didn't want to convey this to the social worker who might feel him unable or unworthy to even try.

Hell, I'm already in Alaska. I'm not going to quit before I even started.

"Did you know that fifty percent of homeless veterans served in the Vietnam War?" the social worker asked Chris.

"No, I didn't know that…by the way, where is he right now?"

"Right now, he's at a homeless shelter here in Anchorage, but he's due to check out in a few days, as he has stayed past the month-period allowed. Who knows where he'll go next? Some winters he goes up to Fairbanks to work with sled dogs—but not always; other ones, he'll just stay here in Anchorage and drink the season away. In the summer, he will *occasionally* try to find side work in fishing or game hunting up at Seward, located a few hours from here. And like many in Alaska, try to work off the tourism industry. He can be rather resourceful when he wants to be. But that sadly doesn't seem to happen too often. Truth be told, the most important thing you can do with these veterans is to just *talk* with them. If they trust you then, they will tell you what they feel is ailing them. And if there is anything you can do to help them—I don't have to remind you that you are not *clinically qualified* to give them any professional advice. But I'm pretty sure your project manager has gone over all that with you. Look, I admit I have largely failed with Tim. Perhaps it's partly because he doesn't trust me or like me. Or maybe it's because I haven't put in the necessary time with him, as I have just too many cases to work on. Anyway, I'm glad you are here…Review his case and details. All the information is there in your folder. Good luck, and, of course, call me if you need anything."

And with that, Chris completed the in-brief of his first veteran. Although he had some more questions for Tim's caseworker, he decided against asking them. Besides, he had heard everything he needed to hear; *Tim was in a bad way—a very bad way. Got it. The social worker's been ineffective in helping him. Got it. Now it's my turn to try and help him. Not sure if I got that one.*

Tim was expecting Chris when he showed up at the homeless shelter the next day to see him. His social worker had notified him beforehand of Chris's visit. When Chris arrived, Tim was standing in the doorway, cane in hand, waiting for him. It seemed he had already packed and was ready to go. But to where?

"Whatta-ya say podna?" Tim asked him in a Texas drawl.

"Hi there, I'm Chris Longo, nice to meet you."

"Name's Tim, nice to meet you too," he said gruffly.

Face to face, looking at each other now, both men quickly sized the other up as most people do when meeting for the first time—or at least when you knew you'd be spending the better part of next month together. They stood at about the same height. Tim was thicker in the midsection. He also had longer and grayer hair that reached down to the back of his neck. Tim's face was a dark pinkish-hue, almost red. And it was badly pocked and scarred, which gave him a ragged look. Chris felt bad that he was accurate in what he visualized Tim would look like. He glanced down at the suitcase sitting upright next to Tim's badly worn-out boots. He then asked him, "You going somewhere?"

"Yep, *we're* going somewhere," Tim replied snidely.

"Really? And where might that be?"

"To Alaska's 2nd largest city and America's coldest: Fairbanks! You'll love it," Tim said with both sincerity and mockery.

"Yeah, sounds *wonderful*," replied Chris sarcastically.

"The Golden Heart of Alaska!" Tim roared, then coughed.

"Let me guess—the city's motto."

"Oh, you're good," Tim said with a hard pat on Chris's arm.

"Come on, I wanna get the hell outta here—which one is our ride?" Tim asked as he hastily picked up his suitcase and began walking with a noticeably big limp out into the parking lot.

"It's the small white SUV to the right," Chris said, while he followed behind him, fumbling to put on his brand-new winter hat and gloves. He saw that Tim was struggling to carry his luggage. He motioned to him with a hand, "Here, let me get that," taking the suitcase by its handle, then placing it in the back of the SUV.

"Thanks," said Tim, "my damn back is out again."

After getting into the car, Tim removed his prosthetic leg. "This thing..." he moaned, "this thing..." he repeated, shaking his head.

"So, are we *really* going to Fairbanks today?" Chris asked thinking that perhaps if he changed the conversation, Tim wouldn't think as much about his lost leg. "That's quite a long drive, especially with more snow coming," he added, matter of factly, to which Tim replied, "Yeah, on a good day we could make it there in six hours, but in this weather, it could take up to eight or even nine. But that's okay podna, gives us more time to get to know each other," he said with a chuckle, then continued, "too bad it wasn't summer, or we could've taken the Alaskan railroad there. But that doesn't run this time of year. Worst case, we could always spend the night at Denali National Park, which is about halfway to Fairbanks—by the way, everyone just calls me 'Til' on the count my last name's Tilly."

"*Tim Tilly*," remarked Chris.

Tim didn't answer but seemed perturbed by Chris's saying his name out loud for no apparent reason besides the fact that it rhymed. "It's just Til, *okay?*" he said crisply.

"Til it is," said Chris unfazed, "and Fairbanks it is, but I need to pick up my suitcase and check out before we hit the highway."

"Fine," Til said in a low, gravelly voice.

As Chris packed up his recently unpacked suitcase, he contemplated calling Tim's, or *Til's* rather, social worker to inform her of their trip, but then decided otherwise. He knew Fairbanks had military lodging where he could stay while he was there. *And anyway, perhaps this was exactly what the doctor ordered—*

40

just me, him, and the open road.

After thirty minutes of driving in quietness on interstate A3, the car's GPS female voice broke it with, "Take ramp right for EAST Airport Way to Interstate A4 toward Fairbanks."

"It's a straight shot from here," Til said, "'bout' three hundred and some miles away." He then reached into his front jacket pocket and pulled out a joint and a lighter, as if reaching the interstate was a mini celebration and justification for him to smoke it. Chris was initially taken aback when he first saw it. He didn't know what to say or do. *Is Pot even legal in Alaska? Can I get arrested even if I don't smoke it? Should I say something to him about it, or will that upset him? Maybe it's medicinal marijuana?* But Til quickly put Chris at ease on the issue.

"Don't worry, kid, weed, in small amounts, is legal in Alaska."

"Kid?" Chris shot back, "I'll be fifty next year, just so you know—I'm hardly a kid," he said with a snicker.

"Nah, that's not what I meant," replied Til. "It's just...I have a son about your age is all." Chris wasn't sure whether he should ask Til about him or not. Til then lit up the joint and cracked the window. The arctic air that rushed into the car felt good and invigorating to Chris. Til then took a large hit off the joint, held it in momentarily, and proceeded to slowly, and evenly, exhale a large amount of smoke that quickly escaped out of the car's cabin. He repeated these steps two to three times before coughing very loudly and violently, which alarmed Chris, but Til then abruptly stopped his heavy coughing.

"Are you okay?" he asked him.

"Ahhh, I'm better now," Til replied, *"much better."*

Now that Til was feeling 'much better' Chris saw an opening to (hopefully) initiate a quality conversation with him. Still, he learned the hard way at the VSA that although a veteran may say that they were feeling better or having a good day, that didn't necessarily mean they wanted to open up and talk to you about their feelings or their problems, but then again, he thought, sometimes it did. *What the hell, that's why I'm here.*

"So," Chris began treading lightly, "you say you have a son about my age? How is he doing? Have you seen him lately?"

"Not in years, it's been tough...but not in years."

Chris decided to then ask about his military service. Perhaps it was a better topic to start on.

It was dumb of me to bring up his son so soon.

"I was told that you served in Vietnam. When were you there? I've read some books about it, but can only imagine what you guys went through—must have been crazy huh?"

"Oh, Nam, right. Well, let's see, I was nineteen—*no* twenty, yeah twenty, when I arrived there in '69. It was at the height of our troop level there at over half a million."

"Wow," said Chris wide-eyed. "I didn't know we had that many troops there at one time."

"Yep. And did you know the total amount of US troops that served in Vietnam is between two and a half to three million?"

"No, I did not," Chris replied. And although those numbers surprised him, the fact that he didn't know them, and Til did; surprised him even more. He then asked, "Were you drafted?"

"I volunteered, the majority of us there did—roughly two out of every three of us," Til said proudly.

"I hate to admit it, but there's a lot I don't know about Vietnam and what you guys went through over there," Chris said somberly.

"Don't sweat it, kid. That was another time, *way* back. But If I'm going to talk about it any further, I'm going to need a few more hits of weed, if you don't mind?"

"Hey, whatever you feel comfortable doing. I don't want you to feel that you're being pushed or pressured. It's your call."

After lighting up and taking a few more puffs of what was left of his joint, Til seemed ready to open up a bit more to Chris.

"Hmm. Well then, let's see what I can remember about Nam. It's been quite a while since I've spoken to someone about it. Maybe it'll do me some good? Can't be any worse. It's been rough going for me lately." Til said, then coughed again out loudly and violently, which again had Chris concerned for him.

"Sorry about that...damn smoke is hard on my lungs. So where was I? Oh, right, Nam. Yeah, it was tough. I was assigned to the One Oh One, the 101st Airborne Division 'Screaming Eagles.' We got into a major battle against the North Vietnamese Army, or the PAVN (People's Army of Vietnam) as they were known. It was called Operation Apache Snow.

"Hey," said Chris, "that wouldn't be a bad name for this drive considering all the snow outside. But I think we'll make it to Denali National Park where we can spend the night as you suggested. Sorry Til, you were saying about the major battle you were in...."

"It was a freakin' mess kid—a *real* mess. We fought for a strategic hill in the A Shau Valley, a ridge in the middle of a thick jungle. It was a mountain really, with its terrain covered by one hundred to three-hundred-foot-high trees and razor-sharp elephant grass that was six to twelve feet high. It'd cut your skin like a knife. Nasty stuff. And there were mosquitoes everywhere—and I mean *everywhere*. And kid, the Malaria from those damn mosquitoes caused beaucoup casualties too. I've seen firsthand what it done to our troops. It was just plain awful, high fever and pure misery. Most cases weren't deadly, but you almost wish you were if you got it. Man, I tell you, it was no place for fightin'."

After a long pause, as if he was thinking of himself back in the jungle in Nam, he continued. "We were met by strong enemy forces in the VC (Viet Cong) that ended up in a ten-day battle. The length of which allowed American journalists to arrive and report the bloodbath there that took the lives of over seventy of our boys; some of which I saw die right before my eyes. I would say it was hell, but that wouldn't be doing it justice."

Chris thought for a moment that he might be feeling a little high from the weed's second-hand smoke but then realized that he probably wasn't, as the cracked open window took out most of the smoke and let in its fair share of glacial air. No, he wasn't feeling high or even elated. It was a different feeling. What he was feeling was love. Not love in the traditional sense of the word; in fact, it wasn't love in *any* sense of the word. It was LOVE the acronym; the one that he was instructed to follow by his boss, Michael Montrose when he was back at the Oklahoma City VSA.

"If you feel unsure about what to do or say to a veteran, just remember love," he told Chris.

43

"Love? Really? Next thing you're going to tell me to hug them," Chris said. "But seriously, *love?*"

"I meant love, as in the *acronym*. L-O-V-E: Listen, Observe, Vocalize, and Empathize with the veteran—love."

Chris had never heard of that one before, but he liked it. It was easy to remember. *And besides, who couldn't use more love?*

As Til continued talking about Vietnam and his youth, Chris, recalling "LOVE," decided he'd do just that. But for now, he'd just Listen and Observe, or LO.

"Yeah, we had close to four hundred men injured in that battle," Til said, as he put up his window, finally done with the remainder of his joint. "Including myself. It was where I lost my leg, and where I began losing my life."

"How so?" Chris said hesitant about asking the question not wanting to upset him, but he couldn't hold it back.

"That kid is for a different day. Right now, I'm just going to enjoy my buzz and crash a bit. Wake me up when we get to Willow. It's about forty-five minutes away, right off the highway— if that's all right with you podna."

"Sure, Til," Chris said, "No problem. I'll wake you up at Willow. We can use the bathroom there and get some coffee."

Til didn't respond. He had already fallen asleep and began snoring. Chris had to do a doubletake as he couldn't believe that Til had fallen asleep so quickly, but he, sure enough, had— *probably the weed that knocked him out.* Regardless, Chris could now concentrate on the road and the snow that was rapidly covering it. He was at least thankful for the other cars and trucks, albeit few, whose lights and tire tracks he could follow behind. Still, he couldn't help but think of everything Til had just told him about Vietnam: the thick jungle, the exhausting battle, the many casualties, the dreadful Malaria, and the loss of his leg. He felt guilty when he thought of his problems in comparison.

The sleepy town of Willow, with a population of only 2000, came up to Chris faster than expected.

What, almighty, are these people doing living out here?

Til then suddenly woke up.

"Can't believe this place almost became Alaska's state capital

44

back in '76," he said rubbing his sleepy eyes.

"Wow, *this* small town. Really?"

"Yup, back in the fifties this area used to be a big gold mining district. Anyway, in the end, it didn't get pushed through."

After stopping off at a local gas station for a bathroom break, filling up the SUV's tank, and picking up some hot coffee, the two were just about ready to get back on the road when Til pointed to a white bird that he spotted on the ground next to a snowbank. "Look-ee there! A Willow Ptarmigan. Our state bird, wouldn't ya know."

"No, actually, I wouldn't," Chris replied. "But it's sure a pretty all-white bird."

"It sure is," said Til, "they're in the pheasant family of birds. That's its winter plumage there, outside of a few black tail feathers, it changes to all-white in the winter from its normal reddish-brown and part-white color. Funny that the same bird in Britain doesn't ever turn the color white. They only do that here in North America."

"Now *that* is neat, but let's go, I'm freezing!" exclaimed Chris.

The remaining three-hour drive to Denali National Park was calm and quiet as the heavy snowfall finally began to taper off. This had Chris pleased since it gave him much better visibility of the road. And the elusive Alaskan winter sun, which had only shone for six hours in the Central part of the state on this day, had already begun its early descent. Til again fell asleep in the warmth of the vehicle.

He must be very tired.

Chris then tried to find an interesting radio station to listen to but was unsuccessful, so he just gave up and shut off the radio. As Til snored, Chris thought of this trip with him as an adventure. Two lost souls going to God knows where to find God knows what. Like in the classic book where Tom Sawyer and his sidekick Jim, float down the Great Mississippi River on a raft. Was Chris romanticizing the drive and his mission? No question. *But isn't that the way it should be? And the way you want it to be when searching for something, or helping someone in life? To have no signs and no people around to tell you which way to go? To just allow fate to play out its hand. This way you can find the true answers to all your questions with definite clarity. Real 'Catcher in the Rye' stuff, like when Holden Caulfield went off on a whim to New York City to just get away after getting booted from Pencey Prep. But really, why not? I'm already missing home and have no clue what I'm doing here. So, if it helps raise my motivation and spirits, why not? At least Mark Twain and J.D. Salinger would understand and be proud of me....*

The White Willow pheasant then came to Chris's mind. *Was that my vision quest sign? — I mean, yes, it was an animal or a bird. But what made it special? Ahh, yes, it was pure white as the driven snow. And it was not only beautiful, but it was also truly pure. So pure in fact that it wore a wintertime only white "state of grace" chasuble coat, or vestment, if you will, not too dissimilar like the one worn by the bishop of Rome, the supreme pontiff, the Pope. Yet, Aunt Sophie told me I would know when I saw my vision quest. And since I am not sure, I guess the bird isn't it...* Regardless, Chris was undoubtedly glamorizing the drive and his mission. And maybe, just maybe, after working the last few years in the doldrums, he was enjoying himself a bit.

In the far distance, bright lights could be seen near a host of hotels lining the entrance to Denali National Park.

"Glitter Gulch!" Til clamored out, waking himself up and startling Chris in the process.

"Glitter Gulch?" Chris asked.

"That's the dubious term I use for the row of overpriced hotels here. They're ridiculous! It's just a big damn tourist trap," said Til.

"Well, I hate to be the bearer of bad news," Chris said, "but I don't have the funds to afford one of those fancy hotels."

"No worries, kid, it's low season, besides we're going to stay at a cheap cabin inside the park, and we'll get in the park free with my lifetime National Parks Pass due to my VA disability."

"Sounds good, then can we get something to eat?" Chris said.

"Sure," Til replied, then added with full assurance, "I know a place nearby that has *great* Elk burgers."

At the restaurant, after eating mostly in relative silence, Til then asked Chris, "So whatta-ya think?"

"Seriously, that was the best burger that I have ever eaten."

"Yeah, I knew you'd like it," said Til beaming.

"You were right...."

"Hey, kid. Before I give you my sob story over the next month. I need to know something about you. For instance, are ya married? Got any kids? Are you a veteran? What's your deal, man? I mean, you came all the way up here to see me. Give me somethin' about you. Not too many people would do what you're doing—what's your deal?"

"All right Til, you win. But I'll need some more coffee first."

"Sure, whatever the kid wants."

"Okay, well," Chris began, "I'm from Oklahoma City. I'm a veteran; served in the Army for five years in the mid to late nineties, but I never deployed anywhere. I'm divorced and have one child. A fifteen-year-old daughter, Sara. I worked in medical equipment sales for a long while, mostly around The Plains states, then I worked for the VSA for the last few years. Now I got this job, working with veterans like you. That's about it, Til. Nothing too exciting, or difficult. I can't complain about my life, compared to the much tougher issues that I saw other veterans face."

"First off, don't do that," snapped Til.

"Do what?" Chris asked, confused.

"Belittle your issues. *They* are important. *You* are important. I catch your drift about other vets with bigger issues. And it's commendable that you feel that way. But we *all* have a cross to bear—even you. And besides, what good would you be to me, or any of us, if you haven't resolved or are working through your own issues?"

"You should seriously have my job," Chris deadpanned.

"So come on, tell me what issues you got kid."

"Well, the biggest one I have is the lack of communication with my daughter. The other was not having a job, or life, with a real purpose. But then, this mission seemed to just fall out of the sky. I'm thrilled about it. All of it. The challenge and reward of working with fellow vets who need help. But to be honest with you, I don't know who this job will help more, them or me."

"Ya see, that wasn't so hard now, was it? So, whatta-ya gonna do to improve your relationship with your daughter?"

"Truthfully? I haven't got the slightest idea. After the divorce, it seems she doesn't trust me or want to be with me."

Til then pulled out a small flask from the inside of his jacket and poured some of its contents into his coffee cup. He then raised the flask slightly, offering some to Chris, who politely declined by waving him off.

"Well, I don't know either. I'm probably the last person on Earth to give you advice on kids as my relationship with my son has always been...poor. And it was my fault," Til said, as he cautiously took a sip of his hot, spiked coffee.

"From the very beginning, when I was just twenty and I got his mother pregnant with him before leaving for Nam, it was *all* my fault. I always put myself, and other things, before him. *Always.* I think it first started when I returned home from the war. I felt as if my family owed me something for losing my leg; and that my country owed me something—even that the *world* owed me something."

"Well *doesn't* your country owe you a huge debt of gratitude for your sacrifice and service to it?" asked Chris.

"I don't want to go down that road...but yes, of course, they do. But I took it to the *nth* degree. I was disgusted by my country and my government on how they treated us when we got back. They didn't care about us and called us everything bad under the sun, including 'baby killers.' My young wife treated me differently too. I thought since my country didn't want me, that my family wouldn't want me either. I didn't think I was worthy of their love. So, I pushed them away; I did so by almost drinking and smoking myself to death. And I spent my time away from them with the wrong crowd. I didn't want anything to do with my wife and son. By numbing myself, and keeping my distance from them, I felt protected from the pain and embarrassment I felt. But I was only making it worse for them, and worse for me until it was too late. Eventually, I lost them: first, my wife left me. Then, over the years, my son and I drifted apart, until he just stopped talking to me altogether. I had nothing left. And that's where I was wrong. You see, for the longest time—most of my life in fact—I never thought

48

that I was wrong, or at least I didn't want to face that I was. I didn't want to be held responsible for my failures. I didn't want to be held accountable for them until it was too late. The damage was done. The unrepairable damage I caused my family was done, forever."

Chris felt bad for Til, but he didn't know what to say. He wanted him to feel better. He then stammered out, "I'm sorry... for all that you've been through."

"Don't do that either," Til said firmly. "Don't you feel sorry for me, I mean, I appreciate the sentiment and all, I really do kid. But please don't. The pain is all that I have left in this world that is truly my own—as dumb as that might sound."

"That doesn't sound dumb," Chris replied, "not in the least. So, what happened afterward? After you lost your family, that is?"

Til then pulled out his flask again and poured some more of the amber-colored liquid into his coffee mug. "I rebelled against my country. I didn't want anything to do with the Army, the VFW, or the VA. Ya know, they weren't as helpful back during the Vietnam era as they are now...Actually, they were crap. The VA hospitals that I was in were dirty and unprofessional. Just crap. I will say that the VA has improved a lot over the years; I will give them that much. Anyway, I couldn't work gainfully, as I would sometimes freak out on account of my PTSD issues that I picked up in Southeast Asia. My heavy drinking and smoking didn't help matters much either. I finally ended up rebelling against the whole world, until I just completely ran away from it. I isolated myself from it up here. I guess I'm still running from the pain and ghosts of my past. Though, I can't ever seem to outrun them. Even way up here." Til then looked out the diner window to the colorful hotel lights and freshly fallen snow which covered everything in sight. "Even way up here," he repeated softly.

Moments later, Til expressed to Chris how tired he felt and that he was ready to go relax at the lodge. Chris was again about to tell Til how sorry he felt for him and for everything that he had been through but now knew better not to say anything.

The drive to the lodge inside Denali National Park was a short, yet picturesque one. Chris wasn't sure that the park would still be open, as it was almost dusk out. But he then remembered the minimal hours of sun that the Alaska winter had. After displaying Til's National Parks ID card for entry, the gate attendant then handed Chris some brochures about the park. They then proceeded to settle into their modestly sized room with its rustic décor and strong woody odor. Til went straight to bed.

At this hour?

Chris considered watching some TV or even reading, but since they had a studio room, Chris didn't want to wake up Til with the TV on, and he wasn't in any mood to read. So, he decided to take a little drive around the park. *And why not?* There was still some light out. And there were a few other cars still cruising the park, which helped create a drivable path on the snowy roads. Also, the park had a few posted map signs around so Chris figured he couldn't get lost if he didn't venture too far away from the lodge. As he began driving around, going up and down several sloping roads, as well as some winding ones, Chris then abruptly pulled over for the view of his life.

Off in the far distance, he could see hundreds of miles of massive snow-covered mountains known as the Alaska Range. And at its peak, soaring 20,000 feet into a violet-blue sky, the largest mountain in North America, Denali (formerly called Mt. McKinley). Adding to the surreal landscape, stretching between himself and the foothills of the Alaska Range, was a vast wide-open valley full of thousands of white spruce trees covered in hoarfrost, which made the view seem something straight out of a fairytale.

Its majestic beauty had Chris overcome with awe and wonder, as its grandeur seemed almost unreal. But it *was* real. He *was* there. He was a witness to it—so much so that he decided to step out of his car and see the view in the flesh. Not through a car window, with the heat blaring, but in person, in the elements and all. And he was glad that he did, as it gave him the unique perspective of feeling both so small in this world, and so big as well. He wished Sara could have seen it. He wished Jessie could have seen it. He wished *everyone* could have seen it.

With the satisfying fulfillment of the singular moment now gone, Chris turned away from his breathtaking view when suddenly, he stopped in mid-turn when he spotted something. There, standing about twenty yards away stood a four-legged creature. It was as still as Denali behind it, and it looked straight at him. Chris then quickly realized what it was. A wolf. A lone wolf. Its coat was mostly black except for some grey and white on its upper chest and backside, as well as on both sides of its mouth. It continued to stare intently at Chris—a peaceful, yet purposeful gaze; not angrily, but not submissively either. Strangely, Chris wasn't scared. And even if he was, he didn't have the time to be, as it all happened so quickly.

The wolf seemed to appear out of thin air and was locked in on him, so escaping to the car for safety wasn't an option. He now understood what this was. What *it* was. It was a sign. *His* sign. The one Aunt Sophie had told him about: how he would go on a journey into the wilderness to seek his calling in life. Then, a sign or signal from the Gods would reveal itself in the form of an animal or bird, thus providing him with a vision and identity of his true purpose in life. A feeling of calm came over him. Chris knew what he was there to do. He felt it. He knew, unquestionably, that he was supposed to be there.

While the standoff continued, Chris couldn't help but be transfixed by the wolf's yellow eyes and small piercing black pupils. In them, Chris saw a savage and wildness that only came from an instinctual need to kill to survive. Chris took the wolf's eyes as a message that his task of helping the veterans wouldn't be an easy one. It would be a fight, maybe even a fight for survival. But it has been said that when one receives their true purpose in life, one can move mountains. Chris now thought that this may be true—that one *can* accomplish anything if one puts their mind to it.

As dusk tried valiantly to hold out a little longer, the gelid, wintery air, which Chris had somehow managed not to feel when he was focused on the beast, then brutishly reminded him of the deadly sub-zero temperatures and that it was time to go. His purpose was confirmed, and his vision quest was completed. He glanced back at the car to see how far he was from it. But when he turned back toward the wolf, it was gone—just like that. Then, as he was just about to open the car door, he heard the wolf let out a long, loud howl that lingered across the enormous valley. It sounded both daunting and rewarding to Chris. *An enchanting, yet dangerous barbarian of an animal, and it was mine.*

Back at the lodge, Chris couldn't sleep—*Til's heavy snoring didn't help any*—but it was more than that. His head was still spinning from all that he had just seen. *How am I supposed to sleep when I'm so ramped up?* Chris then grabbed the brochures about the park that he had been given earlier. He sat in a chair in the corner of the room, turned on a lamp, and began to quietly peruse through them. Some were more interesting than others. Like the one warning park guests to be watchful of certain animals like Bison, Black and Brown Bears, and Polar Bears (which it said were concentrated at the Arctic coastlines). The brochure listed a handful of other smaller animals too but the one that most sparked Chris's interest was the creature that he had just encountered—the Interior Alaskan Wolf, which was aptly named since it said that they were generally found in the inland part of the state. Chris read on as his curiosity with his vision quest sign persisted. He wanted to know more about this type of wolf. He thought it necessary— almost mandatory, considering what had just transpired only moments ago.

When done reading the park's brochures, he recalled the comment by the park's gate attendant, who said that cell service was *only* available within a few miles of the visitor center. And since his lodging was just two miles and a half away, he wasn't surprised that he had service. On his smartphone, he searched for more information about the beast. He discovered that this type of wolf was among the largest in North America and that in Canada the same wolf is called a Yukon Wolf. He also learned that Alaska has an Arctic Tundra Wolf, which is all-white and lives like the polar bears around the Arctic coastlines. And that the wolf can survive in the harsh Arctic region for which it is named.

Chris went on to read that wolf and man have some distinct similarities. Both are known as "apex hunters" since both are at the top of their food chain, and, except for each other, neither has to fight with any other enemy or animal for their biological niche. Another one is the pack. The Hominids (early prehistoric apes that were the ancestors of humans) normally hunted and stayed in clans of 5 to 15, just like wolves. The Hominids would also travel over a territory of 500 to 1000 square miles in search of food, again just like wolves. But what made this fact extraordinary to Chris was that the article also said that few, if any, other animals, ever cover such a large territory, especially with such few numbers in its pack. With all that information about this wolf, Chris was finally satisfied; the bond was reinforced. He then walked over to the large window, pulled aside the curtain, and looked out into the dark stellar night. *Good night wolf. And thank you.*

The next morning Chris awoke to Til's crabby morning voice.

"My head is killing me, and my back is killing me too. Maybe I should go back to sleep. No, I *ought to* go back to sleep," Til said as he slowly began dressing. Not wanting to be a pest, Chris was unsure of what to say, but he also decided he wasn't going to be of any help to Til if he walked on eggshells around him over the next month. He had to be assertive yet careful. They were in this together now, for better or for worse.

"Come on Til, let's hit the road," he told him with gusto. "You can rest in the car on the way to Fairbanks. Heck, you can even sleep if you want to. It's not as if you're that interesting to talk to," Chris said with a snicker. He then walked up to Til, patted him on the arm, and said, "I'm only kidding with you. I enjoy talking with you, *podna.*"

"Well thanks, kid, coming from you, that means a lot. And I'm *not* kidding with you. But, before we leave, I need to take some painkillers, and maybe even have a drink."

"But Til, we just woke up! Can't it wait until at *least* afternoon or this evening?" Chris asked in desperation. Til glanced over at his liquor bottle sitting on the nightstand as if giving the idea a serious thought. "I'll tell you what," he said, "I'll promise not to drink this morning, but as far as the afternoon, *that,* I cannot promise you."

"Okay, good. Baby steps," Chris said, content with the small victory. "Now, let's go get some breakfast."

After a filling breakfast, they were back on the snowy road with a pale gray sky overhead. The drive to Fairbanks wasn't as enjoyable for Chris as the first leg since Til was growing ornerier and more difficult as the day progressed—the opposite of the day before. Chris knew it would be a long day for both of them. He then thought of the wolf and how much more difficult it was for it out there in the freezing forests of Alaska and what it would have to endure just to survive the day, much less the night. Chris wanted to tell Til about the whole wolf incident of the previous evening but decided to keep it to himself, as Til wasn't in the best of moods and Chris didn't want him to put a damper on his perfect story of finding his vision quest in the wilderness. He reminded himself that he was a long way from home, and so if he needed to cling to an improbable story that occurred, then so be it. He also knew that the odds of him succeeding on this mission were minimal at best, so he was going to use everything in his power to make it work. Make it survive, just like the wolf was going to do. But on this drive, on this day, it wasn't easy. Til began to dig into him.

"So, what are you gonna do? Save me from myself?" Chris looked over at him but didn't say a word. He didn't have an answer for him. "No, really, what do you think you can do that someone else hasn't already tried? What the Army hasn't already tried? What my family hasn't already tried? What the VA hasn't already tried? What my VSA social worker here in Alaska hasn't already tried? Don't you get it, kid?!" Til yelled as he lit a cigarette, the smell of which bothered Chris, but he wasn't about to say anything to him about it. "There isn't anything that you or anybody else can do for me, *ever*. And do you want to know *why* that is?"

"I do," said Chris respectfully.

"It's because I'm *too* far gone. I've seen *too* much in war. I've lost *too* much: my leg, my family. I've been hurt *too* much; both mentally and physically. Now I spend most of my time trying not to feel those things. Between the booze, painkillers, and weed, I'm trying not to feel anything at all."

"You have certainly been through a lot Til," Chris said sympathetically "and are *still* going through a lot, more than any person should have to in one lifetime, but I'm not giving up on you. Everyone needs help sometimes. I'm just a veteran trying to help out a fellow veteran. It's true, perhaps I have no special ability to help you, but I have the desire to. Why don't we just start with that for now? What do you say?"

"Well, I'm still drinking this afternoon," Til said stubbornly.

"Your situation reminds me of a quote that I like to refer to sometimes for inspiration in tough times," Chris said. "I assume you don't want to hear it but I'm going to tell it to you anyway. It's by Ernest Hemingway. He said, '*The world breaks everyone, and afterward some are strong at the broken places.*' So, don't you see? *You* are now strong in those broken places of yours."

Til chuckled lightly after he heard the quote. He turned to Chris who was now pushing and turning knobs trying anything to defog the fogged-up windows.

"That quote funny to you?" Chris asked, confused by his response. "A little," replied Til. "That and you trying to defog these windows. It's too cold out there and too hot in here. You have to turn on the AC or put windows down some more."

"Okay, but I already have them cracked on account of you smoking? The stuff stinks to tell you the truth."

"Fair 'nough,"

"What about the quote?"

"The one from his book, *A Farewell to Arms*. It's just, you only said part of it," replied Til. "The cliff notes version of it. The happy version of it. There's more to it, kid, and it ain't pretty."

"Really? I honestly didn't know that. What's the rest say?"

"Hemingway said, '*The world breaks everyone and afterward many are strong at the broken places. But those that will not break, it kills. It kills the very good and the very gentle and the very brave impartially. If you are none of these you can be sure it will kill you too but there will be no special hurry.*'—A rather sobering thought, huh? But if you think about it. He's right, I agree with Papa, as he was called. The world does break or kill everybody impartially. The very good, the very gentle, and the very brave. And although it hasn't killed me yet, it damn sure has broken me. There are some days, well, I just don't know if I can go on in this world. On those days I ask myself, why go on? What for? It's not like anyone out there would care if I were gone. Anyways, that's the rest of the quote."

"I care about you," said Chris.

"Hmm, you're just being kind as I just met you. You don't know me. My scars and wounds run long and deep. *Too* deep."

Chris tried to change the topic of conversation to something Til still had an interest in; to something that he still lived for. He recalled what his social worker had said about how he would sometimes go to Fairbanks to work with some Dogsledders up there.

"So *why* exactly are we going to Fairbanks?" he asked him.

"Come on' you know why," Til said, sounding annoyed by the question. "You wouldn't just hop in a car with me to go up north for nothing. You're too smart for that—heck, *anyone* is smart enough not to do that...Tell you what," he continued, "let's stop and pick up a six-pack, and then I'll tell you all about it."

"Sorry, Til, no can do. Illegal."

Til turned away visibly upset. "Fine, kid, have it your way... Don't matter anyhow. I got some booze," Til said as he pulled out his flask and drank from it.

Chris then said, "We only have about an hour to Fairbanks?"

"An hour?" Til stated or asked, then said, "Good, just enough time to get me nice and lit."

Great, just what we both need.

"I figured in Fairbanks I'd save some money and stay on base at Fort Wainwright. Do you want to stay there too?" asked Chris.

"Thanks, but nah. I'm staying with Gary, Laura, and the dogs."

"The *dogs?*"

"Yep, Gary and his Siberian Husky dog team who participate in all the big dog sledding races in the state."

"Does he know that you're coming?"

"He knows all right, and if he doesn't, he'll put me up anyway—*always does,"* snorted Til.

Chris then said, "The weather is awful here. I can't wait to get up there. Winter in Alaska, Til, you sure keep things interesting."

"I try," Til said dryly. "Wake me when we're there, will ya?"

Sure, no problem. I'm Ok to drive through this blizzard alone.

As Chris drove, the idea of pulling over to a rest stop to wait out the weather crossed his mind, but the other cars trudging on the highway around him, as well as the assumption that the weather probably wouldn't improve much, kept him driving on. He then thought of his dad and wondered what he would have thought about what his son was doing; would he think he was foolish? Or admirable? Chris figured his dad would have said something to the effect of both. 'Well, son it's an honorable thing you're doing, helping out your fellow kind in crisis and all. Yet do you think it wise to travel across the country—even out of the continental U.S.—when you don't even have your *own* house in order? Now don't get me wrong, if it's what you want to do, I support it. I just want you to consider everything before making such a major commitment.'

His father always had a way of showing Chris all the cards on the table, so to speak, so that he could make more of an educated decision on things. Sometimes, however, this would bother Chris, who thought his father was trying to change his mind. But as Chris aged and matured, he understood that his father wanted what was best for him, even if it meant looking at the worst-case scenario of things, just in case. Thinking about it now, Chris saw more and more of a resemblance in the behavior of his father in his sister, Aunt Sophie. Both made him look at the bigger picture, so he could make a more informed, and ultimately better decision on important issues. *So, I guess I have two guardian spirits..*

The 'Welcome to Fairbanks' sign only read 'airbank' as the rest was covered in snow—not a good sign in more ways than one. As Chris entered the downtown area, he couldn't help but think of how similar it looked to any other smaller city in Oklahoma, with its boxy buildings lacking anything remotely close to resembling a skyscraper. Yet, this city was (obviously) snowier and even had a river running through it, which is a 100-mile tributary of the

Tanana River and went right by Fort Wainwright.

On Main Street, Chris drove past a bank with a digital sign that displayed the time and weather: 12:33 p.m. -21 degrees. He shivered at the thought. He then turned to wake up Til.

"Til, *we're heeere!* Rise and shine. Wakey, wakey."

"—I hear ya," Til said, in a low, muffled voice, "I hear ya."

"Welcome to Fairbanks!" Chris said enthusiastically.

"Relax, kid," Til coolly replied, "—not in the mood,"

"All right, no problem, but you have to tell me where the heck I'm going? It's a complete whiteout out here. I can't see crap."

"It'll be okay. All you need to do is get back on the expressway, and head north for another two or three miles; you'll then see a sign for Aurora. That's where we're going. That's where Gary, Laura (his wife), and the dogs live."

"Got it," said Chris thankful that his arduous drive would soon be over. When they finally reached Gary's home, pulling into a driveway that had recently been paved of snow, Chris saw thick smoke coming steadily out of the chimney of a smaller-sized home. There was another structure to the left that resembled a cow barn. It was partially exposed at the bottom of its sides. And it held several dog houses. The extensive yard was mostly snow-filled, minus the path to and from the house and dog barn. There were two pickup trucks and a large shack that was completely enclosed from the outdoor elements. It presumably contained all the dog's gear, such as their sleighs and so forth. The front door opened just as they pulled up; Gary was coming out in an Eskimo jacket to assist Til into the house. Once inside, Chris met Laura; a small, gentle, soft-spoken woman with dark hair with streaks of gray. He estimated her to be in her late fifties. She was warm and hospitable. Gary was a tall, burly man with pale skin and bushy red hair. Chris also thought him to be in his late fifties and, like his wife, friendly to his new guests, as both seemed genuinely happy to see them. Laura soon brought out hot coffee and asked if they were hungry.

"Yes ma'am!" replied Til, almost before she was done asking.

"We've got reindeer sausage," she told him.

"Stuff's damn good too," Gary added boastfully.

"Sounds good," Til and Chris said in unison. Laura then

gracefully left the room with the three men moving over to the dining room: its table was covered with wooden knick-knacks and old newspapers. Gary quickly cleared it by putting it all in a nearby closet.

Til then asked Gary, "Got anything stronger than this coffee?"

"Sure Til, but how about you wait until later? It's just the afternoon?" Til didn't respond but looked over at Chris to see if he would make a face or comment about Gary's request to him. He did neither, which seemed to satisfy Til for the moment, who remained silent. Gary and Chris commenced to small talk about the drive to Fairbanks and the cold weather in Alaska during the winter. Soon after, Laura served the reindeer sausage with some sourdough bread and mustard. She also topped off their coffee cups. No cream or sugar was offered, for, although they were officially still in America, small provisions here were a commodity—even cream and sugar.

Chris thought it better for Til to get settled in at Gary's alone while he headed to Fort Wainwright to check in and regroup. Gary and Laura were more than friendly, but Chris wanted to wash up, rest, and maybe even go to the base gym: though not a gym rat by any stretch, Chris knew he needed to start going regularly as it could only help him with his growing waistline, lower energy levels, and now higher stress levels. *Plus, what else was I going to do? I should let Gary, Laura, and Til catch up until I come back in a day or two when I am better rested and more focused, and they are ready to let a stranger like me in.*

The accommodations at Fort Wainwright were exactly as Chris had expected them to be. And he liked them that way; it was comforting to him to be on base. Sure, it was bland, as most military bases are. But it was also very safe, and cheap, and allowed him the use of a gym almost all to himself. Although halfway through his first modified midlife work out there, he felt dispirited after experiencing discomfort. It first came after he walked on the treadmill in the form of heavy breathing and throbbing knees. Then it was after some sit-ups that his stomach burned. And lastly, after just a few bench presses and arm curls, which ached those muscles as well. Dejected, but not defeated, Chris went to his room to nap. On most days he felt younger than his soon-to-be forty-nine years. But on this day, he did not. On this day, he felt older. He even thought that he looked older with the V-shape of his widow's peak appearing extra sharp, along with some new uninvited gray hairs.

Those are stupid things to worry about. I shouldn't be worried about things like that. Vanity. Please. I should worry about more important things like helping others and my family. But vanity is vanity. We all have it in some shape or form—just some more than others. Besides, who do I need to look good for anyway?

Chris awoke from his nap with a big appetite. He took the base shuttle bus over to the PX (Post Exchange), *no need to take the frozen rental car.* At the food court, there were primarily fast-food options to choose from, and like at the gym, he had it mostly to himself. Since he was so hungry, and it was so slow there, he threw around the idea of eating at different places because one meal, after such a tough workout, may not do the job. But after eating a Philly cheesesteak with fries, he wisely decided against it. He, nonetheless, couldn't resist a piece of cake for dessert. *Baby steps.*

Afterward, he meandered around the main store to kill some time. He didn't want to go to the room and watch TV. He looked briefly at the clothes, colognes, watches, electronic equipment, and even at the snacks and alcohol. But he didn't want to buy anything. He didn't *need* anything. He thought that both a little strange and positive. *Maybe I'm not so vain after all? Or maybe I'm just boring? Whatever, there's got to be something here for me. Hell, anything.* Chris then came across an aisle full of magazines and paperback books. A few magazines might do the trick, but the fonts were always too small which would make him have to use his reading glasses, and make him feel, gulp, *fifty.* The paperbacks were another issue. They were just so long. At least these were, he thought, with some over 400 pages. He just wanted something simple to read occasionally, if at all. The truth was that Chris wasn't that big of a reader. Nevertheless, he looked and looked but nothing struck his fancy. He was just about to give up when he came across a small section of classic books, like, *The Great Gatsby*, by F. Scott Fitzgerald. *A Tale of Two Cities*, by Charles

Dickens, and *The Old Man and the Sea*, by Ernest Hemingway. *The classics stand the test of time and continue to sell for a reason. How can I go wrong with any of these?* He decided on *The Old Man and the Sea*. He even bought an extra copy for Til since he had known the full quote by Hemingway that Chris had partially quoted to him.

A day and a half later, Chris drove over to see Til. He could hear the dogs barking excitedly as he walked up to the house. Gary opened the front door, which was practically frozen solid just as Chris arrived at it. *He's always ready with the door—thank God.*

"There he is," Gary said in a booming voice that seemed fit for the lumberjack kind of a man he was. "How are ya? Come on in. I bet you're not used to this really cold weather. But who is? Am I right?"

"Not me, that's for sure," Chris quickly replied.

"Let me take your coat. And come sit down and relax," said Gary. "Would you like some coffee, water, or hot chocolate? Or perhaps something stronger?"

"Coffee, black. Thanks. Sorry to just drop over unannounced, but I wanted to see how Til was doing."

"He's with the dogs out in the barn," said Gary, "—tending to them, feeding them, grooming them; just being with them. He likes it. Calms him down and calms the dogs down too. And they need it, as I recently ran them in a race here in Fairbanks called: The Midnight Sun Gold Run. It had four sprints in it: two 6.2 milers with four dogs, one 8.1 miler with six dogs, and one 12.5 miler with ten dogs. I ran in the 8.1 miler. Didn't win, but I did okay and sure had fun. A lot of fun, but it's also very tiring. Laura—who's always a big help with the races—is actually in the other room right now taking a nap. Let me get you that coffee, then you and I can sit down and talk until Til returns."

"That'll be great," said Chris, encouraged by the idea of having a stimulating conversation with Gary, not only about him in Alaska and his dog sledding, but also, hopefully, about Til. He wanted to know if he honestly thought that Til could improve from all the issues that hindered him in the past. And if so, maybe even provide some advice on how to help him.

"Here ya go, nice and hot," said Gary handing Chris an off-white ceramic diner-style mug, while holding one for himself. They then sat across from each other; each in a worn, bulky armchair with crochet blankets draped over them: Gary's was a solid brown, Chris's multicolored.

"Thanks," said Chris, who then asked, "so, what brings you and your wife up here to Fairbanks? Or Alaska for that matter?"

"Well, we're originally from Duluth, Minnesota right there off Lake Superior. It's there where I first met Laura at the University of Minnesota Duluth, where they have an extension center—the main campus is in Minneapolis. We both became math teachers and eventually got married. All was good. That is until we found out that she could not have children. That was a tough one to take. *Real* tough. We tried other avenues; even considered adoption. But children just weren't in the cards for us. We accepted our fate. Then, just a few short years later, Laura's younger sister died from breast cancer.

"I'm sorry to hear that," Chris said sympathetically.

"Thanks…Laura took her passing extremely hard. Mable was her only sibling; they were very close. She looked after her until the very end," said Gary, who then paused and looked downward appearing to get misty-eyed. He then let out a small cough, stood up, and took Chris's coffee cup for a refill.

"Appreciate it," Chris said, feeling the sadness coming off Gary. But when he returned with Chris's coffee, he sounded better. "So," he continued, "after Mable passed, that was enough for Laura. And for me too. I mean, we had our teacher's pension, and it was just time for a new start—you know what I mean?"

"I know *exactly* what you mean."

"So here we are, dog sledding on top of the world. Yes, sir, the town of North Pole, Alaska is just 15 miles from here," Gary said with a chuckle. "The actual North Pole is much further north."

"But dog sledding?" Chris remarked, then asked, "Did you know anything about it before coming up here?"

"Truth be told. No, we didn't. But we learned about it, like how Russian explorers were credited for being the first efficient dogsledders in the late 1700s. And we learned about the dogs too, like how there are two main pure dog breeds for sledding, The Siberian Husky and the Alaskan Malamute. Both can withstand extreme cold. And both are used for their speed and endurance. There is also the mixed breed dog, the Alaskan Husky. They are also sometimes referred to as Indian dogs since they originally came from Native American villages in the Alaskan and Canadian regions. Those dogs make the *best* sled dogs. They are unquestionably the sled dog of choice for world-class racers. None of the purebred northern breeds can match them in racing speed and pulling ability. One would probably think the purebred snow dogs would be the optimal ones. But nope, it's the mutt breed here that's best. The good ole' Alaskan Husky."

"When do you race again?"

"Our next race is only a week away. And it's the Big One wouldn't you know? This sprinter race was just a warm-up."

"The *big* one?" asked Chris.

"That's right. The big one. I'm talking about the Iditarod, The Last Great Race on Earth! (As it's officially known)."

"I think I may have heard of the Iditarod before," said Chris. "Maybe, I mean, I guess I have. But it doesn't ring a bell, to be honest. What exactly is it? And when and why did it start? If you don't mind telling me."

"Sure. Be honored to," replied Gary. "Heck, almost seems my duty to, considering I'm in the race this year. Anyhow, it all started back in January of 1925 in the small western Alaskan coastal city of Nome, where an outbreak of the often-deadly disease of diphtheria occurred. As many as 10,000 people (including children) were at risk of death without the proper medicine. The only doctor in the area at the time knew this, but the medicine could not be delivered since the port of Nome was closed for the season when temperatures can reach as low as 50 degrees below zero. Anyway, no vehicles could get there through the snowy terrain (at least not in 1925). To travel there in those conditions, in that winter season, was pretty much impossible. The Nome doctor communicated throughout Alaska and found out that the city of Anchorage had the medicine. But that was nearly 700 miles away, and with no real means to get the meds there, they decided to use mushers and sled dogs. Less than a week later, the medicine had finally reached Nome. The people were saved. It became quite the story. Even our President at the time, Calvin Coolidge, wrote the mushers to thank them for taking part in the dangerous delivery. Fast forward almost fifty years later to March of 1973, when they had the first Iditarod race. It began in the city of Anchorage and ended in Nome, to pay homage to the mushers and dogs who had first delivered the medicine there in 1925. And it's happened every year since. It's a long and grueling race, and the longest Sled dog race in the world, at almost 1000 miles long, that takes about a week or two to finish. It took the first winner twenty days! It's now a big deal all over the state and has been for a while. The real heroes though are the volunteers in the various communities who help out from putting up the mushers overnight, to helping with fundraising, to well, pretty much everything. And there are of course the Seaveys. Wouldn't be right to tell you the story of the Iditarod without including the Seaveys. Heck, they practically *are* the Iditarod itself."

"The Seaveys? How so?"

"Well for starters, Dan Seavey Sr. was one of the pioneers of the first-ever Great Race back in '73. He even raced in it, finishing in third. He ran it again in '74. And would you believe it, he ran in it in 2012 at age 74. He wasn't in the running to win, but still just to finish it at that age is quite incredible. Then there is his son Mitch. He first won the race in 2004. He then won it again in 2013 and 2017, where he beat the Iditarod speed record at age 57 to become the oldest musher to ever win the race. And lastly, there is Dallas Seavey. Grandson of Dan and son of Mitch. Not to be outdone by either of them, he was the youngest musher ever to win the race at age 25 in 2012. As if that wasn't enough, he then won it three years in a row (from 2014 through 2016). So, you can see why the Seaveys are such a big part of the Iditarod."

"A family affair if there ever was one," said Chris.

"The Iditarod is in truth a large family affair," Gary replied. "Especially when you consider all the teamwork and partnership it takes to pull it off every year. Hey, I've got a great idea. Why don't you and Til accompany me and Laura down to Anchorage and see me off at the beginning of the race? It starts on the first Saturday in March. But that's only the ceremonial start. The real start or restart is in Willow, about an hour North."

"Been there!" Chris said excitedly.

"No, really, it'll be a lot of fun, and it's my last Big Race too. At 58, I'm too old to be competitive in it anymore. But not for Mitch Seavey. No, at 59, he's racing in it again this year and always has a chance of winning it. That darn Seavey winning gene is *real*. Besides, I figure you and Til need to eventually get back down to Anchorage anyway."

"I'd be honored to go," replied Chris, gracious of the offer.

"Ok, it's settled then. By the way, Til told me a little about why you're here; how you're working with the government on a program to help out vets. I think that's very commendable of you,"

"Thanks. But frankly, I don't know if I can help Til or any veteran—I'm no social worker. I'm just a regular guy trying to make a difference for some heroes who've lost their way. Do you have any advice or insight that may be helpful with Til?"

"You come across me as a sincere person. I think that just by being with him, you are helping him. I think that's the biggest part. I will tell you that we have only known Til for about four years, and when he visits, he doesn't stay that long. He says he doesn't want us to be bothered by his issues. I mean, we do try to stop him from drinking too much when he's here. We let him smoke his Marijuana since it's prescribed and legal here. Either way, he has a lot of personal issues; Vietnam messed him up, especially at such a young age. And afterward, he lost everything. Even today, he still has flashbacks of the war fifty years later. He continues to display all the classic PTSD issues and more, like avoidance, massive mood swings, and negative thoughts about himself, people, and even the world, including feeling detached from his friends and family from being so emotionally numb—not to mention his homelessness and suicidal tendencies. But I'm sure you're well aware of all this already. And you're also well aware that Til has worked with many medical agencies that have tried to help him. But none have. So, we saw him homeless on the street one day in Anchorage, as I said four years ago, and, as church-going people, told him he could stay with us for a while if he'd like. He agreed to stay for only a few days as that's all he felt comfortable doing. He got a big kick out of the sled dogs and just began helping out with them. So that's what he does. He comes up once or twice a year for a few days, a week at most, and helps out with the dogs. We don't ask him too many questions or bother him when he visits. We figure he's been through enough already. We're always happy to see him. Although we're not veterans, we believe in helping them whenever possible, especially homeless ones."

Gary's story about the big race amazed Chris, and his story about how they cared for Til impressed him.

These were good people.

Chris also wanted to remember what Gary had told him, that by just being with him, you are helping; that's the biggest part....

After the conversation with Gary, Chris went to the dog barn to talk to Til. The short walk from the toasty-warm house to the raw, bone-penetratingly cold air was still too long for him. The dogs began barking wildly upon his arrival. Til turned to greet Chris as he entered the barn rubbing his hands rapidly together.

"Hey," Til said as he stood up with his cane.

"I came to see how you and the dogs were doing," Chris said.

"They're fine; strong souls indeed," Til replied, petting one affectionately. Chris then pulled a book out of his bag and handed it to him. "I found a book to read at the PX, so I thought I'd pick you up a copy too. It's *The Old Man and the Sea* by Ernest Hemingway. I thought it was fitting since you taught me about one of his quotes."

Til accepted the book and studied it as if it were an old artifact that had just been discovered after many years of being buried. "He won the Pulitzer for this one...been maybe fifty years or more since I last read it. Thanks, kid."

Over the next week, it was a similar routine of Chris staying at the base and going to Gary's house daily to see Til. Chris even helped with prepping the sled dogs for the big race. And although these dogs are famously known for being ultra-strong and durable, as well as being able to withstand insanely cold weather, Chris also found them to be smart and loving animals. He now fully understood the connection that Til had with them. They had an unmistakable bond; both were warriors at heart. Both were able to withstand hell. And both had.

One day, Gary came up with what he thought was another splendid idea. He suggested that Chris and Til take an excursion to see the Northern Lights; he added that an ideal place to see them was just twenty miles north of Fairbanks, at a place called, Clearly Summit. He said to see them was magical and mythical, even inspirational. And that they, at least for him, invoked pleasant memories. "It was a *must-see* experience," he explained. "Besides, when, if ever, would they have the chance to see them again?"

Til and Chris agreed. It was all settled.

Later that evening, they headed up to Clearly Summit. As soon as they got into the car, Til lit up a joint. Chris didn't say a word as he remembered that it was legal in Alaska and that Til needed it for his anxiety and other medical issues. *And anyway, if there was any time to be under the influence of weed, it would be while watching the fabled Aurora Borealis.*

At Clearly Summit, they parked at the large, state-maintained parking lot, which faced northward toward the arctic skyline for what was supposed to be a flawless view of the auroral displays. But when they arrived, all they saw was a dark, midnight-blue sky full of millions of little white stars. A picture-perfect backdrop for one of nature's most dazzling shows. Til scoffed at the lack of lights, then puffed on his joint. Chris peered up to try and catch a glimpse of the elusive Aurora, which in Roman myths, was known as the goddess of the dawn. Their view was still spectacular, even without the presence of the Northern Lights. But they came for the show, and fortunately for them, it came just minutes later. It started with a flicker. Then a light lime-green haze appeared faintly in the distance until, finally, it began in all its glory, streams of tall, bright, emerald-green lights were winding through the endless night sky.

Til and Chris were awestruck by the immense occult beauty which they beheld. Til then pulled out his flask, took a swig from it, then, without speaking, offered some to Chris. Though never much of a drinker, Chris figured a drink now would be okay, almost appropriate. He took a good sip and handed the flask back to Til. The wavey green lights then changed in direction and color, replaced by huge curtains of white and purple and slivers of red. A symphony seemingly orchestrated by the Gods for the mortals on Earth to admire.

Mesmerized by the dancing, multicolored lights, Chris and Til began to reminisce about a specific memory of their past. Though barely two feet apart, inside, they were worlds apart; Til was back home, a young G.I. preparing to leave for Southeast Asia. His young, pregnant wife peppered him with kisses. He could vividly remember her soft, velvety white skin and the smell of her enticing perfume around her delicate neckline. She was proud of him for serving his country. That he was going to help stop the spread of communism. That he was going to stop the killing on the other side of the world. They talked about the future. *Their* future. He would go to tech school or college or something. He would provide. She would stay at home. Have more children. They would be happy. All would be okay. She assured him of that. He assured her of that. Til took another, yet larger, gulp from his flask and got lost in his recollections and the polar lights above. And in a very long time, he felt good inside.

Chris's thoughts took him back almost a decade earlier to a hockey game he had attended with his father before his illness. Both were giddy that their city had been awarded a new hockey team in the AHL (American Hockey League), the Oklahoma City Barons. They even talked about becoming season ticket holders. At the game, Chris told his father amusing anecdotes about little Sara, which he couldn't get enough of. Over popcorn, pretzels, and sodas, they talked and talked, all while still paying close attention to the game, pointing when seeing a hard hit, clapping over a good play, and throwing their hands up over a bogus penalty call. Chris recalled how his father would always take the time to listen to him—to really listen to him about things that were bothering him—even on smaller, petty issues, unlike Jessie, who would become infuriated by them.

It was at this game that Chris first told his father that his marriage was going sour. His father took it in stride when hearing this, as if he already knew something was amiss with them. "Look," he said to his son while not changing his ever-optimistic outlook, which Chris always revered. "All you have to do and keep doing is to put *her* first. Period. Not her parents, not her siblings, not even her grandparents. *Her.* Don't get me wrong, I'm not saying you don't have to like her family, friends, or even her dog. But they are all secondary because, in the end, it'll only be you and her. And if she loves you, like the way she's supposed to, she'll feel the same. Likewise, she should always put *you* first. If she ever stops doing that, then that's when you know she no longer loves you. Make no mistake, marriage is tough. Even the best ones need constant work to succeed. Remember, son, put *her* first. How she treats you after that, there isn't much you can do. Either she loves you, or she doesn't. It's just that simple. Your mother loves me. Sure, we have our problems. But she always respects and supports me over anyone, and for that, I am grateful. Hang in there. If it's meant to be, then it's meant to be. True love endures."

Chris always loved that line from his father—the eternal optimist. After the game, they went to see a late movie. A comedy with Zach Galifianakis and Robert Downey Jr. called Due Date. They laughed out loud in the empty theatre, nudging each other at the hilarious scenes. Chris missed laughing like that with his father. After the picture, his father wanted him to promise him something.

"Sure Dad, anything. What is it?" he asked him.

"Whatever happens between you and Jessica, promise me to stay involved in Sara's life. I mean *fully* involved. Got me? She needs her father in her life, especially when she's growing up. I've seen too many of my coworkers not put forth the effort to spend time with their kids. Those dads all have excuses not to: they're too busy or tired they would rather have a drink. Or watch the game, whatever. It's always something. Anyhow, you get the idea, be *her* hero. Got it?"

"Yes, got it, Dad. Is it me, or do you sound extra sentimental?"

"I just wanted to make sure I covered that with you."

"Okay, anything else?" Chris asked kiddingly.

"Yes, as a matter of fact, there is one more thing. If I haven't told you lately, I love you."

"I love you too, Dad."

The Northern Lights continued their erratic yet somehow calculated movements through the night sky. Chris smiled and envisioned his father manipulating the show from the heavens above and smiling himself—the eternal optimist in any world. Tears of joy filled Chris's eyes. For a moment, he felt reconnected with his father.

A few years later, his father received his cancer prognosis. They all thought he would make it. Doctors. Family. God. They were all wrong. He hung on for a couple more years. In the same year of his passing, their new hockey team in Oklahoma City announced that they were folding. They lasted only five years. Chris didn't care. On the contrary, he was relieved that they were folding; too many fond memories of going to the games with his father: talking, listening, laughing, learning.

At the end of the week, they all drove down to Anchorage for the ceremonial start of the Iditarod. It was a frigid Saturday morning on the second of March, under a greyish-blue sky, when each sled team began taking off like old Roman chariot racers through the snow-filled roads of the city. Race fans packed the sidewalks, all bundled up and boisterous, supportive, and jovial. Though it was only the ceremonial start, the real one was occurring the next day—there was still an undeniable atmosphere of excitement in the air similar to that of a college football game or a speed car race: part party, part comradery, part competitiveness, and part danger. Chris enjoyed it, getting lost in the people, their passion, and the terms affiliated with dog racing, such as booties, which were on all the dogs' paws. And the yelp of *hike!* Which was the command to get a dog team to start moving. There were the lead dogs' which are known for their high level of intelligence, drive, and trail savviness. And there were the footboards, which are on the runners, and where the mushers stood. And, of course, the ever-important snow hook which the mushers use to drive into firm snow to temporarily anchor a team without needing to tie them to something that took more time. A large sign, *the 47th Iditarod Trail Sled Dog Race,* hung overhead.

It was finally Gary's turn to go, his last symbolic start to the big race. Chris, Til, and Laura waved eagerly to him as the closely nestled crowd around them roared. When all the starts and festivities were over, Chris and Til said goodbye to Laura. She went on to follow her husband, along with the other spouses and volunteers, until the end of the race, sixteen days later, on March 18th, in Nome.

Though Mitch Seavey didn't win the race, he did finish in the top ten. Gary, however, did not finish the race as he was scratched approximately one week into it due to flu-like symptoms, which, according to Laura, were too much for him to overcome. There was no shame in him not completing the race of all races, especially at his age and in those fierce weather conditions. But, according to Laura, Gary's spirits remained high afterward as he still planned on participating in sled dog races around their home in Fairbanks in the future—albeit much smaller ones.

The remaining weeks in Anchorage for Chris and Til had its ups and downs, but overall, they were not too dissimilar from when they were in Fairbanks. Chris returned to stay on base and even got Til a room there too, at the recommendation of his social worker, who knew he would not go right back to the homeless shelter. As their last days together approached, Chris now focused on the *E* in love (empathize). He looked it up just to be sure; *understand and share the feelings of another and put oneself in another's place.* Chris knew this would not be well received by Til, but he wanted to ensure it was self-evident to him.

They met for the last time at a low-key diner on a snowy Sunday morning in the third week of March. Both seemed semi-upbeat when they ordered their breakfast. Chris, a western omelet with wheat toast. Til, pancakes with a side of bacon. Both had black coffee. They ate in silence until Chris broke it. "I just wanted to thank you for allowing me the time to spend with you over the past four weeks. I know it wasn't easy on you, getting you out of your routine and all. And I don't need to sugarcoat it for you, as you taught me not to do that with you, but…well, Til, I must say it, you have been through so much, and I can only imagine how hard it all must have been for you—and *still* is for you. Anyway, you hang in there and remember that there are people out there, like Gary, Laura, and me, who care about you. So, you don't give up on us, and we won't give up on you. Deal? And who knows maybe one day you will even see your son again."

Til didn't respond to Chris's last statement, so he continued, "Before I go, I have two surprises for you; the first is about your room on base."

"What of it?" asked Til sounding annoyed.

"Well, your social worker and I, worked it out with the DoD, and you will be allowed to stay there permanently if you wish. And they also have a base shuttle that goes to and from downtown, so you'll be all set there."

"You didn't have to do that kid. And I don't know how that will work out for me, but I do appreciate it. What's the other thing?"

"That one I'll have to show you. I'll be right back."

Chris hurriedly got up from the booth and stepped outside. He then waved to someone in a parked car to come over. Til looked up toward the door to see what was going on. He was surprised to see Laura walking into the diner with a dog. An Alaskan Husky. And it was one Til was familiar with. One that he had spent much time with when he was in Fairbanks, helping with Gary's sled dogs. It was his favorite one, Reno. Laura was all smiles when she walked up with him, straight to Til.

"What is this, Laura? What are ya doin' here with Reno?" Til asked, confused.

"Reno is yours now. He's retired from racing, and since you were always so good with him, we thought it would be a good idea if he were *your* dog," said Laura, who then handed him the leash.

"Officially, Reno will be your service dog," Chris explained.

"He'll need to go through some training but that won't be a problem considering how smart and well-trained he already is."

72

"That he is," said Til. "My social worker is okay with this?"

"She's been informed and is on board with it," replied Chris assuredly. Til nodded then asked Laura, "Where's Gary?"

"He's at home. But he wanted you to know that he couldn't think of anyone better to take care of Reno than you. And I agreed." Til took in what Laura said. He appeared moved, then said, "Well, I don't know what to say except thank you. I hope I don't let you guys down."

"I'm sure you won't," responded Laura. "And you take care of yourself Til. We hope to see you and Reno again soon in Fairbanks," she said, before lastly giving him a warm hug goodbye. Til then turned to Chris and thanked him for all his help. Adding, "You know in a way, you remind me of the son I wish I had." He then paused for a moment then uttered with a snort, "But that doesn't mean I'm gonna read that damn book you got me."

The next day Chris was on a flight off to, according to his boss, "One of the most beautiful cities in the country."

"Are you going to make me guess?" moaned Chris.

"You're San Diego bound! Not the worst place to go in late March—wouldn't you say? As always, you'll get all the details of your next veteran's case from the local social worker there. I also emailed you some information."

"Ok, thank you," Chris replied. "I must admit, it will be nice to be in the warm sun."

VI
SOLITUDE IN SoCaL

---

*"Whether you think you can or you think you can't,
you're right."* –Henry Ford

On the five-and-a-half-hour flight to his new location, Chris went over the past month: what he did, what Til did, and what they did.

Did I accomplish anything of value?

He then remembered what his boss had first told him, that this was a pilot program—an experiment. The words hung in Chris's head unsure of how reassuring they were. He decided to take the advice. Although deep down, he knew that it didn't matter if it was a pilot program or not, especially when it came to his desire for it to succeed. He also remembered that Til was supposed to be his toughest case. And a tough case it was.

Looking out the airplane's window, Chris could see that they were flying parallel down the Pacific coast. *An utterly beautiful sight indeed.* It came with the customary bright Southern California sunshine, together with a baby-blue sky that was the envy of the world. But the envy wasn't just from its sun and sky. It was also from its coastal location, year-round mild temperatures, and its highly sought-after low humidity. But Chris again reminded himself that he wasn't on a vacation. He was on a mission. He then felt good about what he had accomplished in Alaska. Or at least of what he had tried to accomplish there. *It was a reasonably good start; I mean, Til was 70 and did have many issues.*

Chris also wondered if Til would make it okay in the end: with his son, with his dog, and with himself. As the plane began its final descent into 'America's Finest City' as it's officially called—per the talky male college student who told this fact to a youthful, pretty woman who sat between them. The student seemed to impress himself with the statement, the young woman not so much. She didn't respond to it at all. Chris thought about it, *America's finest city? Please. The arrogance to call it that. I mean really. There are many fine cities in our great country. Many. What the heck made this one the finest? Anyway, finest city or not, it does make me curious to know if it's true. Nonetheless, San Diego here I come....*

After landing, Chris got a call from his next veteran's social worker, who yelled fervently in the phone, "I'm at the USO, in the airport! —I'll meet you there!"

"Will do," Chris replied, now strangely missing Alaska.

A short walk and several minutes later, Chris met his next social worker at the USO. He led him to a makeshift office in the back which, he explained, he was able to use when he was at the airport. He was young (mid-thirties), lanky, and spoke very quickly—too quickly for Chris's liking. He was also very animated with his hands, which constantly moved when he spoke. It was almost as if he was making a pizza in the air, just without the dough. Perhaps it was due to overtraining in public speaking, or lack thereof, Chris thought.

"How was your trip?" the social worker asked with a hand now appearing to hold a cooked pizza.

"Fine," said Chris, suddenly hungry.

"Good, good, I'm glad you're here. I've been briefed on your mission and am thankful to have you here helping us with a veteran. And one who could surely use your help. I, myself, served ten years in the Navy, then I went to school to do this. You know, give back. Are you a veteran?"

"Army, five years, a long time ago," Chris said, hoping he wouldn't be asked about his combat time. He wasn't. *Thankfully.*

75

"Our casework load here is, uh, extensive. Quite extensive to be honest with you. Any help is appreciated. So, let me provide you with Alex's information so you can get on your way. Alex is a former Marine with two combat tours in Afghanistan. He served six years in total. First, training right here in San Diego at the Marine Corps Recruit Depot. Then, he got stationed just up the coast at Camp Pendleton. He's twenty-six, single, and lives in a small apartment downtown. A *very* small apartment. His current job doesn't pay that much—I don't know how he affords to live here. I've been trying to get him into college or tech school with the G.I Bill but it hasn't been easy; Alex has Post Traumatic Stress Disorder, or PTSD, from all the action he saw. He has the usual symptoms of aggressive and destructive behavior, as well as problems with concentration, and he especially has issues with hypervigilance and exaggerated startled response. I truly don't know how to help him anymore. We tried a service dog but that didn't work out. Well anyway, like I said, I'm glad you're here. Do you have your lodging all set?"

"I do, thanks. I figured I'd stay at the Navy Annex over at Point Loma. I mean the price is right and the location is right on the bay. Do you think I'm okay there?"

"Yes sir, that's a fine military lodging, and like you said, the price is right; hotels in downtown San Diego are *crazy* expensive. Do you have a rental car?"

"Yes, I just need to pick it up."

"Okay, but you may not be driving around here that much. The downtown city area is very compact. You can uber or taxi it almost everywhere; it's still good to have it though, just in case. By the way, are you a baseball fan?"

"No, not really. Why?"

"I got you and Alex tickets to the San Diego Padres baseball game on Sunday, March 31st for military appreciation day. The game is at 1:10 p.m. I got the tickets through the USO. The official opening day game is on Thursday. But I couldn't score you guys those tickets. Too pricey. Hey, did you know that this is the second straight year in which every team will be playing opening day on the *same* day? The last time that happened was in 1968. Can you believe it?" he said with splaying arms, then added. "All but the Mariners and Athletics that is, they began their season openers last week with a two-game set in Japan, at the Tokyo Dome. But that doesn't really count."

Chris then replied, "You sure know your baseball. Sounds like you're a big fan. Why don't you go with him?"

"Oh, I would, as I am a big baseball fan, but he doesn't want to go with me. And besides, it wouldn't be right, going with his social worker and all. Look, I would appreciate it if *you* took him. I have been trying to get him to go out more socially, but he doesn't care about that, with his PTSD and all. But he needs to get back out there. He can't be a hermit forever."

"You mean a recluse," Chris said, hoping not to offend by correcting him.

"Yes, of course, right, a *recluse*. So, what do you think? Will you take him? They will be recognizing the military and our veterans, good stuff. You'll be doing me and him a big favor. And who knows, you guys might even enjoy it. If it doesn't work out, you can leave the game early. There's no obligation to stay for the whole game. If he starts feeling uncomfortable, just leave. It's a win-win. And if the Padres win, it's a win-win-win," he said, amusing himself with the weak attempt at humor, but at least his talking had slowed enough for Chris to follow him. Though not excited about going, Chris agreed, "Sure, fine."

Hey, it's a baseball game in Southern California, not a Sled Dog Race in Alaska.

"Great! Here's your ticket," the social worker said before quickly handing it over. "—Alex already has his. I'm also giving you his cell number and home address. And, oh yeah, a map of the city. Don't hesitate to call me whenever. Good luck on your mission."

"Thanks," Chris said, surprised that he had called it a mission.

A day before the baseball game, Chris sat down at his desk in his room at the Navy base. He needed to make some calls to catch up with Sara and Aunt Sophie. He looked around his room. It was simple, no question, but it was also ultra-clean, recently renovated, and of course, as safe as can be. And the view from his window, which overlooked the northwestern part of San Diego Bay, was certainly relaxing to look at, especially to someone coming from Alaska, where it was negative something degrees out.

Aunt Sophie was Chris's first call. He wanted to call Sara first, he truly did, but he figured his aunt might help him with any concerns he had about his daughter before he called her. He knew this was probably unnecessary, but he had already been gone a month; who knew how well she was taking it? No, he thought, he needed his guardian spirit to help him navigate the treacherous waters that are the adolescent girl. And, he thought, his aunt would want to know how her old pupil was faring in the field with his new job.

"Hey, Auntie. How are you?"

"Me, I'm fine. Same old here. Oh, Christopher, it's *so* good to hear from you. So, how is Alaska? How's it going with you there?"

"I'm well. I just arrived in San Diego about to start my next case. I *was* in Alaska: Anchorage and Fairbanks. It was, of course, very cold—*okay,* unbelievably cold. But it was also unbelievably beautiful. And guess what, Auntie? I found my sign out there, *my vision*, just like you said I would. It came unexpectedly, out of nowhere, deep in the forest. At first, I was scared of it, then fascinated, and finally just thankful that I saw it. It was a striking beast, Auntie. A *wolf* of all things."

"Wow!"

"Wow is right! But don't worry I wasn't hurt. And I'm sorry I can't divulge all the details of my cases to you, but rest assured I'm doing well so far on my mission. Sure, it's been challenging but also very rewarding. And I have you to thank for that."

Aunt Sophie said, "Oh, please, don't even. We are family. It's what families do. By the way, how is *your* family? Have you spoken with Sara lately?"

"Funny you should ask...I was going to call her next, but...."

"But what?"

"I think she may still be upset with me for leaving for so long."

"But I thought you told me that she was okay with it?"

"Well, maybe I misread her." Aunt Sophie then abruptly interrupted him. "Sorry to cut you off Christopher, I hate to be rude, but I remember what my brother, *your father,* used to say to me about you and Sara."

"What he'd say?"

"Oh, just that Sara was the center of your life, but at times your relationship with her was strained because of your bumpy relationship with Jessie."

"Did he say *bumpy?*"

"No…I don't know. I'm paraphrasing. Anyway, that's not the point; your unsuccessful marriage *affected* your relationship with your daughter. Yet, she remains the center of your life is the point. There is no time to worry about the 'what ifs.' Sara doesn't have it, as she'll be in college before you know it, and you surely don't have it. You need to focus on the cans. Like, what *can* you do with her now? —Phone calls included."

Chris said, "I remember what my dad would always tell me, 'Be her hero,' and he would also say, 'true love endures.'"

"Oh, Christopher, now you're just trying to make me cry. How I do miss your father. You know he loved you very much."

"I know," Chris said softly. He was then going to tell her about how he recalled the time his dad told him so after they saw that movie together. But that one he wanted to keep all to himself.

"So," Aunt Sophie said as she cleared her throat which was coated with emotion. "Like I was saying, phone calls too. No more psychoanalyzing when it comes to your daughter. You call her and just tell her how you feel, *always,* about everything; good, bad, or indifferent. She's your child, she may not always understand you, but she will always love you. Your dad was right, be her hero."

"Okay, now you're trying to make *me* cry, Aunt Sophie,"

She then laughed lightly and said, "And after you speak with Sara, be sure to call your mother, though she may not always show it, she worries about you. Now, you take care of yourself hon and I'm glad to hear you're out of Alaska and in better weather."

"Thank you, Aunt Sophie. You truly are my guardian spirit."

Sara immediately answered Chris's next phone call. He was relieved that she did. "Hey kid, how are you doing?" he asked her.

"Kid? Where did you come up with that one Daddy?"

"Oh, that's a story for a different day. Anyhow, tell me, how are you? School? Home life?"

"Well, Mommy's driving me crazy, but you know how that goes…school's boring, but my grades are fine overall. As far as our basketball team goes, we weren't *too* bad this year, but we were no Oklahoma City Thunder, that's for sure," she said with a giggle so sweet that for a quick flash, Chris would have traded anything just to be with her.

Sara then asked, "But tell me, how are *you* doing? Mommy said that you were in Alaska. Is that *true?*"

"It is," Chris replied.

"And…how was it? Tell me! Tell me! Oh, My Goodness!"

"Sara, it's the most magnificent place that I've ever seen. I was there in the middle of winter, so it was freezing, and everything was covered with snow, but what I did see was breathtaking; I saw the tallest mountain in North America, Denali. And the Alaska Range, which is 400 miles of grandiose mountains that would make everyone a believer in God. I also watched the beginning of the Greatest Sled Dog race in the world, as well as met some of its mushers and dogs. And I saw Alaska's official state bird called the Willow Ptarmigan, which is a pheasant that changes its feathers from white in the winter, to light brown in the summer for concealment. And last, but not least, I saw a wolf! It was scary, but it was also very impressive in that it is perfectly made to survive in the wild against some of the world's worst weather, as well as amongst its toughest predators."

"That is *so* cool Daddy! I wish I could have been there with you."

"Yeah, me too, buddy," Chris said, adding, "I miss you."

He wanted to tell her that the best thing he really saw in Alaska—better even than everything he had just told her about— was seeing the spirit of an old man still fighting on one that had been through so much, had given so much, and had lost so much. But one that was still hanging on, *barely*. But how can that compare with the mountain of all mountains? Or with the range of all ranges? Or with the velvety white feathers of Alaska's state bird?

Or with one of the fiercest animals, pound for pound, on the planet? —Sara would have fairly asked him, he thought. To which Chris would have paused to think of an answer that had a scientific explanation. But he couldn't come up with one—not one that was properly supported anyway. The answer then hit him square between the eyes; he'd tell her it was more beautiful because it was the essence of a man doing what he was instinctually born to do in this world, like the wolf, *survive*. To which he hoped she'd simply nod in agreement and say, "Yeah...."

"Are you still there, in Alaska?" Sara then asked.

"No, I'm in San Diego, where the weather is here, and I wish you were beautiful."

"Ha-ha, that's a good one pop. Hey, by the way, I've never been to California either, much less Alaska, you'll have to take me there one day."

"Deal. But you have to keep up your grades and be good to your mother, and your grandmother too. Can you do that for me?"

"Ha! That's asking a lot! But I'll give it a shot. That's, of course, if I get a new sports car next year," she said laughing hard now. To Chris she sounded like all was well, but she then quickly turned serious. "Dad, um..., after these six months are over, or five months now, are you going to travel again? I only ask because I feel like, well, it's just so long. I mean, I'll be an adult in a few years, and I just want you here, while I'm still here, ya know."

Chris immediately got a lump in his throat which made it hard for him to respond. The more he thought about what his daughter had just said to him, the more he got choked up.

"Daddy, are you... crying?"

"No, but close enough though. Look, we discussed this before I left. This job, *my* job, is something I felt I wanted to do, and almost *needed* to do. But make no mistake about it, princess; for although it may not seem like it today, you were, are, and will always be my number one. So, to answer your question, no, *heck no,* I will not be traveling again after I get back. Don't worry, you just hang in there and be a good girl. And wait and see, in the end, we'll all be better, stronger people for it—oh, and if I haven't told you lately, I love you."

81

Ok, now I'm starting to sound just like my dad; optimistic and a little mushy. I like it.

"I love you too, Daddy."

After his calls, with still an entire day left to spare before meeting up with Alex at the baseball game, Chris tried to be productive—*after a nap, of course*—traveling is a tiresome business. Once awake, he went over to the base gym. This was becoming a normal routine, he told himself proudly. But it was then, unfortunately, another abbreviated workout on another treadmill, in another state—again due to heavy breathing and throbbing knees. He tried some sit-ups, but his stomach soon burned. Finally, he tried some bench presses and arm curls, but those were also met with aches and pains. Chris was discouraged by his lack of physical strength and stamina; *maybe I need to exercise more often. Who am I kidding? Of course, I need to exercise more often, as well as improve my diet. And I sure hope this pain goes away soon....*

When the taxi dropped Chris off near the stadium, the streets around it were already buzzing, though it was still two hours before game time. He and Alex had agreed to meet there at noon, one hour before the game. This gave Chris time to take in the atmosphere of the park. He looked up at the mosaic blue sky with a few wispy clouds that were scattered about. It seemed to say to him, in a California coolness way, to slow down and take it easy. He then noticed small brown and yellow San Diego Padres banners hanging everywhere, with their logo of a cartoon monk swinging a bat, welcoming patrons to "Beer Fest." Upon passing through security, he found himself, along with hundreds of others, on a street just outside and adjacent to the center field area of the park. There were makeshift beer and food booths set up and a rectangularly-shaped stage with a DJ on it playing old 80's hits. Looking around, Chris could see it was a party-like atmosphere. Yet, the mood of the crowd also felt laid back and unpretentious which surprised him. Getting a beer crossed his mind, but he decided not to and opted for a hot dog and soda instead. *No diet today.* He sat down to eat, along with about fifty other people, on a grassy knoll on the side of the booths which faced the stage. The DJ reminded the gradually growing crowd of the band that would soon play for them; a few courteous applauses followed. Chris then texted Alex his location.

"Ok, see you there," Alex promptly texted back. A few minutes later, the band took center stage. Chris didn't recognize their name but that didn't mean much since he didn't know or enjoy most bands after 1999. However, after the band began playing, he found the music quite enjoyable. It put him in an even better mood. He told himself to forget about the gym setback and to instead focus on the positive and heartfelt phone conversation he had with his daughter, as well as the opportunity he presently had to help a veteran on such a gorgeous day.

Alex looked and walked like a marine. His haircut was high and tight, *naturally*. He had a long neck that craned side to side that scanned the perimeter, but his body remained straight and erect, like an ostrich. He stood about six feet tall, but his posture made him seem taller and more imposing. Chris knew right away that it had to be Alex walking toward him. He stood up and walked over to meet him, throwing out his half-drank soda just before doing so. As he approached, Chris reached out to him for a handshake. Alex appeared older than twenty-six years of age, and more mature. His skin was taut and deeply tanned as if it had too much sun. Yet his short black hair seemed unaffected by it. His hazel colored-eyes locked onto Chris's briefly as he took his hand and shook it sturdily. He had a tattoo on each arm; on his right upper arm, the U.S. Marine Corp logo was visible under the sleeve of his plain white T-shirt, which he wore tightly. On his left forearm, the Marine Corps motto of 'Semper Fi,' short for the Latin phrase Semper Fidelis, which translated means, *Always Faithful*.

"Hello, I'm Chris Longo, but please call me Chris."

"Hello, I'm Sergeant Sanchez...I mean Alex Sanchez," he said, then nervously glanced around the crowd as if somebody was watching him. Chris thought of asking him if everything was okay but knew better not to. He told himself he needed to *listen,* and he needed to *observe; I need to just shut up and let him speak.*

Which he did.

83

"Hey, would you mind if we left the beer fest and just went straight to our seats," asked Alex, "I'm not really into crowds in small spaces—at least the stadium is big and open—that's if you don't mind?"

"Sure. Do you want to grab a beer to go?" Chris asked him.

"No thanks, doc."

"Doc?" Oh no, please, I'm no doctor by any stretch. Please, call me Chris or Mr. Longo even, but not doc."

"Have you ever served before, sir?" Alex asked as he pointed at a stadium entry gate which he speedily began walking toward. Chris tried to keep up with him, but the dense crowd and the former marine's quick pace made it challenging; he had to constantly bob and weave around people to do so. Alex again, scanned the perimeter with his head from side to side as he marched on, seemingly oblivious of the slightly overweight, middle-aged man with thinning dark and gray speckled hair, trying hard to keep up.

"Yeah, I served. A long time ago. Why do you ask?" Chris said, finally catching up.

"It's just that in the service—especially in the field, or when deployed—we always refer to anyone in the medical field simply as *doc;* that's the way it's always been and it's what I'm used to saying," said Alex, as he was now sidestepping to get through the crowd as they entered the stadium.

"Do you call your social worker doc?" Chris asked while he gathered his belongings from security and rushed to hear Alex's answer.

"Ha, I call him something all right, but it's not doc," he said, looking back at Chris with a smirk. "I hope you don't mind that we take the ramp up. I'm not that big on elevators."

Well, I'm not that big on walking....

"Yeah sure, I'm right behind you," said Chris with heavier breaths now. They continued up several levels of steep ramps before Chris finally quipped, "I guess we're in the nosebleeds."

"No, this is actually where all the rich people sit," Alex said with a laugh. He continued marching up the last incline ramp as Chris dragged behind feeling as if he were climbing Mount Everest;

his shirt soaked with perspiration. They then walked past an Italian sausage stand with the robust smell of peppers and onions wafting past them. Not far from it, a long line of people stood for garlic fries. The aroma of which stopped many in their tracks to consider joining the line, Chris included. They finally made it to their level. Chris then noticed that Alex's shirt was as dry as his throat. He made a mental note to thank Alex's social worker for the great seats *and workout....*

They sat down in their upper deck right field seats thirty minutes before the first pitch. Just as they did, the U.S. Navy Parachute team, the Leap Frogs, descended lazily from the canvas of an almost cloudless, blue sun-drenched sky, most landing on their feet as if they had only jumped from a few feet up.

Though their seats were not located in the shade, they were still comfortable as the day's temperatures hovered in the low seventies. When Alex then excused himself to go use the restroom, Chris thought of his dad and Sara and how he wished that they could be here at this place and time. It made him feel sad for a moment, but the moment quickly passed for he was there for a reason. A purpose. He was there for Alex; a young, honorably discharged Marine, and as he would soon discover, a very troubled one.

The fans who sat around them were mostly working-class families, college students, and middle-aged businessmen who took the day off early to attend the game. A few sections over to the right, sat hundreds of Marines in short sleeve khaki shirts baking in the sun—yet none of them seemed to mind. Alex returned with two water bottles. He handed one over to Chris who thanked him for it.

"Service C's, or *Charlies*, as we call them," Alex said pointing at the sea of tan uniforms with his water bottle. It then came time for them to stand for the national anthem; Chris put his hand over his heart. Alex raised his right hand fast and sharp in salute to old glory. He held it there, still as can be, as if paying extra respect to all the military ceremonies on the field, yet by the end of the anthem, his hand started shaking. He tried hard to stop it from doing so, but apparently couldn't. Then, just as the anthem was about to conclude, a loud, thunderous noise of four F-18 Super Hornets came tearing past the stadium for a tremendous flyover. Many in the stands, including Alex, were startled by them. Chris thought Alex's flinch from the flyover could have been from his PTSD issues. Or maybe it was just from the shock of the passing fighter jets that flew so closely overhead. The act of which seemed to raise everybody's patriotism level instantly. The crowd erupted in approval. It made the hair on Chris's arms stand. He felt the rush of being among other veterans. If nothing else to be among others with whom he had something in common. He missed that camaraderie and esprit de corps that the military was so known for. He figured that Alex must surely miss it more than he did, after all, Alex was half his age, and had gotten out of the service less than two years ago—not two decades ago. The loss of that brotherly bond with whom he went to combat must have certainly left a large vacuum in him, he thought.

As they retook their cheap seats, down on the field, one hundred lined-up service members from all the branches of the armed forces began walking off the field, most of whom shook hands with the ballplayers as they did.

With the pregame festivities over, the game was finally underway. The issue of being called 'doc' now seemed petty and unimportant to Chris.

I mean really who cares anyway, plus he had a point. A medical troop was, in fact, often referred to as "doc" by military personnel. Besides, what was the harm in it if he wasn't being disrespectful and it made him more communicative?

As if he read his mind, Alex then said, "Look, sir, I won't call you doc if it bothers you." Chris then cut in. "Don't even worry about it, calling me, doc is fine. Really." Alex didn't respond but Chris sensed he felt relief from it, however small the concession.

"I wanted to let you know that I appreciate you trying to help me out," said Alex. "I just hope you're not wasting your time. I haven't been very successful in overcoming my PTSD issues."

"Please, I'm *not* wasting my time. First of all, *you're* worth it. And secondly, there is no pressure for any kind of results. We'll just take it day by day and see what we can figure out. Okay?"

Chris said, trying to reassure him of his intentions so they could start on a positive note.

"You know what I was just thinking about?" Alex said.

"What's that?" asked Chris.

"I was thinking that you being here reminds me of an old Afghan fable that I heard over there called *The Handless Man.*"

"I'd like to hear it," said Chris. "It's got to be better than this game; these two teams can't score a run for the life of them. Sorry, I'm not the biggest baseball fan."

"No problem, doc. I'm not a big baseball fan either. Anyway, the story starts with an injured man walking down the street. He has blood dripping from a cut on his hand that's so bad it looks as if he may lose it. Though he was very hurt, he didn't complain about it, which surprised the people in the street who saw him. All of a sudden, on the other side of the street, emerged a man who just had an entire hand cut off. The first man with the cut hand then began to yell out in agonizing pain, 'Ahhh!' Another man in the street rushed up and asked him, why didn't you complain before about your injury? Why did you then shout when you saw the other injured man?' The man replied, 'I didn't complain about my injury because you couldn't feel my pain. When I saw the man without his hand, I started to complain because I knew he had felt the same pain that I was feeling and that we both shared the sorrow of loss that nobody else could understand.'"

"Fine story," Chris said, "short, yet deep." But you thought of it because you think we have felt that same pain? I have to be upfront with you. I have never been in combat. And I've never even been outside the United States. You, on the other hand, have seen a lot; much more than most soldiers have, which has surely been tough on you. But I can tell you that even though I haven't been in war, or lost a hand like in your story, I too have issues and have lost a lot like loved ones, a career, and a purpose in this world. And when you're nearing fifty, I must say, metaphorically, it can feel at times like having your heart ripped out of your chest. Sorry, I didn't mean to steal your thunder."

"You didn't, besides, that was pretty good," said Alex. "And so that's part of what the story means to me. I mean, okay, so you don't have the same injury or issues as me. But what's important is that you're here. In a sense, I'm the other injured man yelling so you can hear my pain and relate to it and the same sorrow of loss that we both had."

Chris said, "I'm glad you feel that way about me—combat vet or not. Let me ask you. Why live in San Diego? Don't get me wrong this place is super, but also *very* expensive."

Before Alex could respond to the question, he and Chris had to stand to allow some fans through their row after another scoreless inning had ended. When they sat back down, Chris noticed Alex again looking around nervously, like he did when they had first met. He certainly seemed uncomfortable, Chris thought, and was sure that something was bothering him. He was just about to ask Alex if everything was okay when Alex continued as if all was fine.

"I was born and raised about an hour away from here," he said. "After I finished boot camp here in San Diego, I got stationed near my home at Camp Pendleton. When I got out, I came back here. Yes, it's very expensive, but it's such an amazing place to live. There is so much to do and see here—though I haven't been out much lately. Besides, I'm not one for the cold."

"I can fully understand you there," said Chris, "I could never understand why anybody would want to live in a place where it's cold six months or more out of the year. But I guess some people don't mind it or they just really love the snow and cold weather. Could you believe I have even met people who love dog sledding in Alaska? I guess it's like my father used to say, '*to each, his own.*'"

Alex didn't respond to Chris's comments, as his attention was now fixated on that of a nearby boisterous fan; a plump fellow in his late thirties whose jersey was a size (or two) too small. The man kept clapping and yelling towards the field with his hands cupped around his mouth, stopping only to take long sips of his light beer from an aluminum bottle. The people around him were growing more and more annoyed by his behavior with long stares and hushed complaints. Chris turned from looking at the irritating fan back towards Alex to see if he was still staring at him, but all he saw was an empty seat. To his dismay, he saw that Alex had gone over to confront the loudmouth and was now standing in front of him with his index finger pointing straight at the man's pudgy face. Chris could hear what Alex was saying, in a stern and even voice. "I'm only going to warn you *once*," he said to the man who looked at him in disapproval. "You better *sit down* and *shut up* or so help me God I am going to make you." The loudmouth then lifted his neck out of his round torso, like a giant turtle. It appeared as if he was going to say something, but he didn't. He just took his ball cap off and on quickly before finally sitting down as if nobody was standing in front of him. Alex continued to stare him down with his raised finger, now shaking. Chris then jumped out of his seat, hurried over to Alex's side, and put a hand on his shoulder. He could feel his body trembling.

"Hey, Alex it's me, Chris. You're all right. Everything is *okay*. Come on, let's go, let's get out of here. He's not yelling anymore. He's not bothering anyone anymore. Besides, it's not worth it."

Alex dropped his shaky finger then quietly walked out of the row and rushed up the stairs and out toward the concessions. Chris promptly followed behind him. As he did, he heard the applause of some of the fans who were thankful for Alex's efforts in shutting up the big, loud turtle man. Alex moved swiftly and nimbly through the crowd, losing Chris a few times; only his bright white T-shirt allowed Chris to spot him as he headed down the first ramp corridor, "AL-EX!" Chris called out, but Alex didn't stop, he just kept on walking briskly down another ramp, presumably towards the exit. Chris could barely keep up with him but was lucky that at least he was walking downward, otherwise, he would have never had a chance of catching him. Yet, with a spurt here and a spurt there, the young veteran was now pulling further away from him.

Why am I even chasing him? Will I upset him if I catch him? What am I even doing here? Gosh, that popcorn smells good....

Despite all that, Chris's inner voice didn't tell him to stop chasing him. On the contrary, it told him to continue to try and catch up to Alex. It told him that he needed to talk to him *now* because if he did, he could perhaps find out a little more about what was bothering him. And what he feels he can do to help himself. It was a good opportunity to communicate with him, he thought. No, he then rethought, it was a necessity.

They finally reached the ground level, but Chris still hadn't yet caught up to Alex as he huffed and puffed after the long decline down the four levels of concrete ramps. Looking up, Chris saw that he now had only one last chance to stop Alex who was about to exit the park. He would have to get close enough to him and yell loud enough not only to be heard but to be heard in a way that would make Alex *want* to stop. He swallowed his dry throat, scuttled up for one last-ditch effort, and cried out in desperation at Alex's back. It worked. Alex stopped dead in his tracks, though he didn't turn around, he just waited for Chris to catch up to him. When he did, they walked side by side past security and out the stadium gate; ending up where they started before the game—at the beer fest. The fest, however, was long over with only a few employees remaining in the area, clearing it of trash and the empty beer booths. Alex walked over to a grass clearing, out of earshot of the cleaning crew who were efficiently going about their tasks. Alex then threw his hands on his head and turned to Chris with a look of despair.

"Doc, I'm sorry about that back there, but I just can't help it. I just can't seem to control myself around people like that—he was acting like such an ass," Alex said as he began to walk in a circle with his hands dropping from his head, then going outward, with his open palms facing the brilliant blue sky. He went on, "I feel like I can't behave normally anywhere. Not anymore. The civilian world just doesn't make sense to me, compared to the military," he said trying hard to gather his thoughts and convey them to Chris.

"My first job in the Marines was as a rifleman, which is ironically their mantra, 'Every Marine is a Rifleman.' My rifle became an extension of me. And I was a good rifleman doc. A *really* good one. I was accurate with it, even deadly at times. And I could always be counted on. I learned early in my enlistment that you *had* to go by the rules because if you didn't, and acted like a Private Schmuckatelli, there were severe consequences to pay; like when a marine has fire watch and doesn't do his duty to standard—that could get someone killed! And that drunk lug back there misbehaving in public like that. If a marine did that *anywhere* outside of a bar, he would have been punched out, maybe even ninja punched by his commander for it. Don't get me wrong, the enlisted do what they do amongst themselves, as do officers, and so on...I just think in public there should be a minimum behavioral standard, but on the civilian side, there just isn't one! Go to your local supermarket or whatever store and see what some people do or wear out in public. It's disgusting; you'll see people in ripped, dirty clothes, disheveled, or even barefoot. In the Corps, there is order. You work hard, you get promoted. Like me. I did, and I eventually became an NCO, then a fire team leader. On the outside, you often have to kiss somebody's ass to get promoted. Look, I'm not a child. I understand that life is not perfect—far from it actually. I get that. I try hard to live by the Marine Corps saying of 'improvise, overcome, and adapt.' And with most other issues I can. But I just can't seem to get over my PTSD issues; one of them being hypervigilance. It originated for me when I had to assess the physical environment in a combat zone—a requirement for any soldier sure, but for a rifleman or fire team leader, it's magnified. It was drilled into us at boot camp. It was drilled into us at rifleman training. And it was drilled into us again at pre-deployment training.

"Sorry, but what exactly was drilled into you?" Chris asked. "Remember, I've never seen combat, so I don't fully understand."

"Doc, it's the *thing* that makes a soldier good, the constant warfighter training, *over* and *over*. To be combat ready. To be ever alert for it. To be on the offensive. To be on the defensive. Order and Rules. Training to Kill. All of it. As well as the feeling you get when you go down range and execute all that training. All that killing. It's..., indescribable. It's just, oorah! Then, Bam! It's over. And I love the Corp, but it's not the easiest life either, even if you're hardcore. So, you finish several tours in the Suck and you're finally ready to rest and put your mind and body at ease. It happens to the best Marines, doc. It happened to me. I got out. Had to. It was not just because of Afghanistan—which was no walk in the park. Anyway, I get back home, and nothing is right. Nothing *feels* right. When I lie down at night, I think about the mortars that might hit my apartment. I think about everything going on outside; cars racing, dogs barking, cats lurking, neighbors with their lights on too late, or off too early. Drunk drivers, elderly drivers, and teenage drivers. Everything in some way, shape, or form, is a threat that I must, as a rifleman and fire team leader, pick out and eliminate, or at least minimize. And it doesn't stop after I fall asleep either. I sometimes have nightmares of the men who were killed in action in front of me or the men that I killed. And if I don't have nightmares, I think about falling asleep on guard duty. Or if our radios went out and we had no comms. Or if we can't hear the enemy about to ambush us. The worst part is that, when I witnessed these things in the service, I was commended for my hypervigilant behavior, which only further reinforced it. And so, when I do finally fall asleep, it's already morning and my eyes are bloodshot and my head is spinning, but not from drinking. It's from lack of sleep and overthinking everything. Then, during the day, when I work as a mechanic, I'm just a zombie. I wonder if they can see through me. If they know how tired I am, or that I'm so aware of their lives—not that I care anything about their boring lives, it's just that my ears are so used to listening to everything around me so I can gauge the danger level. Is that crazy? I have an ear locked in on my boss's conversation even though he's two rooms away and people talking around me. Why do I do that? And what about the nice lady who comes in for an oil change with her cute baby in a baby carriage? I always look at her as a possible terrorist bomber. Is that crazy? Why do I do that doc? Why can't I change my frame of mind? And at the end of the day, I feel the need to pump iron and run a few miles, even if I can't keep my eyes open or if I haven't eaten all day. I feel that if I don't, then I won't be strong enough to one day go back into battle. And when I do finally lay down at night, it all starts over again; the mortars, sounds, cars, pets, neighbors' lights, drivers of all types, until— more nightmares. It's like, I see too much. I hear too much. I think too much. It's all just so...*exhausting*." Alex then plopped down on the ground with his hands on his face looking gloomily down.

Chris was speechless after hearing about Alex's issues. He sat down quietly next to him for a while, the feeling of helplessness tried to creep into Chris's psyche, but he wasn't going to let it.

Not today.

Something had to be done to help this distraught young man, he thought, then asked, "Do you have someone you can share your feelings with? Someone who you can talk to regularly?"

"Well...there was somebody. A girlfriend. A good-looking one too, but it didn't work out. She recently broke up with me; said she couldn't put up with me and my 'problems' anymore. I guess I can't blame her, but it would have been nice to have somebody there supporting me through all this—know what I mean?"

"I do," said Chris, "just curious, are there things, hobbies, which you enjoy doing that help curtail your troubling thoughts when they arise?"

"There are a few things, I guess, but to be honest with you. Right now, I just want to take my anxiety meds and lie down in my dark bedroom. Would it be all right if we caught up in a day or two?"

"Yes, of course," Chris said. "And if you feel the need to talk before that, please call me. Ok?"

"Wilco doc," replied Alex as he stood up straight and held his chin up, ready to battle another day with his inner demons.

Chris thought Alex's idea to go lay down was not a bad one. He planned on doing the same when he got back to his room at the Navy Annex. Besides, it had already been a full day of episodes and emotions for both. But back in his room, Chris couldn't nap. His mind spun. He was too tired to work out—*way* too tired, so he began reading his book, *The Old Man and the Sea*. The simple yet intricate story immediately pulled him in. It was, of course, about the title, but also much more. Chris became fascinated with the book's characters; the overaged protagonist, Santiago, who lives in a shack. "Thin and gaunt with deep wrinkles in the back of his neck," with an unlucky fishing streak so long that he is labeled *saloa*, which is the worst form of unlucky, per Hemingway, who also wrote, "Everything about him was old except his eyes and they were the same color as the sea and were cheerful and undefeated."

But he is not alone. There is a boy who checks up on him regularly. Looks out for him in a large sense to see if he needs any food or drink. But the man is often too proud and tells the boy to worry more about his own home and not his. But they are friends. They also talk about baseball. "Have faith in the Yankees my son," the old man tells him. "Think of the great DiMaggio."

Alone at night, the old man would dream of everything from when he was a boy in Africa, from windswept beaches and brown mountains to women and great fish. And even of lions on the beach, which he so loved to watch play together like young cats in the dusk. Yet now, he only dreamed of them and places.

As Chris read on, he would leisurely gaze out at the sapphire blue waters of the San Diego Bay that lay calmly outside his window. It further absorbed him into the book and the elderly fisherman's life on the waters, as well as his frequently mentioned sunny terrace. Chris also couldn't help but correlate Til with Santiago when he tells the boy, "I may not be as strong as I think, but I know many tricks and I have resolution." He then read that the old man "always thought of the sea as *La mar*" which, (per the author) is what people call her in Spanish when they love her. Chris said the words softly *"La mar"* letting the *r* roll lightly off his tongue which made it vibrate.

*Perhaps I too could learn to love her...*he then lazily put the book down and drifted off for a long nap far, far away.

The next few days went by slowly for Chris as he didn't hear a word from Alex: Not a call. Not a text. Nothing. At first, Chris didn't think much of it, using the time to catch up with his mom and Aunt Sophie, as well as with Jessie and Pat. But as the days passed, he became concerned that he hadn't heard back from him.

He did have a job after all. A life. He didn't need me hanging around him every day cramping his style. Still, I thought we got along rather well. Chris then recollected how Til needed a few days to himself with the dogs.

Maybe he just needed some time too? He was, after all, very upset the last time we saw each other. I had better go see his social worker just to be on the safe side.

"Oh no, you're totally fine," The social worker told him. "He even called me and said he felt comfortable talking with you."

Chris wasn't sure if the social worker had told him this just to make him feel better—either way, it did, *somewhat*. Still, Chris felt the need to further explain his concern.

"I didn't want to badger him, but it's been almost a week and I only have another three here, as I leave at the end of April. I don't want to waste time. Do you think I should call him tomorrow?" Chris asked thinking that maybe he should have called his DoD boss, Michael Montrose, instead for advice. But the social worker eased his worries.

"Don't fret," he'll call you soon. I promise. Please remember Mr. Longo, that with PTSD veterans you *must* have patience. You must let them communicate with you on *their* timetable. On *their* clock. Otherwise, it won't be genuine. It won't be from their heart. And also, keep in mind that—and don't take this the wrong way— you're not a professional mental health counselor. You don't need to *fix* him; he already sees professional therapists and takes medication for that. You're here to get him going in the right direction. At least that's what your Mr. Montrose told me.

Don't tell me...I know...I'm here to help him find his path....

"Look," the social worker continued, "you're in San Diego for goodness' sake! Enjoy it a little. Why don't you go spend a day at the zoo? You'll love it and I have a free pass for you. You know it's said to be one of the best zoos in the world. What do you say?"

The Zoo? Any place but there. I've been there enough lately...

"Thanks, but no zoo. I do appreciate it though."

"Well, what do you enjoy doing?"

"I'm fine. I don't need entertainment while I'm here."

"It's San Di-e-go! Try me, Mr. Longo," he said eagerly.

"Okay, fine. If you insist. I like, or used to anyway, to watch ice hockey."

"That's perfect!"

"How's that?"

"We have an AHL team (the San Diego Gulls) right here! They play just down the road. And I have tickets for their last home game on April 10th that I got from the USO."

"Great. Do you think Alex would like to go too?" Chris asked.

"Hmm," the social worker hummed as he rubbed the stubble

on his chin with one hand, while the other lay uncharacteristically idle at his side. "Well, considering what happened with him at the baseball game, I'd say you go to this one solo. We don't want to upset him unnecessarily," he said, handing over the single ticket.

"And remember Mr. Longo, patience, patience, patience."

It was several days later when Chris finally heard back from Alex. He texted him and asked him if he could meet him over at the USS Midway Ship Museum at 1000 a.m. on Thursday, which would be the day after the hockey game.

"Sure, I'll be there," replied Chris curious as to why he asked him to meet him there.

Alex then said, "Oh, and sorry for not calling you last week. Between work, therapy, and my workouts, it's been pretty crazy."

"Say no more; I fully understand," Chris said courteously.

The apology cleared the air and put both of them back on track. Chris was glad to hear that Alex was not avoiding him. A sense of relief then came over him and he looked even more forward to helping this veteran however he could.

The night of the hockey game arrived a few short days later. Chris was well-rested that night and was still surprised that he wasn't worrying about too much. After getting dropped off by a taxi, he noticed some festivities outside the arena. It was far smaller than what the Padre's beer fest had, but Chris thought it, nevertheless, considerate of the Gulls to do something for the fans on their last home game of the year; discounted food and drinks, as well as games for the kids, all go a long way in showing fans their appreciation for their support of the team.

Being alone at the game gave Chris more time to 'people watch' that evening. He noticed some young service members, pilots probably, with their girlfriends looking excited to see the game. He then wandered around outside a bit before going into the plain-looking, outdated arena which was constructed almost sixty years ago. But once inside, Chris thought it had—though clearly antiquated—an underdog charming appeal to it. It was understated in every way, with an interior that was underlit and cavernous, and which had symmetrical second-level seating. Yet, it also possessed an intimate feel with a roughly 13,000-seating capacity for hockey games. Every seat was a good one. Chris fictionalized that it was somewhat of a cross between the old Boston Garden and the Roman Colosseum, just smaller and more oval. But then discerned honestly that it was probably more like the old Nassau Coliseum where the New York Islanders used to play. Nonetheless, he felt akin to this once venerable building, which, in its heyday, hosted the world's biggest names, from Elvis Presley, Van Halen, and Nirvana; to Madonna, U2, and Lady Gaga; for he knew that it, like him, was beyond its best days.

Focusing now on the hockey game, Chris relished the sport for its fast-paced movement, which kept his mind on the action at hand. For three twenty-minute periods, the game took him away from all the issues and concerns in his world to just the puck, players, and the net. He didn't mind going to baseball games, but the slow pace of the game often allowed his mind to wander to things away from it and, at times, think of the problems in his life. Perhaps if he were more of a beer drinker, he thought; he would enjoy baseball more. Regardless, he also enjoyed hockey games more because they reminded him of the times watching them with his father.

The game turned out entertaining, with the Gulls falling just short, 4-3. And with a scuffle on the ice, a tasty pretzel, and a quality hot dog, Chris left the game more than satisfied.

A fine night indeed. The only thing better was if Sara had been there with me.

When Chris went to sleep that night, he hoped the next day would be productive with Alex. He also hoped that Sara was thinking of him. As he closed his eyes, he felt confident that both could occur.

The USS Midway ship, or aircraft carrier, is anchored downtown in the waters of San Diego Bay. As Chris walked up to it, a large, warm sun, which was still ascending to its highest perch of the day, shone brightly at him. To his left, Chris then saw the 'Welcome

Aboard' sign that was located just above the entrance to the ship. After paying for his entry ticket at the discounted veteran rate, Chris spotted Alex coming off the ship to meet him. He wore a red, short sleeve polo shirt with the words USS Midway Museum embroidered in yellow on the right side of his chest. The word VOLUNTEER was on the left. They both reached out a hand when they met, shaking the others cordially. "Volunteer, huh? Nice," said Chris. "I had no idea."

"Come on, climb aboard. I'll tell you all about it," Alex said as he guided him up an outdoor stairwell, then onto a small bridge that connected the ship to land. "I should have asked them to cover your entrance fee."

"No. It's fine. I got in with the veteran discount," replied Chris.

When they reached the main deck, Alex got them some coffee. They then sat down on a bench just outside the gift shop. "Thanks," Chris said. "I could sure use it. I went to see the Gulls hockey game last night. They lost, but it was fun. Have you ever been?"

"Nah. Hockey is not really my thing. But maybe one day I'll go just to go," Alex said shruggingly.

"So, tell me all about your volunteering here. That's so great," said Chris, who sipped his coffee and looked out at the visitors strolling the ship, most of whom walked in different directions, speeds, and group sizes, yet all had similar expressions of curiosity with gazing eyes and twisting necks, as if on another planet.

"It started last year. I came out here just to sightsee. I had always been interested in military history, but once I was here, it just felt right. And there are other veterans here to talk with, so I guess it's kind of therapeutic in a way too."

"I'd say so," said Chris. "Funny, your social worker never mentioned any of this to me."

"That's because I didn't tell him," Alex replied. "And I would appreciate it if you just kept it between us. There are some things I don't want everyone to know. Know what I mean?"

"Say no more. I get it."

Alex then said, "Let me give you an overview of this amazing aircraft carrier. I think it'll help you understand why I like it here."

"Sure, I'd love that, and I like military history too," said Chris as both now stood, through with their coffees. "But I've got to ask you, since this is a Navy ship, and you were a marine, do the Navy volunteers chide you about that?"

"Oh, sure, but always in good jest. I call them swabbie or squid, and they call me leatherneck or jarhead, even devil dog,"

"I was never sure; is the Marine Corps separate from the Navy? Or are they under them?"

"Good question," said Alex, who straightened his posture as if addressing a group of the ship's sightseers. "Well, the answer is yes *and* no. At the Pentagon, they *technically* fall under the Department of the Navy. But the Marine Corps, like the Navy, is also a separate entity under the umbrella of the Navy Department. The Navy has a Chief of Naval Operations, while the Marines have a Commandant, yet both report to the Secretary of the Navy, who then reports to the Secretary of Defense. The Marines are still mostly on naval vessels and larger ships, like carriers, but they're also the amphibious assault force with their own units, bases, and equipment. They do work a lot with the Navy, so now that I'm fully explaining it, yeah, I guess they're part of the Navy if you really look at it."

"You sure know your stuff, Alex. So, this ship, it's very historical?"

"Heck yeah, it is. And it's named after the pivotal Battle of Midway during World War II in the Pacific Theater of operations in June 1942, which three-day battle was fought mostly by aircraft. Anyway, the ship took about a year and a half to build. It missed World War II by just one week since it was commissioned on 10 September 1945. One week! It finally saw action in 1965 with strikes against the North Vietnamese, where it recorded the first air kill of the war. Unfortunately, due to that tough year, it was decommissioned for four years for repairs and updates. After being put back in service, it served as a humanitarian ship after the fall of Saigon. It saw action again in 1991 in the Gulf war for Operation Desert Storm, where it served as the flagship of naval forces launching over 3000 combat missions without a loss. In April of 1992, it was decommissioned here in San Diego. It then moved to

Puget Sound, where it sat idle at a Navy shipyard in Washington State until 2003; after which it was returned here and opened as the USS Midway Museum in 2004."

"To say this ship is historical is an understatement," Chris said. "This ship has seen so much—has accomplished so much."

"Sure has," Alex said. "This ship is the longest-serving aircraft carrier in the 20th Century."

"Incredible," said Chris shaking his head in amazement. He then asked, "When do you volunteer? Must be tough with work."

"It is," replied Alex, "I try and volunteer a few days a month, mostly on weekends. Though I must say, even though I enjoy coming here and all, there are days when I won't come on account of my PTSD issues. I don't want to be around people then—vets included. Does that sound stupid?"

"No, not at all. I think it's very commendable that you come here and volunteer in your free time, when able."

"Thanks, doc, I appreciate that. Hey, I'm sorry I can't give you the entire tour right now, as I've got to get back to my post, which is on the flight deck today. But I can take you up there and show you some of the jets and helicopters that we have. You can tour the rest of the ship on your own if you don't mind."

"Not in the slightest and thanks for inviting me here. It's truly impressive. I can't wait to see the rest of it."

After showing him the flight deck, which even further impressed Chris, they went their separate ways for the remainder of the day. They would meet up again several more times over the next few weeks. The time passed quickly, and just like in Alaska, Chris fell into a routine of sorts in San Diego as well; he went to the gym a few times a week (the pain notwithstanding) and met up with Alex during the week and even a few times on the weekend. He also called back to Oklahoma to speak to his family and boss. And he slowly but surely kept reading his Hemingway novel. He wondered if Til had even picked up his copy yet.

On his last visit with Alex, Chris asked if they could meet at Old Town San Diego Historic Park. He figured that Alex would like the

100

place for its rich history, though he also thought that he had probably been there before, perhaps even recently. But he was wrong. Alex told him over the phone that it had been many years since he had been there; that his last time there was with his parents when he was little.

Chris was right about Alex liking the colorful, quaint town with its famed adobe structures of a bygone era built in the 1830s. It was mid-Saturday morning, on a clear day, with a radiant sun and royal blue skies, when Alex and Chris met at Old Town. They immediately began walking the roughly mile-long town which boasts as having the state's first Spanish settlement (1769 The Presidio of San Diego), as well as being California's most visited state park. And rightfully so, as it was steeped in over two and a half centuries of the city's history when it changed from Spanish and Mexican rule to finally American land. And there's much to see, like the first brick courthouse and a Wells Fargo Museum that displays old banking exhibits and even a stagecoach. Yet something that stood out to Chris and Alex, that was just as enjoyable to them as anything else there, wasn't an exhibit, an old building, or even historical at all. It was the slow, old-time feel of the place which it exuded and that seemed to affect all the patrons present. But as much as Alex was enthralled with the park, he still gravitated to the military part: The Mormon Battalion Historic Site, which pays homage to the only religious-based unit in U.S. military history and their grueling 2000-mile march from Council Bluffs, Iowa to San Diego, California. Chris and Alex then came across the statue of a Mormon infantryman. Alex stared at it, then slowly began circling it and said, "When I look at this old soldier of the mid-1800s, it reminds me of a part in a book I once read about Ulysses S. Grant when he was a general in the Union army. It was about a confederate soldier who, after he got captured and was taken to the rear, defeated, and demoralized, explained how the union officers would ride by all the confederate prisoners without paying any attention to them. All except for General Grant that is. He did so when he reached the end of the line of some tired, dirty, and bloody prisoners who were lined up along each side of the road. He then lifted his hat and held it over his head until he passed the

101

very last one. The soldier said he was the only officer in the whole train who recognized them as being on the face of the earth."

"What a story!" said Chris. "A general with real compassion."

"Yeah, looking at this ragged soldier stature reminded me of that," said Alex. "But anyway, this place is something. I should have come back much sooner."

"Well, I can see why you live in this city. It truly does have everything one could ask for, which is saying a lot. By the way, how have you been doing lately?"

"Doc, I'm trying. I really am. You know with all that I'm going through, I still don't want it to seem that I'm ungrateful for what I have. I appreciate that I still have my parents, my physical health, a job, and of course, this city."

"That's good you feel that way," said Chris. "Let me ask you something if there was something else you could see yourself doing, say in a year or two from now, what would that be? Something that would make you happy yet still challenge you? What would that thing, or those things be?"

Alex didn't respond right away. He first felt his cleanly shaven face, took off his dark sunglasses, then said, "Sir, if I had to answer that, I would say something with history, probably military history. Maybe be a military history teacher or work for the federal government with the National Park Service, like at a historic military site like this one. Yes, that would be it. A job where I could provide answers to questions about important historical military events, whether it be in a classroom or even, preferably, at its actual location. That's what I think would make me happy." said Alex with a gleam in his eye.

"Then *that's* what I think you should pursue. Look, Alex, you're still young. Now is the time to start. Please don't wait until you're middle-aged to do what makes you happy. Let me be your cautionary tale. I've spent the last ten years largely discontent. Be it in my work or my life. My *only* advice is that you go for it. Whatever that *it* is. And if you think everyone does that, you'd be wrong. Many people, for whatever reason, just don't. And then afterward, are resentful towards the world for it, at a world where anything is possible—please don't be that person, Alex."

"But what about my PTSD issues? Do you think I'll be able to overcome them enough to do what I want?"

"Yes, I do," replied Chris, "at the very least, you could try. I'm not saying it's going to be easy. But remember the saying 'Improvise, Adapt, and Overcome.' That's what you do. What's the alternative? *Not* going for it? To be discontent? I believe in you, Alex. Listen, I'm not telling you what to do. Like someone told me, only *you* can decide that. All I'm saying is you should strive for whatever it is you want to do out there in this world. Otherwise, you'll always regret it. Roger?"

"Roger that," said Alex. "And thank you for believing in me."

Chris's time in San Diego was now coming to an end, which Chris thought went by faster than his time in Alaska—no surprise there. The last few days went by so quickly that he almost forgot to return Mr. Montrose's call about his next case. But he decided to do that the following day as he felt tired from his day at Old Town with Alex. All he wanted to do was relax and read some more of his book. As he did, he read a passage and imagined himself for a moment parallel with the old man who, like himself, was leaving the coast. "The old man knew he was going far out, and he left the smell of the land behind and rowed out into the clean, early morning smell of the ocean." The words jumped from pages so vividly that Chris could almost taste the salt water from the ocean.

The next day he called his boss, who cried, "You're going to the City of Second Chances!" as if he'd just won the lottery.

"Where?" he asked, puzzled.

"You're going to Naw'lins!"

"Never been there," Chris said. They then engaged in small talk about the city before Michael reminded him, "Take notes, submit the case reports, and lastly, your mission summary report."

"Roger that," Chris replied, imitating Alex's sharp response.

VII
NEUROTIC IN NEW ORLEANS

"When dealing with people, remember you are not dealing with creatures of logic, but creatures of emotion." –Dale Carnegie

The first thing Chris saw in New Orleans upon debarking from the plane was a large sign that read 'Welcome to New Orleans, the birthplace of Jazz.'

Jazz? I know as much about jazz as I do combat. Yet, here I am, trying to take care of some combat vets...Maybe I should play in a jazz band while I'm here...Focus, Chris.

After picking up his luggage, Chris went to hail a cab to take him to another base and another military lodge. The location was ideal, as it was just seven miles from the VA clinic where his next veteran's social worker's office was located. And it was just five miles from downtown where most of the famous sites like the St. Louis Cathedral, Bourbon Street, and Cafe Du Monde, with their world-renowned tasty beignets, were all located. But it was also across the Mississippi River in Westbank, far enough away from all the craziness of the area, especially at night. And the navy base was near the Algiers Point Ferry, which would be convenient for traversing the Big Muddy, or the Great River, which derived from the Ojibwe word, *misi-ziibi,* meaning just that.

In the room, Chris studied the view from his window. What a difference, he thought, from the clear blue waters of the Pacific in San Diego Bay to this river: brown and murky, resembling a massive, coiled snake with its eerily moving waters, like skin. Chris recognized it as a force. Of this, he had no doubt. That evening he heard the occasional loud, dull blast of a passing steamboat, which only added to the river's allure and mystique.

The next day, Chris left the base with an upbeat outlook as he set off to meet the social worker at the VA.

And why not be upbeat, he thought. He had completed his first two cases—which meant he was one-third through with the overall mission—and both went fairly well, considering. Sure, I may have come across a little Joel Osteenish at times with Alex, he mused, but deep down, he knew that was just part of his job; to not just tell them what they wanted to hear but also what they needed to hear. He also attributed part of his cheerfulness to simply getting a good night's sleep since he was so tired the day before from traveling. Either way, he thought, he'll take it. Unfortunately, the social worker with whom he was about to meet would quickly change his mood for the worse with her foul demeanor toward him and, it seemed, at life in general.

"Yes?" asked the social worker, a short, African American woman in her mid-forties with short reddish hair and even shorter patience. Her outfit was office appropriate; a burgundy blouse with steel-grey dress pants and low-heeled sandals, but the scorn on her face was anything but.

"Oh, yes, hello. I'm Chris Longo. I believe my boss, Michael Montrose, contacted you about a veteran of yours that I was sent here to help. He said that you emailed him back and that this morning would be the best time to meet with you to discuss the veteran's case." Chris said in an extra nice tone, just to be safe—but it didn't work. The social worker first just looked back at him stoically. She then slowly began opening her eyes wider and wider before finally tilting her head forward as if to say. *Really? You have got to be kidding me.* Chris even thought for a moment that she was about to break into a loud laugh right in his face, which probably would have been a better response than the one he got. She made a frown and looked away in disgust, then went back to her computer, "I don't have time for this right now," she said, as she jabbed heavily at her keyboard a few times, then looked back, "Yeah, I see it now, but things have changed. My *schedule* has changed. By the way, what do you intend to do with Ms. Williams anyhow? I understand that you were sent here to help her, but what do you actually intend to *do* with her? I've been her social worker for almost three years. Do you think you can do a better job than me?" She then stood up, crossed her arms, and tapped a foot, waiting for a response.

Chris thought of himself as largely nonconfrontational when it came to disagreements. This, however, was different. *He* was called for this job. Someone out there thought that *he* was valuable enough, and hopefully effective enough, to be sent around the country to help these people. And he had always told his daughter to stand up for herself, especially when she was in the right. How could he take himself seriously, or this job for that matter, if he didn't follow his words with actions? With his good mood now gone, he decided he was going to give her a piece of his mind.

"You ask me if I think I can do a better job than you? And what do I intend to do with her?" Chris said, trying not to sound angry. "Well, first of all, I'm not sure I can do a better job than you, but I do truly hope so. You do understand that I'm here for a *reason,* not my health. That reason is...." Chris then looked at the folder sitting on the desk in front of him with the name Tashana Williams on it. "I'm here for *her!*" he proclaimed while pointing at the folder. "I'm here to try and help her. It seems she hasn't been sufficiently helped. Maybe that's your fault, maybe not. I don't know, and I don't care. I care about *her!*"

"Oh, and I don't?" the social worker shot back.

"I didn't say that. And as far as what I'm going to do with her, well that depends on her current situation and ailment. You know that I'm not a doctor or psychologist. I'm just a regular person that the DoD hired to spend some quality time with some veterans who are working through their issues. They felt that my past interaction with them at a VSA in Oklahoma City was helpful and effective enough to warrant hiring me to help in these particular cases. So, if this interview is over, can we get on with the important issue of going over Ms. William's case so I can get started with my job—if that fits into your schedule, of course."

"Okay, fine...*whatever*," she said. "But just so you know, if it not for the DoD making me, I wouldn't help you at all, not *one* bit."

"Duly noted," replied Chris, who was about to say something nastier but then judiciously changed his mind. The social worker gave him half-defeated, half-still fighting glance as if she hadn't yet committed to one. She then ultimately did. "Tashana Williams is an eight-year veteran of the Coast Guard. She's a thirty-two-year-old, single, black woman, who was *supposed* to get married a couple of years ago; but ever since 'the incident' she's never been the same. She has become very emotional and now mostly isolates herself from the world. Her fiancé called off the wedding and that was that. She occasionally does have some good days when she'll go out but...Anyway, we've tried various approaches to help her; they ranged from seeing a psychologist and taking medications to group therapy, but she just can't seem to get out of her rut."

"You said the *incident?*" inquired Chris. "What happened to her? I mean, I don't need *all* the details, but an overview would be nice."

"Okay, for *her* sake. If it'll help her, I'll tell you. But it's sensitive so remember your HIPPA confidentiality agreement."

"Of course," said Chris, who felt the reminder insulting.

"It happened when she was stationed in Miami about two years ago. You see, Ms. Williams is a pretty woman: tall, athletic, nice smile; she was an obvious attraction to many of the service members there—especially the officers, being one herself. She ended up getting sexually harassed a few times. Did you know that 55% of women report being victims of sexual harassment while serving in the military? Anyhow, she tried to put an end to it. She even told her command, but her concerns fell on deaf ears. The assault, which came at the hands of a fellow coast guard officer, occurred soon after. The perpetrator was subsequently *only* kicked out of the service after the completion of an incompetent investigation. It makes me angry to think about it. She told her superior officer. She told her chain of command. And what did they do? Diddly squat. I've got much more colorful words to describe how I feel about how they handled the situation, but I'll spare you from hearing them; though if I continue talking about it, I won't be able to hold them back," she said in a tense voice. "Also, let her decide if, when, and where she will meet you. Even though you're employed to help her, she may still feel uncomfortable being alone with an unknown male. So, if she wants to bring her twin sister along—then you let her. *Agreed?*"

"Agreed," said Chris now really wanting to leave her office. The social worker went on, "I'll let her know of your presence here for the next month. You can keep me updated or not. I'll be personally checking up with her concerning your visits, regardless. If there's nothing else then...."

Chris accepted her curt goodbye, and though he didn't like it, it still allowed him to escape the social worker's wrath as soon as possible. Lastly, she gave him Ms. William's contact information, and he was quickly out the door. And not a moment too soon, he thought.

That evening, on base, Chris read some more of his book. As he did, he couldn't help but think of his new veteran when the old man thought of the ocean. "He always thought of her as feminine. The moon affects her as it does a woman." The social worker's words then kept coming back to him. She's *very* emotional.

Chris knew he was no expert with women, not with his mother, not with his ex-wife, and certainly not with his daughter. Either way, he was going to proceed very carefully with this Tashana Williams. He didn't need another woman on his list of failures.

And that maybe, just maybe, the old man was right. The ocean was more feminine than masculine.

It was a full four days before Chris received a return phone call from Ms. Williams. But this time around, he was more patient when he waited to hear back from a veteran. He took heed to what her social worker had told him; to let Ms. Williams respond on her own time. During those days of waiting, Chris went back to his routine of going to the base gym for a workout, if one could even call it that. He didn't feel as good about his workouts as he did his work. Nevertheless, there he was back on the treadmill, walking at a modest pace. He walked almost two miles before his knees started hurting him. But his pain wasn't as bad as it had been over the previous two months. It was the same with the rest of his workout: his upper body, his stomach, and his arms; all still hurt, but not *as* bad as before. He took it as a good sign but knew he was still on the upward side of that mountain.

Besides the workouts and the reading, Chris had some time to catch up on some phone calls back home. He called his daughter first. It didn't go nearly as well as the last time they had spoken.

One step forward, two steps back.

"Where are you *now*?" she asked him sounding annoyed.

"I told you before—New Orleans." Silence then flooded the phone line. Chris stopped the flooding. "So, how are you? How is school?"

"Well, I'm graduating tenth grade at the end of the month. You *do* remember that, right? Are you going to be able to make it? Oh, I forgot, you told me before you left that you probably couldn't make it. Now that I think about it, this reminds me of when I was little, and you were always away with your sales job. Remember?"

—Yeah, I remember. It wasn't like I was enjoying it, kid…and our last conversation went so well, I thought we were going in the right direction. Yet I wasn't there for her, again…but I had already told her that this was a special situation.

He thought briefly that she wasn't being fair; then remembered that she was only fifteen and that he wasn't talking to Jessie. He tried to change the subject. Keep things merrily moving along. But life is not always merry. It can be harsh sometimes. Harsh oftentimes.

He then asked her, "Do you have any plans this summer?"

"Daaad," she replied, clearly irritated. "You know Frank likes to take Mom and me to Branson, Missouri for summer vacations."

"Oh yeah, Branson," he said cynically, "*how* could I forget? Do

109

you even like going there?"

"It's fine. There's a lot to do there, ya know."

Ah, now there's the nonchalant attitude I'm familiar with.

"One day Sara, I promise I'm going to take you to New York City, Miami, and San Francisco. Maybe even Rome."

Sara didn't respond to her father's comment, but she believed him or at least wanted to. She then said, "Oh, speaking of Frank, it seems like he and mom are arguing even more, but whatever. That's *their* problem."

No crap. Jessie is the queen of arguing. It's no wonder she's doing it with him too. Typical Jessie.

"If it gets too out of hand, you'll let me know?"

"I will," she replied unconvincingly.

"Look, Sara, I'm sorry I have to be away again, but it's only a one-time deal. We discussed...."

"Sorry Daddy, but I have got to run. Love you."—Click.

Chris shook his head in disappointment. But he wasn't surprised by it. He was at least half to blame for it, if not all....

He then called his mom, who said she was doing fine. Getting older like the rest of us. She thought Aunt Sophie was the one who pushed him to take this job, which Chris knew was the opposite of the truth. She fished for an argument; cast the bait out, and hesitated on the line, waiting for a bite. Didn't get one. Then they talked a little about his father. How they both missed him. Sara came up. Chris knew better not to bring up his daughter's 'attitude' to his mom. Get her started on him for nothing. They then said their goodbyes until the next time. After the call, Chris felt a concern for his mother that he hadn't felt in a long time. She had lost her husband of many years. But he mostly thought of how *he* had missed him. *Could she have missed him more?*

With his calls over, (Jessie didn't answer) Chris contemplated going downtown to see some of the sights. But since it was already late in the day, he decided he would go the following day. Get up early. Use the day to its fullest, until Ms. Williams called him. And called him she did, the first thing the very next day. Chris was relieved. He wanted to begin what he had come there to do. Besides, there would be another chance to see the sights if he cared

110

to, he thought. This city believes in second chances.

"Hell-o," said a faint female voice into his cell phone.

"Ah, yes, hello. Is this Ms. Williams?" Chris asked clumsily.

"Yes, sir. I'm Ms. Williams,'" she replied, the uneasiness in her voice evident. "Oh, nice to hear from you. I'm Chris Longo," he said trying to ease her along while overcompensating some.

"Thank you for reaching out to me. I assume your social worker told you why I am here and why I'd like to talk with you."

"Do I *have* to?" she asked nervously.

"No. If it makes you uncomfortable, absolutely not. But I am here to try and help you."

"And how, Mr. Longo, are you going to do that?"

"Please, call me Chris."

"Look, Mr. Longo," she said in a stronger voice, "I'm sure you mean well, but I've seen enough VSA and VA doctors, therapists, and counselors to last me a lifetime. Why should I see *you?*"

Chris didn't want to sell himself, or anything else for that matter. His salesman days were long behind him. And anyhow, he knew that she needed to *want* to be helped. All he could do was show her the way.

"Short answer Ms. Williams," he said, "why not give me a chance? I only ask that we meet to talk at a location of your choice. You can bring a friend or a family member if you want—no problem."

If she declines, at least I was honest and straightforward with her. Don't push her. She's emotional and has been through a lot.

"All right Mr. Longo, I will see you. How about today at the Laura Plantation, say 11:00 a.m.? It is fifty miles away at St. James Parish. Can't miss it. Just follow the Mississippi River westward."

Chris wanted to ask Ms. Williams why meet at a plantation. And what a plantation even was. Sure, he'd seen his share of them in movies, but he didn't know the specifics about them, including this one. But he wasn't about to ask her about that now. He was just content that she had accepted.

Once a salesman....

On the highway, now westbound in his rental car, Chris was excited about the day. He was on the road to a plantation to see a

111

veteran in need. It wasn't serendipitous or anything, but it wasn't too far off either. Both needed each other, therapeutically in a sense. At least that's what Chris was telling himself on the one-hour ride up.

Arriving fifteen minutes early, after the faster-than-expected drive, Chris right away noticed the expansiveness of the property. Yes, he expected as much; it was a plantation after all. But seeing it in person was different. It was *real.*

They met at the entrance. Ms. Williams was a tall, slender, and undeniably attractive woman, he thought. She had smooth, butter-scotch-colored skin that was lighter than Chris had envisioned. Her hair was full of dark lengthy curls with hints of gold at the ends. And though they hung casually at her shoulders, they also appeared as if professionally done. Her eyes were a rare aqua blue which contrasted especially well with her skin color oval face and high cheekbones. Chris also couldn't help but notice her full, pink lips. She looked like a model straight out of a women's clothes magazine. Her attire was casual with jeans and a thin gray crew sweatshirt. She wore white, low-cut converse. She waved a hand up at him.

"Hello, Ms. Williams, it's me, Chris. Nice to meet you." He then asked her a question to break the ice, "Why did you want to meet me here? I mean, don't get me wrong this place seems very interesting, but why *here?*"

"Well," she began, "for starters, my family's background is Creole Louisiana, just like this place, the Laura Creole Louisiana plantation. And also, I feel empowered by *not* only what my people had to endure for generations to survive here, but also by what they had to do as families for generations to thrive here as well— as best they could anyway. It makes me think that what I went through is smaller, even beatable in comparison. I mean, if they could overcome such a horrid way of life, then why couldn't I? Why *shouldn't* I overcome my issues? This place gives me strength. And strangely, I feel safe and at home here."

"That's...very inspiring," said Chris marveling at its powers.

"Are you familiar with Creole Louisiana culture?" she asked.

"To be honest, not at all. Can you tell me about it?"

"Okay, Mr. Longo, sure. Well, let's see. It originated with the nomadic Native Americans some 3000 years ago. In this area, there was a small tribe called the Acolapissa. They chose it because it sits above a geologic fault line that puts it almost 20 feet above sea level. Then, in the 1720s, came the slaves from French Senegal, in Western Africa, who were skilled in construction and farming; this was useful to the French colonists who used them on their land. Next, through war, it fell under Spanish rule. But that didn't stop the French-speaking refugees from Canada (called Acadians) from being accepted by the Spanish here as part of the Catholic population. Finally, with the Louisiana Purchase in 1803, it became part of the United States. That sale included so much land that it doubled our country's size. Anyhow, I'm sorry for the detailed answer, but to put it simply, Creoles are mixed-race people who come from a union between the Native Americans, Africans, and Europeans. Their influence in food, music, architecture, and traditions are still prevalent today."

"Incredible," said Chris, "so much history and diverse cultures here over the past three hundred years."

They then walked in front of the Big House, past four massive Live Oak trees that were so big in both size and aura that they eerily brought you back several centuries in time. The trees ranged from 160 to 210 years old and were named after the four different generations of women who ran it: Nanette, Elisabeth, Desiree, and Laura.

Afterward, they turned to check out the Big House, or *Maison Principale*, which was built in 1805 in French Creole architecture. Its old colonial design and mixture of matted colors in ochre, red, green, gray, and mauve were unique, yet typical of the period and area. Besides serving as the office headquarters, as well as a place for social entertainment, it was also the property owners' secondary residence where they would reside during the plantation's high seasons, as it was much more convenient for them to do so; Their primary residence was a townhouse located in the French Quarter of New Orleans.

Chris was highly intrigued by it all, yet his mind would occasionally drift and think about asking Ms. Williams some personal questions, but he knew that that wouldn't have been polite, or wise. Not on this day. This day was about her and allowing her to discuss her background and culture. And it was about him gaining her trust. He knew that wouldn't come easy. He wished that she would address him by his first name but that was also up to her.

The weather was unusually cool on this spring day in early May; a perfect one for seeing this former sugar plantation which, at its largest, was 12,000 acres in size. Ms. Williams then spoke about its former inhabitants, who until the 20th century, spoke French as they preferred to remain separate from the more dominant Anglo-Saxon-Protestant culture.

"The first occupant was a French Naval officer and veteran of the American Revolution named Duparc," Ms. Williams explained. "After it passed down two generations, another French-born man, Locoul, owned the property. When he passed, the family patriarch eventually became Elisabeth Duparc Locoul. She was an amazing woman who ran this place for close to fifty years. Her granddaughter, Laura, then inherited the plantation that her father had named after her and even stipulated that any future sale of it would continue to be called, 'Laura Plantation.' Laura ran the sugar cane business here until 1891 when she married, she then moved to St. Louis and sold it to the Waguespack family who continued to run the property until 1984. After this, it was purchased by investors who planned to destroy the historic buildings and build a bridge across the Mississippi River. Fortunately, the still-active earthquake fault line ruined those plans. It was finally restored by a private enterprise and opened as a Creole culture attraction."

"Wow. That's all so interesting. I'm speechless...," said Chris, who then asked, "How often do you come out here?"

"Maybe once a month, sometimes more, sometimes less," she said, thinking about her answer for a moment as she looked out toward the Mississippi river which was just six hundred feet north of the Big House. She then turned to Chris, and said, "Mr. Longo, I have seen so many different medical people who have tried to help me, and now you show up. Do you truly think you can help me?"

I've sure been asked that a lot lately....

Chris thought about her important question and moment for them. If nothing else, he would have to be blatantly honest with her and tell her the unbiased truth, at least from his point of view.

"No. I don't think I can help you, Ms. Williams," he said matter of factly. "In the end, I think that only *you* can do that. That said, I do think I can help you, help yourself. The rest is up to you. I saw you looking over at the Mississippi. Do you know that in Buddhism they say that 'you need the boat to cross the river, but that once you cross the river, you no longer need the boat.' Ms. Williams, I ask you to let me help you cross the river."

Ms. Williams didn't respond right away, she first looked back at the imposing river, then said, "That's sure one wide river to cross...."

On the way back to see the slave cabins, they passed by two large orchards of pecan trees before reaching the small, dilapidated structures on both sides of a long dirt road. Ms. Williams began talking about them. "Each cabin held two families and had a chicken house and/or pigpen with a vegetable garden outside. At its peak, during the Civil War, 86 slaves resided here."

Ms. Williams then went to go sit down on an old bench located under a low-hanging tree. Chris noticed that she looked especially sad. He was right, for she soon began to cry. At first just a little, but then she had tears pouring down her face. She tried covering them with her hands, but the tears were just too many. Chris assumed Ms. Williams was emotional due to the slave cabins, as he thought them a wicked sight to behold, but he quickly found out that her tears were not from them.

Chris waited a bit, then asked her if she was okay.

"Sorry it's...it's...my father," she said in between sniffles.

"Your *father?*" Chris asked. "Is he okay?"

"Yes—no. He hasn't been supportive of me through all this. He's just been so...indifferent to me ever since all this happened. And especially so after my marriage plans fell through."

She then cried a little more before finally composing herself. "I'm sorry Mr. Longo, but I think I want to go home now. I don't feel that good anymore."

"No problem," said Chris, who then escorted her to her car. Afterward, when he got to his car, he then wondered, how could a father not be there one hundred percent for his daughter. And especially with what Ms. Williams had gone through? Chris then thought of his daughter and how he hadn't been there fully for her either. He now felt further compelled to succeed with this case as well as with the relationship with his daughter. He never wanted her accusing him of being unsupportive or indifferent to her needs. No, he thought, he was going to be there for her and Ms. Williams, come hell or high water.

Back at the naval base later that evening, Chris pulled out his book. He needed a break from overthinking how he was going to help Ms. Williams. Before he began reading, he decided that he would call her in the next few days—even if she didn't call him. He knew that he was supposed to wait to contact her, but he wanted to put an end to her pain and crying as soon as possible. And he knew that he only had a few more weeks to try and accomplish this as his departure in late May was on the horizon.

Now, where was I in this book....

Chris was enjoying reading it not only because he found it engaging, but also because he couldn't help but continue correlating Santiago with Til. He felt a connection to the book's protagonist because of it. He knew it was silly, but he didn't care, it made the book more entertaining, and it also made him think of Til. And he had no problem with that. On the next page, the old man said to himself, "Most people are heartless about turtles because a turtle's heart will beat for hours after he has been cut up and butchered," the old man then thought, "I have such a heart too and my feet and hands are like theirs too."

Ah, now that could be Til as well. A heart of a turtle, with feet and hands to match. Yes sir, that was Til indeed.

The phone call from Ms. Williams that Chris was waiting for never came. So, he called her the next day. *Maybe she didn't call me because she didn't want to get emotional in front of me again.* But when Chris spoke with her, she sounded polite. Even nice. She asked him if he could meet her at the Cathedral-Basilica of Saint Louis, King of France; known better as The St. Louis Cathedral.

"Yes," he told her. *"Of course."*

They met at the church two hours later with Chris immediately entranced by the beauty of its interior. He was going to seek out Ms. Williams in the pews but his eyes wouldn't let him. They were captivated by the ivory-colored walls and columns, as well as the colorful flags that shot out from both sides of the balcony. He recognized most of them: Union Jack, Royal Standard of Spain, U.S. Continental, Bunker Hill, U.S. Liberty, Grand Union, and the flag of France. Just below the flags hung stately chandeliers. On the upper back wall was a large, magnificent mural of King Louis IX starting the 7th Crusade, which began on March 15, 1270. The 1872 painting depicts soldiers kneeling and saluting him on his right, and clergy and family to his left, in addition to several French flags being flown about. Examining the ceiling high above, Chris saw that it was covered with smaller round paintings which were surrounded by rich ornate painted ribbons of red and beige.

The church was only sparsely filled with people and the ones who were present were mostly tourists snapping pictures around the doorway. After he finished viewing its interior, Chris eyed around for his veteran. He found her off to the far right, midway down the main aisle. She was sitting with her hands held together in prayer. She then did the sign of the cross, just as Chris was about to reach her. He sat down next to her. She acknowledged him with a small smile.

"Hello," he said quietly.

"Hello," she replied in an equally low tone.

He then said, "Such a marvelous church," stating the obvious he thought. She didn't respond. He couldn't help but notice that Ms. Williams looked even prettier than the last time he saw her, which made him feel a tad guilty, but the truth was the truth. She wore loose khaki-colored pants with a matching short sleeve top. Her hair looked different; her previously semi-curly hair was now brushed back flat over her head and tied neatly in the back. She had on casual, yet stylish white sandals that unsurprisingly fit well with

117

her outfit. Chris saw that she had a tissue in her hand, which made him assume that she had been crying. Outside, the sound of a strumming guitar could be faintly heard whenever someone opened the front doors. This seemed to lighten the mood inside. Ms. Williams then whispered something to Chris as she remained facing toward the alter, which made it seem as if what she was saying was illegal.

"I was wondering if you would do something for me?" she asked him shyly.

Chris relished the request—anything that would have him in action, doing what he was sent there to do.

"Sure, that's why I'm here," he quickly responded, which he thought made him sound overeager. They sat in peaceful quietness for a bit before she asked, "Are you Catholic?"

"I was raised one. And my daughter had her first sacraments of initiation: Baptism, Eucharist, and Confirmation. But to be honest, I was never too religious as an adult. And my divorce didn't help matters any."

"Sorry to hear that," Ms. Williams said with her head now at a half-turn toward him. "But it's never too late you know. God's always with you—*us*—he's always with all of us."

Chris nodded and pondered her words, her faith. His lack of lately.

"I know it's none of my business," she continued, "but in the Catholic world, you do have a responsibility to keep your daughter attending mass and practicing the word. *His* word. Tell you what, just think about it. I mean she *is* already a Catholic. Both of you getting back in the saddle, it isn't that hard. You just need a push."

"Ok, I'll think about it," Chris said, "no promises though."

"No, of course not," She replied respectfully. "Hey, did you know that *this* cathedral is the oldest Roman Catholic Cathedral in continuous use in the United States?"

"Unbelievable," Chris mouthed to himself, further impressed.

"Yep, it dates way back to 1718. It did have to be rebuilt a few times; once due to The Great New Orleans Fire of 1788."

"It is truly stunning," said Chris, whose knees suddenly began to ache. He had forgotten for a while that he was almost twenty

118

years her senior, but the pain in his knees coldly reminded him. He tried to brush it aside, think of something else, like her.

"So, what is it you want me to do for you?" he asked.

"Would it be Ok if we went to the nearby Café Du monde to talk there," she replied. "Maybe we could even get some Beignets?"

"Well, I guess If you're going to twist my arm about it," Chris said with a chuckle. Ms. Williams smiled back slightly and said, "It's just on the other side of Jackson Square, which is right outside the church. It's less than a five-minute walk from here." She then did the sign of the cross so slowly and methodically that Chris was sure that she had prayed for something specific.

And he would be proven right.

After leaving the cathedral, they walked through the picturesque Jackson Park with its emerald green lots of grass and its monumental statue of Andrew Jackson, which has the general majestically on a rearing horse with his elaborate bicorn hat raised off his head, as if saluting the city.

At the café, they sat outside with the cool and airiness of the plantation replaced by the warmth and mugginess of the city. They drank coffee and ate the world-famous Beignets. Chris had more than she, but she didn't seem to mind. He thought it even polite.

"They're good, right?" she asked rhetorically.

"No question! And great coffee too."

"Yes, and it's their brand too," she said with raised eyes. She then got to the request that both were there for.

"I was wondering if you could talk to my father for me."

"Your *father*? Why? What about? What would you want *me* to say to him?" Chris didn't mean to ask those questions out loud. Sure, he was thinking them in his head, but the shock of the question made him blurt them out—a rookie knee-jerk reaction.

"I'm sorry," he said, feeling embarrassed by his comments.

"Why? Don't be," she said, "It's understandable. They're fair concerns—oh, just forget it. It was a bad idea anyway."

"No, it's not," said Chris. "Look, I'm sorry. Sometimes I shoot my mouth off when I shouldn't. I will gladly talk to your father for you—just let me know what you'd like me to say."

Ms. Williams then slumped her shoulders and lowered her

head as if she now felt down and distressed. She remained that way for a while. Chris stayed silent and waited. He thought she was going to cry. But she didn't, though she seemed very close. When she finally lifted her head, Chris could see her sad eyes. He waited for her to compose herself, which she eventually did, her eyes now steadfast.

"I want you to tell him to respect me. And to love me."

"Ok, but don't you think he already does?" Chris asked.

"Yeah, you're right. I guess in his own way he *thinks* he does, but after I was sexually assaulted, my father began treating me differently. At first, he was just a little distant. He kept pretty mum about it. Then, after my marriage fell through, he completely disowned me; wanted nothing to do with me. I asked my mother and sister to talk to him about it, but they weren't much of an influence. I was then going to ask my social worker or even my psychologist, but that just didn't feel right, not with them anyway. But with you, I feel a different sentiment. I feel you somehow understand the importance of our relationship more. And that you can put some sense into him as his approval and love are very important to me. Maybe he wants to distance himself from me because he thinks I failed in the military from it and failed in my prospective marriage from it too. To him, I'm just damaged goods."

That's an awful thing for her father to think Chris wanted to say but didn't. He just listened and observed while she vocalized.

"If you could just tell him the truth, that all this wasn't my fault: the assault, leaving the service, losing my fiancé. I need someone in a position of strength, with nothing to gain from it, to tell him that I'm a good person. That I'm worthy of him and his love."

Chris couldn't believe that her father was treating her this way. *Hey, I'm no angel, but this was just wrong. Ms. Williams was right, she was worthy. Worthy and then some.* He then asked her, "Is there anything else I should know before I see him?"

"Well, yes, there is. He's a very formidable man. He's highly educated and a master debater who is not easily persuaded."

"To be honest, that doesn't help me much," Chris said. "I

kinda feel like David going against Goliath here."

"If that were true then you would be fine," she replied. "David was not scared of Goliath. When the Giant blasphemed his God, David was eager to stand up for what was right. He ignored the danger and trusted in God to help him fight the mighty Goliath. And in the end, as you know, David slung a stone between the Giant's eyes, bringing him down. You see, David trusted in God to help him fight Goliath. That was the difference. *Trust.* Trust and faith."

"Now that *does* help me. Thank you, Ms. Williams."

"No. Thank *you*," she replied, "and please, call me Tashana."

A day later, Chris stood at the front door of Mr. Williams's fine home on the outskirts of the city. He had reluctantly agreed to meet with his daughter's 'veteran counselor' at the urging of her twin sister. As Chris stood there, waiting for someone to answer the front door, he wondered if he should have called his guardian spirit for advice. But he had no time to. Like David at the battle when he came across Goliath. No time to think, just fight.

"Good evening," a tall, dark silhouette said in a deep voice upon opening the door. "Come in, come in." A handshake wasn't offered. It was past dinner time but not by much. Mr. Williams led them to a den. Not an office and not a living room. On the surface, he appeared a venerable man; gracefully aged and sharply dressed, with a sweater vest over a long sleeve dress shirt, round spectacles, tie, wingtips, and a Rolex that he made sure was easily visible. He was an intimidating figure, no question. But Chris had to stay on track, he told himself. He had traveled far. *Way* too far.

Mr. Williams had short, all-white hair and a large head. His skin was much darker than Tashana's, which made Chris wonder if this caused animosity between him and his daughter. Chris knew that this shouldn't matter and that he was probably even wrong, but he thought it anyway—though he wished he hadn't.

"Scotch?" Mr. William's stentorian voice asked.

Chris despised the drink but at that moment thought it wise to partake. Be on his level. "Yes. Thank you," he answered to which the big man then grunted and stomped off.

Chris peeked around the half-walled mahogany room, looking

at some pictures and paintings. Mr. Williams then abruptly returned, handing Chris his drink. "Please," he said pointing to a leather chair, which Chris cordially sat down in. Mr. Williams seated himself in a chair directly across from him, sitting back, and crossing his legs slowly. He then nosed his Scotch to admire its quality before carefully taking a measured sip.

Goliath indeed.

"I deduce," Mr. Williams began, "that you are here for not only the betterment of my daughter but to speak to me about *me*."

"That's right," said Chris taking a sip of his drink while trying not to make a face from its hardy odor and taste. It wasn't easy for him.

"Ok then, what is it you want from me Mr. Longo?" he asked. "I'm a busy man, so please get to the point of why you're here."

This is when David would have slung a stone right between Goliath's eyes, Chris thought. He took a bigger sip of his drink.

More courage never hurts, even in the liquid form.

"I'm here, sir, because, according to your daughter, you have neglected her in her time of need. Furthermore, she says that you have not been there for her lately. That you have been distant with her. Even cold. She needed you—she *still* needs you."

Chris waited; waited for the fury to come.

It did.

Mr. Williams sat up in his chair. Pushed his glasses in and then pointed his index finger upward, "Why the effrontery of you! The gall! I *love* my daughter! I would do anything for her! Shame on you for suggesting otherwise."

"I'm not suggesting that you don't. But I *am* suggesting that you haven't been there for her after her ordeal. And I'm asking, or rather your daughter is asking, that you be there for her *now*."

Mr. Williams settled back into his chair like he knew he now had the upper hand—or maybe he was bluffing or was just apathetic. Chris couldn't tell which.

"Tell me, Mr. Longo," he said. "Do *you* have a daughter?"

"I do," replied Chris. "One."

"And you think that if something, God forbid, like this ever happened to her, you would be there for her unconditionally?"

"I would *sure* hope so," Chris countered.

"But there was more to this that changed things. The outcome of things. And they would change it for you too—I'll explain. See, Tashana was a good kid. Smart. Quiet. Nice. Well behaved. She then went away to college. Afterward, she became a Coast Guard Officer. And in the service, she stood out because of her good looks—not her fault—but soon, she began to relish in the attention that she received. She went out with too many men. Flirted. Misbehaved. Her twin sister went to see her in Miami. They went out for a few nights. She told me the stories…I won't share them."

"So *that* justifies what happened to her?"

"No, it does not. But it *does* explain a lot," said Mr. Williams. "And when she finally found a nice, conservative, well-respected man that both her parents strongly approved of. Well, she, with her improper behavior with other men, pretty much threw it all away. After the incident, that fine man, from a fine family, couldn't be allowed to marry her."

"Doesn't sound like a fine man," Chris snapped back. "And are you *not* Catholic? Do you *not* forgive? Though I still don't know what Tashana did wrong. She didn't deserve what she got. I hope you're not implying that."

"I am implying no such thing," shot Mr. Williams, "but it didn't help matters. Also, and you may disagree, as a father you work hard to make, grow, and keep your family name intact. Tashana, though not purposely, tarnished that name. Her name."

"You mean *your* name," Chris said snidely.

"*Our* name," Mr. Williams stiffly replied, then said, "Is that it? Are you through? I had agreed to meet you because of my other daughter. But I don't revel in rehashing all of this. Anything else?"

Chris couldn't think of anything else to say, yet he wanted to give Mr. Williams one more gut punch, so to speak, so that he would remember this conversation about Tashana. Remember to help her. As he was getting up from his chair, he thought of something.

"I do have one more thing to say, Mr. Williams," who had stood up, put his drink down, and waited.

"Okay, what is it?" he said, then rudely glanced down at the time on his Rolex.

"It's simple," said Chris eyeballing him. "Be *her* hero. And oh yeah, *Love* her." Chris then abruptly walked out of the den, and out of the house. He was a little shaken and wondered if he had done enough. Said enough. *Was it enough?* He wasn't so sure. Chris then hopped into the car and began to drive off. But just seconds later, he stopped, got out of the car, and picked up a single rock from the many that adorned both sides of the luxuriously paved driveway. The rock was just a tad smaller than a golf ball.

Perfect.

Like David in his story of yore, Chris heaved the stone. He aimed it at a small side window, as hurting someone was not his intention. The stone hung longer than expected in the humid night air. Then, *"Crash!"* A nearby dog barked instantly as if on cue. A light in the house came on. Then another.

Time to go.

But Chris didn't run. He casually walked over to his car. Slid in it, and slowly drove out of the driveway.

Now that was enough. He was sure.

A small, sly smile then crossed his face. Chris wasn't proud of what he had just done. But he wasn't ashamed either. A mark had to be left. A memory. A stain. A statement. Something Mr. Williams would soon not forget.

Tashana and Chris met a week later as she didn't want to meet again until she had first heard back from her father. This was off-putting to Chris since he had half-planned to sneak away to Sara's tenth-grade graduation, but he wasn't going to inform Tashana of this so as not to rush her to meet with him. This month was about her, not Sara, Chris reminded himself. Still, it wasn't easy. Teenage daughters don't take too kindly to being second.

Especially by their father.

They met this time, not at a property of historical significance or archaic church, or even an acclaimed café. No. This time they met at a dull, unimportant place—the on-base bowling alley. It was Memorial Day weekend, so the place was empty. It would be the last time the two would meet before Chris's departure for his next case and next location. And as usual, he still hadn't been informed as to where that was yet.

Tashana Williams looked comfortable to Chris, almost at ease. She dressed in simple summer clothing: a T-shirt, shorts, low-cut socks, and running shoes. It was clear that she ran and worked out often.

I need to get back on track. I'll be forty-nine next week....

"Hello, Mr. Longo," she said. "Thanks for seeing me, again."

"Please, call me Chris."

"*Chris.* I wanted you to know that my father finally reached out to me. It seems you left quite the impression."

Chris expected to hear about the rock and the broken window. But she didn't bring them up. "How did that go?" he asked.

"Well," she said, "he thought you were an *ornery* fellow. And a person with a chip on his shoulder. A *big* chip."

Guilty as charged.

"—But a person who ultimately had my best interest at heart," she said joyfully, knowing both would benefit from the statement. When Chris heard this, it made his heart swell. Maybe not to the extent of the Grinch's tiny heart, which, as the fictitious tales went, grew three sizes on that jubilant Christmas day, but it swelled, nevertheless. And it wasn't just because of the compliment—though that didn't hurt—it was because he was understood and that it was the truth: a rare state of grace exacta. He beamed inside.

"How else did it go?" Chris asked, hoping to stay clear of the topic of his combative visit with her father.

"Actually, much better than expected," she said wide-eyed.

"Really?" Chris remarked, genuinely surprised. "How so?"

"In the way that he wants to begin a dialogue about us. It's a start. A positive start. I don't want to get ahead of myself. I've been kicked so many times in the past. I want to be safe. Guarded."

Chris was just about to say that she shouldn't ever need to feel that way with a father but then checked himself. He told himself to leave well enough alone—an idiom his father used to say. Chris would tell him that the saying sounded old fashion. But now that he was older himself; it no longer did.

"I'm not ignorant about this situation," she said. "I understand that we still have a long way to go. And that I must learn to forgive him. And that my father, once he shows improvement, can one day forgive himself. I know it won't be easy but, as I said, it's a positive start—thank you for what you did."

"I didn't do that much," said Chris "You did the hard part. You faced your fears and grew a lot in the past month. You were brave. I'm proud of you."

"I appreciate that," she said, "and my psychologist tells me that my neurosis, or mental state, will improve once my distress over my father improves. I look forward to not being so, emotional."

"I think you are going to be fine," Chris told her. "I really do."

Back in his room later that day, Chris couldn't help but compare cases. He knew he shouldn't and wasn't supposed to, as they were all so very different. Yet what stood out with this last veteran was her desire to improve. Her will. She *wanted* to improve.

Even a medically unqualified freewheeler such as myself could figure that one out.

He then called his boss regarding his new destination.

"Hello Michael, it's Chris Longo. How are you? It's the end of May. My time to fly...."

Chris was going to tell his boss his sob story about missing his daughter's graduation but then skipped it. It was done, he thought. No need to further upset himself about it.

"Yes, Chris. Right. Wow, how time flies. Let me see now. You are going to, oh yes, the city of brotherly love, Philadelphia!"

"*Oh...Ok...thanks,*" replied Chris, unsure how to take the news. He then automatically added, "Well, please email me the social worker's information."

Celebrating my birthday in Philadelphia..., could be worse.

126

VIII
NONFEASANE in PHILLY

"Fall down seven times, get up eight."
–Japanese Proverb

The clichés about Chris's next destination were difficult for him to avoid thinking about. They were the unruliest of sports fans. They had a strong animosity toward the more revered nearby sister city of New York. They were obsessed with Rocky. They were crazy about their cheesesteaks. They had an attitude. And, of course, they overindulged in alcohol.

But Chris knew that most of these were outdated myths. Okay, sure, there was the incident there in 1968 at a pro football game at Veterans stadium when irate Eagles fans, upset over their bad team and bad weather booed Santa Claus (the halftime guest) and then pelted him with snowballs. They did it again in 1989, only this time, with ice balls at the Eagles archrivals, the Dallas Cowboys, who played there for "Bounty Bowl II." The first of which was played earlier in the year in Dallas; the name came from the alleged bounty that the Cowboy's head coach said the Eagles put out on the Cowboy's kicker who had, earlier in the season, played for the Eagles. During the kick-off to start the game of Bounty I, an Eagle linebacker leveled the Cowboys kicker so hard that when he got up, shaken and wobbled, he headed to the wrong sideline. It was no wonder that the "Vet" as the stadium was so affectionally called by the locals, had a makeshift jail cell located in the basement for out-of-control fans known infamously as "Eagles Court." But that was all in the past, Chris told himself, as it was now just days from June 2019. And even if some of these *were* adages, he thought, that was fine too. A city, like a person, isn't perfect, thus what makes its character and its personality.

Besides, what did it matter if Philadelphia was a good or bad place? What mattered was the veteran I was there to help. Period. That was the mission. Not the famed liberty bell.

Although this was Chris's undeniable view, he also felt a persisting responsibility to see some of the historic sights outside of his primary task there. He felt that appreciating them, even to a small degree, be it a quick viewing or short tour, would make him a better-rounded counselor or whatever he was. Perhaps, he thought, it was Alex Sanchez's interest in history that influenced him, or maybe he just wanted to share some of what he saw in his travels with Sara. Regardless, he decided that between his primary mission, light workouts, and occasional reading, he would try to go sightseeing when able.

That night, as he nodded off in his hotel room in the aptly named Center City area located in the heart of Philadelphia, (no military lodging to be found; Fort Dix, in the bordering state of New Jersey, was the closest at 50 miles away) Chris dreamt of how excited Sara would be to hear of all the old sites he had seen and how he would one day take her there to see them too.

The next day, Chris called the social worker at the local VSA office, but no one picked up. No answer at all, not even a voicemail message option. Nothing. Just ring, ring, ring.

He tried again. Same.

That's strange.

Chris was told that his visit was expected. But the fact that the social worker wasn't answering his phone wasn't a big deal. Chris figured that he had probably just stepped out for a late breakfast or an early lunch. Yet, instead of calling the VSA again later, he decided to take a cab to the VSA and speak to the social worker in person. He figured that he'd have to go there anyway.

It was a cool, cloudy day out with rain threatening, however, Chris didn't mind, he was just content with the lower humidity compared to that of New Orleans. But Chris wasn't fooled; he knew summer was only three weeks away and that the Northeast can get quite humid in July and August too—at least that's what all the weather channels were always reporting, he thought.

When he walked into the VSA center, Chris both liked and disliked its layout. The doorway and halls, he felt, were too narrow which gave it a crowded feeling, yet this also gave it a warmth; like as if you were in a cozy diner with friends. But it was still too crowded. He saw an example of this when a wheelchaired veteran had to wait on the foot traffic before going through. The veteran didn't seem to mind though. Veterans, Chris found, were patient people, contrary to what some said.

The line moved steadily, and before he knew it, Chris was up next. "Yes, hello. Chris Longo here with the DoD. (He felt strange not saying VSA, though he technically, albeit only partly, still worked for). I'm here to meet with Mr. Johnson. I called for him this morning, but nobody answered."

A portly, aged male clerk with a saggy face and a laissez-faire disposition suddenly straightened up when he heard Mr. Johnson's name. "Mr. *Johnson,* did you say?"

"Sure did," Chris said.

"Oh, um. I'll be right back," said the clerk rushing off so spryly that it surprised Chris.

Moments later, a professionally dressed woman in her late forties hurriedly stepped forward. She held a folder in her hands.

"Chris Longo?" she asked.

"Yes?" he replied.

"Can you please show me two forms of ID and confirm to me who your supervisor is?"

"That would be a Michael Montrose, of the DoD."

"Okay, thank you. Here you go," she said, handing him the folder. "I regret to inform you that Mr. Johnson will be out of the office for the next few months. He is presently in the hospital with a medical condition."

"I'm sorry to hear that," Chris said, "but...."

"I spoke to Mr. Montrose this morning," she said, "And he is aware of Mr. Johnson's condition and the situation. I also informed him that the veteran you are here to assist, Vincent Mancuso, has yet to have a new social worker assigned to him. And to be honest, it could take weeks or longer before he gets another one. Considering all this, Mr. Montrose and I agreed that it would be best if you began working with the veteran immediately, especially since you're only here for a month. All his detailed information: telephone, home address, medical issues, and a summary of the recent support he's received here is all in the folder. Please keep it safe and private."

"But...," Chris said again, unnerved.

"Look, Mr. Longo, I understand this is not an ideal situation for anyone involved, especially the veteran, but we will just have to make do. If you have any issues, questions, or concerns, you can call me, I'm Ms. Daley, the Operations manager here. And you can also call your supervisor. Now if there isn't anything else...as you can see, we have a full house today."

Chris was dumbstruck. He muttered something to himself that he didn't even understand, or Ms. Daley hear. He walked off in a daze wondering what he was going to do next, but all he could do was what Ms. Daley had suggested they do, '*Make do.*'

Back in his hotel room, Chris went through the information in the veteran's folder. It was exactly what she had described it to be, detailed. Vincent Francis Mancuso: age 30. Veteran U.S. Army. Served four years in Germany. Presently resides in Philadelphia with his mother and younger brother. Employment status: Unemployed. Primary ailment: Alcohol use disorder. Has a pattern of alcohol use that involves problems controlling his drinking, being preoccupied with alcohol, continuing to use it even when it causes problems, and having to drink more to get the same effect; also has withdrawal symptoms when he rapidly decreases or stops drinking entirely. Has been attending AA meetings, as well as VSA support groups for the past 36 months. The results of which have been unsuccessful. Higher medication doses and one-on-one counseling sessions are highly recommended. The veteran is at times unwilling to conform.

Unwilling to conform? Oh boy, this should be an interesting case. A thirty-year-old man, who still lives at home with his parent and sibling. But who am I to judge?

The De facto Pathfinder then called the first number listed.

No answer.

The Philadelphia Experiment was not starting off well, he thought. He tried the second and only other phone number listed. This one at least went into voicemail. "Yo, Yo, Yo! You've reached Vinny Mancuso. That's right! You got *the Man*-cuso! Ha-ha-ha, leave a mess—beep!"

Chris couldn't help but let out an unexpected laugh.

Yep, this was going to be an unusual case. Something different for sure. I could feel it. Hell, I just heard it. He tossed around the idea of just showing up at the Mancuso residence or waiting a few days until someone had answered his calls. To wait or not to wait, seemed often the decision to make. Sometimes it was better to wait, but other times not. Chris then remembered what the social workers had told him, to let them reach out to you.

But how could I wait for the veteran to contact me if he didn't even know who I was? The answer was obvious to him.

He needed to go meet the *Man*-cuso ASAP. Get this show on the road. Looking again at the veteran's folder and information, Chris wondered how his mother was dealing with her son and his ongoing alcohol issue. Was she supportive of him? Or was she an enabler with whom he drank? These questions swirled around his head, but that was okay, he thought, as it was all part of the process that he was still learning.

Later that day, Chris went to the hotel gym to resume his dedicated, or somewhat dedicated, workout. After two miles of walking on the treadmill, he felt relatively good, but towards the end of it, he began to feel a little aching in his knees; though not as bad as when he was in Alaska or San Diego, he still felt some lingering pain that he had in New Orleans. It was the same with his bench presses, his biceps, and his ab workout. Better? Sure. Lesser pain? No doubt. Room for improvement?

Absolutely.

The next day, after again being unsuccessful in trying to reach his veteran by phone, Chris set off to try and locate Mr. Vincent Mancuso in person. As the cab drove through the streets of Philadelphia to his destination, Chris noticed that the streets had become narrower and tighter. And the neighborhoods grew unattractive and uglier.

"If you have never been, you should see Little Italy here." said the talkative retired cab driver, who also told Chris that he only took the job because he liked talking to people. "It's right next to Little Saigon, which is two miles and less than ten minutes from your hotel—have you ever been?"

"No, never been," said Chris flatly, not in the mood to appease the cab driver's people-talking hobby.

"Good people there," said the cabbie, not taking Chris's hint for silence. "Working class. The South 9th Street Market is there, or the Italian Market, as it's widely known, dates to the early 1900s. It has covered sidewalks, restaurants, cafes, bakeries, dessert shops, cheese shops, and butcheries. It's got everything—nice." said the cabbie with a bobbing head.

"I'll have to check it out," Chris politely replied.

"So, you're going to the...*Olde Richmond* neighborhood huh," coed the cabbie while rubbing a hand over his head as if the news wasn't good.

"I guess," said Chris, who caught himself from saying anything else in hopes of stifling the conversation, but he had no such luck.

"They have a large Polish community there, as well as an Irish one too. Did you know that?"

"I did not."

The cabbie seemed to finally take the hint as they rode quietly for the rest of the short thirteen-minute ride, or maybe he just felt sorry for Chris as the neighborhood he was taking him to wasn't a preferred one; as for the talking, Chris didn't mean to be rude, he just had a lot on his mind and was in no mood for chit-chat.

When they arrived the cab driver asked, "Do you want me to wait in case no one is home? Looks like it's about to come down pretty hard out there."

"No, I'm fine. Thanks," said Chris, eager to exit the cab and begin his work. The driver shrugged, then drove speedily off, leaving Chris at the short front steps of an unpresuming two-story brick row house. It looked as dismal as the gray skies above, which had begun drizzling. Glancing down the street and back at the front door, which he was about to knock on, Chris then realized what the street, and the house reminded him of. *Rocky*. It all looked very much like it, eerily much so. In fact, apart from it being two-story, instead of Rocky's one-story apartment, it all looked *exactly* like it, Chris thought, as he knocked on the door with the rain starting to pick up.

"Vincent, the door!" cried a woman from upstairs. Moments later she said it again, only louder. VIN-CENT, the door!" Chris then heard hard steps coming slowly down the stairs. Next, the unlocking of the front door, to finally it being opened "Yeah, can I help you?" asked a yawning man in a robe peering out from the cracked open door who was presumably Vincent Mancuso.

Chris was caught off guard. Maybe it was because he was suddenly thrust into a Rocky movie, but he had to pull it together and fast if he had any chance of getting into the house and out of the rain. *Get right to the point Longo. No time for games here.*

"Yes. Hello," he began. "Sorry to show up unannounced, but I tried reaching you by phone. I'm Chris Longo. I'm working with your local VSA office and the DoD."

"The DoD?" the young man of medium height, and seemingly to Chris, medium build, responded, now opening the door wider while closing his robe tighter. "What do they, *you,* want with me?" he said moving his dark shaggy hair away from his eyes.

With the rain coming down hard now, Chris noticed that all the connecting row houses didn't have any awnings on them to shield anyone from the rain, should they ever need the protection from it, like today. Bizarre, he thought, and just plain wrong.

Chris said. "I am supposed to work with you and your social worker, Mr. Johnson, but he'll be out of the office for a while. I spoke with Ms. Daley about it yesterday. Anyway, that's why I'm here. To help work with your VSA-related issues."

"Vincent!" the woman screamed again, "Who's at the door?"

"I got it ma!" the man yelled back.

"Anyone who knows Mr. Johnson and Ms. Daley surely wouldn't be lying. And if they were, why would they come here? To this house? In this neighborhood? Nothing to see here. Okay, Mr. Longo, come on in, you're getting soaked. Go ahead and have a seat," he said, motioning to a table that was littered with empty beer bottles. A staircase, which stood awkwardly in the middle of the room, divided the living room and dining room areas. Uncommon setup, Chris thought. He had never been inside an old row house before, not many, if any, of those in Oklahoma.

"Thank you," Chris said shaking off the rain.

"I'm Vinny. Vinny Mancuso," he said with his chin raised, obviously proud of the fact. "But I guess you figured that out already, huh?"

"Yes," Chris replied.

After clearing the table of the empty beer bottles, Vinny said, "Be right back. I gotta get changed."

Chris sat there looking around the bland room. There was nothing on the off-white walls except a large picture of a woman with two children. She was smiling, the children barely; on the corner of the family portrait hung a large silver medal from a colorfully striped ribbon. Chris then heard footsteps slowly coming down the stairs. It was another person in a robe and slippers, a woman. A very lovely one, Chris couldn't help but think. She was small, almost petite, but undoubtedly a tough cookie. Her Italian U.S. Northeast accent was thick and to Chris appealing.

"Um. Excuse me, sir, but can I help you?" she said, with her fingers running through her long black hair. She had a small, almost round face with a slightly pointed nose and chin. Her eyes were dark, her skin clear and light. She had a few wrinkles under her eyes which showed her age (*pushing fifty*), and although mature, her eyes had a youthfulness to them. And as beautiful as Chris thought she was, he would soon find her personality equally as attractive. But he wasn't there for her, he told himself, *or was he?* No, he was there for her son, Vinny the Man-cuso.

"Um, sir?" she repeated with a small courtesy cough, *"Who* are you? And *why* are you in my house?" she then turned to her son and said, "Vincent Francis Mancuso! *What* is going on here?"

"Ma'am, I apologize for the intrusion," Chris said. "Please let me explain who I am and why I'm here...."

Vinny then returned, dressed in jeans and a red Phillies shirt. "Ma, it's okay. I just got off the phone with Ms. Daley at the VSA. This man works with the VSA and the DoD. He's filling in for Mr. Johnson, who will be out of the office for a while. Mom, meet my new social worker, Chris Longo."

"Really?" She said with her arms now crossed. "I need a cup of coffee for this. Would you like one Mista Longo?" she asked, already pulling two mugs from the cupboard.

"Sure. Thank you," he replied.

"Ma!" whined Vinny.

"You go upstairs now," said his mother, "and let Mr. Longo and me talk. Vincent, DO NOT mess with me—ya hear?" He obliged, begrudgingly, and with slumped shoulders walked slowly up the stairs without saying another word. The woman placed two cups of coffee on the table, she added some milk to his and a spoonful of sugar to each. Chris liked that she decided how he'd be taking his coffee, which he didn't understand why since it wasn't his usual way, but he liked it, nonetheless. She then sat down next to him. Close but not too close. He thought she might apologize for her attire, but she didn't. He tried to pay close attention to what she was saying, but he kept wondering if she knew that he found her, in a way, special.

She knew. Hell, they always know.

"Alright, Mista Longo,"

"Chris, please."

"Ok, *Chris*. Before I begin. *Who* exactly are you? I mean you some kinda *fixa?"* she said while holding her mug with both hands and blowing on her coffee, then cautiously sipping on it.

"Excuse me?" asked Chris.

"A *fixa*? You some kind of *fixa* for my son?"

"Oh, you mean a FIXER?"

"That's what I said, didn't ya hear me right?"

"No, ma'am. I'm not a fixer."

"Then what are ya?" she asked, with long, blinking eyelashes.

"I'm sorry, but I didn't get your name," he asked courteously.

"Didn't give it...All right, it's Linda."

"Linda, you can think of me simply as a helper."

"Like an elf?" she said, smiling amusedly at her silly comment. Chris then noticed her pearly, straight white teeth. He liked them that way. Jessie had them as well. *You take care of your teeth, you take of yourself, and other things too* was his philosophy for liking them that way, besides them also being aesthetically pleasing.

"Yes, like an elf—*no!* Not like an *elf!*" Chris said, correcting himself, smiling now as well. "Just think of me as someone sent to help your son."

"So, you're more like Santa Claus then?" she said in a deadpan fashion. Chris didn't respond but laughed inside at what she said. They then just looked at each other for a moment, with one not believing the other. Chris thought that he could have looked into her eyes forever. They drank some more coffee in silence. He waited to listen; waited longer than expected. He was getting better at it.

"I don't mean to bust your chops mista," she finally said. "But you gotta understand my standpoint. I've been dealing with you VSA people trying to help my son with his drinking problem for the past few years, and I'm here to tell ya, that he hasn't improved any. Not one bit. Now I don't want to blame the VSA for that, Vincent needs to step up too, but it's all been so disheartening. I'm sick and tired of dealing with it, to tell you the truth. I just want my boy better so he can get on with his life, and I can get on with mine," she said as she then looked sullenly down into her empty coffee cup.

Chris sat there, observing, waiting.

"Oh my God, I gotta go," Linda then said, quickly rising to stand. I'm going to be late for work. Besides my regular job, I also work part-time as a waitress at a local diner. A Polish one. This is a big Polish neighborhood, ya know, and an Irish one too." she added in a lower tone as if there was a sad story there. "Hey, why don't you and Vincent, head over to the diner for lunch? You can talk to him on the way; ya know, get to know him. Let him tell you all about himself. Don't worry, that shouldn't be a problem," she said, with a wink and a smile before abruptly going up the stairs. Chris meandered over to look at the family photo and hanging medal. He looked closely at the latter. It was a wrestling medal: 2nd Place, 145 lb. PA State (Class AAA) Wrestling Championships. Hershey, Pennsylvania. March 9-11, 2006.

Linda then came downstairs dressed for her diner shift. He was surprised by how quickly she had gotten ready and how much even better she looked. She wore an almond-colored skirt, with a matching-colored blouse. On her feet, she wore dark clogs which exposed her feminine ankles and toned calves. Her hair was up in a tight, neat bun. Chris's heart couldn't help but skip a beat.

If she looks that good wearing that?

"Oh, you *must* ask him about that thing!" she said, catching Chris studying the medal. "Or maybe not," she added, revealing possibly another sad story. Chris felt momentarily embarrassed about his nosiness. "Can I walk you?" he then asked her, moving away from the medal. "It's raining pretty hard out there."

"No, I'm fine. I think the rain has mostly stopped, but thank you," she said while opening the front door. "Walk with Vincent there. He'll be down shortly." She then grabbed an umbrella, grinned, and said, "Just in case," and went out the door.

This woman has spunk. Or something, whatever it is.

Vinny then scurried down the stairs. He looked a bit more refreshed, like he had splashed some water on his face, and hair, but it wasn't enough, Chris thought. He still looked as if he'd been up late last night and that he had drank too much.

"My mom leave already?" he asked. "Did she say anything?"

"She said that we should head over to the diner for lunch."

"What was your name again?" Vinny asked, pointing at him.

"Chris Longo—call me Chris."

"Are you hungry, Chris? Wanna go eat there? It's good," said Vinny, quickly putting on his high tops while standing.

"Lunch would be great," Chris replied, "I can always eat. Hey, I was looking at that wrestling medal. Is that you? Second place in the state? Wow! That's impressive."

"Yeah, that's me...." Vinny said glumly. "Come on, let's go— I'll tell ya all about it on the way if that's all right with you."

"Sure," said Chris, "Let's go."

A light sprinkle fell when they stepped outside, umbrellaless, under a dreary, gray sky that matched both the color of the street and the neighborhood vibe.

"This way, I wanna show you something," Vinny said, as he bopped up and down like a teenager half his age. Chris caught up next to him hoping his knees would hold up. "I won that medal senior year of high school, back in '06—second place in the entire state of Pennsylvania in my weight class. I was a good wrestler. *Damn good.* I should have won first place that year, but...well...I screwed up."

They then walked without speaking for a while.

Chris thought Vinny may have gotten sidetracked about thinking back to how he had screwed up. Chris had to bite his tongue not to ask him how.

"So, where are you staying? Hotel?" Vinny then asked him.

"Yes, in the Center City area."

"That's close by, only five miles and fifteen minutes away," Vinny said, seemingly acceptive of the hotel's location. "And it's in a safe, touristy area," adding, "you'll be fine there."

After a few blocks of sad streets and some more light rain, they reached their first stop. "Ya know what this is?" Vinny asked as they looked at a small, one-story corner-row apartment.

Happy it was not.

"Should I?" Chris asked, confused.

"This was *Rocky's* apartment!" declared Vinny. "You know, like, as in *Rocky Balboa's*, from the movie—the original one."

"Oh my God, so strange to be right in front of it," Chris said.

"Pretty crazy right? We're now in the Kensington area, just a mile north of my home in the Olde Richmond district," said Vinny. "I used to stop by here sometimes on my way to the gym; to get some motivation," he said, twisting his torso and dragging a leg in a quasi-wrestling move. Chris walked with him a few more blocks past some Polish delicatessens and bakeries. Across the street, he saw a few locals duck into an Irish pub, probably trying to cheer themselves up on this downcast day, or perhaps their humble lives; it was probably a little bit of both, Chris thought. A man from across the street then stopped, threw a hand up in the air, and

138

called out "Yo, Man-cuso! What up? You stopping by later?" Vinny raised a hand back to him as if to say, maybe? The man waved him off appearing unconcerned with his answer. Vinny then looked over at Chris, thought he might be judging, and said, "Did you know that Sylvester Stallone had only 106 bucks in the bank when he was offered $300,000 for the rights to the Rocky movie? He, of course, famously didn't give in and take. That amount back then is equivalent to one million dollars today! He wanted to make it all on his terms—I mean he did write it and star in it. The *cojones* he had for making a gusty decision like that. And did you know that he was thirty years old when Rocky was filmed? Yep, the same age that I am right now. What a coincidence huh?"

With the many coincidences here, that's the one he tells me?

"Yeah, that's *quite* the coincidence," said Chris agreeably.

"There it is!" Vinny said with some newfound energy. "That's the gym that I'd go to for wrestling practice."

With Chris following close behind, Vinny then sat down at a nearby bus stop bench which was covered and protected them from the rain that had again picked up. Both stared over at the gym across the street. It looked as if it was condemned or closed, but it wasn't. It was open to the surprise of both. Above the place hung a faded, half-busted, sign which simply read, *Grady's*. It appeared as if it had been pulled out of a dumpster twenty or more years ago.

With his knees now unexpectedly panging, Chris placed his hands on them. He was, however, optimistic about them since their pain level wasn't as bad as it had been in the previous months. Yet the pain, like any unwanted presence, was still there, hanging on, like the hard dirt on Grady's old, rotting sign.

"Which brings me to the medal," said Vinny, suddenly serious. "That second place medal...that was my life in high school, wrestling. I started in middle school, but I wasn't any good. In truth, I was bad, *really* bad. And *too* skinny. Hell, I think they only let me on the team because the coach felt sorry for me, but my dad pressed me to stick with it. He supported me; was there for me—at least in the beginning. At first, I just wanted to make him proud. But then I enjoyed it. And at school, the bigger kids wouldn't bully me since I was on the team. The jocks stood up for me even

139

though I wasn't part of their crowd. Most of them came from money and lived on the rich side of town. But on the team, for a few hours a day, I was one of them." Vinny proceeded to pick up a rock and appeared as if he was going to throw it through Grady's front window. He then brought his right arm down and threw it softly sidearm into the wet, litter-strewn street. Little did he know that throwing rocks through windows was a De facto's Pathfinder's job, Chris amusingly thought to himself.

"Anyhow," Vinny continued, "I began to slowly improve. It didn't help that I was a late puber—*just sayin'*. Anyway, freshman year I had a losing record on Junior Varsity. In my sophomore year, I wrestled the first half of the year on JV and the other half on Varsity. Still, I lost as many matches as I won. Junior year was when I began to get good. Strong. But it was also the year that my father began to travel more and more for work, and see my mother and me, less and less…And so, I began spending practically every afternoon after school right there," he said with a slight tilt of his head and look of disdain on his face, then added, "—and many evenings too. Not much to do in Philly during the winter in high school except drink and wrestle—know what I mean?"

"Yep," said Chris nodding, though he didn't. Not a clue. But he listened, closely. *And besides, his question was surely rhetorical.*

"So, I wrestled, and I loved it," Vinny further explained. "But things changed. My father, when he finally came home from his long road trips, would drink more," said Vinny looking down now and scanning the ground around him, probably looking for another rock, Chris thought. But all he saw was trash and small pebbles. Nothing to waste his time with. He then brought his head back up and said, "My mother and father began arguing a lot. About him not being home. About his drinking. About her working double shifts at the diner to make ends meet. After a while they would argue just to argue—know what I mean?"

"Yes, I do," Chris replied without hesitation thinking of his own failed marriage.

"Anyway, in my senior year, I was unbeatable. The closest I came to losing was a draw. It's true, I have my father to thank for getting me started in wrestling, but Grady was the one who honed my skills. Instilled discipline in me. Made me a winner. I breezed through the district and regional rounds. Won them both. I had colleges knocking on my door. My mother was elated. So proud. My father, however, left; moved down to some Gulf state, Alabama or Louisiana. Said he was working at some refinery, but who knows the truth? He wouldn't tell us anything and after a while, we no longer asked. Besides, by then my parents were already going through their divorce. I don't want to blame my drinking on my dad, or my parents splitting up, but it sure didn't help matters any. I began to drink more and more. Grady saw a difference in me right away. He was tough with me, but he believed in me. He believed that I was special. I didn't tell him about my dad, but I assume he knew. I came to practice hungover and tired. I just wasn't into it. This went on for weeks leading up to the state tournament. I still wanted to show my dad that I was the best. That I could be number one. That was a big motivator for me, as well as to make my mom proud. But inside, I was still hurt that he was gone. We barely talked anymore. The drinking helped me with that then, it helps me with that now, *or not*. Anyhow, it all came to a head when I drank heavily just nights before the state tournament. I kept thinking about our family and how it was now broken and lost. I was good enough to get the final match—it's just...I needed everything I had to beat my opponent that day, and I didn't have it. He was the total wrestling package. Still, if I was a hundred percent, I *know* I could have beaten him."

"You still got second place! And scholarships, no?" Chris asked.

"That brings me to the worst part of my story," said Vinny. "After not winning state, I had some run-ins with the law: DUI. Drunk and disorderly. I was a mess. I was barely eighteen; young, immature, and stupid. My future looked bad. I lost my scholarships. I couldn't afford college. That was also when Grady and I had our falling out. I came to the gym one day and he laid into me. He said he wouldn't train me anymore if I didn't get my act together. He yelled at me and even called me a bum. I told him I was his star protégé. I won second in the state; had been training there for four years and *this* is the way he treated me. I told him that he wasn't my father and that he had no business talking to me like that. I told him to go to hell, walked out, and never went back in there again. I joined the army a week later. I got stationed in Germany, which was cool: beautiful country, gorgeous girls, and great beer. I enjoyed my four years there for sure, but the army...not so much. Have you ever served?"

"I did. One five-year tour at Fort Sill. It wasn't for me either,"

"Right? So, you know how strict that lifestyle is. There's the constant training and frequent field duty, and if you stay in it, it only gets more intense. So, I got out. Came back home. I didn't want to go to college, just not my thing. I bounced around jobs for a while. The longest job I had was working security over at the Sports complex. You know, where the football and baseball stadiums are, along with the hockey/basketball arena. But in that atmosphere, I was again drinking too much. The VSA has been trying to help me with that, as well as trying to find me a job. Though we haven't gotten anywhere with either. That's it. That's where I am at today." said Vinny somberly. "Come on, let's go to the diner, I'm starving, it's just around the corner," he said with an unexpected pep in his step, considering his bitter story.

They walked under the sidewalk overhang, which offered cover from the pesky rain; walked further on by a few stores, then a laundry mat. All of which seemed to be in a similar condition to Grady's gym, shabby. After another turn, and one more block, they reached the *Polonia* diner. Although it was nothing extraordinary it seemed to stand out, even shine. It was not quite a diamond in the rough, but in this neighborhood, anything with some pride or dignity in it stood out. Seemed brighter, taller. Vinny opened its door for Chris to enter. Inside he saw Linda taking a lunch order from an elderly couple. She then tucked her notepad into her apron and walked off toward the kitchen. Vinny recognized someone sitting in the back of the diner and headed over to them. Chris took a seat at the counter as Linda returned from the kitchen with a pot of coffee. She smiled at Chris and asked him if he wanted a cup. "Please," he said, smiling back. Linda then spotted her son in the back and didn't seem surprised that he hadn't sat down next to them.

"So, whatta-ya like for lunch mista?" she asked Chris.

"What's good?" he swiftly replied.

"Well, the breaded pork cutlet, or *kotlet schabowy*, as it's called in Polish—sorry I don't speak the language—is incredible. And it's the oldest of Polish foods they tell me. We serve it here the traditional way, with buttered potatoes and cabbage salad. You can't go wrong with that dish."

"I'll take it!" Chris said, adding, "can you take a break and sit with me?"

"No," she replied, "but I can stand across the counter here and talk with you. It's not that busy so the boss won't mind. Let me go put in your order."

Gazing around the diner, Chris guessed that most of the patrons were regulars. The Polish ones were obvious, as he could hear them speak the language fluidly with each other. The others were city workers, retired folks, and the likes of Mr. Mancuso, young and unemployed.

Linda returned with a side salad, placed it in front of Chris, and put her hands on her hips. "Tell me, did Vincent tell you his story?"

"He did."

She then asked, "Can I ask you if you're married? Sorry, I didn't see a ring."

"It's Ok. I'm divorced," Chris said as Jessie's face suddenly appeared. He still missed her. He missed her love. But her feelings for him ended years before they even got divorced, he told himself.

Did she ever really love me?

"Do you have children?" she then asked him.

"One. A daughter, fifteen," he replied.

"Then you know how important they are to us."

"Of course," said Chris, "they're everything."

"Exactly," she said, "so you can understand how tough it is for me to see my son going through his drinking problem again. Again, and again. He has honestly tried to kick it many times in the past, but he just can't seem to turn the corner on it. Ya know, he was a good kid in high school. *Great wrestler.* When his father left, he was never the same. He could have won the state tournament that year but something inside Vincent changed. Maybe he felt responsible somehow for him leaving, which of course, doesn't make sense. I even had my name changed back from Calhoun to my maiden of Mancuso so that he wouldn't think of him so much—move on, ya know?"

Chris said nothing, wasn't sure what to say. She continued, "First my husband left me, then my boy left me for the army. Went overseas. I didn't want to be alone, so I dated. It wasn't easy, but eventually, I met somebody. He was fine, no big spark, but we got along okay. And being in my late thirties at the time, I figured I should hold on to what I had while I was still relatively young. We were going to get married. We even had a child together, Joseph— he's ten now and in school today—but then my boy's father cheated on me and left. Whatta-ya gonna do? Men: can't live with em' and you can't live with em'...So, I focused on my baby and my studies. I became a paralegal so that I would have a decent job to pay the bills and not have to rely on anyone else in my life, except my boys of course—oh I'm sorry, let me go check on your lunch. It should be ready."

Thinking of Linda's life—her ups and downs—and here she was still fighting the fight to keep some semblance of a life for herself, and her family made Chris feel jealous of her strength, but it also made him feel bad for her too. True, he was there to try and help her son, but she also needed help.

Stay focused Chris...remember, by helping her son you would be helping her too—and like I could do anything for her anyway.

Linda set a big oval plate full of hot food down in front of Chris. And for a split second, he felt that warm, satisfying feeling of being given a good meal by an attractive woman his age who cared about him; even if it was by someone who was still more of a stranger than even an acquaintance to him. He still, nevertheless, felt the warmth of it. *Of her.* "Thank you," he said, trying not to sound too thankful. He didn't succeed. She sensed his sincere gratitude not only for the meal but also for her presence. She let him eat in peace, and as he did, they both thought about what they would say to each other next, and what they would not say.

Vinny's voice and laughter could be heard from the back of the diner, along with the smash of the closing cash register from another transaction. The occasional ringing of the bell from the opening of the front door was a reminder to the patrons that this was still a diner and not their home, though most didn't seem to pay any attention to it. To them, this was surely their home in a sense; even Chris was feeling more comfortable there.

"Paczki?" Linda asked after Chris finished his meal.

"Excuse me?"

"It's a popular Polish dessert. It's basically just yeast dough that's fried to a golden brown that's filled with yummy jam, then topped with powdered sugar. It's good—try one," she said encouragingly.

"When you put it like that, how can I not?"

Linda took his finished lunch plate and then replaced it with a smaller dessert one.

"Oh my God, it's *delicious*," Chris said, with jam dotting the corners of his mouth. Vinny then started walking towards them. Linda, seeing him, made a half-left turn and faced him.

"And where are *you* going? Don't forget you gotta pick up your brother today from school," she told him firmly.

"*Half*-brother," Vinny said lowly with his head turning away. Chris expected a harsh response from his mother to the remark, but none came.

"I know ma. I know," he said.

"And *no* drinking before you get him. Do you hear me?" she said sternly, yet in a hushed tone so that no one around them could hear. Chris was then about to ask him where he was going since he was there for him, not to talk with his mother over lunch and dessert, however much he was enjoying it. Linda acknowledged this by asking the next obvious question for both.

"Why don't you tell Mr. Longo when you'll see him again? He is, after all, here to help you," she said, which Chris thought was considerate of her to say.

"Sure," said Vinny. "How about Sunday afternoon after the Phillies game? We could talk at the house or the park with Joey. He likes to play catch after church. Or we could go to a pub?"

"Vin-cent!" Linda hissed.

"Just kidding, ma," he said smiling, "I'll see you Sunday," he said and walked out as the doorbell rattled. Linda and Chris then looked at each other blankly. She then said, "Hey, you may not think so, but that was a lot of progress for one day. He opened up to you and he's fine with meeting you again. He doesn't do that with everybody. Look, for what it's worth, I appreciate what you're trying to do here, help my boy out and all. It's just with booze, it's tough. He's been on and off the wagon more times than I can remember. Anyhow, we'll talk again on Sunday. Take care."

"Wait," said Chris, "I'm sorry to be so forward. It's just I only have a month here. I really need your help. You heard his social worker will be out for some time. Where should I start with Vinny? His father? Do you think I should try to find him? Have them hash out their past issues?"

"Don't make me laugh…his father is long gone, as is Joseph's," Linda said. "What? Did you think this was a classic 'daddy' issues case? Because I assure you it's not. Okay, it may be partly—but it's surely not the big part or even the most important part with Vincent. Understand Chris that many, many kids have had inadequate, bad, or unworthy parents; trust me as I have seen my fair share of them in court, as well as in my personal life. Yet many grow up just fine. What you need to focus on with Vincent are two things that I think will help him: I tried to tell the VSA and AA this, but they have their policies and procedures and wouldn't hear of it. You seem different. You seem like you really want to help him, no matter what."

"Yes, I really do want to help him," replied Chris. "Though you give me too much credit. So, Linda, please tell me, what are the two things I can help him with?"

"Well," she began saying, "the first one would be to talk to Grady."

"Grady?" Chris asked, confused.

"Yes, Grady. He was more of a father to him than his real father; see if you can iron out the fallout that they had, as they haven't spoken in years. Both are stubborn. Both think they were right. I don't know the details, except what Vincent told me. He was drinking too much, and Grady wouldn't put up with it. Said he was wasting his life. My son got upset and…stuff happens. People have differences. It's just…they were so close. My boy looked up

146

to him and Grady looked after him. They were a good team. Who knows? Maybe you were sent here to fix it? *Them.* You're a fixa, right?" she said with a cute smirk.

"I want to help, but maybe *you* should talk to his old coach instead?" asked Chris.

"I thought about that for a long time," Linda explained. "I even called over there once or twice. Grady is old school. I mean *really* old school; he won't listen to a woman. He'll only listen to another man."

Chris didn't know what to say. This wasn't like when he was going to talk to Tashana's father, he thought. That was for a specific reason and her *actual* father. Grady was only his coach.

No. Think Longo. She just told you that he was much more than just his coach to him. You could even argue that he had been more of a father to Vinny than Mr. Williams had been to Tashana lately. Still, Grady and Vinny haven't spoken in a long time; it won't be easy, but then again, that's why you're here.

"All right. I'll speak to him, Linda." Chris said, accepting the request and challenge. "Just remember they haven't spoken in years, so who knows how receptive he'll be...but I'll give it a shot."

"Thank you," she replied gratefully.

"And what was the second thing?" asked Chris.

"That would be helping my son find some purpose. Something in this life that will keep him occupied and busy. And most importantly, proud. Something he has a real passion for; we already know it's not college or the military, but he has to do more with his life than just drink. I don't want his life to be a joke, or even worse, tragic. Honestly, I think he's heading in that direction. Whatever you can do would be greatly appreciated."

Chris just nodded back, the words not there.

"Listen," Linda then said, "I gotta get back to work here. Why don't you go see the city or get settled in and we'll see you on Sunday? Say around oneish? On Sunday we go to church mass at 11:30 a.m. very close to here. You can attend with us if you'd like."

"Maybe next time," Chris said appreciative of the offer.

"Well, let's exchange numbers before you go," she said. "In case there are any issues with my son while you're here in Philly."

147

Chris liked that she wrote her number down on a napkin, and with a smiley face.

As he walked out of the diner and into the misty rain, Chris was thankful to have a break from Vinny and his case. Not that he needed one yet, as he had just arrived there, but after hearing all the details of it he felt he needed to step back and gain some perspective on the situation. And he thought he had a routine that was fairly successful in how he could achieve that. So, he stuck to it: a little resting of the knees, a little reading of Hemingway, and maybe even a little sightseeing.

I mean, I am staying within blocks of one of our country's original capitals during the American Revolutionary war and of some of its most famous sights. Think of what Sara would say.

Chris then thought of Linda. Her smile. Her humor. Her sly way. Her care for her family. Her care for him.

Well maybe she doesn't care about me, but she was nice, even invited me to church. And that's something. Ok, it was probably nothing, but I should be nice back. Cordial, at least.

With his mind set on his routine, Chris cabbed it back to his hotel to execute his simple plan for the day. He felt unusually secure and free of any worries about his case in Philadelphia, and even briefly, of the other worries in his life too. In the hotel room, he was content and relaxed; so much so that he sat far back in his room's desk chair and kicked up his feet on the corner of the desk as he read about the old man who was now slowly maneuvering and fighting to slowly bring in a big, hooked Marlin. The old man was experiencing cramps in his hand which he felt was bothersome and embarrassing. Chris thought of his knees. He could understand how the cramping would be bothersome and embarrassing, especially for a fisherman who needed his hands to function. He thought again of his knees and how they had improved some since Alaska.

In the book, the old man began praying ten Our Fathers and ten Hail Marys in hopes of obtaining the prize fish. Chris then peacefully dozed off for a nap. It didn't last long. He was awakened by a knock on the door. For a second, he thought he was in a dream, but he wasn't. The knocks came again and harder.

148

"Who is it?" asked Chris. "Who's there?"

A voice answered. A familiar voice. "Hey Longo, you there? It's me, Pat. Come on, open up."

"*Pat?*" Chris said as he opened the door. "What are you doing here? How did you even? —*Jessie.* I texted her the hotel where I am staying."

"You're a regular Columbo," said Pat laughingly. "Yes, she told me. And why wouldn't she? It's your 49th birthday tomorrow! I flew up here to surprise you. To spend the weekend with you; let loose a little bit. Have some laughs. It'll be like old times working on the road, remember them?"

"How could I ever forget? It's a miracle we survived them."

"That it is, my friend," said Pat, already unzipping his bag, "that it is...."

Chris was still in a small state of shock. "You *do* know I'm working up here," he said boldly. "I'm supposed to be here for my veteran 24/7."

"No worries pal, I understand. I'm not here to get in your way of that. If you can hang out tonight and tomorrow, I'll be out of your hair by Sunday. Will that work?"

"Guess so," Chris said. "But if my veteran calls me and wants to see me at any time, I'll have to go."

"You got it," replied Pat. "You always did put work first. That was always your first mistake, along with many others...."

"Very funny. It's nice to see you haven't changed in years, always the comedian." Chris said part kidding, part serious.

"I aim to please," said Pat who then conducted a half bow in jest. Chris was actually glad to see his old friend/coworker. He had already been gone from home for three months and so was happy to see a familiar face. That evening the two went out for a steak dinner. Afterward, they went to a sports bar that was full of local fans watching a late baseball game that was being played on the west coast between the Philadelphia Phillies and Los Angeles Dodgers. Phillies fans booed and fumed when the Dodger's Will Smith hit a towering home run in the bottom of the ninth to cap off a comeback victory.

Chris enjoyed the game and catching up with Pat, who drank

many beers, while he had yet to finish his second.

"So, you ever going to date again?" Pat then asked him. "It's time you know. You need to get back on the horse—Jessie has moved on."

Chris knew he was right. But Miss Right hadn't come along yet. What was he going to do?

Online dating, maybe? No, that's not my style or way.

"It's not that easy and you know it," said Chris. He wanted to tell him about Linda. That he thought he had a connection with her.

"I know it's not," Pat said. "But you've been alone too long. No more! I'm going to line you up with one of Stacey's friends!"

Now was the time to tell him about Linda, Chris thought. If for no other reason than to get him off his back. He probably wouldn't buy it, but he told him anyway. To his surprise, Pat thought he should pursue her. Ask her out. But how could he? Chris explained. He was the mother of his client. It didn't seem right, or ethical. He wasn't there to fulfill his loneliness. He was there to work with her son. He was the priority. No more, no less.

"Life doesn't work like a puzzle, Longo. Pieces don't always fit perfectly into place like they're supposed to. And so, what if you met her under these circumstances? So what? All I'm saying is never say never. Oh, I get it. You *still* love Jessie, don't you?"

Chris didn't respond.

"Yes, yes *you* do...I knew it! Well, you could always wait for her. But she might be married to her boyfriend by then."

"Ok, Ok. I get it. Can we change the subject?" Chris pleaded.

"Sure buddy, I'm just looking out for you. Hey, let's get out of here. It's kinda dead." Pat then asked the bartender for a good bar that was still lively at this hour. The bartender recommended an Irish Pub a few miles north, an oldie but goodie. "Great," Pat barked, "we're there! But first, line me up with two shots of whiskey for my friend and me before we go."

Chris shook his head in amazement as Pat carried them over to their table. "Come on Longo. A few shots. For me. I flew all the way here from Oklahoma. And you're not working tomorrow. Besides, it's your birthday in a few minutes. You *have* to!"

150

"Fine. *Whatever.* But Sunday can't get here fast enough."

"That's the spirit! Laugh—even at my expense! And most importantly, *Re-lax,*" said Pat grinning widely.

After the shots, they ubered it a few miles north to the Irish pub where they were dropped off right in front of. "Out of the way!" Pat hollered to a few people standing in front of the bar's entrance, "Got a birthday to celebrate here!"

Chris couldn't believe how immature his friend was acting, yet he also thought he was pretty funny as he was feeling a bit buzzed from the whiskey shot.

"Over here," yelled Pat who had found them two stool seats at a round high table. "Now *this* is the type of place to celebrate your birthday at, good music, good crowd, and good booze."

"Aren't we a little too old for this?" asked Chris.

"Oh, the hell with that," Pat frowned back. "You're never too old for a good time."

And with that, the two former coworkers laughed about their salesmen days together. The peculiar towns. The bad hotels. The eccentric customers that they would come across. All of a sudden, in the middle of their reminiscing, somebody pushed up against Pat and accidentally split beer on him. Pat didn't take too kindly to that, so he pushed him back. The two then exchanged harsh words. It seemed the heated argument was going to end in fisticuffs. Chris swiftly jumped in between them. "All right, break it up you guys. And Pat take it easy, will ya?"

"*Chris?*" said a voice in the loud, dimly lit pub." Is that *you*?" At first, Chris was unsure of who it was as he was a bit out of it. Then it hit him. He was in Olde Richmond. He was at the Irish pub that he had walked by with Vinny earlier in the day. "Vinny is that *you*?" he asked back, though he already knew it was the *Man*-cuso.

"Yo, yo, yo, it's *me!* Hey, what's wrong with your friend? He starts shoving me for nuttin.' Better tell him to calm down and shut up, before I make him."

"*Oh yeah?*" said Pat. "And what are you going to do about it, punk?" then added, "I'd like to see you try."

Chris then cut in and said, "I'm sorry about this Vinny, my friend flew in today to celebrate my birthday with me. He just had

151

too much to drink. No hard feelings, huh?"

"You and I are cool," Vinny replied. "And happy birthday to ya. See you Sunday."

"Yes. See you Sunday," said Chris who was going to ask Vinny to not tell his mother that he saw him at the bar but then thought that sounded too desperate. He then turned to Pat and said, "That was who I am here for. *He's* the veteran that I am here to help. Please just take it easy. It's bad enough I'm at a bar at this late hour. I'm asking you to back off and cool down. I'm going to go get you a towel from the bar to wipe off the beer. Just calm down. *Okay?*"

"Yeah, sure," said Pat, "Oh, and can you grab me another beer while you're up?"

"I think you've had enough tonight, don't you?" Chris replied with raised eyes. With the situation diffused, Chris went to the bar and waited for the busy bartender to get him a dry towel. He then looked back at Pat and Vinny and saw, to his astonishment, that not only were they talking to each other, but they appeared to be getting along. After waiting too long for the bartender, Chris returned to the table sans towel.

Where did Pat go? He scanned the bar. Nothing. He scanned again. Something. He saw that Pat and Vinny were now playing darts and laughing. Chris could only shake his head at the crazy night. They were carrying on as if they had known each other for years. Pat then mentioned to Vinny how Chris thought highly of his mother. Chris hushed his friend behind Vinny's back. Vinny however wasn't surprised by the news. "My mother thinks the same of him too," he explained. "But you'll know if she *really* likes you if she ever asks you to go see a hockey game with her to see her Philadelphia Flyers—then you'll know."

"Hey Longo, aren't you a hockey fan too?" Pat said to Chris, who didn't respond; though he thought what Vinny had said about his mom liking hockey pretty coincidental considering his connection to the sport through his dad. Still, that could have also just been the booze talking, he rationalized. Chris didn't think any more about it. He had enough to think about, like getting his friend back to the hotel room safe and sound.

In the morning, Chris was awoken by a phone call from Sara wishing him a happy birthday. "Thanks, and I'm sure feeling older today," he said weakly—his hangover the reason for his sentiment—though he didn't relay this to her. She then told him that she, Jessie, and Frank, were all leaving for Branson next week. It was an unintentional cruel reminder that someone else was taking his daughter, as well as his Jessie, away on vacation. *It should be me doing that. And only me....*

He thanked her again for the birthday call, wished her fun on her trip, and reminded her to keep in contact with him throughout the summer as he missed her very much. She reciprocated the feeling. Chris then felt grateful that Pat was there with him, besides not being alone on his birthday, it kept his mind occupied from thinking too much about not being with his daughter.

His next birthday phone call of the morning came from his mother. She was polite, albeit stiff. And she was judgmental; judgmental of her son's job, which caused him to be away from his only child who, adding saltily, '*really* needs him at this age.' Chris knew she was right, but he also knew that his job would help his daughter financially and himself professionally. Maybe even personally. He thought of his father, of what he'd think about his wife's stinging yet truthful remarks to their only child. "Be respectful to her," he'd say, and "that's just the way she comes across, but you know she only wants the best for you."

When Chris heard his cell ring again just minutes later, he envisioned, or *hoped* rather, that the birthday well-wisher was Jessie. "Hello, Chris, I was just thinking about when we celebrated your 30th birthday together," she'd tell him. But it wasn't her, it was his guardian spirit, Aunt Sophie. "Were you expecting someone else?" She asked him intuitively.

"Hello, Auntie. How have you been?" Chris asked, trying not to sound disappointed.

"Fine, fine., thanks for asking," she replied. "Just wanted to call and wish you a happy birthday. And so, what new location are you at now, hon?"

"Philadelphia," he said, not sure yet if he was going to tell her about Pat's surprise visit, but then decided he would. *Why not?*

"Well, I'm glad to hear that," she said. "You should enjoy your friend's company, as much as you have time to anyway. Life can't be all work and struggle; even the patriots in Philadelphia who were going through the revolutionary war still found time to blow off some steam and have some fun. Helps keeps your balance *and* your sanity," she said, with a snicker.

"Aunt Sophie, you sure put things in perspective for me—like the way my dad always did."

She paused for a moment, thinking of his words, then said, "And you make sure to visit some of the many historical sites that they have there...Did you know that the city is also known as The Birthplace of America? —former history teacher, remember? Ok, Christopher, I'll let you go as I know that you're very busy. Enjoy your birthday, and take care of yourself."

"Thank you, Auntie. It's always a pleasure to hear from you."

As advised, Chris and Pat went to see some historical sites, including others that people often saw when visiting Philadelphia. They first saw Independence Hall, proclaimed the birthplace of the United States. since it was where the Declaration of Independence was signed and where the U.S. Constitution was created.

In the Assembly Room, Chris and Pat were both in awe when they viewed where these paramount documents were signed by the Founding Fathers. Next was the Liberty Bell, or the Old State House Bell, as it was originally known until the late 1830s. It was renamed the Liberty Bell when it became a symbol of the anti-slavery movement. The Bell pre-dates The American Revolution as it was made by the Pennsylvania Assembly in 1751 to mark the 50th anniversary of Williams Penn's 1701 Charter of Privileges, which served as Pennsylvania's original Constitution. The Bell is also cast with the lettering, "Proclaim Liberty Throughout all the Land unto all the Inhabitants Thereof," a Biblical reference from the Book of Leviticus. As far as when the Bell first cracked is up for debate. Many believe it occurred in 1752, when it was tested upon its arrival in Philadelphia.

With so much seen in such a short amount of time,

the two sightseers were now ready to eat. They ventured over to the intersection of South 9th Street and Passyunk Avenue, where the famous Cheesesteaks rivals, Pat's King of Steaks and Geno's Steaks, serve the masses daily. Since Pat and Chris couldn't decide on which place to eat at, they decided that each would order from the other so that they could conduct an impromptu taste test. And they did. Pat liked Pat's. "Of course, you would," chimed Chris.

"Not true. I just find Geno's a little greasy. And, of course, the name's all wrong," Pat said with a chuckle.

"Same old Pat...Hey, before I forget to tell you. Thanks for flying out here for my birthday. It means a lot to me."

"You got it, buddy. Anytime."

"Yeah," Chris said, "but next time please try not to fight with anybody. You can be crazy sometimes. Do you know that?"

"Now you sound just like my wife," said Pat chuckling again. "Hey, let's head over to see the Rocky statue and go up the Rocky steps. I can't go home without seeing it. The boys would kill me. What do you say?"

"Sure," Chris said, "though I read that they moved that statue off of the top of the steps a few years back. It's now at the bottom of the steps, off to the side somewhere."

"Yeah, I heard that too," replied Pat. "It probably got too busy with people taking pictures up there next to it, but who knows? It did look pretty cool on top though."

Five miles and seventeen minutes later, they arrived by cab at the Philadelphia Museum of Art where the Rocky steps and statue were located. And since it was a Saturday, there was a line to take a picture next to the Rocky statue, but Chris and Pat had no interest in doing that anyway. They eyed the three levels and seventy-two steps of the famous "Rocky steps." Pat took off first and jogged it up modestly at an even pace, stopping only once, halfway, to catch his breath—not too bad Chris thought, for a fifty-year-old out-of-shape salesman. When he reached the top, Pat turned and faced the Benjamin Franklin Parkway which was modeled after the Avenue des Champs-Elysees in Paris. And like the Parisian boulevard, the tree-lined Parkway is broad, and lush with greenery, as well as brimming with grand buildings, monuments, and fountains. It also offers a tremendous view of downtown Philadelphia, which in Greek means, *brotherly love*.

At the top of the steps, Pat held his hands up high and danced around some, like the way Rocky originally did back in '76. Seeing him, Chris laughed out loud. He then headed up the steps himself, though instead of running, he walked them briskly; even with his knees improving lately, he didn't want to risk straining them. Together now at the top, both stood in silence catching their breath and admiring the spectacular view. Soon after, Pat joked with Chris about not running up the steps. "Not happening," Chris said firmly back. "But you, you almost looked like Rocky, and I'm using almost *very* loosely," he said with a pat on his friend's arm.

Upon descending the steps, they decided to go back towards the Center City area to check out the 126-year-old Reading Terminal Market, which is set below a former railroad terminal and today serves as a sensational tourist destination that offers a wide variety of mouthwatering foods from fresh produce, meats, seafood, and cheeses, to appetizing desserts. There are also dozens of restaurants to choose from. Inside, they each picked up a cup of coffee and walked around the colorful and lively market while trying different foods. Afterward, they went to see their last attraction of the day, Penn's Landing, located at the city waterfront next to the Delaware River. There they stumbled across a festival that had live music that they both agreed was very good. It capped an end to a perfect day of sightseeing and catching up. At the hotel, later that evening, the friends said their goodbyes as Pat was getting up exceptionally early the following day for his flight back to Oklahoma City. But before he did, he reminded Chris to not let an opportunity, *any* opportunity, slip away. Chris thought he was surely talking about Linda or assumed so anyway but left it at that. He thanked Pat for the advice, as well as his surprise visit for his birthday, and his enduring friendship. "Don't go changing," he told his friend lastly as he liked him just the way he was, which was pretty much the complete opposite of himself.

The following afternoon, the now forty-nine-year-old Christopher Longo left to go see Vinny and his family. He was looking forward to it too, though he was a little concerned about what Vinny might have told Linda when he saw him at the Irish Pub Friday night. This was however out of his hands. Besides, he thought, Linda would understand, at least he hoped that she would.

The sky was a ribbon blue with the air fresh and the winds low when Chris knocked on Vinny's door. Early June weather in the Northeast was a contrast to that of Oklahoma, where the blazing heat had already begun, so Chris appreciated his current location's weather that much more. On this Sunday he wore slacks, a short-sleeve-collared shirt, and comfortable shoes. He remembered that the Mancuso family would be coming back from Church, and then afterward, were going to the park so he tried not to be under or overdressed for the occasion; it was still a working visit, he told himself, no matter how relaxed things seemed between him and his veteran. He knocked again. The door was opened by little Joey who was still dressed in his Sunday best. "Ma, it's for you," he said lowly, leaving the door open as he lazily sloughed off.

"No, I'm here for Vin—" Chris was about to finish saying before Linda appeared in the doorway. She too was in her Sunday best. Chris was taken aback by how stunning she looked in her mint-shaded, short-sleeved, V-neckline dress that had a soft pastel floral print. With it, she wore white sandal heels that not only made her taller but look at least ten years younger, if not more. "Well, hey there, mista," she said. "You've been behaving yourself in our city I hope," she said while waving him inside.

"Ah, yeah. I think so—hope so," Chris replied awkwardly back. "Smells delicious," he added, trying to redeem his composure and, hopefully, his standing with her.

"Come sit down here with Vincent and Joey. Are ya hungry?" she said motioning him to a chair.

"Hey," Vinny then said, looking up from his cell phone. "Sorry, just checking the Phillies score from last night. You'd think that now that we have Bryce Harper, one of the game's best, we'd be better than .500. But sadly, we're not."

"That's crap!" said little Joey, lifting his head out of his cereal

157

bowl. "Enough with the language, Joey!" snapped Linda from over a sizzling frying pan.

"Sorry, ma," Joey said dejectedly, then lowered his head back down to his spoon, continuing its steady flow from bowl to mouth.

"What are you cooking there?" Chris asked, sitting down with the tough, yet colorful table of characters. "Pork roll," said Linda, rubbing her chin artfully with her shoulder with both hands occupied. "Do you like it?" she then asked.

"Like it?" Chris asked incredulously, "I've never heard of it,"

"Where are you from again?" Linda asked him, which now got the attention of both her sons who looked up emptily at him.

Chris said, "I'm an Oklahoma boy through and through."

The boys, clearly uninterested in his response, returned to their respective involvements of cell phone and cereal. Linda, who saw this without seeing it, said, "Well, it's a regional thing; southern New Jerseyans, to include us Philadelphians, call it Pork Roll. Northern New Jerseyans call it Taylor Ham, though it's *technically* not a ham. It's a processed, smoked pork product."

Vinny, after cursing the Dodgers for beating his team, interjected, "Well, whatever it is, it's the greatest breakfast meat ever, and my mom makes it the best and only way; fried egg and cheese on a Kaiser roll, with some salt n' pepper, and ketchup. That's it—perfect."

"I like Scrapple better!" exclaimed Joey, his words hard to make out through his full mouth.

"That stuff's gross!" objected Vinny.

"Now *that* stuff is really old Pennsylvania," said Linda as she served everyone at the table a pork roll sandwich just as Vinny had described it. But she didn't make one for herself. She just sat down with an elbow on the table, resting her head in her hand, waiting to hear Chris's verdict of her esteemed creation.

Everyone took a bite at almost the same time. Little Joey, after pushing his cereal bowl off to the side, grunted his approval first. Chris's verdict was next, as cheese oozed out evenly from the sides of his sandwich. The salty meat, he thought, was tasty. *Very* tasty. "Vincent was right," he said, "it's *perfect."*

Linda smiled, then blushed faintly.

Vincent remained silent, his thoughts on the subject already conveyed. A small smirk of being right then appeared on his face. Little Joey saw this and then started laughing, lightly at first, then uncontrollably. This made Linda start to laugh as well with a hand over her mouth, the other cutely touching the back of Joey's head. Vinny came next. Saw them laughing. Couldn't help it, was contagious. He seemed to enjoy it. As if he *wanted* a reason to laugh. He took it. Leaned back now hard in laughter holding his stomach. The bare room was now filled with the sounds of joy, Chris thought, by a broken family, but still a family. Chris laughed too. So hard in fact that his eyes watered; he wasn't sure if it was from the laughter or the joy he felt. It didn't matter, for in that fleeting moment he recalled that old, loving feeling of being together with Jessica and Sara: the feeling of being home.

The Park was scarcely occupied. Medium in size. Oval in shape. With its grass too short and closer to brown than green. City Park. Hollering was heard from kids playing basketball without nets across the street. Sixers' jerseys abound. A few dog walkers hovered the park's perimeter. One hand on their leashes, the other on their cell phones. The dogs sniffed around oblivious to everything except the scent they were eagerly trying to locate.

The Mancuso family had all changed to casual wear for the sunny day at the park; shorts, T-shirts, and sneakers, as little Joey called them. Vinny had a catch with Joey. Chris then said to them, "In Oklahoma, we say *play catch*,"—to which both sneered, saying nothing. Little Joey shook his head in further disapproval. Chris noticed they had name-brand gloves on and were using a real baseball. And that they threw the ball properly.

Linda casually watched her sons *having* a catch. She and Chris stood alone off to the side as they did. Chris wanted to put his birthday night bump in with Vinny behind him, so he mentioned it to her; had to, he thought. She replied coolly, "Boys will be boys."

"That's right," said Chris, anxiously sliding dirt back and forth with his foot. He thought of the wolf in Alaska, its eyes, the focus. Then, of Til and Reno, to finally, the old man in the book still fighting to bring in the Marlin.

"By the way, happy birthday," Linda said with a devious smile. "And don't worry about last night. Vinny told me everything. He knows (thinks) you're a good guy."

Chris, never good with compliments, even smaller ones, didn't respond. He waited for the topic to pass...brought up the touristy stops he had seen with Pat. She nodded in concurrence. "Those are nice to see," she said, "and I like the Reading Terminal Market, but my favorite place in the city is the Italian Market which runs about ten blocks along Ninth Street in South Philly. It's one of the oldest and largest open-air markets in America. It has it all and is quite the experience. You should go." she said as Little Joey dropped a fast-thrown ball from Vinny. "Hey, not so hard!" he yelled out.

"Yeah," said Chris, "a cabbie mentioned the market to me when I first arrived here; said there was a lot to see and eat there."

Linda then grew quieter as the snapping sound of the baseball hitting the leather gloves grew louder; an uncomfortable moment lurked. She then said, "Um, I'm sorry. I'm a little preoccupied with work at the Law Office. We have a big case coming up, which means I'll be working long and late. I just wanted to tell you that in the next few weeks, I won't be around much. I'm even sending Joey to summer camp for a few weeks because of it, but I still want you to try and take care of my Vincent as we discussed."

"Yes. I remember, *Grady* and *purpose*," Chris said dutifully. He wasn't sure if what Linda had told him about working late over the next few weeks was just an excuse to brush him aside, or if she was truly working late.

What did it matter anyway that I wouldn't see her much? I will work with Vinny and then I'll move on from Philadelphia and from her....

Linda picked up on Chris's dejection of her news by his body language and by the fluctuation in his voice. She didn't understand it at first, then did. "Listen, Chris," she said sincerely. "I wish I could be around more to see you and to hear the progress updates of my son, but I've got commitments at work too."

"I understand," said Chris sliding around some more dirt.

"Know what?" she then said, "The case should be over in

about three weeks or so. Why don't we catch up then? We could even go to the Jersey Shore for a day—it's only an hour away. Just you and me. You could fill me in on progress status of my son. Does that sound Ok?"

Chris then became filled with contentment. He didn't know why she made him feel that way. Did he like her that much?

Maybe she could be the one to finally fill the void or lack of companionship in my life since the divorce. Either way, he thought, he'd like the company. *Her* company. "Yeah, that sounds fine, and it'll be a nice break," he said, trying not to smile too widely at the idea.

The topic of if they should tell Vinny about Chris's upcoming talk with Grady then arose. They went back and forth on the subject before finally agreeing to tell him, though they knew he would strongly disagree with the idea. Linda insisted that she be the one to tell him since the talk was her idea. "Sure," Chris said. "What? *Right now?*" he asked her slightly startled.

"Yes, now. Why not?" she asked. "Next week will be busy for all of us. Might as well let him know ASAP. You can have a catch with Joey while I talk to Vincent about it."

So, while little Joey and Chris had a catch, Linda informed Vincent of Chris's upcoming meet with his old coach, and how it was her idea. As she talked to him, Chris glanced over to see how their conversation was going. Vinny, as expected, shook his head and walked away from his mother, then stopped, shook his head again, and walked back to her. The body language from both was easy to translate, Chris thought. Linda then wagged a finger in the air as if underscoring to her son the importance of the talk, and the plan, to get his life back on track. Back on the right path. They then hugged tightly. Chris saw this not only as a sign of love for one another but also as an understanding that both were at a crossroads in their lives with Vinny's drinking. And that anything short of positive results from him would be a high price for both to pay. Maybe too high.

Chris thought it better to call ahead to Grady and inform him of who he was and what he wanted to talk to him about. *Surely that would be more appropriate than just showing up unannounced. Seemed only fair and just considering the circumstances.*

"Grady here," said a raspy, aged voice answering the phone. Chris gave him the who, what, where, and why for the call but was still asked. *"Who is this?"* He went over it again, this time slower.

"I'm Chris Longo with the DoD. I'm here to help Vincent Mancuso. You were his wrestling coach. Do you remember him?"

"Oh, you mean Vincent Calhoun?" Grady said. "That used to be his last name. His mother changed back to her maiden name of Mancuso after Vincent's father never returned—can't blame her."

"Mr. Grady, could we...."

"*Grady*," he retorted harshly, "name's just Grady."

"Grady...could we meet to talk about Vinny?"

A pause followed; Grady gave the request some thought. He then uttered, "Tomorrow, here, 0530 hours," which Chris thought sounded more like an order than an answer.

"In the morning?" Chris asked, dead serious.

Grady didn't answer the question. He only added, "And don't be late."

Before he did anything else that evening, Chris set the alarm clock for 0430 hours the next morning. He also set up a wake-up call with the hotel front desk for the same time—better safe than sorry was a lesson he learned the hard way when he worked in sales. He then went about his normal routine, trying not to think about the brutally early hour he'd be up at.

During his walk on the treadmill at the hotel gym, Chris reminded himself that Grady was not Mr. Williams—no David and Goliath underdog, God, faith, and trust story here. No, this was almost the opposite in the sense that this person was a positive father figure to the veteran. But they were however similar in the way that Grady wasn't there for Vinny either when he needed him most after he hit rock bottom. Still, that was a long time ago. And Chris wasn't there to assign blame. He was simply there to get

Vinny past his past, stop his drinking, and push him toward a purpose in life. He thought of Linda; didn't want to let her down. He didn't want to let Vinny down either. Or Aunt Sophie, or Sara, or his mother, or Mr. Montrose, or Pat, or even the wolf. The list went on and on...but only Vinny should matter here, he thought, but then remembered that life's long insensitive tentacles reached over into everything, always.

Chris still had some residual pain after his workout, but it was a little bit less than last week, and the week before that. He then read some. The old man was again thinking of the Yankees and the great Joe DiMaggio, as he called him; the old man then wondered if DiMaggio would stay with a fish as long as he will stay with this one. And how DiMaggio's father was also a fisherman. Seemingly, only moments later, the hotel phone rang, then the annoying beeping sound of the alarm clock. Chris squinted. Saw the alarm clock: 0431 a.m. He had fallen asleep with the book still resting on his chest. Thought of Rocky getting up early to begin his workout for his fight with Apollo Creed and his drinking of the five raw eggs; how he started strong but limped back by the end of the run—out of shape and pathetic. But you have to start somewhere, Chris then thought. That was Rocky's start—now, if he could only get Vinny to begin his. But how?

Within the hour, Chris was at Grady's gym, arriving ten minutes early at 0520 hours. He noticed a small FOR SALE sign in the corner of the big window. He opened the old, squeaky doors and saw a huge picture on the back wall of Philadelphia's own Joe Frazier, the champion boxer. He was made famous by being the first man to beat Muhammad Ali in a fight, which occurred in 1971. Chris then saw in the middle of the gym a huge square wrestling mat with three separate wrestling matches going on at once. Grunts and moans echoed off the walls of the empty cavernous room. A takedown here. A takedown there. A whistle here. Then two quick ones. Then silence. Then the squeaking of wrestling shoes on the worn-out mat. The stench of sweat. Saliva. Testosterone. Burnt coffee. Mold. Hope. Misery. All mixed pungently together.

The man blowing the whistle had to be and was Grady.

163

He looked to be in his mid to late sixties. A pale Irishman who was just slightly less than medium in both height and weight. And he hunched a bit; wore a crumpled kelly-green colored Eagles hat that clung loosely to the side of his head. Clumps of white hairs crept out from under each side. He wasn't Rocky's Mickey, but he wasn't too far off either. He coughed like Mickey, and maybe even shook a little like him too, Chris thought. He waved Chris over and pointed to an upside-down bucket for him to sit down on, which he did. Grady slid another one over for him to sit on as well. He blew the whistle long and loud then squawked, "Break!"

Half the wrestlers immediately collapsed to the floor as if they were wind-up toys that had just expended all their energy. The thuds on the mats were almost simultaneous. The others stood, or bent over, with their hands on their hips breathing heavily. All sniffed, stretched, and moaned.

"All right. What-cha want? Oh yeah. You want to talk about Calhoun, I mean Mancuso."

"That's right," Chris said.

"Ok. What then?" asked Grady.

"Well, Vinny isn't doing so well, he's still drinking as you might know. I'm here, as I told you, to help him and his mother asked me to also try and help him find a purpose."

Grady stood up, took a few slow steps, and pondered his words. He then pointed up to Joe Frazier and said, "One of, if not the best boxers ever. Really. 32-4 record. 27 by knockout. His only four losses came from Ali and Foreman. Each gave him two. That era—*his era*—was the toughest boxing era, bar none. Did you know he used to spar here over fifty years ago? I used to see him here. Yep, smokin' Joe. A real champion. And do you know what it takes to be a champion before talent and before brains?"

"I don't," replied Chris honestly.

"Three things. The three *most* important things. Number one, Character. Number two, Will. And Number three, Discipline."

The down wrestlers slowly began peeling themselves off the mat. They listened to Grady as if he were giving them a lesson. But they also wished they weren't there to watch this stranger get an earful. Chris took no offense. He thought Grady, like Mickey, was just cantankerous, but ultimately, a likable person.

"Character, Will, and Discipline. It's what separates champions from the rest. Joe had it," the old coach said throwing a hand up at the poster. "And it's something Vincent never had. He could have been state champ. He could have had a career in the military. He threw everything away because of his drinking." Grady scowled, then sat back down on the bucket. All the wrestlers were now still. Waited for more. Wanted more.

"Maybe he just needed, or *needs*, somebody to believe in him," Chris said. "That somebody could be you. I know it's been a long time, but he just needs a second chance with you and with life."

Grady then stood back up, blew his whistle, and cried out, "Team up!" The wrestlers reacted swiftly to his command; each grabbed an opponent and began their wrestling dances. Round and round. Grady then walked Chris over to the far end of the gym, out of earshot of the wrestlers. "Look, I hear ya. I do. And Calhoun—*damn it,* I mean Mancuso—was one of my favorites. I always had a soft spot for him. He was a tough, talented wrestler. One of my best...." He then pursed his lips, rubbed his barely visible white goatee on his chin, and looked around the gym as if it were a close family member he would soon be saying goodbye to forever.

"You know I've been part of this gym for most of my life. Hell, owned it for half..., but it's time. It's time to sell it. Move on. You know, I would love to hand it over to someone special in my life: a son. Grandson. Or someone who I had a real connection with. But to be honest with you, I don't have anyone like that. I would *maybe* consider letting Vincent start running the wrestling program here at the gym. Maybe even take it over. If...."

"If?" Chris asked, almost biting at the word and its implication.

"If he showed progress with his drinking," replied Grady. "AA or something. I don't know. I've always said that when you fall down, you get back up. No matter how many times. That's will. That's fight. That's what he needs to do. Get back up. Get back up and stay there!"

"Ok Grady," said Chris. "I will personally see to it that Vinny attends his AA meetings and that he hopefully stays off the booze."

"*Hopefully?*" Grady asked, taking his cap quickly off and on.

"That he *does!*" Chris said correcting himself for Grady's sake. "But don't you want to see him first," he then asked him. "Talk to him before he takes over your wrestling program?"

Grady eyed Chris sharply. "Oh, he'll have to do better than that. I want Vincent to talk to the wrestlers. *All* of them at the same time. I want him to tell them his story. So they can learn from him and how he is trying to back up from being down. Then I'll talk to him. Even take him back in if he's serious."

"Won't that embarrass him?" Chris asked.

"No," said Grady, "and that's not my intention. He needs to learn. To teach. To grow. If he's going to run this gym one day, he needs to understand that. Period."

"Do you realize what you would be doing for Vinny?" said Chris. "You would not only be giving him a second chance with you but would also be providing him with a purpose in life. Thank you." Chris then put his hand out for a handshake with Grady and said, "I will be back here with Vincent (clean and sober) in three to four weeks for his talk with the wrestlers and you. And thank you again, sir, you are a true saint."

Grady said nothing. He just turned away, blew his whistle, and yelled, "Break!"

A few days later, Chris was alone with Vinny outside his home. Linda was busy at work on her big case while little Joey was off at camp. Chris told the Man-cuso the news about his talk with Grady. As expected, Vinny wasn't initially receptive to Grady's proposal, but he eventually came around to it. Besides, Chris thought, when would he ever get such an offer again that would address his past, present, and future issues?

"Really?" said Vinny. "He wants *me* to take over?"

"He just said taking over the wrestling program, for *now*," said Chris. "But I have to be upfront and frank with you. If you don't already know this, let me remind you. This is the time for you to get back up and as Grady put it, stay there. Look, we all fall. All of us. Do you hear me? ALL OF US. But you need to decide if you want to get up or stay down. I'm sure you tell yourself you don't want to stay down, but if you don't stop drinking now, then getting back up later, when you are older, is going to be that much harder, and the damage much worse. I'm not trying to scare you Vinny, but your situation could turn out disastrous if you don't...well turn it around now. So, for your mother, brother, and you. Please, please, *try*. Grady believes in you enough to give you this great opportunity. What do you say?"

Vinny thought about what Chris had just told him. He thought long and hard about it. Chris hoped that something would click inside him. "Also," Chris went on, "you will continue to have support from AA, your family, Grady, the VSA, and me. Remember, you are not alone here."

Vinny then looked at Chris as if he was already thinking about his next goal. He spit at the ground, turned, and said, "I need to get back in shape if I'm going to run Grady's wrestling program, or even his gym one day. I need to be in shape. And you're right, that includes no drinking. You know Mr. Longo, inside, I have been wanting to stop for a long time. And you're right, this may be my best and possibly last opportunity for me to do that."

"You could do this," said Chris encouragingly.

"I could do this," Vinny said, repeating him. "Hey, I gotta go. I want to go tell my friends about this."

"Ok—just don't forget about your AA meeting tomorrow."

"Don't worry. I'll be there. And thank you for all this. You know..., maybe you wouldn't be the worst guy for my mom." He then smiled and darted off down the street.

The first week in Philadelphia for Chris was busy, yet for whatever reason, went by slowly. The last three weeks, however, were the opposite. Not as busy, yet went by quickly. But after four months on the road, Chris wasn't surprised by this. Things never stayed the same, he told himself. They changed from month to month, week to week, day to day, and even minute to minute.

Vinny attended his AA meetings twice a week and spoke to Chris sometimes before them, and sometimes after. Chris was impressed with how eager Vinny was to get back into wrestling. And he was glad to see this for he was aware that this newfound purpose in Vinny's life was not only a positive thing but also an essential one if he were to overcome his drinking problem.

One night in his hotel room, Chris received a phone call from Linda. She told him she had finally finished her work on the big case and wanted to take Chris to the Jersey Shore that upcoming Saturday like she had promised. And that she wanted to be filled in on what had occurred over the past month. She said that Vincent had already informed her of some, but she wanted to hear it from him, adding, "You need a day off too. To relax and get away from the city."

"That would be nice," Chris told her. The plan of going to the beach on a warm day made him feel excited, even youthful. Or maybe it was just that *she* was asking him to go together.

Regardless, I'm just going to try and enjoy her company.

"Late June down the Jersey Shore, I feel, is the best time there. July and August are too hot and too crowded. June is just right," Linda said to Chris on the roughly hour-long car drive down. She then searched the radio for a song she liked before finally finding one. "Oh, I *love* this one by The Dobbie Brothers. Do you know it? You must. I remember listening to it and songs like it when my dad would take me down here; it must have been what? Forty years ago? My, oh my, how the time has flown by."

"What a fool believes, classic," Chris said flatly. Linda got caught up in the song's contagious beat and the lead singer's, Michael McDonald's, entrancing voice. Her fingers tapped lightly on the steering wheel. Chris enjoyed it too, until the lyrics got too close and stung, then hurt: *Jessie.* Was he a fool? What he believed?

> *And nothing at all keeps sending him somewhere*
> *back in her long ago*
> *Where he can still believe there's a place in her life*
> *Someday, somewhere,*
> *she will return...*

They arrived at the beach under a high orange sun that looked right at home against a boundless baby-blue sky. On the beach large, colorful umbrellas contrasted against the wheat-colored sand with endless towels that dotted the beach's landscape as if filling in the blank spots on a canvas. The Atlantic water looked darker than expected to Chris, but that also made it seem cool and refreshing, which it was. The nautical breezes tied it all together by causing the ocean scent to crash like airwaves against the smells of the nearby boardwalk foods, which included everything from straight-out-of-the-oven pizza, funnel cakes, and soft ice cream to salt water taffy and the aromas of peppers and onions cooking over a smokey grill; to then be carefully laid atop a cheesesteak, and lastly, slid inside a soft, fresh hoagie roll for serving.

It was there, sitting on the beach, where Chris told Linda of what had transpired over the past three weeks with her son from the AA meetings to his talks with Grady. And how he kept referring to her son as Calhoun.

"Took me a while to get over that name too," she said.

They talked about Vinny possibly taking over the wrestling program, then of the talk that Grady required her son to give to the wrestlers.

To Chris's satisfaction, Linda also filled him in on some of Vinny's thoughts and opinions on these matters and more that he had shared with her at home in the evenings.

The talk at the beach turned out, a productive one for both.

"I'm so proud of Vincent for going along with this," Linda said. "I told him it wouldn't be easy, that actually, it would be hard. *Very* hard. But also, that anything in life which is valuable always is."

"You're a really good mother."

"And I bet you're a really good father."

"…I don't know about the *really* part," he said, not jokingly.

"Well, I know that you're a good person to Vincent. That I know for sure," she said, nudging him with an elbow.

Over the next few hours, they laid down on their towels, took in the sun, and talked some more. First about their children, then themselves and their youth, to their present lives. They eventually went into the water. Linda, in her one piece, was still one of the most beautiful women on the beach, even in her middle age, Chris thought. Her face radiated, especially when she talked about going to the Shore as a teenager, "My first kiss here," she said sheepishly.

Later, with the sun going down and the beach quickly emptying, Chris and Linda strolled down the boardwalk, stopping occasionally to play a spin-the-wheel game, and ducking into an arcade to play skeeball. The game played by rolling a ball up an inclined lane over a ball-hop, or hump, that jumps the ball into bullseye rings for competing points.

"I got you mista!" Linda said to him after landing a ball inside the highest fifty-point hole, which had Chris already missing her with his days in Philadelphia numbered to a few.

Then, before going to dinner at an unassuming Italian restaurant on the boardwalk for linguine with clams, they decided to ride the Ferris wheel. With the sun long gone and a mysterious starless sky out, they boarded the ride enveloped by loud, pulsating music and a festive mood.

When the ride stopped at the very top, they both peered over the side to see the flashy lights below; the rides, games, and eateries, all shown brilliantly against the dark sky. They quietly took in all the scenery. She then turned to him, and he to her, and paused for a second and looked into each other's eyes. The breezes off the boardwalk suddenly picked up, sending her hair seductively blowing about. She nervously tucked them behind her ears, then both slowly leaned into each other, and with slightly tilted heads, kissed long and warmly. Her lips, at first a little hesitant, with the faintest hint of saltwater still on them, felt soft and alluring to him. His lips, a little unsure at first, with the slightest bit of sand still on them, felt stern and passionate to her. Afterward, she licked her lips lightly, then smiling bashfully, turned away and said lowly, as if to herself, "That was nice." She then took his hand and placed it on her lap and held it there. They stayed silent for the remainder of the ride with both savoring the romantic moment.

On the drive home, they spoke again about Vinny's upcoming talk to the group of wrestlers that he would soon be taking over. Chris said, "You know, I've been thinking about it. But really, the most important thing is that he just gets up there. What he says is secondary. Still important, but secondary; him getting up there is the hard part."

"I agree with you," she said. "Anyway, thank you for doing all of this for my son. It will, of course, be up to him to fail or succeed with—this chance—this *big* chance. But thank you, regardless of what the outcome is."

"You're welcome, Linda. Vinny deserves another shot to get back up, like all of us. I wish him the best. And for you as well."

Two days later, at a minute past five p.m. on a Tuesday afternoon, with Chris and Linda standing nervously at the far end of the gym, Vinny finally went up to give his talk. Vinny, at first, didn't want his mother or Chris to be present. But she *wanted* to be there; she insisted on it. And she wouldn't take no for an answer anyway. Eventually, Vinny agreed on the condition that they stay at the far side of the gym so he could concentrate on what he was saying to the wrestlers and Grady, without seeing his mother or his DoD counselor, which Linda had no problem with. She wanted him to feel positive, as well as comfortable about the experience.

Vinny stood with his hands in his pockets in front of the wrestlers, some of whom stood and some of whom took a knee. All were ready to hear this former protégé of Grady's, who most knew from around town. And most not in a good way. He looked back at his mother and Chris before beginning. The atmosphere was tense; Grady pensive; the gym eerily silent.

It was time.

"Um. My name is Vincent Mancuso. You can all call me Vincent. It's not the *Man*-cuso or Vinny or Calhoun or *The Man*. It's just plain, Vincent. You know, when I was younger, similar to the age that many of you are now, I thought I had life all figured out." He then paused, and went on, "Towards the end of high school, I was a talented wrestler with exceptional speed and strength, so I thought that I could win my way through everything. Girls. Grades. Friends. College. Family. Even my future. But I was naïve. I didn't consider two important things. One: I knew nothing, *seriously,* nothing. And two, I underestimated something: *Life.* It happens to all of us. Me, you, and even Grady. Okay, maybe not to Grady. (A few chuckles came from the group). When I say life, I mean life events that happen to you that will affect it. For me, it was my dad leaving, so I drank. And I wasted my chance at something special. Sure, it hurt when he left, but I bet if I asked any of you if you have ever experienced a loss, or some major life-altering event in the last few years, most of you would say yes. And if it hasn't happened to you yet, I hate to tell you this, but it's only a matter of time before it does. The point is the tough parts of life are something that we all have to accept and get back off the mat from, so to speak. So today, with the support of my family, friends, and others, I'm here to start over. To do something I have always enjoyed and was pretty good at. Wrestling. I stand before you here today and ask you for the opportunity to be your coach. And lastly, I want you guys all to be like Smokin' Joe up there (all heads turned back to the huge picture of Joe Frazier in a boxer's pose wearing the belt). *Champions!*" he shouted out.

Everyone erupted in applause. Grady himself clapped wildly. His protégé was back. Loud Cheers of Vin-cent! Vin-cent! rung out and verberated off the stained gym walls. Vincent then turned around and walked back half the length of the gym toward his mother. His face flushed; tears imminent. His mother, already walking towards him, met him in the middle and embraced him. The applause grew louder; tears then fell for both. Even Chris got a lump in his throat from the scene. A person finding their path back, he thought, was truly a remarkable sight to witness.

Later that day, Chris said his final goodbye to Vincent and Linda at their home. After Chris left, Linda rushed outside and told him that if he returned to town this fall, she'd love to take him to a Flyers hockey game. Chris was flattered by the offer. *Very* flattered. But he told her he wasn't sure of what his future held. He then took her hand and whispered in her ear, "You're one of a kind, Linda," then softly kissed her on the lips goodbye.

Leaving Philadelphia felt different to Chris than the last three places that he had left. But he wasn't fooling himself, it was Linda who made him feel this way. For she, he told himself, now held a place in his heart. Would he feel that way a month from now? Six months from now? Time will tell, he thought, Time always tells.

Back at his hotel room, Chris received a call from his boss, Mr. Montrose, about his next location. "You ready?" he asked him.

"Is this where I'm supposed to say *always?*"

"I like your sense of humor. Keep that up."

Chris said nothing, thought of Pat, the King of Funny.

"Well, you're headed to...The Mountain State!"

Chris thought about it but wasn't sure, *"Colorado?"* he asked.

"Nope. West by Golly Virginia!"

"West Virginia?" said Chris, half repeating, half questioning.

"Yep. God's country!" replied Michael. I emailed you all the information—you know the drill, contact me if you need anything.

More mountains. Great.

IX
ANTSY IN THE APPALACHIANS

Every child is an artist. The problem is how to remain an artist once he grows up." –Pablo Picasso

On the short one-hour and fifteen-minute flight to West Virginia, Chris pulled out his book. He wanted a distraction from his new case. From his new location. And he discerned, from Linda too.

He read that the old man had dispatched a dolphin while still hooked to the great fish. And that the old man was thankful that he had, as he would need the nourishment from it, as well as the two flying fish that he pulled from the dolphin's belly after efficiently cutting it up. He proceeded to wash the fillets in the water and eat them raw, then said, "What an excellent fish dolphin is to eat cooked...And what a miserable fish raw...."

The reading worked as a distraction—though it put him out of the mood for any seafood—Chris was ready for his new location with a refreshed, crisp mind, He was ready for the 'Wild and Wonderful' state, which was one of its official nicknames. But was he ready for his next veteran? A meeting with his VSA social worker in the city of Beckley was already set for the following day. Yet before that could occur, Chris first needed to land in the state's capital city of Charleston, which turned out to be no small task as its landing strip sat atop *Coonskin ridge*, 1000 feet up between two deep ravines, with the end of the runway only mere feet away from a frightening cliff drop-off. Chris was fortunate enough to be unaware of this. But he was, nevertheless, white-knuckled upon the plane's abrupt landing on its short runway due to its precarious location.

God's Country?—seems more like Devil's Country so far.

Next came the long and winding drive down the mountain.

Long and Winding....

So much so that the curvy roads nearly made him nauseous. When he finally reached the bottom of the mountain, under a hazy, dull slate-blue sky, Chris headed southeast in his rental car toward the town of Beckley, roughly an hour away. As he began his sixty-mile journey out of Charleston, he saw the city's unimpressive skyline; it was not a good first impression of the state. In fact, it was a bleak one. It did, however, gain some luster with the sight of the Kanawha River, which ran along I-64, the city's largest highway. That and the Elk River, a tributary of the Kanawha which ran through downtown Charleston, added a touch of nature and charm to the city, as well as being its primary drinking source. On his drive, Chris occasionally saw industrial factory conveyor belts from coal mining plants protruding monstrously from atop the Allegheny mountains; A common sight for the native, but for the visitor, a steely, if not uneasy reminder that they were in a different, even strange land.

Arriving in Beckley, Chris found a small (17,000 pop.) town with a quaint main street which displayed some historical pride and significance. Tree-filled and hilly, he judged Beckley a likable place. He did, however, notice that it was uncomfortably muggy out on this late June day. Nevertheless, without a military base nearby, he checked himself into a local nameless motel, though he would have preferred a chain hotel like the ones he used to frequent when he traveled around the Plains.

Though it was mid-afternoon after he got checked in—too late for a nap by his calculation—he decided to take one anyway on a count of feeling overly tired. During his nap, he had another zoo dream. He was back at the cages. He looked around for someone, anyone. Even his duplicate self or clone. Saw no one. He looked down to the left, then to the right. Again no one. He then heard voices coming from the cages. Was one of them *him?*

Strange dream. But aren't they all if you really think about it?

Then from a cage, he heard, "Hey kid over here."

"Til?" is that *you?"* he asked in disbelief. Then heard from a cage behind him, "Whatta-ya-say, Doc?"

"Alex? Is that *you?"* Chris asked, confused, then heard lowly from another cage, "Mr. Longo, can you help me, please?"

"Tashana?" is *that* you?" he asked, bewildered, then heard in another nearby cage, "Hey Chris! It's *me*—need some help here." "Vincent?" is that you?" he asked, now completely shocked. "What are you doing here? What are you *all* doing here?" he asked frantically. But no one replied. They just stood in their cages, ominously silent now with each leaning forward with tight grips on the cage bars, with their faces grim and despondent wedged in between them looking hopeless, Chris ran to the zoo entrance to see if Aunt Sophie was back at the booth, but she wasn't there. He then went back to the cages where all his veterans were now saying to him at the same time. "Chris! Help us! Please!" Desperate and scared, Chris began shaking each cage, one by one, until he fell to the ground in exhaustion. He then repeated defeatedly, "I can't help you! I can't help you! I can't help you!" Chris then abruptly awoke from his nap, shaken with a face full of sweat. He thought about the dream.

What? I can't help them. Why? I sure hope I can help them.

That night, Chris had planned to go out to eat, maybe even make some phone calls or go for a walk since the motel didn't have a gym. But after his bad dream, he wasn't in the mood for anything except watching some mindless TV and going to bed early. Besides, he thought, he wanted to be well-rested for his meeting in the morning with his next veteran's social worker. Chris got his wish for a good night's sleep as he, fortunately, didn't have another disturbing dream about his caged veterans at the zoo. But he didn't think those dreams were done with him either.

176

The following day, he walked into the Beckley VSA feeling refreshed and ready for his next case. And with four cases now behind him, Chris thought that maybe he was getting the hang of this job. That he was even perhaps becoming halfway good at it. But like all things that go up—he would soon be brought down.

"Chris Longo, is it?" asked a short, studious, older-looking man who gave a professional handshake. And although he was close to being elderly, he showed no signs of retiring anytime soon. He was sharp and displayed a genuine concern for the veterans he served.

"Hi there—I'm James Lipton," he said with a warm smile, "your veteran's social worker, but everyone here just calls me Jimmy. Please take a seat. Coffee?"

"Yes, please. Black is fine," said Chris courteously.

"You got it," said Jimmy, who then walked out, returning shortly with a small Styrofoam cup of coffee that Chris was familiar with seeing at the VSA center in Oklahoma City.

"Thanks," Chris said, accepting it.

"So, Mr. Longo."

"Chris, please."

"I know why you're here. I've spoken with your supervisor, Mr. Montrose, about it. I must say this is quite an unusual undertaking. I mean the DoD using a regular admin, medically unqualified, VSA employee to work with some of our most severe veteran cases? That's unusual, to say the least. Yet, however unorthodox it may be, I'm on board. I've been doing this for a long time. A *very* long time. And although our counselors and social workers are educated and specially trained to deal with these issues, sometimes, for whatever reason, they just don't get it done so, using a different approach—as long as we are careful not to hurt or worsen the veterans in any way—is totally fine by me."

Chris said, "Thank you, I appreciate your support," to which Jimmy nodded a 'you're welcome' back. He then reached into a filing cabinet, pulled out a manila folder, and handed it over to Chris. "That's the veteran's information there," he said before pausing briefly, then continuing. "His name is Kyle Barnett—*Major* Kyle Barnett, Air Force pilot, retired (medically). He's 45, married, and has three children."

177

Jimmy then paused again, gathered his thoughts, and went on. "The major was in an accident in 2011. A bad one. It happened when he was stationed in Southwest Asia (Iraq) in 2011. He was flying in a F/A 18 Hornet Fighter jet—no sorry, that's Navy and Marines. He was in an Air Force F-15E Strike Eagle when it crashed due to mechanical failure; something about the engine igniting, which then shut down its hydraulics and electrical power that made it unflyable. He was severely burned, but luckily, did eject, though late, which meant his landing went awry. He was severely injured upon impact. He got a TBI (Traumatic brain injury) and lost his right arm below his elbow, as well as his left hand at the wrist."

Jimmy then sat back with a sorrowful expression that didn't fit with his initial rosy demeanor. He paused to let Chris take in the information.

"You see the major was an expert with his hands as a pilot, a farmer, and a hunter. In fact, as a pilot, he was an 'Ace' which I didn't know was a fighter pilot who had at least five air-to-air kills. He got those during Operation Iraqi Freedom in 2003. But his biggest talent and passion was as a drawer."

Chris thought of the old fisherman and when his hands had cramped up and how they wouldn't open, who said, "It is treachery of one's body," and, "If I have to have it, I will open it…whatever the costs."

"A *drawer?*" Chris then asked, very curious.

"Yes, a drawer," replied Jimmy. "It's an artist who primarily makes drawings, and he was a master at it—has had the gift since he was a child. He studied it in school too. You've got to see his drawings; even though they are mostly black-and-white sketches, they are exceptionally detailed and amazing. But an artist's salary most often won't pay the bills. So, since he was also very patriotic, being from West Virginia and all, he went into the military (Air Force flight school) after college. He then married his high school sweetheart, Sally. Anyway, after the accident, he went through extensive physical therapy; got prosthetics for his arm and hands, which he can use to a fair degree, but nothing like he was able to before, and of course, his TBI doesn't help the situation.

178

Thus, his issues and your challenge.

"Not sure I follow you," said Chris.

"He was a master with his hands, now he isn't, nor will he ever be again—his issue is simply that. But that still doesn't mean he can't find something he's good at or even enjoy again."

"Let me get this straight, you want me to help him find a passion, one that could replace his others, like drawing?"

"Well, more or less, because of the loss of abilities, he's having a hard time with his identity—as I said, he was an ace pilot and a talented artist. What is he now? he asks himself. His wife and I remind him that he's a good father. And of how useful he is on their small farm in helping with tasks. Yet nothing has come close to fulfilling what he once was. This leads to other issues when he can't feel comfortable with who he is outside of his everyday physical challenges. Sally and I are concerned about him. We need to help him become at least part of what he once was. That is what he needs. To somehow become an artist again."

"I will do my best," Chris said holding up the manila folder.

"That's all any of us can do," said Jimmy. "Oh, and I would recommend you talk to his wife first about meeting up with the major. She'll let you know when it's best to see him and how he's feeling."

"Got it. Thank you. I'll call her later today. And would it be Ok if I contact you if I need any help or advice with the veteran?"

"But of course, anything you need. Take care, Chris. And thank you for being here and doing this," Jimmy said with a parting, two-handed handshake.

In his motel room, Chris sat in a chair, pulled it up to a small round table, and carefully went over the veteran's folder his social worker had just given him. As expected, Jimmy was spot on. He had covered it all thoroughly. Chris saw the date of the aircraft accident back in 2011 and realized that the major was 36 when it happened. In the prime of his life. Then, bam! The rest of his life forever changed. Chris couldn't help but think of his own life at 36. Back when he was still passionate about his job in sales. Back when he was still passionate with Jessie. Sara only three at the time. Her precious smile. His life was promising. His life was fun. His life was fulfilling, he thought, until one day, it no longer was.

Chris shook off his self-pity, then thought, this was a *real* loss; of a great pilot, of a gifted artist, but it was not the loss of a good man. No, that man was still here with us, alive. Down, but not out.

Looking inside the folder again, Chris read that 10 to 20% of Iraq and Afghanistan veterans have suffered a traumatic brain injury and that the consequences of this internal injury vary from personality changes and suicidal thoughts to anger; then read on that some physical handicaps, as a result of injuries sustained during deployment to the Middle East, also included amputation, disfigurement, and scarification. In addition, he read that the psychological effects of these traumatic experiences may inhibit personal and professional growth.

Chris located Sally's number in the folder. Called it. She answered. Said she was grateful to him for what he was trying to do for her husband. Told him to come over tomorrow at 10 a.m. and that their home and farm were in the town of Daniels, located just a few miles outside of Beckley. She ended the call by saying that she was looking forward to his stay in West Virginia, for Kyle, over the next month.

It was a splendid sunny morning the following day, when Chris pulled up to The Barnett Pig and Poultry Farm. As soon as he got out of the car, Chris could hear the clucking of chickens coming from behind the small pink house. He also heard some young children laughing wildly as if they were chasing them. He decided to forgo the front door and walk around to the back of the house toward the activity. He smelled the farm before he could see it. It was a smell he wasn't too familiar with, even being from Oklahoma. It was strong and rude, but also compelling. There he saw Sally. She had short, frizzy, sandy-blonde hair, and wore denim overalls with a white T-shirt, work gloves, and cowboy boots. Her skin had an agreeable tan which made her look under forty. Her smile was big and friendly. She was laughing at her three young children, all in a frenzy, trying to catch a chicken. Sally removed her gloves and introduced herself. She then laughed some more at the kids. Chris identified them right away as her true love and passion.

"So, this is it!" she said, with her arms raised, out wide, "this is our little slice of heaven—*or hell*—depending on what day it is," she said with a small snort. "The goat pen is up that-a-way. The pigs and chickens are here. And those little devils, over there are our kids: Travis, Caroline, and Preston. Hey, kids, come here and meet Mr. Longo." Each child then ran by Chris, one behind the other, still chasing the chickens, with each waving a hand up as they did. "Hello, mister!" said one. "Hey, Mr. Logo!" said another. "Hi, Mr. Logan!" said the last one. Chris couldn't help but laugh now too.

"Sorry," said Sally, they're just...." Chris waved off her apology and thought of Sara when she was young, which brought an unexpected lump in his throat. He coughed, clearing it.

"This place is really beautiful," Chris said, looking out past the relaxing pigs in their pens, past the bustling chickens in their coops, and into the gracious sloping hills of the many green-leaved oak trees which dropped down into a scenic valley that had a creek running through it; the blazing sun's rays from high above made the creek's clear water shimmer and sparkle as the occasional cool breeze came passing through.

"Mr. Longo, Kyle is down over there by the water. You can go straight down that way," she said with a quick point, "and go talk with him if you'd like."

"Please, call me Chris," he said, but Sally didn't respond. Chris thought of repeating himself, but since he was sure that she had heard him, he decided to let the request go so as not to bother her.

Walking through the high grass down to where there was nothing but dirt, Chris saw Major Barnett standing there with his arms crossed, staring into the glistening water. Medium in height and build, Chris could see, however, that the major was in excellent shape with the muscles in his neck, arms, and chest evident through his snug, short sleeve polo shirt. He could also clearly see a long, deep scar that ran up his almost entirely shaven head. His prosthetic hands matched well with his skin color, Chris thought, which was lighter than his wife's.

"Hello. I'm Chris Longo, nice to meet you."

"Nice to meet you too," replied the major affably, who continued looking out at the dazzling water, which made Chris take a peek. After some silence, Chris said, "The views here are stunning, really amazing."

"They are," said the major, scratching his arm. "You should bring a camera next time. This state has gorgeous landscapes—I take it you're not from these parts."

"No. Oklahoma."

"Oh. Mostly flatlands there. But you do have some mountains way up west in your panhandle what they used to call 'No Man's Land.'"

"That's right, most people don't know that," said Chris.

The major said, "Yeah, get a camera and take pictures. You'll want to capture the state's beauty while you're here. I think you'll be impressed with what you'll see."

That is a great idea. Why didn't I think of that before?

"I talked to Jimmy at the VSA," said the major, changing topics. "He filled me in about your visit. I appreciate you coming here, but...well...yeah."

Chris, unsure of what to say, finally replied unsteadily, "Oh, it's...it's my honor to be here."

"—Look," the major said. "In the afternoons, I sometimes like to walk around the indoor track at the Beckley YMCA, and afterward do a small workout. Would you like to join me there later today?"

Chris remembering his motel didn't have a gym, jumped at the offer. "Thanks, that sounds great."

"All right," the major said, "I'll see you there at about 1400?"

"Ok," said Chris, who got the abrupt hint to leave the farm early, but he nevertheless felt good about the invite for the walk. He left feeling positive about his start with his new veteran.

Three and a half hours later, the YMCA employee didn't even nod when Major Barnett displayed his membership card for entry, as if it required too much effort. The major unsurprised or unconcerned by the employee's passivity, just held an arm out to allow Chris in and past the lethargic young man. The indoor oval track at the Y was unique, at least it was to Chris. It was located on the second floor and connected only to the wall, which came out about six feet. It gave the feeling of being suspended in mid-air since you could see down to the bottom floor if you just merely looked over the side. They started walking around the track right away. The major set the pace, which, luckily for Chris, was the same speed he was used to walking at.

The major said, "Sorry I can't walk any faster; if I do, my TBI makes me dizzy. I must take occasional breaks when walking, when I start feeling lightheaded."

"No problem," Chris said. "This pace is fine, and please, stop whenever you need to." The major said nothing, just kept walking.

They walked together for a while before finally talking some. They talked about Chris's sole Army tour at Ft. Sill, which Chris tried brushing aside, but the major wouldn't let him.

"You served your country. That's commendable," he said. They then talked about the major's father, who had also served and, like his son, was also a fighter pilot. He now lives with his wife in a retirement community near Charleston.

"Quite the landing strip at the Charleston airport," Chris said.

"You mean Yeager airport?" said the major rhetorically. "It's named after West Virginia's own Charles 'Chuck' Yeager, the United States Air Force General—you know, the one who became famous for being the first pilot ever to break the sound barrier in 1947. He also served in World War II as a highly decorated combat pilot. An ace."

Just like you.

"My father flew with him a few times," the major said, beamingly, then pointed to a door and walked off the track into an adjacent exercise room, where he sat on a long metal bench. Chris followed behind and then sat down next to him. Though slightly winded, he didn't feel any pain in his knees, which pleasantly surprised him.

"Call me Barney," the major said, looking down at his hands as if he had just lost them yesterday.

183

"*Barney*?" Chris asked, "How'd you get *that* nickname?"

"Well, first off," the major began, "I only allow veterans to call me by it—but it's my fighter pilot call sign. You get it assigned to you (informally) early in your aviation career, often during initial training. And you cannot pick it, it's chosen for you. The more you complain about it, the better chance it'll stick; often it's a spinoff of your first or last name. So, since my last name is Barnett...they chose Barney. It's an old tradition and it also keeps things light between pilots. You've got to have a sense of humor up there: at those speeds, on those missions; you better or it will bury you."

"That makes sense."

"I'm Ok to continue now," said the major, who got up and walked to a nearby water fountain for a drink. He then turned around and asked, "Are *you* ready?"

"I'm ready," Chris replied, standing up and thinking about how the major's pilot call sign didn't quite fit him. Yet after talking to him some more, he realized that it indeed did; for even with all his aviation combat accomplishments and wide range of skills and talents—which would surely qualify him as a Renaissance man— he was at the core a simple, humble, mountain man who put everyone else before himself. Chris hoped that some of this would rub off on him. As they walked on, Barney told Chris that on rare occasions, he missed the adrenaline rush from flying fighter jets. Whenever this occurred, he explained, he would have one of his pilot friends take him up in their Cessna. Or he would go whitewater rafting down the Gauley River or the New River Gorge, but usually the latter, as it was closer. "But not to worry," he said reassuringly, "I always go with experienced guides and never above the easy-to-navigate Class II Rapids level."

"Those sound like lots of fun," Chris mused.

"No biggie," replied the major, "I only do those to scratch an itch every blue moon."

"Still, fun is fun."

"Then you'll have to go with me the next time."

"I'm in!" said Chris excitedly.

Meeting at the YMCA several times a week for walking and talking soon became a routine for the two. On some walks, however, they barely spoke at all, which Chris didn't mind. This was when he would think about his own life: of what he would do after this traveling job was over: of what, if anything, he would do about Linda. He thought about his father and his progressively aging mother. And he thought about Sara's birthday at the end of the month.

Wow. She'll be sixteen. How I miss those days at Lake Hefner. from pushing her around in a little plastic car to watching her learn to ride a bicycle to just going for walks there where we would talk about everything from her school, sports, and friends, to upcoming family vacations.

One day at the YMCA, Barney confided to Chris that he had become increasingly tired over the years of his inability to do something creative. He used to draw artistically, he told him, as well as enjoy other hobbies with his hands ever since he was young. But after his accident, he was simply unable to do those things again. "And trust me, I've tried everything." he said. "It's just too difficult to move my fake fingers in those intricate, precise ways for me to be any good and enjoy them like I used to."

Chris listened, then nodded as Barney continued. "Listen to me…going on about what I'm tired of…about what I can't do anymore…I should just be thankful that I'm alive. And that I have what I have; a loving family and the ability to see, speak, hear, and walk. I should be grateful for that and stop complaining."

"Don't be so hard on yourself. You're not complaining," said Chris. "You're simply stating a hard truth. That your life has forever been changed. And for someone with your extraordinary abilities, it's especially hard."

"I guess you're not wrong,"

"Exactly. You've been through *a lot*—I know you don't need any reminding of that—but maybe today, you do. Sometimes an outsider can see things clearer than someone on the inside."

"You just make that up?"

"Actually, yes I did."

"Well, I like it. Jimmy couldn't have said it better himself."

185

They both chuckled at that then decided to head over to the universal gym room as they both agreed that they had walked enough. After some chest presses and sit-ups, Barney told Chris that he should see more of West Virginia than just the inside of a YMCA. He then asked him if he'd like to see Little Beaver state park, which was just five minutes away from the farm. Chris, who was surprised that he was feeling minimal pain in his chest and stomach, replied, "Sure, love to."

"Great," said Barney. "Come by tomorrow morning at 0700. And don't forget your camera, some beautiful country out there."

That evening, Chris went out to buy a camera. He tried a big box store, but the ones he saw were either too expensive or too complicated. He left the store thinking he really didn't need one anyway. On his way back to the motel he reconsidered this since Barney had strongly suggested that he get one. He decided to stop by a drugstore in search of one. Unfortunately, all he found was a disposable camera—the very last one. The thought of what Barney would say when he showed it to him made Chris laugh to himself.

Oh well, it's this or nothing.

Arriving at the Barnett farm a few minutes shy of seven the next morning, Chris figured all would be quiet there.

It wasn't.

After Barney had opened the front door to let Chris in, he saw that the little ones were already up and rambunctious. Sally scolded them loosely, but they didn't seem to listen. Her attention turned back to the cast iron skillet on which she was frying thick strips of bacon. Already on the table was a large platter of fluffy scrambled eggs, which still had steam coming off them. The smell of both made Chris's stomach move with hunger. Sally then laid her spatula on the counter and wiped her hands on the front of her apron.

"Are you hungry, Mr. Longo?" she asked while taking two slices of rye bread out of a toaster, then replacing them and pushing down on the lever. Next, she reached into the refrigerator and pulled out some real butter and a glass quart milk jug. She then generously buttered the toasted rye bread.

"Yes, Sal, he's hungry," Barney said plainly.

"Then both of ya, sit down," Sally called out. "Do you like goat's milk Mr. Longo?"

"Not sure I ever had it," replied Chris, thinking about it.

"He's having some," said Barney. "You'll like it—promise." Sally then placed a glass of goat's milk in front of each of them and went on to fill their plates with eggs, bacon, and toast. Lastly, she kissed her husband on the head, said goodbye to Chris, and walked out of the kitchen seeking to regain control of the house from her clamorous young children.

Sipping the goat's milk with apprehension, Chris was unsure of the taste. He took another, bigger sip. He thought it tasted sweet and clean and a little grassy. "You were right. I like the goat's milk," he said. "It's good—different for sure, but very refreshing. And this bacon is just incredible. Crispy and hickory smoked to perfection. Actually, this entire breakfast is fantastic, and I didn't even get a chance to thank your wife."

Barney said nothing, just hummed in acknowledgment. When through with eating, they went out to the backyard where Barney said he had to restock the pig feed. Chris helped him fill up the big plastic tubs which prompted the grunting swine to waddle over in excitement. Barney then threw some fishing poles into the back of his pick-up truck and instructed Chris to jump in. They arrived shortly after at Little Beaver State Park, where they pulled up to a large, pretty lake with its water still and reflecting. Next to them lay a twenty-foot canoe with oars, which Barney instructed Chris to help him pull into the water. For the next hour or so they sat in the canoe quietly fishing. They exchanged words every so often, but not much. Chris then tried to get Barney to open up and talk more.

"What type of fish have they got in here," he asked him.

"Bass, Trout, and Catfish," said Barney. "And Bluefish,"

"Oh," said Chris, though he didn't know one from the other. Sitting there watching nature and Barney cast his line every so often, Chris began to appreciate the peacefulness of being on the lake as a balmy sun danced between sporadic woolly, white clouds. Barney then came to life with a tug on his line. Moments later, he reeled in a decent size trout, then dropped it into a bucket of water

187

inside the canoe. "These are *good*," he said, sounding better. "But you have to be careful when handling them. The bigger ones have teeth and will bite and draw blood—well, not from my hands anyway...." He then laid his fishing pole across his lap, taking a break after his catch. Soon after, he put his hand straight out toward the top of the tree edge line, then slowly began moving it across to the right and slightly up and down as if he were drawing.

"You know," he said, dropping his hand. "There are five basic skills in drawing. The first is identifying edges, like at the top of the tree line there. The second is recognizing non-object shapes or spaces, like the sky. The third is to calculate proportions and angles, like the lake width and tree heights, as well as the ground around it. The fourth one is judging light from shadow. That one may sound simple, but you must get the right depth which makes what you're drawing seem more realistic. The fifth, and final skill, is to unconsciously pull them all together." He then paused, as if in careful thought, then said with a wince, "You know, it's hard when you've had something you loved and then lose it. It seems like you are never the same after. You're always trying to fill that hole, that loss."

Thinking about what the major had said, Chris didn't have a response. Not then anyway, so he remained silent, thinking about his loss. His hole. His Jessie.

A jiggle from his line moments later took him back to the lake. Pulling lightly on the line, he felt resistance. "Reel, reel, reel," instructed the major. Chris did, again and again, until finally from out of the water, he yanked out a small, yet lively catfish.

"Whoa!" said Barney. "You got one!"

Chris cracked a smile and laid his fishing pole across his lap. He then took the catfish off the hook and put it back in the lake—per Barney telling him, "It's not yet ready for cookin'."

The catch, however modest, did improve their moods, or at a minimum, changed their attention from losing something each had loved. They then went back to the topic of drawing.

"About drawing, you were saying about pulling it all together," said Chris. "What's it all for? What's the ultimate goal?"

"To *capture* it!" proclaimed the major. "To capture what

you are drawing so that whoever views it, sees precisely *just* how you see it, so they too can feel what you are feeling about it. That's the art. That's what an artist does. That's their goal. Their ultimate goal."

Wow. How can something be so detailed, yet so elementary?

"Speaking of capturing, did you by chance bring a camera?"

"I did! I had forgotten about it, but I got it right here in my cargo pocket," said Chris, happily pulling it out and then remembering that it was only a disposable one. His joy further dissipated with Barney's tepid response. "I haven't seen one of those in forever," huffed Barney, "but you gotta work with what you got, right? I'm sure it'll do fine."

Chris clicked back the small plastic roller to prepare it for picture number one, then asked, "So what should I shoot first?"

"Are you *kidding?*" asked Barney, baffled. "Just look around you. There's beauty here everywhere."

"Oh no question," said Chris. "It's just, exactly *what* should I shoot?"

"Here, let me show you," Barney said as Chris handed him the camera. "Please, be my guest," said Chris. "I never take good shots anyway." He then noticed that the major held the small disposable very carefully so as not to drop it, as it was surely not due to its monetary value, but probably his stiff prosthetic fingers, he thought. Once he asserted his grip, he turned the camera vertically, peered inquisitively into the small square viewer, and rotated 180 degrees, slowly back and forth, until he was satisfied with a picture to "capture."

I was unaware there was that much to picture taking. I just aim and shoot. I guess that's what happens when an artist does it.

Barney ended up taking a few extra pictures, just to be sure. When through, he brought the camera back down and looked at it as if it had just done something extraordinary. Chris wasn't quite sure what the major was thinking. Was he making fun of the camera, or did he think it was something special? Either way, he thought, the camera interested him—whether as a joke or not. And since Chris wasn't that interested in it, he asked the major to hold on to it until the next time they met at a scenic place.

The major put up a small protest, but Chris wouldn't hear it.
"You'd be doing me a favor," he told him.
"Fine," shrugged Barney, "have it your way."

The next two weeks went by as usual, with Chris and Barney meeting up during the week at the YMCA. Chris was now mostly absent of any pain from his walks and workouts, outside of the occasional twinge in his knees that lingered ever so slightly. On the weekends, they met up at the Barnett family farm. Their conversations were friendly and expressive, yet Chris didn't feel he had gained much ground with the major since their first week together.

Perhaps it was me who was in a rut. Here in the quiet yet spellbinding state of West Virginia, lulled by its warm summer and peaceful natural surroundings. No. The major was in a rut too. But what could I do for him? He was a smart man. He had a great family and even some interesting hobbies. Still, he was missing that spark. That thing that he used to have before his crash.

Am I even helping him at all here?

The next time they met at the farm, after another hearty breakfast, Chris asked Barney about going white water rafting with him. He remembered the major telling him that he would go sometimes. Chris thought the excursion might be just what they needed to shake things up a bit. And with just a week left in West Virginia, he thought, what could it hurt?

The major said, "Sure," and that they could go in a few days. Sally overhearing this, chimed in, "So help me, Kyle—if you go above Class II rapids with Mr. Longo—you will never go again! "

"Relax Sal," he told her, "Mr. Longo is a professional. He wouldn't put me in harm's way," he turned to Chris with a wink.

With the whitewater trip a go, Chris felt content for now. So, with a few days to himself before the trip, he decided that he would catch up on some phone calls as well as with the reading of his book, both of which he had neglected over the past few weeks. Thinking about who to call first, the answer became obvious. With their daughter's birthday just a week away, it had to be Jessie.

"Hello Jessica," he said from inside his plain motel room, which he grew unexpectedly fond of—outside of its unsightly bed cover, thin pillows, dated bathroom, and persistent unrecognizable odor.

"What? No *Jessie?*" she wisecracked.

"How are you?" he asked. "How are you and Frank doing?"

"What? No *Fred?* All right, where's Chris, and what have you done with him?" she quipped.

"He's here...," Chris replied meekly.

"Are you feeling all right?" Jessie then asked him, now serious.

"Yeah. No. I mean, I'm fine. I've just been thinking a lot about Sara, with her big birthday coming up, and about you too. I guess when you're on the road you think about what you've left behind." Chris then heard Jessie breathe a sigh into the phone. A long pause ensued. He expected her next words to be harsh or crass. He almost deserved it, he thought, but they weren't.

"I...I...have been thinking about us too," she said. "And to be honest with you, it's partly because Frank and I aren't doing that well. The Branson vacation was pretty rocky for us. Don't worry, we kept most of it from Sara, but you know, that's not easy to do."

Chris said nothing. What could he say? he thought. She had left him. He had missed her terribly since the divorce. She had hurt him. He had recovered some, *maybe*. Moving forward without each other was all they could do. They still had Sara to bind them. Keep them connected. She was their only bond now.

"I know you've always taken great care of her," he said, "but she'll soon find out that life isn't always rainbows and butterflies, no matter how hard we try to make it that way for her."

After another sigh and another lengthy silence, Chris frowned. Jessie was at her head games again and he wasn't in the mood for it. Not anymore, no matter how much he missed her or loved her.

"Um yeah," he said, not wanting to listen to more dead air. "About Sara and her birthday gift...would it be okay if we discuss her (gulp) car when I return home in a month; month and a half?"

"Of course, Chris," she replied rather nicely, he thought, or maybe that was just wishful thinking. He continued, "Oh, and I'm sorry to hear that you and Frank are having troubles."

191

"Thanks," she said. "That's nice of you to say. We'll see what happens—if it's meant to be, then it's meant to be—but don't worry about anything except getting back to Oklahoma and Sara."

He wanted to hear her say, "Oklahoma, Sara, and *me,*" but he didn't. She just said lastly, "And Chris, Sara is very proud of you, of what you're doing, helping out veterans and all, as am I."

"*Thanks,*" he replied humbly, unsure if her praise was genuine.

When finished catching up on all his phone calls, which included calls to Aunt Sophie, Sara, and his mother, Chris settled in to read his book. The old man was finally getting close to catching his big fish. *Real close.* Still, the prized marlin wasn't done putting up a fight just yet, as Santiago tried with all his strength to pull him in, the testy fish continued to resist, swimming back and forth from the skiff. This got Santiago worried that he may not have enough in him to complete the job. "I am not good for many more turns," he thought. The old man then told himself, "Yes, you are," which brought Chris to the next, and to him, the best line in the book, "You are good forever."

For some reason, this again made him think of Til.

A few pages later the old man, at last, kills the fish: driving a harpoon deeply into it, which discolors the sea with its red blood. The fish is left floating stilly in the waves. But the job wasn't finished yet. The old man still had to take it to the shore. And since his catch was so big, running longer than the length of the bow to the stern, he had to tie it up along the outside of the boat. Nevertheless, that part of the book was for a different day. For now, the beaten fish was secure.

Several days later, Kyle Barnett and Chris Longo were together on the rapids of the New River Gorge. Their guide, however, informed Chris that this was a misnomer as the river was 340 million years old and one of the oldest on the planet. Adding to the river's ancient history on this abundantly sunshiny day, was the New River Gorge Bridge; a strikingly impressive sight sitting high above the heavenly views below that spanned over 3000 feet across and almost 900 feet high. Chris couldn't help but marvel at its size, as well as its deceiving simplicity. Also, he thought the vast steel bridge somehow fit in with the natural surroundings; be it by its majestic presence or by brute force. It seemed to have an inherent right to be there, amongst everything else in the angelic setting.

Floating smoothly down the river, the two veterans conversed as their guide kept a keen lookout for any possible danger, however minimal that was on this route, his attention not at all on their conversation. Perhaps overhearing too many in the past on the same route was the reason for his disinterest. Or perhaps it was the twenty or more year-old age difference between him and his passengers. Either way, Chris and Kyle didn't seem to miss his input as both knew this was their last full day together since Chris would be saying goodbye to the Barnett family in a few short days.

But they still had today.

The soothing sounds of the streaming waters within the enclosed green mountains had all aboard the raft in a pleasant state. Even the guide, while still on duty, couldn't help but notice.

"You know," the major began saying to Chris as he moved his oar lightly through the clear waters next to him, "your position is normally done by a doctor, someone with a Ph.D." Chris couldn't help but be slightly offended, though he knew he was right.

"Mine?" he replied, not understanding the exact reason for the comment. "I guess, but this is a new, unusual position, so who knows what the qualifications should be?"

"You're right," said Barney, "I didn't mean you aren't good at your job or that they should have sent somebody with a Ph.D. here. It's just that nobody can *make* somebody do something— except God, that is."

"Well maybe I should have a talk with him," joked Chris.

"Well maybe you should," Barney replied with a smirk. "No, my point was that a person just needs to want to do it on their own. But you know that already. Look, for what it's worth I think you're good at your job. And I have enjoyed our time, our talks. And I also wanted to let you know that I appreciate you coming to our glorious state to try and help me."

Chris nodded and replied politely in kind, but he still wasn't ready to concede defeat that he was unable to help this combat

ace/ farmer/ drawer/ hunter/ fisherman/ renaissance man find
something in his life that he would enjoy doing as much as some of
the other things he had done so exceptionally well in the past. And,
equally important, one that would also give him peace and
satisfaction.

*But maybe that was just a pipe dream. But then again, maybe
not? And what would my father have said? Thought?*

The major suddenly pulled his oar out of the water, placing it
in the raft. He then took out Chris's camera from the inside of his
lifeguard vest. He held it up so the guide could see that he would
be taking some shots with it and that he wouldn't be paddling. The
guide lifted his chin back to him in acknowledgment. Barney then
surveyed the area around him, and, with detail and intensity,
began taking pictures. At first, he took only horizontal pictures,
holding the camera securely with his stiff hands. But he soon
turned his hands and began taking them vertically and diagonally.
The guide didn't pay the major's action any mind, he just patiently
waited for him to finish. Chris, on the other hand, couldn't help
but be curious about Barney's attention to detail with his picture
taking as the major was now twisting his head and upper body
around for his shots. Chris then brushed the thought aside,
thinking simply that he was, after all, a true artist.

As they approached rougher waters, the major tucked the
plastic camera back into his life vest away and picked up his oar as
the guide warned them to be ready. When the raft hit the first
sudden rush of crashing waves, Chris glanced over at Barney to see
his reaction. He saw that he had the same one that he had; an open
mouth, followed by a wild laugh. Though the rougher rapids
didn't last long, they both relished the experience.

On the drive back, the major gave the disposable camera back
to Chris and said, "Hope you don't mind; I also took some pictures
at the state park and around the farm."

"No problem, even better," said Chris accepting it. With the
drive almost over, he then asked his fishing/walking/talking and
rafting sidekick over the past month if there was anything else he
could do for him before he left West Virginia.

"No. You were here. And that was enough for me. Just ensure

you stop by the house and say goodbye to the family before you leave in a few days. Sally would appreciate it. And, oh yeah, don't tell her about the *rougher* rapids or me driving on the highway. She'll get on me about those things," he said soberly.

Chris nodded. Understood.

A short while later, after thanking Barney for the special day, Chris picked up his rental at Barnett farm and drove to a pharmacy to drop off his disposable camera for processing. The employee, a drowsy 20ish-year-old woman with big glasses, walked over to look at the relic inquiringly for a moment, then, after quickly losing interest in it, said, "It will take a day or two. You can check back tomorrow." She then shuffled off in a sleepwalk.

"Thanks," said Chris, reminding himself that his daughter's birthday was now only a day—not two—away.

Here you are again, another missed birthday due to another traveling job. I lost my love, and I lost my father. I can't lose my daughter. I can't lose my daughter. I won't lose my daughter.

Early the next morning, Chris called Sara to wish her a happy birthday. "Happy sweet sixteenth angel!"

"Thanks, Daddy. What time is it?" she said with a yawn.

"It's early, sorry I was eager to call you."

"It's all right. Mommy was going to wake me up early to make me a special breakfast. Anyway, so, *where* are you now? Virginia?"

"I'm in West Virginia," he told her.

"Oh," she replied, unenthusiastically.

"Sara, I wanted to tell you how sorry I am for not being there for your birthday, but you already know why I'm here and not there. Not that that's an excuse...I just wanted to tell you that."

After a pause, she said, "You're not off the hook yet, just come home to stay this time. Okay?"

"I just have one more case, then I'll be coming home."

"Well, you better because I want to buy my car!"

"Oh yeah. That's right, my little girl will be driving soon."

"Yep. But I need you here too. Mommy's been a little nutty lately. I'm not sure if she and Frank are going to make it."

"I got you," said Chris. "But you don't worry about that. *Them.* They're adults, they'll figure it out one way or the other. You just enjoy your teen years while you can. Deal?"

"Deal. But don't you ever wonder if you and Mom will ever get back together?

Yeah, about every day of my life.

"Um. Of course," Chris replied, "but I also want to live in reality and focus on what I *can* do. Understand? Oh, I almost forgot to tell you. I went whitewater rafting the other day. It was fun. You'd love it! We will have to go sometime."

"I'd *love* to do that! Well, I gotta go. Mommy's calling me for breakfast. Thanks for calling for my birthday—love you."

"I love you too kiddo. Thanks for understand—"

"—Click"

Shaking off the abrupt hang-up, Chris remembered he had to call his boss about his next assignment. He had been so caught up with his current case and his daughter's birthday that he had almost forgotten to call him before the month had ended.

"Good to hear from you," Michael Montrose told him, adding, "Your next and last case is near Second City!"

"Chicago?" Chris asked him, not sure.

"That's right. But you'll actually be north of it, forty miles away at Naval Station Great Lakes (NSGL). Opened in 1911 and located on over 1600 acres that overlook Lake Michigan, NSGL is the Navy's largest training installation and the home to its only Boot Camp. The base is basically a small city, with its own fire department, police force, and public works department."

"I appreciate it," said Chris, knowing his boss would email him the specifics about his next case and next plane ticket.

"And, as always," Michael went on, like clockwork saying, "remember to submit all your reports after this last case is complete. By the way, do you miss Oklahoma yet?"

Chris thought about it for a moment. He wanted to convey to his boss exactly how he felt, "I'll put it like this," he said, "in a way not at all, yet in a way, more than anything else in the world."

"Well, I can understand that. No place like home. You keep up the good work and take care of yourself. See you next month."

That afternoon, Chris went to the YMCA for the last time, though this time alone, without the major. Afterward, he went to check on his pictures with mixed feelings; he felt good as he experienced almost no pain after his walk and workout, and it was, after all, his daughter's birthday. But he was still bothered that he hadn't succeeded fully with his present veteran. Thinking that there was nothing else for him to do about it, he picked up the developed pictures from the same sluggish employee from whom he had originally dropped his disposable camera off.

In his motel room, he placed the envelope of pictures down on a table—uninterested in them at the moment—he thought he might read some that night but found that he wasn't in the mood. Too much in his head. He decided to go to bed early since he was asked to stop by the Barnetts to say goodbye on the way to the Yeager airport for his flight out to Chicago. He fell asleep right away. In the middle of the night, however, he again dreamt. But not of the zoo. No. This time he was in the heart of a thick forest with tall trees and high soft snow, the silence frightening as he stepped reluctantly onward, unsure of what he was looking for or doing there. Then suddenly, from behind a tree, out came a wolf.

His wolf.

It stared at him. Chris stared back. Their eyes locked. Without any action or sound, a communication of sorts occurred. Then in a flash, the wolf disappeared, like it did when he saw it in Alaska. Seconds later, he heard the long howl of the wolf with the forest lit by a bright moon that reflected glaringly off the satiny white snow that looked especially exquisite, he thought, even if it was a dream, even if it wasn't real. But if it looked real, and felt real, then was it not real? He asked himself. Then yes, he told himself, it was real.

Chris then abruptly awoke covered in sweat.

But what of the wolf in the dream? What was its message?

Then it hit him, fight. Fight and Hope.

Glancing over at the sealed pictures on the table, which were visible from the moonlight that gently came through the window curtains, Chris then pulled off his bed covers and rushed over to view them. He quickly turned on the desk lamp and looked at the first picture. It was one from when they were on the lake, fishing.

And it was *perfect*. Not the quality of the print. Nor the quality of the film. Nor even the color. What made it perfect was something more important. It was as if the major had given the picture a soul. Maybe it was something just as simple as the way he allowed everything in it to have a say, yet at the same time not say too much. Or how he caught the shadows at the right angle. Whatever it was, it was something special. It was nature written. It was poetry captured. Chris looked at more of the pictures. Same. And all this with a cheap disposable? Why was he surprised? he thought.

Well, why would anyone expect this? Amazing photos with each, also, practically telling a story. From the trees to the waters to the farm animals. All were beyond good.

Flipping through the pictures again for the third time, Chris finally put them back on the table, shut off the lamp, and slid back under the covers. Tomorrow he would tell Sally what he had seen tonight, of what he had learned. He knew that Barney wouldn't want to hear that Chris thought he could be a real pro with the camera. And he was not only talented with it but, more importantly, that he *enjoyed* doing it. Chris knew that these things didn't just fall out of the sky. Yet sometimes, on rare occasions with enough hope, fight, and luck, he thought, they indeed did.

Good night wolf. And thank you again.

It was like when he had walked up to the farm for the first time a month prior; Chris could hear the chickens clucking wildly along with the kids yelling playfully in the backyard. As he got closer, he heard the grunting of the pigs. The feeling that he might even miss this place then hit him: this place that was so far from the rest of the world. Far from the big city lights and the rat race for wealth and power. Far from it all. And yet, curiously, everything anyone needed was right here. Chris tried to identify what he was feeling. It wasn't hard to pinpoint. It was envy. He was envious of Barney. Of his happy kids. Of his content animals. Of his loving wife. And then Chris remembered that even with all this, Barney still needed more. *Wanted* more. Life wasn't that simple—like Aunt Sophie had told him—it was complicated. So here was Chris, with the hopeful future of retired Major Kyle Barnett in the palm of his hand, literally; for in his palm, he held the pictures that would perhaps change his life and follow photography as a new artistic passion and one that could even replace his drawing.

"Hello Mr. Longo," Sally said gleefully as she handed him a hot cup of coffee. "Kyle will be right down. Will you be having breakfast with us?"

"Sorry, but I can't. I have to leave shortly to catch my flight. But thank you. Your breakfast meals are something I'll never forget from my time here."

"Then you'll have to return in the future," she said. "Hey, whatcha got there?" she then asked.

"This?" It's something I actually wanted to show you."

Sitting down now next to him at the kitchen table, Sally began going through the pictures. At first just casually, then sensing something special about them, she got up to grab a pair of reading glasses from the kitchen drawer. "These are...very good,"

"They are," Chris said.

"Are these pictures from your disposable camera that Kyle was telling me about?"

"They are," Chris said again, "and every one of them was taken by your husband. Look, Sally, I know how this may sound a little pushy, but I think, *really* think, that Barney has a special knack for photography, I mean look at them. They are just spectacular. He somehow even made the plain ones look captivating."

Sally didn't say anything. She just looked at Chris in wonder, considering his opinion. She then went through each picture again. When done, her eyes filled with tears and began to fall down her tanned cheeks. "Thank you for this," she said softly. "Thank you," she repeated. "And I agree with you. I do think he has a special skill here that he could pursue. I will talk to him about this seriously." Sally then stood up and hugged Chris just as Barney came into the kitchen and, upon seeing them, said, "—Nothing left but the cryin' as we'd say in the military."

"That's right," Chris said with a laugh as Sally wiped away her tears. They then all sat down for a last cup of coffee. Sally and Chris discussed the pictures with Kyle. They told him how good they were and how they both agreed that he was a natural at photography. Yet they both stopped short of telling him that it was something that could fill or replace the void of his drawing. That was a subject for the major and his wife to discuss in private. Still, like in New Orleans, Chris had to leave a reminder, or mark, just to be sure. So, just before leaving, Chris took out another disposable camera that he had picked up that morning as a last-minute gift. The major, holding it with a grin on his face, said, "See, I told you that you were good at your job."

X

LANGUISHING AT GREAT LAKES

---

*"The secret of change is to focus all your energy,
not on fighting the old, but on building the new."*
–Socrates

When the pilot announced the plane's final approach into Chicago's O'Hare airport, all Chris could see through the heavy rain was the industrial setting of hundreds of monotonous rectangular structures. It was the first week in August of 2019. Almost one year to the day since Chris had come up with his plan or epiphany for a change. A fresh start. Now, here he was, about to begin his last case. He tried telling himself that he had done a satisfactory job so far with his completed cases. And that his future employment, and his relationship with his daughter, looked promising. Even so, he wouldn't feel comfortable until both were facts. It was just the way he was wired. He wasn't carefree like his friend Pat, he reminded himself. He worried about things until they were done. Until they were right. But he'd get there, he told himself. And once he worked this out in his head, he then felt better about his future with work and with Sara, and even with Jessie.

Walking with the other passengers to baggage claim, Chris peered into an airport bar that showed tornado warnings, but the mid-day drinkers inside didn't seem concerned. At a closer look, Chris saw that they were only for the central part of the state, so he moved on to pick up his luggage, get his rental car, and pull out a map.

Same old, same old. Like when I was traveling in my thirties.

Chris wasn't unhappy that he was driving out of the mega city that was Chicagoland. He had been there once, twice, or thrice before working in sales at the downtown convention center. He wasn't impressed with all the movers and shakers trying to get rich. *Everybody wants to rule the world....*

Reaching the outer Chicago city limits, Chris saw that he was now only twenty miles away from Naval Station Great Lakes. He was glad that he would be staying at a military base for his final case, thought it fortuitous in a way.

About thirty minutes later, he arrived at the base's main gate with the dogged rain finally stopping. After showing his credentials, the guard pointed him to the base lodging quarters, as well as the whereabouts of his next veteran's social worker's office.

Upon entering the spacious base, Chris was fascinated by the ground's enormity, as well as by the tall and stately red-bricked clocktower building, or Building 1, officially which was built in 1905 in Classic Revival architecture and which loomed over the giant parade field, adding a sense of both authority and history to the prospective, young seamen who were marching orderly about.

Unloading his things in his prosaic yet adequate room, Chris couldn't help but wonder why he was called to a training site. Though he knew he'd soon be briefed, his curiosity still purred.

"Aren't all service members on the base active recruits?"

"Well, yes, they are. The vast majority anyway," said the stout, mid-fiftyish-year-old social worker, who reminded Chris of Santa Claus, just without his signature white beard. He did have Santa's belly down pat, as well as a reddish nose, just like good ole' Saint Nick's. His hands were large and he used both when he shook Chris's hand, just like Jimmy did. "Sit, sit," he rumbled before sitting at a hulking desk. The move made him huff and puff

202

before finally catching his breath. "Welcome to NSGL!" he said grandly. "We got trees on the left. We got a parade field in the middle. And The Great Lakes to the right. And, well, that's about it," he loudly cackled. Then, with a gigantic fist over his mouth, he cleared his throat, and, with his other hand, he picked up a folder and said, "Excuse me, this is an uncommon case."

Aren't they all....

"I say this because the officer, in this case, is still on active duty; I know the obvious question is, 'Why are you here for someone who is not officially a veteran yet?' Well, that's not the only reason it's uncommon. It's also uncommon because the officer is the present base commander, Captain Matthew Dobson. This is actually his office, which he lets me use when I'm up here. My VSA office is in downtown Chicago. Do you think they would ever give me such a nice desk? —Ha!"

"So, what are his issues?" Chris asked, getting him to the point.

"Transition to retirement: he's having a hell of a time with it. He began the out-processing seven months ago, where he'll soon transfer command to the new base commander at a change of command ceremony at the end of the month."

"*This* month?" asked Chris, partly stunned.

"Yes! And that's why you're here," blurted the social worker.

"—As you've been unsuccessful with helping him, I assume?"

"Bingo." replied the social worker. "Hey, I'm not proud of it, but I do have other veterans too—not that that's an excuse."

"Sorry," Chris said. "I didn't mean to offend. I was just trying to understand all the facts."

"Facts? Oh, I'll give you all those. They're all in his folder here. Let's see. Captain Matthew Dobson. Age 54. He entered the service late at 28. After graduating from Annapolis in 1993, he served in the Navy for 26 years. He has had tours and commands all over the world."

"Captain? Is that normal after 26 years in the Navy?" asked Chris. "Seems that he'd have a higher rank after so many years in."

"In the Navy, the rank of captain is equivalent to colonel in the Army, Air Force, and Marines," explained the social worker, who went on. "And in the Navy, the next rank after captain is rear admiral, which is equivalent to general in those other branches of service. So yeah, after 26 years, it's normal, even distinguished."

"Oh, absolutely," said Chris, "now that you've explained it to me. Sorry, you were going over his case...."

"Right. So now, after a long career, he's finally through, retiring. But instead of looking forward to his post-military life, he's distressed about it. He's become more and more dispirited the closer he gets to leaving—to the point of being depressed. I know what you may be thinking, 'Why would a squared-away senior grade officer, who's about to retire with full benefits, need so much emotional support from the VSA, VA, and the DoD?' It's a fair question. I mean, really. There are many veterans out there who have nothing and who are in urgent need of support. So why all this fuss about one retiring navy captain?"

"You're right, I was thinking that."

"Well, then you've probably begun thinking of the answer."

"Right again."

"The answer, of course, being," the social worker began saying, "is that we are *all* worthy of help and support, regardless of rank, race, and time in service. Just because an individual, even an officer, was successful in his military career, and served longer than most, doesn't mean he should be penalized for it. And why should he be? —Because he has secured retirement and a pension at a younger age that some of us will never get to see? Or enjoy? And who, I might add, most are envious of? To that, I say, Hogwash! Service members like Captain Dobson are deserving of all and everything we have available to help them. Hell, he's earned it. The years, sometimes decades even, those military lifers must spend overseas away from their country, family, and friends are unfathomable for civilians and even to most military non-lifers."

"I, for one, don't disagree with you," Chris told him. "And nor could anyone else when you put it so fairly and so bluntly."

"Yeah. Sorry," said the social worker rubbing his face roughly with his big hands, which caused it to turn red and match closely with the color of his nose. "I get a little worked up when I hear what some people say about lifers like, 'Hey, they signed up for it!' Or if they didn't want to go to war, they shouldn't be in!' You know Chris, if I can call you Chris, it seems today all anybody cares about is themselves and money, not country. It's a 'me, me, me' society. Sure, we'll clap at a ball game or fly a flag on national holidays, but if people knew, I mean *really* knew, the deep, intimate sacrifices, as well as the long-term consequences that service members must deal with so we could keep our freedom and our cushy American way of life, soldiers would be thought of in even higher esteem. Like we did in World War II, where my grandfather served and died. The way it is today, you're only highly esteemed if you have money. Period. The more you have, the more you're esteemed. Nobody cares about morals, values, or country. Not anymore. Not for a long time, actually."

"Jeeez, again, I don't disagree with you," Chris said, a bit surprised by the social worker's zeal and patriotic speech.

"Sorry, sorry," the social worker then said with his face quickly losing its flushness though his nose remained a jolly red. "I get sidetracked sometimes," he revealed with his zeal now dissipated. "Here, let me give you Captain Dobson's folder and let you go get started. Oh, and by the way, this is where you will be seeing the captain. *This* office is the captain's secondary office, which is far from his primary one that is on the other side of the base. He uses this one only occasionally, like when he gives out NJP (Non-Judicial Punishment) or Captain's Mast, as it's sometimes referred to in the Navy. The Army calls it Article 15, which is just a commander's direct punishment for minor offenses. He also uses it for quiet time to read or just get away. Lately, we've been using it for his counseling sessions. And now, since I'll be going back to my own office for good, it'll be yours to use over the next month."

Chris said nothing. He just took a brief look around the long, dark room with its full-length wood-paneled walls and lower-than-normal ceiling that resembled the interior of a ship. He then noticed the only thing that hung on the long wall to his left. It was a shadow box filled with various knots. "What's that?" he asked.

"That? Oh, those are boating knots. Yeah, the captain, he *loves* his knots, and his ship stories."

Thank you for the in-brief on the soon-to-be veteran," said Chris. "Is there anything else that I should know about him?"

"Well, let's see," replied the social worker while pulling folders and other office supplies from out of the massive desk and into a cardboard box. "—I apologize, I have another appointment with a veteran in my office today, and I'm running a little late. Let's see…is there anything else…well he's married and has two kids in college. Oh, you should know that the captain achieved his success all by himself, at least initially. His father also served in the Navy and was also a lifer. But his father was a drunk. A career enlisted sailor who partied wildly and often at ports all over the world. The captain's upbringing as a military brat was unstable at best, what with his dad's ways and all. Anyhow, when the captain became old enough to enlist in the Navy, he chose instead to go to college, which was against his father's wishes. Even worse, he went to Annapolis Naval Academy, which was another slap in the face to his father, who was a career enlisted man."

"His father should have been proud of him," Chris interjected.

"Of course, but people are imperfect. Flawed. That's why we're here. Anyhow, those are the highlights," said the social worker, who stood up with his now full cardboard box resting on his protruding belly. "Good luck to you, Chris," he said, before walking out the door with some more huffs and puffs.

A few hours later, Chris was in his base room monitoring the status of the tornados, which had begun moving north up the state. He then received a call from Captain Dobson on his room phone, which surprised him, but then figured that he was, after all, the base commander. After exchanging pleasantries, the captain requested that they meet at his office, his secondary office, the same one Chris had just received his in-brief at. Chris obliged, telling him that he would be there ASAP. The thought of walking to the office crossed his mind, but since it was over a mile away and the rain had returned with ferocity, he wisely drove there.

"Come in, take a seat," the captain said.

Chris shook off the rain as he approached the ajar office door. He peeked into the dark office and saw a small lamp atop the wide desk that gave off a cozy light. And sitting regally behind the desk in his service dress blue uniform was Captain Dobson. He then stood to greet his new, temporary DoD counselor/ therapist/

social worker. The captain wasn't sure what Chris's position was, nor did Chris, for that matter. But the captain knew that he was there to help him. And so, for this respected him, though truthfully, he didn't want his or anyone's help. He was a proud naval officer, after all. Maybe a little bit too proud. The captain knew this; tried to keep it at bay. But it came with the territory, he thought. It's what helped him all those years in the service, he told himself. And it's what helped him in the years before it. Now he was being told that it was no longer helpful. That it was no longer needed after the service. That being too proud as a civilian or a military retiree would make him appear arrogant, aloof, and even aggressive. He needed to now fit in with everyone else, he was told. He would no longer be the base commander who received VIPs and rubbed elbows with high-ranking officials and politicians and was the desire of many of the officers' wives if even just to be a friend of a person in power.

The captain wasn't always this way. As a teenager he was humble. Humble to a fault. It was only when he was old enough to understand who and what his father was; a womanizing drunk who cared more about himself, partying, and the navy, that young Matthew Dobson changed. He did what most people did in these situations. He rebelled. And later in life, he achieved. He rebelled by not enlisting in the Navy at 17. He rebelled by attending Annapolis and becoming a naval officer, which he never understood why his dad was against, except to think that he was upset that he may have to look up to *him* one day and even salute.

After getting commissioned as a young officer, he slowly grew more and more confident. And he grew strong. And he grew proud. He soon began achieving success to underscore what his father wasn't. To underscore what his father would never be. To underscore what he had become and what he had accomplished despite him. As his lengthy career went on and he became more successful, the captain eventually forgave his father for all his wrongdoing and failure as a father before he passed away. And now that his military career was coming to an end, here he was being told that his point of view, which he had been so successful and familiar with, not only needed to be changed and forgotten about but that it was even wrong and harmful. That his once fierce Lion pride and chip on his shoulder, which he knew deep down was what motivated him to succeed in the first place, would now be frowned upon and unwelcome. He's told what few, if any of us, ever wanted to hear, that he needed to change.

This would be a tough task and the primary one Chris Longo had with this soon-to-be veteran whose desk he now sat squarely in front of. The captain remained standing as if giving Chris a moment to take him in, which he did.

Chris thought his uniform resembled that of an airline pilot. Dark blue suit with six gold, petticoat arranged buttons. White shirt with a black tie. Gold piping on each forearm. The only redeeming feature was the colorful, multirowed set of ribbons displayed over the right side of the captain's chest, directly over his heart. Chris couldn't help but be impressed by their sight. He estimated his height to be similar to Vincent's. His build was slightly slimmer than that of Kyle's. His posture was similar to that of Alex's; stiff yet able. His dignified manner reminded him of Tashana. A quiet intelligence that needed no selling but demanded a degree of deference. He wore his short, thinning hair handsomely, lightly grayed at the temples and dark on top—there was nothing about him that reminded him of Til.

No handshakes were offered as introductions were understood to have already been covered over the phone; politeness was nevertheless in the air. The captain then sat with the torrential rain pinging loudly against the windowpanes. It was followed shortly after by the sound of shrieking winds, which blew angrily outside.

Chris flinched at the unnerving noises, the captain, who didn't flinch at all, then said, "Storm's heading this way, but don't worry, we'll be okay, just need to keep an eye out for the tornados. We'll probably lose power in the area soon, though, the base won't. We have industrial generators in place for that. The entire base does, except for this room. I had them keep the generator back up disconnected in it since it's the last original room in this entire historical building, which dates back over a hundred years. Look at these walls, they're from wood that they used to make old ships with. Cedar and Teak. It's why I call this the *Ship* room. Do you see how the planks curve slightly inward at the bottom and the top of the walls? This makes it feel as if you're on an old ship."

"Oh yes, I see that," said Chris, barely seeing anything in the low light. He wanted to ask him about the knots on the wall but waited. Waited and listened. But all he heard was the hideous rain and violent winds that didn't seem at all concerned with the room's antique walls or the two people sitting silently within them.

Moments later, the power suddenly went out. The captain then quietly struck a match, which Chris always liked the smell of, and proceeded to delicately light a white candle that appeared out of nowhere and which threw a long shadow over the broad desk.

"When it's like this out, I can't help but think of the SS *Edmund Fitzgerald,*" said the captain morosely, as the candle then flickered, as if doing so due to hearing the name of the ill-fated ship.

"I know it!" Chris said gleefully, excited to contribute to a conversation with a navy officer about a ship and a body of water. "That's the large ship that sank in the Great Lakes. Did it sink out there, in *that* lake?" he asked, with a finger toward the current pitch-black view of a Great Lake, which, in good weather, would have been easily visible due to its proximity.

"No. That's Lake Michigan there. The Edmund Fitzgerald, an enormous iron ore carrier, went down in Gitche Gumee."

"*Gitche Gumee?*"

"Yes," replied Captain Dobson. It's what the Indians named Lake Superior, which, when translated loosely, means Big Sea or Huge Water. It is the largest of the Great Lakes. Yeah, *The Fitz,* or the Titanic of the Great Lakes, as it was also called, was *enormous.* It was the biggest cargo vessel ever built at the time. But on that stormy night in November of '75, with wind gusts reaching 86 mph (75 knots) and swells 35 feet high, it didn't have a chance. It split in two just like the Titanic did. All 29 crew members perished, and no bodies were discovered. And that voyage was to be the ship's master, Captain McSorley's, final one before retiring. The Coast Guard did send a rescue vessel, *Woodrush,* from the Duluth port, but it took 21 hours for it to arrive on the scene. Captain Hobaugh, who commanded the ship, says a life ring from the *Fitzgerald* popped up to the surface just as they arrived. That life ring is now located in a museum off the coast of the wreckage. But the Fitz still sits today 530 feet deep at the bottom of the lake, which, with its treacherous waters, has sunk 6000 ships to date. It's like the Gordon Lightfoot song goes,

Superior, they said, never gives up her dead
When the gales of November come early...

Maybe it was the frightening storm outside or the old wooden ship walls, or the heart-rending story told by candlelight, either way, Chris was riveted by it all. The social worker was right, the captain liked his ship stories. And, he thought, he was good at telling them. But the captain, who now removed his Dress Blue jacket and loosened his tie, was through with his ship stories for the evening.

With the storm still raging outside, and the hour getting late, Captain Dobson recommended that they spend the night right there in the ship room. When Chris then asked him, "What would we sleep on?" the captain unhesitatingly replied, "On cots."

"Sure, whatever," said Chris, assuming it would be fine but then reconsidered when he thought how uncomfortable it may be.

As if sensing his concern, the captain replied, "Don't worry, they're more comfortable than you'd think if you're tired enough...." Then added, "Not much of a choice right now anyway, not until the tornado warnings cease."

"Is there a bathroom nearby?" Chris asked.

"You mean the *head?* That's what it's called on a ship. It's through that door in the back, then to the left."

"I heard that term before, but why do they call it that?"

"The forwardmost of a vessel was called the ship's head. It normally protruded beyond the bow (the front of the ship). That was where the grate, used for human waste, was located and which then went into the ocean."

Chris hummed, then nodded, satisfied with the explanation, which added to the feeling that he was on a ship. He wondered why he wasn't more concerned about the dangerous storm outside, fighting nastily to get in, but he wasn't. Unable to resist

210

any further, he finally inquired about the knots; encased in glass and framed in wood, hanging lonesomely on the wall as the now steady and brighter than before candle flame shone glowingly on them, providing them a sort of temporary company. The light on the knots also reminded the viewer that each was different. Each had its own purpose and distinctive origin.

"Oh, those...those are called nautical, or sailing knots, but also often referred to simply as sailor knots."

Here, I wouldn't expect them to be called anything but.

"They look interesting. Can you tell me about them?"

"Ok, but how about tonight I just tell you about one?"

"That's fine," Chris replied, forgetting briefly why he was sitting in the office across from a senior naval officer by candlelight in the first place. He was there, of course, to help him become a veteran and to become a civilian. To help him become somebody different. Essentially, he thought, to become somebody else.

That was like asking each sailor knot to be something different from what it has ever known to be. And each of these knots, just like the captain, had a long history in the purpose they had served.

Captain Dobson leaned over and pulled out the desk's left, large bottom drawer, taking out a shoebox-sized, clear plastic box full of knots and placing it on his lap. He looked briefly inside the box, spotted the one he wanted, picked it up and set it on the desk between him and Chris, and said, "Remember these knots are not to size, like the ones on the wall, they're small examples. I would be remiss if I didn't start with the King of Knots; one that's been used continuously by sailors for the last 500 years, the bowline (pronounced *boh-lin*). It's also one of the most useful knots to know. It forms a secure loop, like so. And it will not jam and is easy to tie and untie. It's a great all-around knot that's often used for water rescues. Some people remember this knot by forming the loop and saying the end of the rope is a rabbit. The rabbit goes out of its hole, around the tree, and down the hole again. It's said that in following the rabbit's route, you'll remember it every time."

"Anything to help remember is fine by me," said Chris, who picked up the ancient yet simple knot and looked at it closely.

"Give it a shot," the captain said, which Chris did though he was unsuccessful in his first few attempts, he finally did get it, once.

The captain then returned the box of knots to the bottom left drawer but curiously placed the bowline separately in the bottom right drawer. With their talk and evening coming to its inevitable end as the storm persisted outside, Chris watched the captain walk to the back of the dark room and open a closet door. He returned holding two folded cots, two wool blankets, and two pillows but no pillowcases. He placed one cot and one set of bedding on the desk. The rest, he handed to Chris, like a private in the army or a seaman in the navy. The captain then gave Chris a nod, looked behind him, and said, "You can set up your cot back there. I'll set up mine here. You know where the head is already. If you need anything else, just let me know. Good night."

It must have been twenty years since he had set up a cot, Chris thought. Nevertheless, he walked to his area in the back of the room, placed his gear down, and began to set it up. As he did, he recalled that the front and back bars of the cots were always difficult to put in their holed metal notches. The trick he learned was to first stretch the canvas of the cot by prying it with pressure from one of the bars. He did this now, and, like decades ago, it worked. He next took off his shoes and placed them just underneath the cot.

With the candle still burning brightly, the captain walked over to Chris and said, "Here's a little something in case you're hungry. Sorry, I forget about dinner." He then handed Chris a small bag of beef jerky and a canteen of water, for which Chris thanked him. Afterward, the captain returned to his desk, blew out the candle, and laid down on his cot. Chris heard squeaking from across the room as the captain moved around to find a comfortable position; it then became silent. The captain had fallen fast asleep.

It only took a few strips of the packed with-protein beef jerky to vanquish Chris's hunger, yet the hickory smoke and peppery beef flavor remained strong in his mouth, so he drank some water. As he did, he could smell the plastic of the canteen. He tried some more water. He liked the feeling of the canteen in his hands. The surprising comfort he felt drinking it with two hands made him feel like he held a present that few else had; this peculiar-looking container, so different from the more common and more attractive water bottles out there today, from spring and flavored waters to everything else in between. Yet at this moment, nothing looked as charming or tasted as satisfying as what he held and drank. He didn't think this. He *felt* this. How it also—from the time it roughly took to hear the thunder from after a lightning strike—brought him back to his mid-twenties. It was almost as if the canteen's water and its slight plastic smell had something in it that made him do so. But it didn't. It was something else. Something much more powerful: nostalgia. His mood soon changed as the nostalgia ran rampantly through his veins. His eyes suddenly filled with tears, which took him by surprise as he didn't know why they did. Then, like the lightning before the thunder, it struck him. His eyes swelled from the emotions he had suppressed for the last twenty years. Why they chose to manifest themselves tonight while he sat there on a cot, in the dark, with a tempest outside, was beyond his control or understanding. He decided not to fight it but, rather, to let the emotions play out their sweet, cruel, happy, and bitter parts. And they did so to a T: ranging from remembering his little girl pulling on his leg asking to be picked up, to his last suffering years of marriage when his wife had stopped loving him, to spending quality time with his father, to the present spotty relationship he had with his daughter, and, he confessed to himself, with most everybody else it seemed.

Chris laid his head on the striped, military pillow with his body encased rectangularly by hollow aluminum posts and suspended off the ground by taut, olive-drab canvas. The waxy smell of the candle was still present. He took a deep breath and felt the last of nostalgia leave his body and leave his mind. He thought the captain might have heard him, so he listened closely to hear if he was still sleeping. His low, steady breathing told him that he still was. Chris was now all alone with the blistery storm banging rudely outside in a seeming attempt to penetrate the ship room. But this didn't frighten him. He respected its noise, its fight. He almost admired it. If it could do it, he thought, then let it be.

He then thought of the crew of the Edmund Fitzgerald and what they were thinking of as the ship swayed and bobbed in those

213

immense swells and winds. Did the ship's captain know what their fate would be? Or was he taken by surprise? Did the bowline knot participate in a rescue attempt in this infamous story? Chris then felt guilty that he tried to make the horrific ordeal seem more interesting to him than what it really was; sea-hardened men, both brave and scared, tragically engulfed by a once-in-a-century storm.

A feeling of grief then came over him, but it was quickly followed by a feeling of appreciation. *I, we, all, should look at our present situation and understand that it could always be worse. That we could be entombed at the bottom of a Great Lake.*

That night, in this bare, vintage room, on a stiff cot with a monsoon outside and only a snack for dinner, Chris slept like a baby. He awoke thinking it a cliché; in an uncomfortable, scary setting, against all reason, he gets his best night's sleep in years.

Only in the movies....

Then he realized that all the distractions he had that evening—after his visit with nostalgia was over—aided in allowing him to forget his ails for a night, the unique room, the horrid weather, the gripping *Fitz* story, and the stern, military bedding. He glanced over to see if the captain was still sleeping, but he wasn't there. He then walked over and peered out between the thick wooden blinds to see if the storm had stopped.

It had not.

Though the weather wasn't as bad as the night before, steady rain and strong wind continued.

"Good morning," the captain said as he opened the door and entered the room with a white paper bag. "I got us some breakfast: hard-boiled eggs, bagels with cream cheese, and OJ," he said while emptying the contents onto the desk. "Sorry I couldn't do better, but the DFAC had a limited breakfast today on account of the storm last night."

"Thank you," said Chris, who sat down in the chair at the desk across from the captain. After making short work of their meals from strong appetites due to the night's lack of a proper one, the two men got to the main topic.

"Less than thirty days..., in less than thirty days from now, I change over command," said the captain.

"Change? Change to what?' Chris asked.

"Well, that's the $64,000 question, isn't it?"

"Yes, I assume it is. But isn't *all* life about change?"

"Sure. Of course, but that doesn't make it any easier."

"True," said Chris. "Very true."

"You know, it wouldn't be the worst thing if you couldn't help me. I mean, I'd be okay."

Chris pondered this, then said, "But you should want to be better than *okay*. Right?"

"Yes, I guess I should. It's just…the Navy runs in my blood. It's everything I am and ever was about, but soon it no longer will be."

Chris didn't have a response to this, so he just continued to listen to the captain, who went on, "You know, I've sent many a sailor and officer back out into the world. I provided them letters of recommendation, helped them secure employment, and now here is their commander, worried about it himself."

"It's normal. You're only human."

"That's the problem. A navy captain needs to be more."

"But soon, you will no longer be a navy captain."

"That's right. Soon I will only be human." The captain then pulled out a knot from the box located in the desk's bottom left drawer. "You know, if you think about it, these knots also tell us life lessons, like this one here," he said placing it on the desk. "This one is called the Impossible Knot, or Double Fisherman's Knot, technically. The irony is that it gets its name *not* for how difficult it is to tie, for which it's pretty easy, but for how nearly impossible it is to *untie,* especially once wet."

Chris then asked, "And that life lesson would be…?"

"Well, me tied to the navy, of course. And yes, it's a wet knot."

"Oh, yes, I see," said Chris. "Perhaps you can pull out a more optimistic knot next time," he added with a chuckle.

"Sure, but no more today," replied the captain. "I'm booked all day with appointments. Besides, one knot a day is enough. Plus, you need time to get settled in. Let's meet up again in a few days."

Over the next ten days, with the weather still rainy and windy, Chris and the captain met in the ship room seven times. During those meetings, the captain showed Chris a different knot each day, placing each afterward in the desk's bottom right-hand drawer. One of them was the *Cleat Hitch,* which was used to tie to the cleats on the deck of a sailboat, as well as to the cleats on a dock to secure a boat. Another one was the *Oysterman's Knot,* which is a stopper knot used at the end of a rope to prevent it from slipping through larger holes.

Besides discussing the knots, and a little about their lives, the captain would tell Chris the occasional ship story. One was about one of the U.S. Navy's first man-of-war ships, the USS *Constitution,* which is the oldest commissioned warship still afloat today, moored at the Boston harbor as a floating museum.

"Man-of-war?" Chris asked.

"Yes," replied the captain. "It's a term for a warship originally used by The Royal Navy. It means any warship from the 16th to 19th Century that ran by sails and was armed with cannons. Anyhow, after our country's revolution, the Continental Navy was disbanded in 1784 as it was thought to be too expensive and largely unnecessary. It wasn't until several years later, with the slew of Pirates in the Mediterranean demanding money and the frequent capture of our ships and enslavement of our crews that a navy, under the direction of President George Washington in the late 1790s, was formed. That was when the U.S. Navy's first ships, including the USS Constitution, were built and launched."

"That's amazing," said Chris.

"It truly is," said the captain. "And the Constitution's fighting against Barbary pirates and French privateers was impressive. But it was in her third conflict, the War of 1812, where she was extraordinary. Understand, we had no business declaring war on Great Britain—okay, they deserved it as they were constantly harassing our ships and taking or *impressing* our sailors, as it is officially known, into their Royal Navy. It was part of the reason we went to war with them. But, as I said, we had no business going to war with them since they had 500 man-of-war ships to our measly 20, yet instead of being annihilated, we fought hard and well. Especially the frigate ship Constitution, which outran a large British squadron and then defeated four Royal Navy ships in combat; it's also where she picked up her nickname of 'Old Ironsides' when in a battle and subsequent capture of the British ship, the HMS Guerriere; a sailor on that ship was said to have seen British cannonballs bouncing off her hull and exclaimed, 'Huzza! Her sides are made of Iron!' But, of course, they were not. They were made of oak: American oak, which is denser than English oak. Think about that. The framing inside that ship is still original. And that ship still floats today from trees cut down back in 1795 and 1796, over 220 years ago."

"Now, *that's* incredible. Thanks for telling me," Chris said.

"My pleasure," said the captain.

Chris then asked, "Um. I know it sounds like an odd request, but would it be all right if I spent one more night here in the ship room? Sorry, it's just such a quiet yet curious room and...."

"Say no more. I get it," said Captain Dobson. "And to be honest, I'm a little jealous. I wish I could crash here again too. But my wife wouldn't like it. You know, the peace and simplicity of this room are relaxing, and it lends one to introspection, which in today's age of ultra-busyness, is a rare and good thing in my book."

"In my book, too," Chris concurred with small nods.

The captain then said, "You've still got your cot set up there with your canteen, and I'll get you some more beef jerky to snack on in case you get hungry. Also, just so you know, the pesky storm that's been sticking around is reported to have one last hurrah before the weather is finally supposed to clear. The ship room may lose power again, almost surely. Do you *still* want to stay here?"

"I do," replied Chris thinking of the wolf in the snowy woods.

On the tenth and last night of the turbulent weather, Chris set up in the ship room for his requested solo sleepover. Why he wanted to sleep in the room again, he wasn't quite sure. Yes, it was peaceful, and yes, as the captain said, it helped with pondering one's inner thoughts, Yet Chris also felt that somewhere in that room held the answer, or at least a clue, to the captain's transition

217

from the service concerns. Nevertheless, he told himself, he wasn't going to sniff around the room looking for it. He planned to, perhaps, finish reading his Hemingway book and probably—*no, definitely*—ponder his inner thoughts, especially considering that his own transition from his current position was also fast approaching. But that was secondary. *He* was secondary. The veteran always came first, he reminded himself.

Inside the office, Chris turned on the small lamp atop the enormous desk and took the tall candlestick stick, along with a book of matches lying next to it, over to the far end of the long, dark, wood-paneled room and placed them on the ground next to his cot. He then got comfortable, or at least as best as one could on a stiff cot, and weighed the past week and a half without any distractions—none, that is, except the nasty thunderstorm pounding outside. Yet for whatever reason, the storm also seemed to make his attention more acute to his thoughts, which were of the amicable conversations he had with the captain of engrossing ship stories and various types of sailor knots. They also spoke briefly about his wife and children. Still, the conversations were just that, amicable; nothing specific to pinpoint how he could be helped. Chris tried telling himself that perhaps not every veteran, or soon-to-be one, can be helped. Or at least not clearly, that some of the answers to their issues weren't as identifiable as others. Perhaps *this* was his hardest case? Chris thought.

No. That distinction went to Til. No debate there.

After a lengthy period of trying to think of a viable solution to the captain's transition woes, Chris decided instead to contemplate his own life, thinking that maybe the prior's answer would somehow find him. This room, he recalled, had a special power. And so, find him soon it would.

As the heavy rain and winds outside grew louder, the small lamp across the room flickered on and off, threatening another power loss. Chris secured the book of matches from off the floor and put them next to him on the cot, just in case. He then laid down, interlocked his hands behind his head, and took stock of his life: of the important people, events, and decisions he'd soon face upon his return, like his daughter, who would soon be driving.

Then, in a few years, attend college. He wasn't ready for that, he admitted to himself. Yet what parent ever was? All he could do was be there for her. That meant working at a job that had *absolutely* no travel. At a complete minimum, not until she started college. Even then, he didn't want to think about traveling again for work. But one step at a time. He then thought of Jessie. His true love no more.

Maybe things wouldn't work out between Frank and her, and she would have a change of heart. And that deep down, she had always only loved me and was miserable without me.

Silly thoughts, he knew, as she had stopped loving him years ago, but he hadn't stopped loving her. Not yet. Next, he thought about his mother. How she should be in a nursing home at her age, or whatever they were calling them now. And how she wanted to stay independent and that going to one of those meant the end. Maybe she was right, probably was. But there comes a day for all of us when we just can't take care of ourselves. Lastly, he thought of his next job after this one was over. Would he like it? Would it be as exciting? As rewarding? As demanding?

Doubtful, he guessed, to all those questions. His father and his eternal optimistic view then crept into his head, changing his doubt. The lamp then flickered again after the night sky briefly lit up with streaks of lightning, followed by a ferocious boom of thunder that seemed to rock the ship room. Next, loud, heavy rain pelted the windows, which made Chris uneasy, but that quickly vanished when he sat up and began nibbling on some of the captain's flavorful beef jerky. He then took a satisfying swig of water from his canteen, after which another flash of lightning peeked through the room's thick blinds that, again, was followed by the unsettling sound of rumbling thunder. Only this time, it took out the room's electricity with the sudden darkness of the desk lamp from across the room. Chris clutched his matches tightly, ensuring their presence, then opened his palm and proceeded to strike a match and light the long, wax-dripped candle. He thought that now was a good time to read. No, he then rethought. It was a *perfect* time to read. By candlelight amidst a mighty squall.

He had left off with the old man securing the prize fish aside to his skiff. This required him to kill it, leaving behind much blood in the water that eventually brought hungry sharks to its scent. Over the next few hours, Santiago fights off several 'hateful' sharks, killing some valiantly in the process, yet, when one of the biggest *dentuso* (big-toothed shark in Spanish) he's ever seen rips off a forty-pound hunk of flesh from the marlin, he realizes his efforts are futile. He's so disappointed that he will no longer even look at the mutilated fish. Also, he thinks that when the fish was hit, it was as though he was hit. Next, the old man sailed on toward the shore for a couple of hours while trying to cheer himself up a little, but the sharks returned with a vengeance, with most getting their share of his once-in-a-lifetime catch. This went on past midnight until, with his energy gone and few weapons lost, he acknowledges defeat, thinking, 'What beat you?' then says out loud to himself, "Nothing, I went out too far."

Chris put the book down with mixed emotions. He was near the end, but not quite. He then thought, was Santiago's long, epic battle with the marlin all for not? Or was there some kind of poetic justice to it? He wasn't sure, and though he asked himself these questions, he wasn't in the mood to try and figure them out. He only knew that he felt for the old man after all his struggles, but he also knew that the sharks had as much right, maybe even more, to the fish as he did.

With his reading over for the night, Chris focused his attention back on the unsettling commotion of the storm outside. It seemed enraged like it wouldn't stop until it got what it wanted. *But what did it want? Probably what all violent things want—destruction.*

He turned to the candlelight for comfort, his shipmate and miniature beacon of support for the night, with the warm glow of its four colors: white, yellow, orange, and blue, burning steadily.

Moments later, an unexpected eerie silence filled the room, making Chris wonder if the storm had ended. Then, without warning, a bolt of lightning, loud and vicious, struck the ship room, followed shortly after by crackling thunder. The candlestick then fell over, putting out its flame. But Chris could still make out the damage. The strike had blown a hole in the inside of the wooden wall. Oddly, there didn't seem to be a hole from the outside as there was no exposure evident to the outside elements. The electric jolt had luckily only caused it to blow out on the inside. Chris was naturally shaken by the event, but was very fortunate he was not hit or injured.

But then something did hit him.

He was strangely hit with a crystal-clear moment of clarity at this frantic hour after the lightning strike on the ship room. Chris suddenly knew what had to be done. This now-damaged room had to be replaced and rebuilt, just like Captain Dobson's life had to be. And not rebuilt in the form of another ship room. No. It had to be built like all the other rooms and buildings on the base.

The captain had to build the new.

And something else came to Chris's mind, or someone, Linda. He now missed her and wanted desperately to see her again. He thought of her pleasantness, her funny wisecracking ways, her love for her family, and her kiss. But mostly, he thought of how she made him feel. Like how she had paid attention to him, even around her kids. She made him feel that he was special. Being with her made him feel as if he was somebody.

Outside, the storm's rage and rain died down to a whimper before, finally, after ten long days, ceasing altogether. Chris then heard the urgent sound of sirens and fire trucks scrambling about the base. He wasn't sure what to do. It was very late, and he didn't think it wise to go back to his room, not unless he was instructed to, yet the possibility of fire remained an obvious concern.

Chris then heard loud stomping steps rushing up the stairwell, then the slam of the office door being opened. In rushed four firemen, each yielding axes and with lights beaming brightly from their helmets. Chris, initially startled by their hasty entrance, was however grateful for their presence. One fireman asked him some questions about what he saw occur, while the others did a quick inspection of the room. Afterward, one shook his head at the antique walls while the others carefully examined the interior hole in the wall. "Strange. I have never seen it before where there wasn't an entry hole from the outside, only one on the inside. "Unbelievable!" he said while removing his helmet and scratching his head. The senior fireman agreed and said, "Me either, and I've been doing this for 30 years!"

After checking the walls for any signs of heat or fire with a thermal imaging device, of which they found none, a curious fireman asked Chris why he was sleeping in this old room anyway. Chris explained that he was there with the approval of the base commander, working late, and that he didn't want to go back to his room in the middle of the storm. The fireman just raised his eyebrows and said, "Okay...wow, I haven't slept on a cot in years. Anyhow, with all the downed trees and lines around the base, you're better off here until morning. And you're also safer here with no electricity on in this room. Stay safe." And as quickly as they had rushed up the stairs, the firemen were gone. Chris then laughed to himself lightly, though there was nothing funny about it; it was just that he couldn't believe what had transpired that evening. He thought that if he had read it in a book or seen it in a movie, he would have found it hard to believe, but then shrugged and told himself that that's just real life sometimes, surreal.

In the morning, Chris awakened by bright rays of sunlight coming through open blinds. He squinted, blinked, and rubbed his eyes and saw, standing at the window with his back to him, was Captain Dobson.

"Good morning, Captain," said Chris, who sat up and began getting dressed.

"Matthew. It's just Matthew."

Chris didn't respond, though he sensed the captain felt down.

Matthew then asked, "You, okay? Are you injured?"

"I'm fine, thanks."

"He's here," said the captain as he stared out at the Great Lake.

"Who's here?"

"The new base commander—my replacement." The captain replied, almost as if it were a question, with the words floating around the room seemingly waiting for someone to deny them as factual. After a long, uncomfortable silence, he then turned around and told Chris, "I got you breakfast. There in the bag on the desk. And a coffee too. Come on and eat. You had quite the evening last night, I'm told."

With the room full of light, Matthew headed over to look at the damaged wall. Once in front of it, he tilted his head, inspecting it briefly, then he slowly felt around the large hole with a curious, careful hand. He then walked over to the desk and sat down in his chair. Chris thought now was the time to tell him.

Now or never.

He sat down in the chair across from the captain, thanked him for breakfast, and proceeded to take out the bag's contents, then said, "I was thinking...after the lightning strike here last night that this would be a good time to take down this room; the walls and all, and build it back up, new."

Matthew looked back at him in bewilderment, then as offended. *"Really?"* The one thing, the *one* legacy I have to pass on to the new commander, and you want it destroyed? Am I hearing you correctly?"

"It's an office. A room. A very cool, old one. But a room nonetheless." Chris said, not wanting to offend Matthew, but the storm had passed, and the sun was out. It was time for him to move on with his life. It was time for both of them to move on with their lives.

"No. I will not," Matthew said stubbornly. "It'll be used by the next commander anyway. He'll appreciate it. Like it even, I bet."

"Sir," Chris began saying, with his mission skills being put to the test here and now, he thought. "You have had a long, impressive career. *Very* long and *very* impressive, but I feel as someone sent here to help you that it's vital that you use this room, or the moving on from it, as a stepping stone to move on with your own life. We all move on in our lives, some better than others. What are you afraid of, Captain Dobson? What is your real fear? Why am I really here?" The captain then stood up, walked over to the window, and stared out at the blue water of the Great Lake made refreshed by the long storm. "Why you ask? I'll tell you why," he said, turning around with concerned eyes that quickly turned upset. "I have nothing after this. Nothing. No base. No sailors. No command. No training. No navy. Nothing. I'll be back to what I was before I graduated from Annapolis. *Nothing.* Today, I have it all. But in a few weeks, I will lose it. And now *you*

223

want me to tear down the ship room?" he asked, then glumly sat back down in his chair.

Chris knew now was the time to Vocalize.

"Do you want me to remind you of everything you have? And have accomplished?" he asked, knowing full well that the captain knew these answers already and that asking them would surely annoy him.

He was right.

"So, I'm now allowed a bad moment here?" he replied.

"Of course. I'm sorry." Chris said.

"No. I'm sorry," said Matthew, who continued. "Do you honestly want me to have the ship room torn down?"

"Yes, I do," said Chris assuredly. "We will do it together. You and I will take apart the room. The walls, plank by plank, and build anew. You and me. And you could get electricity put in here too."

"And you know how to do all this?" asked Matthew.

"Not a clue," Chris replied, smiling, which put a subtle smile on the captain's face. "But we'll figure it out. The first step is to say yes!"

Matthew looked back at him, unsure. Then sure.

"Okay. Yes! Jesus, you're persistent. At a minimum, we'll be bringing it up to code…, but I won't have time. I'll be side by side with the new base commander for the next two weeks, showing him the ropes, the sailors, the instructors, the equipment."

"Can we possibly do it at the end of each day?" Chris asked.

"I guess I could work an hour or two after 1630."

"Sounds like a plan. I don't want to sound patronizing, but I'm proud of you, Matthew. Rebuilding this room to make it new from what it is now, considering what it meant to you, I think that's a big first step. And some say, the most important one.

Over the next week and a half, while Chris waited to meet with Matthew each day at the ship room after COB, he worked on his final reports. He also spent time at the base gym or walking on the outdoor track as the skies remained clear after the long storm. He was pleased because he no longer experienced any pain during his workouts or walks. Slowly but surely, he had improved physically over the past six months and had even lost weight. He felt better and healthier; nothing to boast about, he thought, but perhaps, it was. And it was, at this time, during the evening hours, that he spoke almost daily with Jessie. She called him to discuss issues concerning Sara, such as the purchase of her car. But they also discussed other topics outside of their daughter, like how she and Frank were thinking of calling it quits since they were arguing more lately; that and his unwillingness to commit long-term didn't help matters either, which she spoke scornfully on the topic of.

Is she trying to come back to me? But what about Linda? Relax stud. You don't even have one of them yet, never mind both.

On the first day of tearing down the ship room, the captain showed up, after work, in his service blue uniform. He did the same every day after. Chris, with a lighter schedule, would always arrive a little earlier. Before starting to pry the wooden planks from off the walls, Matthew took off his uniform jacket and placed it attentively on his desk chair without a word. Chris considered asking him why he didn't change into something more appropriate for the task but then realized that he probably wanted to wear his uniform until his very last day, the same day as the change of command ceremony. So, it was, for this reason. Chris didn't bring the issue up to him.

When they were done rolling up their sleeves and putting on their protective eyewear, they commenced with the business at hand. It was not smooth sailing from the get-go. There were minor issues to overcome: the room wasn't bright enough, even with the afternoon sun still out and the blinds fully opened. They would have to be removed. And the planks were difficult to take off. More tools were needed: hammers, pliers, etc... But just a day or two later, after all the appropriate adjustments were made, the planks then came off at a rate that would allow them to meet their goal date. This seemed to lift Matthew's spirits, who Chris thought was mostly pensive during his first few days of work. It was then that Chris felt that the captain had truly begun to accept his fate. He had even started telling a few more ship stories that Chris couldn't get enough of. He told him of one Christopher Columbus in 1504 when his two ships got stranded on an island in what would later be Jamaica. "This happened due to an epidemic of shipworms which ate holes in their planking," the captain narrated. "The native islanders helped feed and stock the crew with supplies. But over time, tensions between the crew and natives mounted. This resulted in bad behavior and even atrocities against the islanders at the hands of Columbus's stranded crew. Unable to get back the support of the natives, which Columbus and his crew so desperately needed so as not to perish from starvation, Columbus used his knowledge of the almanac to determine that a lunar eclipse was soon approaching. He warned the islanders that if he and his crew weren't again fed and supported, the Gods would be angry with them and turn the moon red forever. The islanders didn't believe him, yet when the lunar eclipse did occur just days later, the terrified natives, so as not to anger the Gods, quickly agreed to help the crew again. This allowed Columbus and his men to be supplied and well fed until a relief caravel from Hispaniola was able to rescue them from the island."

"That was very clever of Columbus," Chris said.

"When you're the captain of a ship, you always gotta be...." quipped Matthew.

"Touché!" said Chris.

They used their time working on the ship room productively, and by the start of the second week, the two were already installing the electricity (with the help of navy electricians). Next, they put up drywall, and lastly, the painting. They choose the light color of bone white. When completed, both men were satisfied with the result, especially the captain, who said excitedly, "Wow. It looks so modern and fresh! Maybe the new base commander will make *this* his primary office. I would! You know, I feel strangely relieved that I (*we*) did this: not only for me but for the new captain as well. I mean, look at it! It's a brand-new room!"

Yet even with the fine outcome of their project, it was Chris who was surprisingly melancholy afterward. He felt that each of his other veterans had a breakthrough moment that showed progress, however small. With Til, it was when he observed the Northern Lights, though Chris thought he had even more. With

226

Alex, it was at the historic park where he affirmed that he wanted to work at a state or federal military park to teach about its history. With Tashana, it was the conversation, the *good* conversation, that she finally had with her father—the stone and broken window notwithstanding. With Vincent, it was at the gym during his speech to his wrestlers. With Barney, it was on the lake that he discovered his joy of photography. But Matthew? When was his breakthrough moment? Chris asked himself. Was it the completion of the new room?

Okay, yes, that was progress. A lot of progress, but I wanted to see something more for him, something concrete that showed that he had truly turned the corner with his transition woes.

Chris resigned to the idea that there would be no breakthrough moment for Matthew as the change of command ceremony had now arrived, and his upcoming departure for home was just days after. Nevertheless, he was curious to hear what the captain would say in his outgoing words.

As expected, the ceremony was full of grandeur and rich with symbolism. It included everything from an inspection and review of the sailors to gun salutes to the military band thumping patriotic beats. When it finally came time for the outgoing commander to speak, Captain Dobson, looking dapper in his Officer Service Dress White uniform, took his place behind the podium, yet before speaking, as if a calculated surprise, a rear admiral presented him with The Legion of Merit for his exceptional service, he then read through the captain's tours and career accomplishments. The assembled audience clapped politely as the captain then gave the traditional thank-you to all the people and parties who had supported him throughout his career. His words, though admirable, were customary, nothing that anyone in the military hadn't heard before. It was when he brought up the knots that everyone listened more closely.

"When I was very young, my grandfather, who was also a bluejacket, or sailor—for all you non-navy folks out there—taught me about the many nautical rope knots that he used out at sea and on the shore. He would intertwine my education of them with old ship stories. Both of which I found fascinating. Over the years, I kept the knowledge of those knots as a badge of honor, almost as if the knots were mine, as crazy as that may sound." The captain then paused, took a small step back, and looked down, slouching a bit while keeping his hands on the podium. The continued silence became uncomfortable. It seemed to Chris that he was on the verge of a breakdown.

Breakdown? Breakthrough.

Captain Dobson, at last, recomposed himself. And after a small cough looked out confidently into the crowd in a dignified manner as if he had something important to say. And he did.

"Over the past several weeks, as I've prepared for my transfer of command and retirement from the Navy, I had the opportunity to revisit my knowledge of these knots, as well as tell some old ship stories to a new friend. Then it dawned on me. But it wasn't until *after* I went over every knot that it did. These knots *didn't* belong to me. And they never did. Nor do they belong to the sailors, the equipment, or the cargo they so strongly hold, pull, and secure. But they do belong to something...," the captain said, with the crowd now in the palm of his hand wanting more; wanting to hear to what or to whom these knots belonged. He continued with his skilled oration. "These knots were born and originated out there!" he cried while turning back slightly and pointing to the Great Lakes. "They belong to the high seas and the waters to which you, I, and this great navy serve. Besides their purpose, they are a symbol, a reminder of that. Of the vast oceans and why we are all here. Like the Military Oath that each of the recruits took before arriving here, which states in part, to support and defend the Constitution of the United States against all enemies, foreign and domestic. And if you remember nothing else from me today, remember that. You are here to fight out there, for the citizenry of these United States of America. You are our defenders. You are our hope. And *you* are our future! Thank you." Chants of USA! USA! yelled out as the crowd erupted in applause. The incoming commander then stood up and headed to the podium to say his remarks. As he did, Captain Dobson reached down into the podium and pulled out a shadow box that displayed knots, and said into the microphone, "And this, Captain Flores, is for you, they're nautical knots as a reminder of today. Of your start as commander of this base. And of its waters, and most importantly, of its sailors. Congratulations." He then handed the framed knots over to Captain Flores who held them up for the crowd to see, then said, "Thank you, Captain Dobson, I'll treasure this. And good luck and Godspeed to you."

Shortly after the conclusion of Captain Flore's remarks, with the majority of the crowd already dispersed, Matthew stood alone on the side of the parade field, looking at it as if in remembrance. Spotting him, Chris headed over to him to say goodbye. He was pleased to have seen the captain's breakthrough moment during his fiery speech; his perfect record still intact, he thought with a self-smirk. But he would be proven wrong as the captain's breakthrough moment would actually occur moments later.

As he approached Matthew, he noticed that he was holding a book. "I enjoyed your speech. Very inspirational," said Chris.

"Thank you," replied the captain graciously. "Here, I got you a book. I remember you saying you were close to finishing yours."

"I am," Chris said, accepting it. "You didn't have to do that, but I appreciate it." He then looked at the title, *Master and Commander,* then looked at the author's name, Patrick O'Brian. Next, he turned it over to read the back cover blurb. Set at the turn of the 19th Century during the early era of the Napoleonic Wars. It follows a young Royal Navy captain who has just been promoted to the rank of Master and Commander and then oversees combat action with his men and Man-of-War ship in the Mediterranean.

"Sounds interesting. This book will always remind me of you."

"My intent exactly," said Matthew happily. "Hey, there's a reception over at the officer's club. Are you going? You're invited."

"No, if that's okay. Not really my thing."

"That's fine. I don't blame you. I don't want to go myself."

"Captain Dobson, I wanted to come over to say goodbye. I've enjoyed our time together: your stories and working with you on the new room. Everything. And I wish you well in your post-military life. I'm sorry I wasn't more of assistance with your transition concerns. Will you be all right?"

"Well, I'd be lying if I said I still didn't have my worries," the captain said. "But you did more for me than you know. You listened to me. You listened to me talk about the knots; you listened to me talk about the ship room, and you listened to me tell old ship stories. You may think that wasn't much, but it was. Your listening allowed me to figure out what those knots really meant. It also allowed you to come up with the constructive idea to tear down the ship room and build it new. The action of which greatly helped me. It gave me confidence. The confidence to know I can change going forward, however small the step. You were here for me, and for that, I sincerely thank you." Matthew then snapped to attention and rendered a sharp salute. Chris, unsure of what to say after hearing the kind words, silently saluted him back. The captain's true breakthrough moment was confirmed, he thought.

Matthew then said, "I know you're leaving soon, but I will be in the area for a few days. You should let me take you sailing. It's the least I can do, and you can see firsthand some of the things that you've learned about nautical knots and sailboats."

The comment gave both a laugh.

"Yeah, sure. I'm in," Chris said.

That evening in his base room, Chris couldn't have felt better. He had just finished his last case of individual case reports for his boss., Only the mission summary report of 'what he's learned' remained undone, which he planned on completing after going sailing with Matthew. Chris couldn't believe his good fortune. All had worked out well in the end. If this were a movie, he thought, he couldn't have written a better ending for its screenplay. He had helped all his veterans. Granted, he had not *completely* healed them, but he helped them. And besides the favorable professional aspect, there were also the physical and financial ones which also ended up favorable. And if those weren't enough, Jessie and Sara were warming up to him as well.

Absence does make the heart grow fonder. And warm is warm; compared to what I've had with both in the past, I'll take it.

He pulled out his book in hopes of finishing it, not a tough task seeing that he only had a few pages remaining. He began his reading with Santiago finally sailing into the harbor very late that evening while the town slept. Once docked, the old man went on to un-step the mast and furl the sail, and when off his skiff, saw the giant skeletal tail of the marlin by the reflection of a streetlight. The large skeleton was proof of both his triumph and defeat.

Adding further to his pain and suffering, the elderly fisherman must carry the heavy mast home on his shoulder, which had him stop and rest several times. He eventually reaches his shack, where he places the mast against the wall and then lays down in his bed atop newspapers, falling asleep with his face down, arms out, and palms up.

The next morning, the little boy came by to see him, but he was still sleeping. The little boy then noticed his cut-up hands which made him cry after he left to get the old man some coffee. The little boy is impressed by Santiago's skeletal catch, but that's not his concern. His concern is the condition of his old friend, who, at last, awakes. They then talk briefly, catching up from the past few days and answering each other's questions. The boy is told, by his old friend, that he suffered plenty, which then causes him to cry again when he leaves to get him some food, the papers, and medication for his hands.

Chris was just about to finish reading the book, but like the old man did after the boy left to fetch him supplies, he fell asleep and dreamt. He dreamed again of the zoo, which would turn out to be his last zoo dream. But this one was enjoyable, with everyone close to him present and all in high spirits, even if, inexplicably, nobody recognized him. He tried interacting with his mother, who sat contently on a bench people-watching but got no response. It was the same with Pat, who was laughing at an elephant relieving itself. Again, no response. He then stopped introducing himself, accepting the situation; this, however, didn't detract from the cheerfulness of the dream. He next saw his veterans walking individually amongst the crowd. He also saw Aunt Sophie, Jessie, Sara, and even Linda, as well as his boss, Michael. It was nothing short of the perfect day and the perfect ending to Chris's journey. Yet come morning, reality would turn out far differently.

The phone in Chris's room rang on and on while he slept in. He would have normally set an alarm, but since he was finished with all his cases, he thought he'd reward himself with some extra rest. When he finally awoke, he wondered why his base landline phone was even ringing in the first place. He figured it was probably just Matthew calling about their sailing plans.

Who else could it be? But he was proven wrong when he heard his boss's voice. Still half asleep, he didn't fully believe it. *"Michael? Is that you?"*

"Yes, it's me," he replied.

"Did you not receive all my case reports?" Chris asked him, now sitting up and wondering why he had called. He already had his plane ticket home. *What else could it be?*

"Yes, I've received them, but that's not why I called," Michael said, with a dejection in his voice that told Chris that it was concerning a doleful matter. He waited for his boss to elaborate, but all he heard was silence, so he pressed him, "What is it? What's wrong?"

"It's...it's Tim."

"Tim? You mean Til?"

"Yes. Mr. Tilly, your first veteran."

"What of him?"

"He's...in the hospital."

"What happened? Is he all right?"

"All I know is he's in a hospital in Anchorage from a suicide attempt."

With what felt like a huge weight fall on his heart and shoulders, all Chris could muster was a faint whisper, *"Oh my God."*

"I'm sorry," said Michael. "I truly am. I read your report on him and spoke with his social worker. You did a great job with him. Remember, he was suicidal before you met him."

"I...I have to go see him."

"Don't be so hard on yourself. You did everything you could for him. Do you really think going up there now would help any?"

"No, probably not. But I told him I would be there for him."

"It's not going to be cheap," Michael warned. "I highly doubt Uncle Sam will pay for this one."

"I've saved a fair amount while on the road, staying on base at times and all—I'll pay for it."

"I guess I can try and run it through. Hold onto your receipts."

Upon hanging up the phone after the call, Chris immediately picked it up again to book his plane ticket to Alaska, with a return ticket home to Oklahoma City. When finished, he then sat down and thought about the mission and its veterans.

I had done so well up until the very end. Was I just living a dream thinking about me, my success, and my perfect record?

Did I lose sight of the reality of the situation?

He wanted to do right by all his veterans, especially Til.

But how?

The idea then came to him. And it was a grand one. He would ask each of his veterans if they would fly to Alaska to meet him and see Til. On Chris's dime of course). It was a long shot, he knew. And some may not go, but that was his plan. He wasn't sure if he should tell Michael of his plan. But he also knew he probably couldn't afford to pay for all the veterans to fly to Alaska, so he called him back.

"*What?*" said Michael, shocked. "Are you serious?"

"I am. I think this is needed. For all of us, as a team."

"Let me guess. You want me to run those tickets through too."

"If you can. I would appreciate it."

"I'll try. No promises, though."

"Thanks, Michael, it means a lot to me."

After the phone call with his boss, Chris called each of his veterans and asked if they would like to go to Alaska to visit with a hospitalized veteran. Alex said a resounding "Yes!" Tashana gave an affirmative, "I'll do it!" Vincent replied enthusiastically, "Count me in!" Kyle answered, "I wouldn't miss it for the world!" And lastly, Matthew declared, "Aye-aye-sir, I'm with you."

With everybody on board, Chris was eager to see Til, along with the rest of his veterans and his mission, through to the end.

XI
ALL HANDS IN ALASKA

"Individuals play the game, but teams beat the odds."
–SEAL Team saying

Following everyone's arrival into Anchorage, which was no small logistical feat that required four full days, Chris and his gang of veterans set foot in the hospital just after six in the evening. They all took a seat in the mostly empty hospital waiting room. No one spoke as all were on edge, waiting to hear about Til's condition. While they waited, Chris thought that the veterans were, perhaps, reflective of their conditions as they mulled over Til's grave circumstance: that his possible death could have easily been their own. And even if every veteran there was not thinking this, he then thought, they all knew that Til was a fellow veteran in need, which was enough for them to be there, for they were all soldiers once, and thus, knew the code of never leaving one of their own behind be it on the battlefield or not.

Chris went up to speak to the nurse at the front desk to see if there was any update on Til's status. Upon returning, he then informed the group of her response. "She said the doctor will be out shortly." Sitting back down, he placed his chin in his hand and took a deep breath. A few of the veterans looked up at him with hope, while the others remained somber, staring down at the mundane tile floor. Tashana then asked everyone if she could lead them in a prayer for Til and that whoever didn't feel comfortable doing so didn't have to. Everyone agreed to pray. They all held hands while remaining seated as Tashana said, "Let him know that he is not alone with what he's going through, that there are people who care about his well-being, including God."

Soon after the prayer, Gary walked in with Reno obediently on a leash at his side. Seeing Chris, he walked over and sat down next to him. After shaking hands, Chris said, "I knew you'd come." Then petting Reno, asked, "Are dogs allowed in the hospital?"

"Service dog," replied Gary. "So, I assume so...have you heard anything on Til yet?"

"Nothing yet," Chris said, shaking his head despondently. Moments later, Til's doctor, a tall Indian man in his late forties, walked out to the waiting room. He flipped a page back from his clipboard, studied it quickly, and then asked, "Who here is the family member of Tim Tilly?"

Nobody responded. Unsatisfied, the doctor turned away and started to walk off when Gary suddenly stood up and said, "*I* am his family." Chris followed suit by standing up and saying, "*I* am his family." Next was Barney, "*I* am his family." he said firmly. Then Alex stood and proclaimed, "*I* am his family." Next came Matthew, who stated, "*I* am his family." Then Tashana announced, "*I* am his family." And lastly stood Vincent, who said, "Yeah, yeah, *I'm* his family too."

The doctor paused, looked at them all as if in appreciation for their concern for his patient, then said, "But if you are not his next of kin, then I'm sorry but *none* of you are his family."

All who stood knew that the doctor was right and that he was only adhering to hospital protocol. Still, his words took the wind out of their sail. Gary was about to object when somebody from the back of the lobby walked up and said firmly, "I *am* his family."

"And may I ask your relation to Mr. Tilly?" asked the doctor.

"I'm his son," said the man who strongly resembled his father, albeit younger. The doctor then pulled up his clipboard and read out loud, "You're John Tilly?" he asked, looking back up at him.

"That's me. And call me Jack," he said, evidently perturbed, then asked, "Can I see my father now?"

"Yes, of course," replied the doctor. "Come with me,"

Gary and the standing veterans then all sat down, one by one. Only Chris remained standing, shocked by what he'd just seen. He wondered if Gary had anything to do with the presence of Til's son. When he turned to ask him if that was the case, Gary responded before the question with, "I have *no* idea," adding with raised eyebrows, "I'm just as surprised as you. And I knew you'd come too. I told Laura so. Anyhow, she and I were thinking that…, we'd like you to take Reno here for good."

"Me?" Chris asked incredulously. "What about Til? That's *his* dog. He loves him."

"Yeah, but he also told me that Reno was too playful for him," said Gary. "Don't worry, I'll give him another dog, one that's more suited to him, like Ares perhaps."

Chris said, "I guess I could take him. My daughter would love that, though I have no idea how to travel with him or anything."

"I'll take care of all that for you," replied Gary.

Approximately twenty minutes later, Til's son came back out to the waiting room. He told everyone who came to see him that his father had overdosed on painkillers but that he was now stable. He also said that his father was also going to swallow his dog tags, which would have choked and killed him; how it had something to do with his battle at Hamburger Hill

"Wow," Chris whispered to Gary, "I didn't know he fought at Hamburger Hill. So dumb of me not to put it together: '69, The A Shau Valley, all those deaths, not to mention the huge political fall from it after we inexplicably abandoned the hill after winning the battle. Til's son then turned to Chris, "My father would like to see you, he's in the third room on the right."

Chris nodded and headed that way, after which Gary asked Jack if he could speak to him outside. He said that it was about Til.

Outside the hospital, with overcast skies and cool summer temperatures in the low 60s, Gary asked Jack if it would be okay if Til stayed with Laura and him until he fully recovered. Jack thought about this and then agreed that that would probably be the best for him. He thanked Gary for his care and generosity.

Sitting next to Til inside his hospital room, Chris noticed that he appeared thinner in the face, almost gaunt. He also saw that he had an IV bag connected to him and some sensors stuck to his chest. Til's defeated eyes then met Chris's concerned ones. It made him think of what Santiago had said to himself in the book. "Man is not made for defeat. A man can be destroyed, but not defeated."

Was this Til, not defeated, but destroying himself?

"Hey Til, how are you feeling'?" Chris asked to cheer him up, or at least change the mood from the grim one.

"You didn't have to come all the way here for me," Til grumbled lowly, then said, "I messed up podna."

"You're going to be fine," Chris said, with his eyes beginning to water. "You had a rough patch, that's all. You're going to be Ok—you gotta be."

"You don't get it. I'm no good. And I never was...."

"Don't say that!" Chris staunchly replied, "Don't *ever* say that Til. You're good. You're good forever."

A hushed stillness then filled the room. Chris then thought of his mission. Where he was before it. Before he met Til and the other veterans. And where he was now, after it. After he had met them. Spent time with them. The importance of which was now magnified by the present situation. Chris, overcome by emotion, got up from his seat, reached over, and carefully gave Til a short yet compassionate hug. As he did, a single tear from each eye came trickling out. Til, surprised but receptive, then patted Chris lightly on his back and said, "Thanks, kid."

Sitting back down quickly, wiping his eyes dry, Chris said, "Speaking of kid. That's so great yours is here now."

"Yeah," Til replied. "He made me promise him, no more stupid stunts like this again, or else he won't introduce me to my grandkids, and I wanna see them. I wanna see them bad."

The topic of the veterans in the hospital lobby then came up. Chris told Til that they had all flown in from around the country just to see him, for they thought he, like them, was part of the same special family of veterans, some of whom were disabled vets just like him. And they wanted to ensure that he was all right.

"Well, bring 'em in, and let me meet 'em," he said.

"You sure?" Chris asked, thinking that he may not be up to it.

"*I'm* sure," Til replied assertively.

In the waiting room, Chris let the waiting veterans know what Til had said about meeting them.

"Are you sure that's a good idea?" asked Matthew.

"Well, *he's* sure," said Chris.

Soon after, Chris and the five veterans entered Til's hospital room. Gary and Jack remained outside discussing the details of Til's care upon his release.

"Hey," said Til with a slight hand wave to the veterans who now stood in front of him. Matthew spoke first. Then Barney. Then Alex. Then Vincent. And lastly, Tashana. All just said a few brief words, but all were heartfelt. All of them. Especially the ones from Barney, who was perhaps most connected to him since he had also lost a physical part of himself. He said, "I came from West Virginia to see you in person. Chris told me that you were a hell of a guy who has been through a lot. That through your sacrifices for our country, you had lost a lot. But we don't want to lose you. And when I saw we, I mean not only us here, but our country and the entire veteran family too, and of course your own family, who I'm told is here today. So please, on behalf of all these, get well, sir, and stay well."

Til, eyeing him closely, gave a sincere nod back.

After saying their goodbyes to Til for the evening, Chris and all the veterans went to their hotel rooms, as Gary and Jack then returned from outside to be with him, before doing the same.

Over the next two days, they all again visited with Til in the hospital before his discharge. Gary also took the whole group on a scenic trail walk as well as the zoo and city museum. By day three, everyone had left for home. And after six long months away, Chris was finally going home too.

XII
OK IN OKLAHOMA

"It's a funny thing, coming home. Nothing changes. Everything looks the same, feels the same, and even smells the same. You realized what's changed is you." –F. Scott Fitzgerald

Chris's long flight home included a two-hour layover in Salt Lake City; this, however, didn't bother him, as he was pleased by his boss's news that all his veteran's costs to and in Alaska were going to be covered by the DoD—and thank goodness, he thought. But somehow, he knew that it would be. Maybe it was because he knew that Mr. Montrose supported him and understood the significance of the group trip, considering the severity of what happened to Til. Either way, the news came as a relief to Chris as those finances were already earmarked for his daughter. Nevertheless, he concluded that he would have paid for it if necessary as he felt the collective trip invaluable.

During the layover, Chris remembered that he had yet to complete his mission summary report. And he knew that his boss would be asking for it before he would be allowed any time off before he started the second part of his one-year term position: a six-month home stint at Tinker Airbase. So, he and Reno walked around the terminal, looking for an empty gate where he could work, and one that was free of people. He eventually found one that was only occupied by an airline employee who was eating her lunch and an older couple who just sat there quietly, not speaking a single word to each other. Forty years of marriage would do that, Chris amusingly thought to himself. Content with the location, he pulled out his laptop and was about to begin typing when he decided to handwrite the report instead. Why he opted to do this, he wasn't sure as this wasn't his regular way. But, like the different way he took the coffee that Linda made him, it just seemed more appropriate or better. Perhaps it was because the topic was a personal one, he thought. He wrote two full pages. When through, he felt good about the report; that it reflected what he truly thought had transpired during the mission, as well as what he had learned. And it was important to him that he did it articulately.

It was a hot and humid 93 degrees out when Chris landed in Oklahoma City in the early evening. He had wanted to surprise Sara at home that night of his arrival but was told by Jessie that she was playing at a volleyball tournament in Tulsa with her high school team. Jessie further explained that depending on how far they advanced in the tournament, she would be back roughly around 7 or 8 p.m.——tack on the 90-minute drive home with the school bus, and Sara should be home at about nineish.

"That works out perfectly for us," Jessie said to Chris over her cell phone while on the way to pick him up at the Will Rogers World Airport.

"You don't have to pick me," he told her. "I can take a taxi home and see you guys tomorrow. It's no big deal."

"Did you not hear me? This works out *perfectly* for us!"

"How so?" Chris asked, confused.

"The OU home football game against South Dakota is just about to start. They're playing at 6 p.m.——that's in half an hour."

"——And you want *me* to go with you to the game?"

"Ha-ha, no silly," Jessie chuckled. "I thought you could come over and we could watch the game together; like how we used to."

Like how we used to? Why would she want us to do that?

"Okay, sure," Chris said, not wanting to spoil her plan or dampen her OU game day spirit, which he probably couldn't do anyway even if he tried, he thought.

"Great!" she exclaimed. "We can come straight back to my place from the airport and order takeout."

You mean *our* place Chris wanted to correct her and say but didn't. He knew it was no longer his place since the divorce, and even years before it too.

When Chris stepped out with his luggage into the sweltering Oklahoma air, he sensed something was amiss. What it was he wasn't quite sure. Sure, the air, heat, and airport were all the same, but something else wasn't. He quickly brushed those feelings aside remembering that he was, after all, a veteran of the road with many miles under his belt from his years of traveling for work. He recalled how back then he would also feel a little different upon returning home even after just a short business trip, so he wasn't completely surprised by how he felt. Par for the course, he thought. Nevertheless, he couldn't help but feel that this was something different; that maybe his hometown, after all these years, had somehow, finally, lost its invigorating ability. And this affected him some. Almost saddened him.

Get it together, Chris. Jessie is pulling up any second.

When Jessie pulled up, she got out of her small pickup and went straight to the back, and dropped the back gate in preparation for Chris's bags. She then walked back to the front and gave him an unexpected embrace and a kiss on the cheek. "Oh My Gosh!" she cried in a strong Oklahoma twang that Chris always had a sentimental weakness for. "You look *amazing!*"

Unsure of how to respond, Chris replied, "You look good too."

And he meant it, from her tight blue jeans, which accentuated her shapely legs and backside, to her brown leather cowboy boots and low-cut crimson red T-shirt, which read OU football est. 1895, he thought she looked better than ever.

"And *who* might this beautiful creature be?" she then asked.

"That's Reno...it's kind of a long story."

"Well, all right. Let's get you and *Reno* out of here.

In the truck, she asked him, "So, how does it feel to be back

241

home? Did you miss us?"

Miss you? I've been missing you for years....

"Um. Yeah. Of course," he stammered. "And it feels great to be home. It's just a little strange too. I've been gone so long."

Jessie didn't respond to Chris's comments which didn't surprise him. She was never one to elaborate on them, he thought.

"This will be great tonight: the game, us catching up," she said as she touched his arm.

Chris didn't reply. He was speechless. He had been waiting for a night like this again for close to a decade. Them. Alone. Happy.

On the 30-minute drive from the OKC airport to Norman, Chris still felt off as they passed familiar buildings, roads, and landmarks he could have remembered blindfolded. This landscape was far from majestical Denali and the awe-inspiring mountains of the Alaska Range. Or the deep blue sea of the Pacific in the coastal, scenic, picture-perfect city of San Diego. Or the Creole-influenced structures of New Orleans's French Quarter with its Spanish and French Colonial architecture. Nor was it Philadelphia, with its Federal-style brick buildings. And row houses that originated in the Colonies just after the American Revolution, and its gritty yet colorful neighborhoods full of many different ethnicities and foods. Neither was it West Virginia, with its seemingly own dialect and view of the world from within its glorious mountains, rivers, and magisterial bridges to its warm, hospitable people. And it wasn't The Great Lakes with its prodigious waters that not only serve as an essential water source for millions but also as recreation and key maritime commerce. No, this landscape was certainly not any of those, but it was home, Chris thought. But after everything he had seen, experienced, and learned on his mission, was it really his anymore? he asked himself.

But that didn't matter right now, he then rethought. Right now, he was headed to his old home with the love of his life to watch an OU football game. Something that he had wanted to do with her again for a long time. But now that it was *actually* going to happen, he had mixed emotions about it.

Stop it, Chris. You're just tired and not thinking clearly. You still love her and have never stopped. Relax. Relax. Relax.

At their old home, Chris took his old position on the sofa with the TV already on the game as Reno lay down lazily beside him on the floor. Jessie left to go put on some comfortable shorts and grab some drinks and snacks. She would have her customary vodka cranberry while he would nurse a beer.

"All right, now *this* is more like it," she said, returning with the goods and her jeans changed. She sat down close to Chris, offering him some chips. He turned them down and then couldn't help but notice her smooth, sexy legs, which she then flexibly folded under her.

Yes, this was how it used to be..., and how nice it was.

Then, from the kitchen, in strolled an orange tabby cat. It seemed oblivious to the Alaskan Huskey lying on the floor as it plopped down in front of the TV and began licking its front paws. Reno briefly surveyed the cat, then returned his head to the floor.

"You got a cat?" Chris asked, stunned. "I never thought you would replace Moses."

"It was time," Jessie said nonchalantly. "It's been years."

"I guess it has," Chris muttered. "What's its name?"

"Joshua," she replied. "You know, in keeping with the theme of taking over after Moses when he led the Israelites in the Bible.

"Wow, you sure put some thought into that name."

"Moses was my baby. You know that."

"Yeah," he said. "He sure was."

It was midway through the first quarter when Oklahoma quarterback Jalen Hurts threw a touchdown pass for the game's first score. Jessie was as giddy as ever for her alma mater. "Touchdown!" she yelled with both her arms raised high as she inched closer to Chris, who could now smell her seducing perfume; her bare legs then unfolded for him to see in plain sight. He considered putting a hand on them, yet he couldn't figure out her signals. Did she *want* him to? It sure seemed like it. She sure looked good, he again thought. With less than a minute left in the first quarter, OU scored again on another touchdown pass. Jessie celebrated by getting herself another vodka cranberry then reassumed her cozy position next to Chris. She then leaned over him to reach for her cell phone, and as she did, Chris felt her firm body brush up against his thighs. "Why don't we order Chinese take-out?" she asked him.

"Yeah, that's fine," he replied, not thinking at all about food.

"You still like Lo Mein noodles with shrimp and beef?"

"Yes," he said, to which she nodded and placed their order.

"Be here in 30-45 minutes. Just in time for the third quarter," she said as she again reached over him to place her cell phone on the end table. Only this time, she stopped after she placed it down. Her body was now right over his, with their faces close. He saw her glossy lips next to his and thought, at that moment, that she wanted him to kiss her. He wasn't sure what to do in that split second. It was now or never....

But it was not to be, for as much he thought about how he missed her and how attractive she was, he discovered—in that split second—that he no longer wanted to be with her. He learned at that moment that he wanted to be with Linda. Jessie then turned her head away and sat back down next to him as if nothing had almost occurred. Chris was still confused by her signals, but no longer of what he wanted, of *who* he wanted.

"So, the reason I asked you here tonight," she then said to him, "besides just catching up, was to tell you that Frank asked me to marry him...and I said, well, *it's about time!* And that I would."

What? Really? After all this? I thought you wanted me?

With conflicting thoughts suddenly thrashing through him from disbelief, anger, and sadness to finally relief, he said, "That's, that's great, Jessica. Congratulations."

"Thanks," she said blasély. Adding, "Yep. He finally did it."

"Have you told Sara yet?"

"No, not yet. I wanted to tell you first. I'll tell her soon. I don't think it'll be a big shock to her though."

"No. I guess it won't," Chris said, pondering the implications.

As they ate their Chinese food, and Oklahoma continued its drubbing of South Dakota with the score now 49-0 in the middle of the third quarter, all Chris could do now was think of his daughter, who was due home shortly. Jessie was still excited after each score. Chris could only shake his head.

Some things never change.

Joshua then began jumping around on the sofa, which was more interesting than the game or Jessica's conversation, Chris thought. The feline got Reno back to his active self, and he started pawing harmlessly at him. Chris then asked Jessie a question he had wanted to ask her for a long time. With the game's result assured and his old flame's future sealed, why not? He told himself.

"Did you ever, *ever* consider you and me getting back together? After the divorce? Dumb question, I know, but I was just curious."

She paused, picked up the remote, put the TV on mute, then turned to look at him. "I don't know what you want to hear, Chris. I mean, with everything we went through with the divorce and all. I honestly never thought that we could get back together again. But I will say, I never stopped loving you, I still love you." She then laid her head on his chest and took a long, deep breath.

Chris then softly stroked her rich amber hair that he had so sorely missed doing. It felt the same way it did when they were dating and when they were married. He loved that smell. He was about to tell her that he also loved her, but she already knew that. And that might even ruin the moment, he thought. He would probably never be this close to her ever again. A sudden surge of unhappiness shot through him, but it was stifled by a sudden thought of Linda. Thinking of her made him happy, and he wanted to be happy.

The front door then burst open with Sara running through it. This sent Joshua scrambling out of the room and Reno barking. Sara stopped in her tracks in front of her parents, who were still sitting close next to each other. She didn't seem to pay any attention to that or the dog though. She just dropped her hands and opened her mouth wide without saying a word as she stared at her father. "Daddy!" she finally cried. "You're finally home!" Chris then got up as Sara rushed him for a big, long hug. "You're finally home," she said again, as she rocked him from side to side. "I missed you sooo much."

"I missed you too, kiddo," Chris said while trying to keep his emotions in check. Only Jessica's presence kept this possible as he didn't want to make a spectacle of the reunion. He was aware that she had been there for their daughter while he was out on the road, both recently and in the past. Besides, he thought, he would have ample time to reconnect with his daughter alone, and she did have some big news to tell her later that night as well.

"Is this your dog? From Alaska?" Sara asked.

"Yep. His name is Reno."

"He's *so* cute—and *so* spending the night here."

"Ok. *One* night. If your mom agrees. I've got a lot to do tomorrow anyway. And *do not* feed him anything. He ate already."

"Come to my room," Sara said, pulling him by the arm. "I've got so much to tell you about."

Chris looked back at Jessie for approval to go. She nodded yes.

As he was being pulled back into his daughter's life, Chris recalled six months earlier when she had hugged him a tearful goodbye in almost the same spot. The thought made him feel even more grateful that he was back.

After listening to Sara cheerfully tell him about what had happened in her life while he was gone, Jessie then drove Chris home. There, she helped him with his luggage. As Jessie stepped outside his front door to leave, Chris, feeling suddenly spirited, pulled her close and said, "You tell *Fred* that he better take care of my old girl and then kissed her quickly on the lips."

After the kiss, Jessie grinned and walked off leisurely back to her truck as Chris watched. She then turned around and said, "Now *that* is the old Chris I know."

Not the old Chris honey, the new and improved.

The next day, Chris went to see his mother first. Following a hug, he told her, though they often didn't see eye to eye, how much she meant to him and how thankful he was to have her as a mother. He also told her that, even though he was always closer to his father than her, he still loved and cared for her very much. Chris wasn't sure if he said these things to make himself feel better, or make his mother feel better, or if he did it for his father, who would have wanted him to say those things. Either way, he thought, he said them, and it seemed to make both of them feel better. And that's what mattered, he thought. Still, his mother couldn't resist the jab of "Now that you're home, you could take care of your daughter, like you were supposed to, and ensure to bring my little girl over to see me. It's been a while."

Yes, Mother....

After the predictable yet good-natured chat with his mother, Chris stopped next to see his Aunt Sophie. He would have just called but considering that he hadn't seen her in a long time, he thought it only appropriate to see her in person.

"Oh, Christopher, what a nice surprise! It's so nice to see you," she said. "You look wonderful. So, tell me, how have you been?"

"Fine," he said. "It's a little odd being back after traveling for so long; things feel different...but I'm very glad to finally be home."

"Understandable. So, I'm dying to know, what's next for you?"

"That's a good question. First, I'm going to finish the second part of my DoD job at Tinker Airbase. Then we'll see. I'm told that I will more than likely have a full-time employment opportunity with the DoD afterward, though I'll probably not be working with veterans directly."

"But won't you miss doing that?" she asked, concerned.

"I would, so that's why I'm going to start volunteering at our local VSA a few hours a week. I'm sure my boss will be supportive of that."

"Well, you did it. You took the risk of going for what you wanted, and you *got it!* All while helping others. I'm very proud of you, Christopher, and your father would be too."

"I couldn't have done it without you, Aunt Sophie. Really, from the bottom of my heart, I want to thank you for all your guidance and support in helping me through all this.

"You're very welcome, dear."

Chris was then going to tell his aunt about his new dog and the news about Jessie but decided he would do that on another day. Besides, he had to leave for the VSA to drop off his mission summary report to his boss, who he called on the way.

"Hello Chris, and welcome home," he said.

"Thanks," Chris replied. "I'm on the way over to drop off my report. Do you want me to drop it off at the VSA?"

"Yes, that'll be great. But I won't be there. I'm headed to Tinker for a meeting, but I will let Mr. Arnold know you are coming. I'll have him let you in my office so you can put it on my desk. After that, you've got two weeks off. Enjoy them. You've earned it."

Chris said, "Also, I was wondering if it would be possible for me to volunteer a few hours a week at the VSA while I'm employed with the DoD for six months at Tinker? I know it's asking a lot, as I'm sure I'll be busy, but I would like some face-to-face time working with veterans."

"I'm sure we could work that into your schedule."

"I appreciate that. By the way, just curious, did OMP finally come up with a job title for my position?"

"They did—though the position hasn't been approved for the long term yet—it's Veteran Temporary Companionship Provider, something or other. But I like the one you came up with better."

"Me too," replied Chris with a small laugh.

For the remainder of his drive to the VSA, all Chris could think about was Linda. He decided that he would call her right after dropping off his report. *Why wait?*

At the VSA, Chris was greeted by Mr. Arnold, who was in an unusually good mood.

"Hey, Longo. I see you're back from saving the world."

"Yes, sir."

"I'm just kidding with you," he said, leading him to the back. "I heard you did some good things for us in the field. Nice job."

"Thank you, sir."

"Here you go," he said, unlocking Mr. Montrose's office with a key card to allow Chris to place his report on his boss's desk. They then walked back to the front of the VSA, where Mr. Arnold told him of his impending transfer to a VSA in Providence, Rhode Island, which explained his chipper mood, Chris thought.

"Yeah, it's only 50 miles outside of Boston," Mr. Arnold said, adding, "So, I'll be pretty close to home."

Chris heard Mr. Arnold say this, but he didn't need to. He already knew it. He knew that that's what he had wanted badly for the past four years. He was happy for him. And he was glad that he was leaving. At least he wouldn't be a jerk to anyone there anymore, he thought.

"For what it's worth," Mr. Arnold then said, "You leaving for greener pastures affected me. I thought about it for some time. I thought, why couldn't I leave too? Why couldn't I go for what I wanted as well? It wasn't easy, but my wife and I had a heart-to-heart and came up with something that worked out for both of us. Anyway, I wanted you to know that." Mr. Arnold then put out his hand for a handshake. "Take care, Longo."

"I wish you well at your new location," Chris told him, then turned and walked out through the VSA doors.

In the car, he called Linda.

"How are ya doing mista?" she said in her northern accent that Chris had grown to enamor.

"Hello Linda," he said. "How are you?"

"I'm fine. Busy with work, you know, nothing special."

"And Vincent? Joseph? How are they?"

"Both doing well, thanks for asking."

"And you? Are you still traveling with work?"

"No, I just got home yesterday. Look. I'm not sure why I called, but…, I've been thinking about you and…."

"And you miss me? And you can't wait to see me again?"

"That's right," he said with a light laugh. "I miss you and can't wait to see you again."

"So, what are we going to do about that?" she asked.

"I haven't thought that through yet, but before we figure that out, I want you to know that I never had any intention of trying to meet someone while I was working with your son. I mean, it was unexpected, meeting you and all."

"You don't need to worry about that, Chris," she said. "I do appreciate you saying it, but I know you're not that type of guy."

Chris took a deep breath, then said, "Also, it's been quite some time since I've been with someone. I was hanging on to my ex-wife long after our divorce. Anyhow, it hasn't been easy for me to meet someone new. Or even try to."

"And you're telling me this, *why?*" she asked.

"I just didn't want you to have high expectations of me."

"Sorry, but you already screwed that up with your kindness and your cuteness. And your kiss. I *do* have high expectations of you, Chris, as I find you a special person. But as far as what I expect from us, let me put your concerns at ease right there. I'm not looking for someone just to be with someone. As a matter of fact, I'm not looking for anyone at all. I have my job or jobs. I have my kids. I have a life. And I certainly don't need another failed relationship on my résumé. But if Mr. Right came along out of nowhere, or even Oklahoma, then I'm not cynical enough yet to not give it another shot. To not give it another chance. At our age, with all that both of us been through, we owe it to ourselves."

"I should just shut up now," Chris said.

"Ha-ha, probably. But seriously, it's important to talk about how we feel. Expression is key."

"Sorry, I didn't mean to get so serious," he said. "But thanks for listening. So, when can I see you again?"

"I thought, maybe, that we could meet up in Dallas in October or November over a long holiday weekend. It's only a few hours away from you by car, and I could get a direct flight. And we could even catch a professional hockey game there as well. Whatta-ya-say?"

Chris replied without hesitation, "I say yes, Linda. I say yes."

Several hours later, Mr. Montrose returned to his VSA office in Oklahoma City and read Chris's final report. When finished, he nodded to himself with pride and approval.

Mission Summary Report

What I've Learned by Chris Longo

Sept 7, 2019

Over the past six months, I met with six veterans, one per month, who needed support for various reasons; The goal of my mission was to help them find their path back: back to where or who they were before their aliments occurred or to assist them in finding a new path. This mission, as well as my hire in this position, was under the understanding and agreement that this was an experiment of sorts, a pilot program. But this did not mean that the veterans were undervalued, or the end goal taken less seriously, even with my lack of clinical qualification in the field. On the contrary, considering all the past failures that these veterans have had with their social workers and/or medical agencies, one could argue that this experimental mission was a valiant attempt to remedy those past failures with the goal of actual success or at least progress toward that goal.

I met Alex, a former marine sergeant who suffers from PTSD from his combat tours in Afghanistan. His internal wounds run deep, which reflect him, at times, harshly externally. I met Tashana, a former coast guard officer who was sexually assaulted and then emotionally so by her father. I met Vincent, a former army soldier who's an alcoholic. An addiction he's been battling for a long time, though he's still young. I met Kyle, a medically retired air force fighter pilot who had a violent crash in a combat zone. This left him with several amputations as well as a traumatic brain injury. I met Matthew, an accomplished navy captain, at the end of his military career. The transition has given him severe anxiety. And lastly, or firstly actually, I met Tim, an army Vietnam veteran who suffers from almost all the ailments that the aforementioned veterans do. And that's not an overstatement.

251

When I met each veteran, I was fortunate to have their full attention and cooperation, which aided greatly in our communication. We did have our challenges at times, but I witnessed each make progress with their respective ailments. This was largely due to them, not me. The former marine sergeant vocalized his next career goal. The former coast guard officer is bravely working through her assault experience through therapy, as well as continuing to reconnect and forgive her father. The former army soldier, through strong support, opportunity, and willingness, has stopped drinking and rediscovered his purpose. Which, ironically, was the same purpose he had lost due to his drinking in the first place. The medically retired air force fighter pilot, a Renaissance man with many talents, yet none of which fulfilled him as much as the one he preferred most before his crash, and is no longer capable of doing, has discovered a new interest. One that he enjoys and is, of course, talented at. The navy captain, and his vast knowledge in his field that he started learning from his family as a child, to throughout his long career, is embedded in him. But that isn't all he is. He is also his own man. He was able to figure that out, thus, giving him the confidence to help him face his fears of his transition. And the army Vietnam veteran, who was almost killed by his own hand. Maybe this was because, like he had told me once, he would not break. But in the end, he was a survivor, like he was then, and somehow, against the odds, he continues to be. But that's what teams do; they beat the odds.

What I've learned during the challenging, joyous, and rewarding time with these veterans is that they all have a gift and that they have helped me as much as I have them, maybe more. They also showed me love, not LOVE as in my boss's acronym, but real love. They are, despite all their distressful experiences, true warriors. For, though their struggles continue, they courageously fight on. I am not sure if I have succeeded in helping them find their path back, but I am sure that they are headed in the right direction. Each is what my father would always tell me to be to my daughter, a hero.

The following Saturday, Chris brought Sara to Lake Hefner with Reno. It felt like old times as they walked around the lake and talked about her school sports and upcoming events. They even discussed possibly going to Church on Sunday. To Chris's delight, Sara also mentioned how she remembered him taking her there to learn how to ride a bike. As they were walking, Reno suddenly broke free from his leash and ran to the top of a nearby mound, where he howled longingly to the crystal blue sky; this made Chris think of his vision quest wolf in Alaska. He then did what he pictured the old man had done at the end of the book while sleeping and dreaming about the lions of his youth and what he saw his daughter do in the shining light. He smiled.